W9-BNY-472

Books by Charlie Donlea

SUMMIT LAKE

THE GIRL WHO WAS TAKEN

DON'T BELIEVE IT

SOME CHOOSE DARKNESS

THE SUICIDE HOUSE

TWENTY YEARS LATER

THOSE EMPTY EYES

Published by Kensington Publishing Corp.

TWENTY YEARS LATER

CHARLIE DONLEA

KENSINGTON
PUBLISHING CORP.

www.kensingtonbooks.com

KENSINGTON BOOKS are published by

Kensington Publishing Corp.
119 West 40th Street
New York, NY 10018

All Kensington titles, imprints, and distributed lines are available at special quantity discounts for bulk purchases for sales promotion, premiums, fund-raising, educational, or institutional use.

Special book excerpts or customized printings can also be created to fit specific needs. For details, write or phone the office of the Kensington Sales Manager: Attn.: Sales Department. Kensington Publishing Corp., 119 West 40th Street, New York, NY 10018. Phone: 1-800-221-2647.

The K with book logo Reg US Pat. & TM Off.

First Kensington Hardcover Edition: January 2022

ISBN: 978-1-4967-2720-6 (ebook)

ISBN: 978-1-4967-4271-1

First Kensington Trade Paperback Edition: January 2023

10 9 8 7 6 5

Printed in the United States of America

From invention is born progress
From reinvention is born freedom
—Anonymous

Catskill Mountains

July 15, 2001
Two Months Before 9/11

Death was in the air.
He smelled it as soon as he ducked under the crime scene tape and stepped onto the front lawn of the palatial estate. The Catskill Mountains rose above the roofline as the early morning sun stretched shadows of trees across the yard. The breeze rolled down from the foothills and carried the smell of decay, causing his upper lip to twitch when it reached his nostrils. The smell of death filled him with excitement. He hoped it was because this was his first case as a newly minted homicide detective, and not from some perverse fetish he had never known he possessed.

A uniformed police officer led him across the lawn and around to the back of the property. There, he found the source of the foul odor. The victim was hanging naked from a second-story balcony, his feet suspended at eye level, and the white rope around his neck angling his head like a broken-stemmed lollipop. The detective looked up to the terrace. The rope stretched over the railing, tight and challenged by the weight of the body. The twine disappeared through French doors that led, he presumed, into the bedroom.

The victim had likely twirled for much of the night, the detective imagined, and now had unfortunately come to rest facing the house. Unfortunate because, as the detective walked across the back lawn, the first thing he saw was the man's naked buttocks. When he reached the body he noticed welt marks covering the man's right butt cheek and upper thigh. The contusions flared a faint lilac against the livor mortis blue of the dead man's skin.

The detective reached into his breast pocket and removed a pair of latex gloves that he slipped onto his hands. Rigor mortis had bloated the man's body to the point of explosion. His limbs looked like they were stuffed with dough. A bundle of rope bound the victim's hands behind his back, preventing his swollen and stiffened arms from extending out from his torso. Cut this rope, the detective imagined, and this guy would unfold like a scarecrow.

He gestured for the crime scene photographer, who waited at the periphery of the lawn.

"Go ahead."

"Yes, sir," the photographer said.

The crime scene unit had already been through the property, taking photos and video to log everything at the crime scene as the *before* evidence. This second time through would be after the detective had his initial look. The photographer raised his camera and peered through the viewfinder.

"So what's the initial thought here?" the photographer asked as the camera's shutter clicked redundantly as he snapped a series of photos. "Someone tied this guy up and threw him over the balcony?"

The detective looked up to the second story. "Maybe. Or he tied himself up and jumped."

The photographer stopped shooting and slowly took his face away from the camera.

"Happens more than you'd think," the detective said. "That way, if they have second thoughts, they can't save themselves." The detective pointed at the dead man's face. "Get some clicks of that gag in his mouth."

The photographer squinted as he walked around to the front of the body and looked at the dead man's mouth. "Is that a ball gag? Like, S and M stuff?"

"It would certainly go hand in hand with the whip marks on his ass. I'm heading upstairs to see what's holding this guy in place."

In addition to the latex gloves covering the detective's hands, plastic wraps now enclosed his shoes as he walked into the bedroom. The balcony doors opened inward and allowed the same breeze that had earlier filled his nostrils with the smell of death to gust through the bedroom. The pungent odor was less noticeable here, one story higher than where death hung in the morning air. He stood in the door frame and moved his gaze around. This was clearly the master suite. Vaulted ceilings were twenty feet high. A king-sized four-poster bed stood in the middle of the room with a night table on either side. A dresser sat against the far wall, its mirror reflecting his image back at him. Through the open balcony doors, the white rope curved up and over the railing to run at waist height across the room and into the closet.

He stepped into the room and followed the rope. The closet had no door, just an arched entryway. When he reached it, he saw a spacious walk-in filled with neatly organized clothes hanging from scores of identical hangers. Shoes filled the thick pine cubbyholes that covered the back wall. Amid the cubbies was a black safe about five feet tall, likely weighing close to a ton. With an ornate knot, the end of the rope was tied to one of the legs of the safe. The other end, the detective knew, was attached to the man's neck, and whether he jumped off the balcony or was pushed, the safe had done its job. The four legs indented the carpeting with no adjacent depression marks to suggest the weight of the man's body had moved it even an inch.

A large kitchen knife lay on the floor next to the safe. Morning sunlight spilled through the balcony doors and into the walk-in closet, painting his shadow across the floor and up the far wall. He pulled a flashlight from his pocket and shined it at the carpeting, highlighting the small fibers next to the knife. He crouched down and examined them in the bright glow of his flashlight. They appeared to be bits of frayed nylon from when the rope had been cut. Within the carpet fibers was a small puddle of blood. A couple of droplets had also landed on the handle of the knife. He placed a triangle-shaped yellow evidence placard over the blood and fibers, and another next to the knife.

He turned and walked out of the closet, noticing a nearly empty wineglass on the night table. He was careful not to disturb it as he placed another yellow evidence marker next to it. Lipstick smeared the rim. High-stepping over the taut rope, he walked past the mirrored dresser and into the bathroom. He slowly looked around and saw nothing out of place. Soon, the forensics team would be in here with luminol and black lights. At the moment, the detective was interested in his first impression of the place. The toilet lid was open but the seat was down and dry. The toilet water held a yellow color, and the pungent smell of urine registered now as his nose caught up with his eyes. Someone had used the toilet but failed to flush. A lone segment of toilet paper floated in the bowl. Another evidence placard found the toilet.

He walked from the bathroom and into the main area, once again surveying the room. He followed the rope out to the balcony and looked down at the dead man hanging from the other end. In the distance, the Catskill Mountains were cloaked by early morning fog. This was the house of a very

wealthy man, and the detective had been handpicked to figure out what happened to him. In just a few minutes he had
identified blood evidence, fingerprints on a wineglass, and a
urine sample that likely belonged to the killer.

He had no idea at the time that all of it would be matched
to a woman named Victoria Ford. And the detective could
not have predicted that in two short months, just as he had
every bit of evidence organized and a conviction all but certain, commercial airliners—American Airlines Flight 11 and
United Airlines Flight 175—would fly into the Twin Towers
of the World Trade Center. On a sun-filled, blue-sky morning,
three thousand men and women would die, and the detective's case would go up in smoke.

Lower Manhattan

September 11, 2001

It was a bright, cloudless morning with blue sky as far as the eye could see. On any other day, Victoria Ford would have considered it beautiful. But today, the cool morning air and fresh, clean sky went unnoticed. Things had gone terribly wrong and today she was fighting for her life. She had been for the last few weeks. She took the subway in from Brooklyn and climbed the subterranean stairs into the brilliant morning. It was still early, and the streets were not as crowded as normal. It was the first day of school and many parents were absent from their normal morning commute, dropping their kids off and snapping first-day photos. Victoria took advantage of the open sidewalks and power-walked through the financial district toward her attorney's office. She pushed through the lobby doors and entered the elevator, which took forty-five seconds to shoot her to the seventy-eighth floor. There, she rode an escalator up two more levels and pushed through the office doors. A moment later she was sitting in front of her attorney's desk.

"Straight talk," Roman Manchester said as soon as Victoria sat down. "That's the only way I deliver news."

Victoria nodded. Roman Manchester was one of the best-known defense attorneys in the country. He was also one of the most expensive. But Victoria had decided, now that things had gone to hell, that Manchester was her best option. Tall, with a thick head of dark hair, Victoria had a surreal moment as she stared at the man now and remembered the many times she'd seen him on television, either answering questions from reporters or staging a press conference to proclaim his client's innocence. Her name would soon be in the same category as the other men and women Roman Manchester had defended. But if it meant that she would avoid conviction and prison, Victoria was okay with that. She knew from the start that it would be that way.

"The DA reached out to me yesterday to let me know they've convened a grand jury."

"What does that mean?" Victoria asked.

"Shortly, likely this week, they will present to a jury of twenty-three private citizens all the evidence they have against you. I'm not allowed to be present, and the proceedings are not open to the public. The district attorney is not attempting to prove guilt beyond a reasonable doubt. The DA's goal is to show the jury the evidence she has to this point in order to determine if an indictment is warranted."

Victoria nodded.

"You and I have covered this before, but I'll give you a quick overview of the case against you. The physical evidence is substantial. Your fingerprints, DNA via blood evidence, and urine were found at the scene. All of this appears to be unchallengeable because they crossed their t's and dotted their i's with search warrants. The rope around the victim's neck matched rope the investigators recovered from your car. There is other, more minor, physical evidence, in addition to a great deal of circumstantial evidence that will be presented to the grand jury."

"Can't you challenge it? That's part of defending me."

"I'll defend you, but not at the grand jury. Our time to shine is when the case goes to trial. And there will be a lot of work to do to get to that point. I'll be able to challenge a lot of the circumstantial, but the physical evidence, quite frankly, is a tough obstacle to overcome."

"I already told you," Victoria said. "I wasn't at that house the night Cameron died. I can't explain how my blood and urine got there. That's your job. Isn't that what I'm paying you for?"

"At some point I'll get to see all the evidence and sink my teeth into how strong it is. But we're not at that point yet. For now, I expect the grand jury will rule in favor of indictment."

"When?"

"This week."

Victoria shook her head. "What should I do?"

"The very first thing is to figure out how much money you have on hand, and how much more you can get from friends and family. You'll need it for bail."

"How much?"

"Hard to give you an exact amount. I'll argue that you have no prior record and are not a flight risk. But the DA is pushing for first-degree murder, and on that charge alone there is precedent on bail. Minimum, a million. Likely more. Plus the remainder of my retainer."

Victoria stared out the window of her attorney's office and looked at the buildings of New York. She made a mental list of her assets. She had just over $10,000 in a joint savings account with her husband. Her investments would wring out another eighty thousand, although she'd likely have to fight her husband tooth and nail for every penny since the account was in both their names. They hadn't spoken since the details of her affair came out during the investigation, which she knew was inevitable. The media had salivated over every dirty detail, spreading them far and wide. Her husband had moved out soon after.

She could borrow against her 401k, where another hundred thousand resided. The equity in their home might yield five figures. Even with all that, she'd still be well short. She could ask her parents and sister, but Victoria knew that wouldn't get her far. Victoria's best friend had all the money in the world, and a million dollars would not be a stretch for Natalie Ratcliff. It was Victoria's only option. The weight of the situation drooped her shoulders and brought tears to her eyes. Things were not meant to play out like this. Just a short couple of months ago, she and Cameron were happy. They were planning a future together. But then everything changed. The pregnancy and the abortion and everything that followed. The jealously and the hate. It had all come so quickly that Victoria barely had time to digest it. And now she was in the middle of a nightmare with no way out. She pulled her gaze from the window and looked at her attorney.

"What happens if I can't come up with the money?"

Roman Manchester pursed his lips, picked up his coffee mug, and took a slow sip before carefully placing it back on his desk. "I think you should find a way to secure the money; let's leave it at that. It will be much easier to mount a viable defense if you are not in jail prior to trial. Not impossible, just easier."

Victoria's mind buzzed. An actual, audible vibration. She imagined it was the neurons of her brain attempting to grasp the gravity of the moment, until she realized it was something else. The vibration was real, a growing flutter that rattled her chair and shook the desk. The sound that accompanied it changed from a far-off buzz to a screaming whine. Suddenly, an object streaked through her peripheral vision but was gone before she could bring her gaze to the window. Then, her attorney's office rocked and swayed. Pictures fell from the wall and glass shattered just as the concussion of an explosion filled her ears. The lights flickered and the ceiling tiles rained down on her. Outside the windows, the blue sky that had been visible just a moment before was gone. In its place was a wall of black smoke that erased the brilliant morning sun. That same dark smolder spiraled through the vents as an ominous odor filled her nostrils. She recognized the scent but couldn't immediately place it. It wasn't exactly the same, but the closest she came was that it smelled like gasoline.

Manhattan, New York

Twenty Years Later

The New York City medical examiner's office was located in a nondescript, six-story white brick building in Kips Bay on East Twenty-Sixth Street and First Avenue. If offices had occupied the top two floors they would have offered views of the East River and the north end of Brooklyn. But the upper floors were not meant for the scientists and doctors who roamed the building. They were instead reserved for water and air purification systems. The circulated air within the world's largest crime lab was clean, pure, and dry. Very, very dry. Humidity was bad for DNA, and DNA extraction was one of the crime lab's fortes.

In the cold, damp basement was the bone-processing laboratory. A technician opened the airtight seal of the cryo tank, releasing liquid nitrogen fog into the air. A triple layer of latex gloves protected the technician's hands. His face was safe behind a plastic shield. He reached into the tank with a pair of forceps and lifted the test tube from the fog. It was filled with white powder that had minutes earlier been a small bone fragment specimen. The liquid nitrogen had been used to freeze the bone, and then the frozen specimen was shaken violently in the bulletproof test tube. The result was total pulverization of the original bone sample into a fine powder. The technique allowed scientists to access the innermost portion of the bone, which made the chance of extracting usable DNA more likely. The concept was remarkably simple and had been developed based on two of the basic concepts of physics—the law of motion, and thermodynamics. If an apple were thrown at a wall, it would break into many pieces. But if the same apple were frozen solid by liquid nitrogen and *then* hurled at the wall, it would shatter into millions of pieces. When it came to extracting DNA from bone, the more pieces the bone could be broken into, the better. The finer the powder, better still.

The tech placed the test tube into a rack with a dozen others containing pulverized bone. With the nitrogen fog still spiraling from the latest tube, he dipped a titrating syringe into a beaker of fluid, drew ten cc's into the chamber, and added the extraction products to the pulverized bone. The next day, instead of bone powder, a pink liquid would fill the tubes. It was from this liquid that a genetic code would be procured—a sequence of twenty-three numbers unique to every human on the planet. Their DNA profile.

In the room next to the bone-processing lab, a continuous bank of computers lined all four walls. It was here where scientists took the DNA profiles generated from the original bone fragments and attempted to match them to profiles stored in the Combined DNA Index System databank known as CODIS. But this was not the national databank the FBI utilized to match DNA profiles gathered from crime scenes to previously convicted criminals. The databank searched here was a stand-alone archive of DNA profiles provided by the families of 9/11 victims who were never identified after the towers fell.

Greg Norton had worked at the Office of the Chief Medical Examiner for three years. Most of those years were spent in the computer lab. Each morning he was met with a stack of DNA profiles recently sequenced from bone fragments that had been collected from the rubble of the Twin Towers. He entered each sequence into the CODIS databank and searched for matches. In three years of employment he had never made a single match. But this morning, just as he sat down with his second cup of coffee and pecked away at the keyboard, a green indicator light blinked at the bottom of the screen.

Green?

A red light meant no matches had been found on sequences entered, and Greg had become so accustomed to misses that the red light was all he ever expected. He'd never seen a green indicator light during his tenure at the OCME. He clicked on the icon and two DNA profiles popped up onto the monitor—white numbers against a black background. They were identical.

"Hey, boss?" he said in a careful tone, keeping his eye on the set of twenty-three numbers in front of him to make sure they didn't change.

"What's up?" Dr. Trudeau asked as he worked his fingers over a keyboard on the other side of the room.

As the head of Forensic Biology, Arthur Trudeau was in charge of identifying the remains of mass casualties from across the state of New York. For nearly twenty years it had been his mission to identify every specimen collected from those killed in the World Trade Center attack.

"We got a hit."

Trudeau's fingers stopped tapping the keyboard and he slowly looked over to Greg Norton's station. "Say that again."

The tech nodded and smiled as he continued to stare at the numbers on his screen. "We got a hit. We got a frickin' hit!"

Dr. Trudeau stood from his desk and walked across the lab. "Patient?"

"One one four five zero."

Trudeau walked to a standing computer station, pulled the keyboard toward him, and typed the numbers.

"Who is it?" Greg asked.

Other technicians had heard the news of a confirmed identification and gathered around. Trudeau stared at the monitor and the small hourglass that spun as the computer searched. Finally, a named appeared on the screen.

"Victoria Ford," he said.

"Next of kin?" Greg asked.

Trudeau shook his head. "Parents, but they're deceased."

"Any other contacts?"

"Yes," Trudeau said, scrolling down the page. "A sister. Address in New York State."

"Want me to make the call?"

"No. Let's run it one more time to be sure. Start to finish. If it hits a second time, I'll give her a call."

"First one in how long, boss?"

Dr. Trudeau looked over at the young technician. "Years. Now run it again."

PART I

The Sting

CHAPTER 1

Los Angeles, CA
Friday, May 14, 2021

Avery Mason was not looking for fame. With a graveyard of secrets in her past, fame was the last thing she needed. Still, she had found it. Whether this had been by accident or with intent was a question that only counseling could answer. It would require a deep dive into her tumultuous upbringing, an examination of her complicated relationship with her father, and some honest soul-searching and self-reflection—none of which Avery had time for. Because *however* it came to be, what Avery knew for certain about fame was that it arrived like a colossal wave rolling toward shore. You either rode it, or let it drown you. She chose to ride it, and in spectacular fashion.

Avery Mason was thirty-two years old and the youngest woman to ever anchor *American Events*, the most popular prime-time newsmagazine program on television. Her ascension to the top of the ratings was improbable, statistically unheard of, and something Avery never expected. Mack Carter had been the long-running and popular host of *American*

Events. His death the year before while on assignment covering the Westmont Prep slaughters had rattled the television news industry. It also produced a vacancy at the top of *American Events.* In a panic, the network tapped Avery to fill Mack's massive shoes until a more permanent anchor could be found. As a frequent contributor to the show, Avery's segments had consistently earned high ratings. So high, in fact, that she was named as the first co-host in the show's storied history. Avery had held that position for exactly one month before Mack Carter died. Thrust into the hottest of spotlights and widely expected to fail, Avery Mason had stepped into the lead anchor role the previous fall and killed it. *American Events* not only stayed at the top of the ratings, but the audience grew by 20 percent.

Critics explained away her success as a fluke of morbid curiosity. People tuned in, the critics argued, to see how this inexperienced woman would handle the crushing pressure of replacing one of America's most beloved anchors on television's longest running news program. The problem with their argument was that Avery's ratings never came down. That she was young and attractive certainly didn't hurt her rising star, and Avery admitted that her looks likely drew a certain male demographic that might not normally tune in to a newsmagazine show. But her looks were not the source of her success. It was her talent, her charisma, and the content of her show that kept the ratings sky-high. The abundance of press hadn't hurt either. During the past year she graced the covers of entertainment magazines, gave countless interviews and photo shoots, and was the subject of a three-part exposé by *Events Magazine* on her natural abilities in front of the camera and her rise to the top of the cable news food chain. And yet somehow, through it all, she had managed to keep her past hidden.

Avery's forte was true crime, finding an unsolved mystery

and dissecting it for her audience in a way that hooked them and refused to let go. Her dark and edgy foray into some of the country's most sordid crimes was where she made her name. But to contrast the sinister stories she covered, Avery also told stories of survival and hope. It was these stories of miracles and beating the odds that kept people tuning in. Not a week went by without Avery featuring some sort of real life, plucked from Middle America, feel-good story—like Kelly Rosenstein, the woman who sank her minivan into Devil's Gate Reservoir in Pasadena after a drunk driver forced her off the road. The indomitable mother of four had not only managed to escape the sunken vehicle, but had miraculously done so with all of her children in tow. Avery interviewed the woman a week after the accident. With as many as six hundred people dying each year in the United States due to a submerged vehicle, how had this soccer mom managed to escape? It was simple. Years earlier Mack Carter had demonstrated the best way to escape a car after it sank to the bottom of a lake. Kelly Rosenstein had watched the episode and remembered what she saw.

So moved by the story, Avery decided to look up the old footage. It was how she ended up this afternoon strapped behind the wheel of a minivan that was parked inside a high school aquatics center, with a television crew ready to film the action. Today, the action would be a giant crane lifting the van over the pool and dropping it, and Avery, to the bottom. Cameras situated under the water would capture Avery's attempt to escape from the submerged vehicle. She was, without doubt or shame, scared to death.

She knew America had loved Mack Carter for the stunts he performed, and Avery could think of no better way to wrap up her first full season as host of *American Events* than with a nod to her predecessor. Today's taping was her right of passage. This would be her last episode before summer sabbatical. A summer that was sure to be the most trying of her life. She was following a lead out of New York that she thought had potential—the remains of a woman killed in the 9/11 World Trade Center attacks had just been identified using promising new DNA technology, and Avery wanted the chance to tell the story. If she made it through today's stunt, she was off to New York to chase some leads.

At least, that was her story. She thought it was the perfect cover.

CHAPTER 2

Los Angeles, CA
Friday, May 14, 2021

The Honda minivan was parked on a hydraulic lift on the side of the Los Angeles high school swimming pool. Avery chose the make and model because of their connection to the middle class. The minivan was among the most commonly driven vehicles in the United States. Sinking a sixty-thousand-dollar BMW in a high school swimming pool might be exciting to watch, but demonstrating to stay-at-home mothers how to escape their sunken vehicle was much better accomplished using an average, run-of-the-mill automobile.

Avery checked the seat belt buckle for the third time in less than a minute. Christine Swanson, her executive producer, leaned through the open driver's side window.

"Good?" she asked.

Avery nodded.

"Show me the abort sign again," Christine said.

Avery took the four fingers on her right hand and waved them back and forth in front of her throat.

"If you ever get panicked, or just can't remember what to do, give the abort signal and the divers will have you out in ten seconds. Got it?"

Avery nodded.

"Words, Avery! I need to hear your voice."

"Yes, Christine! I've got it, for Christ's sake. Let's go."

"We're about to sink you, and the car you're sitting in, to the bottom of a swimming pool," Christine said in a calm voice, trying to control the panicked moment. "I want to make sure your head is in the right place."

"Of course my head is not in the right place, Chris. If it were, I wouldn't be doing this. And if we don't do it soon, I'll lose my nerve. So let's get this show on the road."

Christine nodded. "Okay. You've got this."

Christine backed away from the minivan, stuck her fingers between her lips, and whistled. It was an ear-splitting screech that echoed off the walls of the cavernous aquatics center.

"Let's roll!"

A loud buzzing filled the indoor plaza as the crane's hydraulics activated and jolted the platform, and the minivan parked on it, upward. Avery grabbed the steering wheel and white-knuckled it as if she were driving through a torrential downpour. She rolled up the window and the noise outside the vehicle—the producers yelling instructions, the engineers guiding the crane operator, the ring of the hydraulics, and the murmurs from three hundred spectators that filled the retractable bleachers and made up the studio audience—went silent. All she heard now was her own exaggerated breathing. Even the smell of chlorine disappeared.

Her ascent finally ended, and then the car jolted again as the back of the platform started to rise, pitching the nose of the minivan downward toward the water. A slew of engineers who consulted on the stunt had decided that thirty-eight degrees was the most accurate pitch angle to best represent a vehicle careening off the road and plunging into a body of water. To Avery it felt like she was hanging vertically off a cliff. The seat belt was tight across her chest as gravity pulled her forward. She straightened her legs on the floorboard to keep her position in the driver's seat.

The whole of the eight-lane, NFHS-approved, competition-size swimming pool came into view through the windshield as the minivan tipped forward. The surface of the water reflected the stage lights that were erected around the indoor pool. Red lane markers swayed in wavy images made brighter by the underwater lighting. She saw the rescue divers hovering near the bottom, the bubbles from their SCUBA tanks rippling the surface as they waited for Avery's arrival fourteen feet under the water. She had imagined during the planning phase that their presence would ease her nerves. That knowing help was just a few feet away would provide a sense of comfort as the minivan sunk to the bottom. That knowing all she needed to do was give the abort signal and the divers would immediately extract her from the vehicle would settle her nerves and give her confidence. But now, as she hovered above the pool with the weight of her body heavy against the seat belt, she felt no such comfort or confidence. Things *could* go wrong. What if she wasn't able to successfully pull off the techniques the survival experts had taught her? What if her mind froze and she simply couldn't remember what to do? What if the seat belt locked up because of the force of the impact? What if the window did not break like it was supposed to? What if the divers didn't see her signal? What if—

The sensation of falling abruptly interrupted her thoughts. The harness holding the minivan in place had been released. She was in free fall. It felt like a hell of a lot longer than the three seconds it was supposed to take to roll off the edge of the platform and drop fifteen feet before impacting the water.

During those frozen seconds Avery noticed the television camera across the pool, one of eight that were positioned around the aquatics center. Another four GoPro cameras were mounted inside the vehicle, their red indicator lights suddenly bright and voyeuristic. Just before impact, Avery caught a glimpse of the movie-theater-sized screen that would display her progress to the captive studio audience who lined the poolside bleachers. And then, there was a crash.

The impact was jarring. The seat belt dug into her breastbone as her head snapped forward. The minivan speared through the water and then, as if a rubber band were attached to its back bumper, began a backward trek as the natural buoyancy of the air trapped inside the vehicle pulled it back to the surface. The van rocked and bobbed as Mother Nature found the center of gravity and then began to slowly pull it under the water, engine first. Water poured in through unseen breaches and began filling the interior. Avery worked hard to control the panic that was growing with each second. Panic, though, was good. It meant she was aware of what was happening and had not suffered "behavioral inaction," a symptom described by the survival experts who had consulted on the episode. Also called "dislocation of expectation," it was the mind's response to a traumatic situation. The brain attempts to correlate the current situation with a known experience from the past. As the frontal lobe loops in repetitive circles, trying but failing to find a similar situation to work from, the body freezes and waits for directions from the brain. It's the science behind the proverbial "deer-in-the-headlights" phenomenon.

Fortunately for Avery, she was suffering no such dislocation from her surroundings. The synapses of her brain fired back to a previous experience when she found herself fighting the relentless water that tried to drown her. She remembered the day her sailboat sank off the coast of Manhattan and she came within an inch of losing her life. It was impossible to remember that day and not think of her brother. And now, those thoughts of Christopher brought her back to her current situation. The minivan was sinking and water was quickly filling the interior of the vehicle. She considered waving her hand in front of her throat and putting an end to this madness. But then she remembered Kelly Rosenstein, the mother who didn't have the option of calling it quits when her car, filled with her four children, sank to the bottom of Devil's Gate Reservoir. It was a miracle that Kelly had stayed composed enough to save herself, let alone her children. It was even more amazing that she credited her survival to watching an episode of *American Events*. If what Avery had learned from the survival experts over the past week could be used now to show anyone else how to save their own life, it was at least worth her best effort.

As the van filled with water, Avery unsnapped her seat belt. She turned sideways in the driver's seat, lifting her legs out of the collection of water that filled the driver's side leg well so that her feet were facing the door. She braced herself on the middle console and aimed her heel at the corner of the driver's side window. The bottom right bend of the window was key, the survival experts had told her. The junction where the tempered glass met the frame represented the weakest part of the window. Struck properly, the window could be dislodged from the door frame in one piece. Striking the center of the window, on the other hand, would put a hole in the tempered glass and slice her foot to pieces. Opening the door would be impossible, as already the water had crawled halfway up the window and the external pressure would be too great.

Avery bent her leg, bringing her knee toward her face, grabbed the steering wheel with her right hand and the driver's side headrest with her left, and kicked the corner of the window. She closed her eyes on impact and waited for water to pour through the opening. When nothing happened she opened her eyes. The kick had done nothing. The van sunk lower in the pool, with the waterline now bouncing above the driver's side window. She closed her eyes and kicked again. This time a spiderweb fracture twisted from the corner of the window. Sensing the lenses all around her—from the GoPro cameras mounted inside the van to the underwater cameras positioned in the pool and focused on her—she pulled her leg back one more time and kicked with all her strength. Immediately she felt the rush of water. It was colder than she imagined and the force of it was so great that it was over her head in an instant.

More panic followed when she realized she'd forgotten the survival expert's instructions to take a deep breath first, *before* kicking the window, as the intrusive water would come fast and furious, preventing her from taking a good lungful of air before it was over her head. They were correct. Not only had she forgotten to fill her lungs with air before the water had found her, but the three kicks it took to blow out the window had exhausted her. She desperately needed a breath. A frantic moment followed before she looked around. It was peacefully quiet under the water, and her vision was less blurred than she imagined. She forced herself to calm down. When faced with a life-or-death situation, being calm was the number one rule of survival.

As the van completed its fourteen-foot descent to the bottom of the pool, Avery shut her eyes and allowed her ears to adjust to the pressure. When the van kissed the bottom, a much softer impact than a few seconds earlier when it crashed through the surface, she opened her eyes and saw the cameraman pointing his lens through the missing window. She saw the rescue divers watching closely for Avery to give the abort signal. Instead, she stuck her feet through the window frame, wrapped the fingers of her right hand around the grab handle, and launched herself through the opening in a smooth glide that took her into open water. Then she brought herself upright, gave the cameraman the thumbs-up, and kicked to the surface.

The underwater footage was spectacular. Christine produced the hell out of the episode, and the network leaked teasers across social media leading up to the run date, which would be during May sweeps week. When "The Minivan" aired, as the episode was titled, Avery Mason and *American Events* earned the highest ratings in the show's history.

CHAPTER 3
Playa del Rey, CA
Saturday, June 5, 2021

Mosley Germaine's backyard was the Pacific Ocean. It was actually a flamboyant stretch of beach and the ocean, but the first thing anyone noticed upon entering the Playa del Rey home was the magnificent views of the water visible through every floor-to-ceiling window. The open concept design included a kitchen island that spilled into the vast living room. The retractable glass patio doors were open this evening, having disappeared into the walls as if they never existed and allowing the ocean breeze to gust through the house. The back patio was made up of multiple levels and built from imported Italian stone. A long, rectangular table that looked to have been plucked from a boardroom dominated the middle of the stone just a few steps from the pool. Fixed for forty guests, each place setting was meticulously ordered with two plates, three glasses, silverware at perfect ninety-degree angles, and a nameplate dictating a seating arrangement created by Mr. Germaine himself.

Tonight was the annual end-of-season gathering for the

faces of the HAP News network, the current ratings leader. There were no close seconds. At the helm of the media giant was Mosley Germaine. He had been the head of HAP News since the nineties, hired when the prime-time lineup was headlined by no-name personalities, the ratings were in the tank, and the network barely made a blip on the radar. But Germaine possessed a vision for delivering the news. He chose the personalities and dictated the content. If a program failed to attract a proper audience, he replaced the hosts with someone new. If a hard news hour failed to compete with the major networks' evening newscasts, the anchor was pulled in favor of a new face. He did this often enough to keep his people in line and on their toes, and to let them all know that folks tuned in to HAP News, not just a single personality. But when a show succeeded and stood out from the rest, he made sure to keep the host happy—cornered and with no other options, but otherwise happy. Mosley Germaine was the master puppeteer controlling everything that transpired at the network. Tonight was a celebration of another successful season at the top of cable news—all of cable programming, in fact. It was an annual gala at the boss's impressive waterfront property where success was celebrated, wealth was flaunted, and the idea that with dedication, hard work, and loyalty, anything was possible for the select few who were invited. Avery Mason hated every minute of it.

She arrived alone. She wasn't in a relationship—another topic to be discussed with her therapist—and even if she had been, bringing a date to this annual ordeal was a bad idea. She needed to be sharp. She needed to be on her game. She could allow no distractions when she entered the lion's den. Mr. Germaine was notorious for cornering his talent and coercing them into agreements to which they had not planned to commit. With Avery's contract ending in a short couple of weeks, there had been only light negotiations to this point regarding her future at HAP News and as the host of *American Events*. Avery had turned down the contract extension that was offered to her a few weeks back. It was a feeler offer meant to see what sort of resistance the network was up against. Avery, with the help of her agent, rejected it outright under the argument that she wanted to concentrate on the final two months of *American Events* and keep it at the top of the ratings before she worried about something as juvenile as money and the future of her career. It was nonsense. She knew it, Mosley Germaine knew it, and every other suit at the network knew it. But Avery had framed the rejection in such a way that made it difficult for Mr. Germaine to push back. So he hadn't. But tonight, in his own home, he surely would.

As far as leverage went, the move was golden. She ended the season on the highest of highs, and could now go back to the negotiation table with some ammunition. Avery and her agent were working on a counteroffer but, up to this point, had left the network hanging. Now, as Avery drove toward her boss's beach house, she was on edge. Her presence at Mosley Germaine's home was sure to lead to a discussion with her boss about her plans for the future. The night was billed as a celebration, a time to put business on hold and enjoy the success they had all found at HAP News. But Avery knew better. Tonight was a well-choreographed ambush, and she needed to be prepared.

She pulled her red Range Rover through the gates and into the circular drive. Germaine had hired a valet service for his guests' convenience and Avery surrendered her vehicle—a gift she had purchased for herself after she signed on to host *American Events*—to a polite young man who handed her a tag in return. Avery had dressed strategically for this evening's event. She wore tapered slacks that accentuated her long legs. At five-ten she didn't need much help. A white, sleeveless blouse displayed her toned arms and gave off an aura of strength, which she always needed when dealing with Mosley Germaine. Her auburn streaked hair was pulled back in a stylish ponytail to keep it out of her face when the Playa del Rey winds kicked up. Standing face to face with Mr. Germaine and constantly having to swipe wild strands of hair behind her ear was a disadvantage she would not allow. She headed up the front steps, her high heels clicking on the stone as she went—another tactical move. The heels put her squarely at six feet. When Germaine managed to find her, she would be eye to eye with him.

A hostess greeted her at the front door with a tray of champagne flutes. Avery took one and sipped it. As usual, it was some of the best she'd ever tasted. Germaine spared no expense at these annual galas, to which Avery had been invited twice before.

She had just passed through the entry foyer and walked to the edge of the kitchen when she spotted Christine Swanson.

"Ah, you made it, girl!" Christine said.

"Thank God." Avery grabbed her hand. "Give me some recon. A quick lay of the land."

"Ooh, you're in fighting mode. I love it."

"I should have worn camouflage."

"Germaine is on the patio and in a festive mood. And Mr. Hillary has honored us with his presence, as well."

"Hillary?"

David Hillary was the billionaire owner of the communications conglomerate HAP Media, of which HAP News was one of many affiliates. As executive chairman, very little happened at the company that did not contain his stamp of approval.

"Yes. He's in a white seersucker suit, looks like he just came from the tanning booth, and has his fifth wife on his arm. She looks like she just graduated from college."

"Probably with a degree in communications."

This made Christine laugh. "She won't need a degree. If she's smart, she'll divorce him in a couple years and take a hundred million with her."

"I always love when one of his exes takes another chunk of his fortune," Avery said. It had happened twice before during Avery's short tenure at HAP News.

"Why are fabulously rich men so stupid when it comes to women?" Christine asked.

"Because they think with their groins and can't help themselves."

An image of Avery's father popped into her mind. She quickly pushed it away. She could allow no stray thoughts tonight, and the hatred she carried for her father was the biggest stray of them all. Her father was another topic to discuss with the therapist she would someday hire. But tonight she needed to be focused and calculated. Avery took a long sip of champagne as she scanned the crowd. She would allow herself just a single glass before she switched to seltzer on the rocks with a twist of lime. She wanted to blend in freely but needed a clear head. Champagne was her drink of choice for such an approach. It loosened her up in ways vodka and wine could not, and it took no more than a few ounces to do so.

"What's the plan?" Christine asked.

"Let's sneak down to the beach and hide out until dinner."

This, too, was strategy. Avery wanted Mr. Germaine, and now Mr. Hillary, to know she had arrived. But she also wanted to stay out of sight. She would avoid them as long as possible. Long enough for them to drink too much and lose their edge. Then, when dinner was served she'd find her pre-assigned spot at the long table, don a big smile, and sit with all the other personalities that made up the lineup at HAP News. Out of reach and untouchable. At least for the night. Tomorrow was another day.

"Hiding out on the beach sounds delightful," Christine said. "I'll steal a bottle of Dom, or whatever this glorious stuff is, and meet you down there."

They gave each other a quick peck on the cheek before heading off in opposite directions. Avery started her careful advance through the party, doing her best to avoid the land mines she knew were waiting.

CHAPTER 4

Playa del Rey, CA
Saturday, June 5, 2021

In addition to her executive producer, Avery had also re-cruited Katelyn Carson, a morning show host, to hide out with her on the beach. The surf cascaded toward them in ro-bust waves that crashed onto shore before sputtering out a few paces from where they stood. The roaring surf compli-mented the acoustic harmonies that spilled down from the three-man band playing on Mosley Germaine's patio, some sort of folk music—a Lumineers cover, or maybe Mumford and Sons. The setting tempted Avery to have a second glass of champagne. She resisted.

When viewed from the beach, the house was a magnifi-cent structure with a slate roof and stucco siding brightened by the setting sun. The straight trunks of palm trees painted long shadows that flanked the property. A wooden gang-plank cut across a short belt of rubble and cattails that sep-arated the home from the beach. With every window and door open, the interior living space blended with the patio, which was populated by the talent at HAP News, from morning to midday, from prime time to weekends.

"Your final episode was insanity," Katelyn Carson said. "I have no idea how you did it. I was scared to death for you."

Avery's sunken minivan episode, which she had dedicated to her fallen predecessor, continued to be popular. It was not only the most watched hour of the season, but had racked up millions of views on the network's online streaming service.

"What you couldn't see on television," Avery said, "were the rescue divers surrounding the van and ready to save me if I ran into any trouble."

"I don't care if Aquaman was in that pool, I would never have been able to do it. Everyone here was talking about it earlier."

"I have Christine to thank for making it look so good."

Christine shook her head. "I didn't need to do much other than roll the tape. You did the rest."

"I heard ratings were through the roof," Katelyn said.

"Through the roof, indeed," came a deep voice from behind them.

Avery felt the smile fall from her face as she looked over her shoulder to see not just Mosley Germaine, but David Hillary as well. She quickly recovered and forced her lips upward again.

"*American Events* has really brightened your star," Mosley said.

The subtle jab—that the *show* had created Avery's popularity—did not go unnoticed. Nor did the fact that she had removed her high heels in order to navigate through the sand. She badly wanted the inches back as Mosley Germaine approached her.

"Mosley," Avery said, still smiling. "The house looks beautiful, as always."

"Thank you. It begs the question of why you're hiding down here on the beach."

"Not hiding. Just enjoying the ambiance. It must be amazing to have the ocean as your neighbor."

"We hoped you would have joined us for drinks before dinner," David Hillary said, steering the conversation despite Avery's best efforts at small talk.

"I didn't see you when I arrived," Avery said to Germaine. "And, Mr. Hillary, I didn't even know you were here. What a treat." She pointed at his white seersucker. "I love your suit."

"Dinner is about to be served," Mosley said. "So I guess we'll have no time for drinks."

"Already? I feel like I just got here. Christine and I were catching up with Katelyn. We don't get to see her much these days."

Mosley smiled. He looked at Katelyn and Christine. "Would you mind giving David and me a moment alone with Avery?"

"Sure," Katelyn said.

Christine nodded. "Of course."

"Everyone is getting seated," Mosley said. "We'll just be a minute."

Despite her best efforts to avoid this very situation, Avery found herself alone with not only her boss, but her boss's boss as well.

"Avery," David said after Katelyn and Christine were gone. "I wanted to take a moment in private to let you know how very impressed I've been this year with what you've done on *American Events*. You've really leaned into the show and allowed it to display your strengths as a journalist and host."

Avery smiled. Another backhanded compliment. She bit her tongue and didn't take the bait. This could get ugly fast if she wasn't careful.

"Mosley and I are confused about why you rejected the contract extension."

"Yes, about that. My agent and I are preparing a counteroffer but we don't have everything finalized just yet."

"We offered the extension weeks ago."

"I know. I was concentrating on finishing the last few episodes of *AE* and, unfortunately, all my focus has gone into the show."

"Understandable," David said. "But the season has ended and we need an answer from you. You're either in, or you're out. You see, we run one of the most successful networks on television for a reason. We plan things out for the future and don't like surprises. We're trying to lock in the fall lineup, and we need to know if that includes you or not."

"Of course. I'm meeting with Dwight this week."

"What was the problem with the offer? We heard only that you had rejected it, but no specifics were given," Mosley asked.

"Well . . ." Avery said. "You know, I wasn't prepared to discuss this tonight. Maybe we could put it off until next week when I can bring Dwight into the discussion."

"Time is of the essence," Mosley said. "We're working on a tight deadline to get things organized for the fall. Perhaps you could hint at what the holdup is about."

It was more a statement that a question.

"Dwight was hung up on the dollar value," Avery said.

"*Dwight Corey* was hung up?" David asked.

"At first glance, yes. But he and I were going to rework the numbers now that the show has wrapped for the season."

"The yearly compensation offered pays you handsomely and puts you in line with your contemporaries. After just your first year hosting the show, we believe that's quite generous."

An overwhelming urge flooded Avery's system to point out that putting her "in line" with her competition was an insult. She had beaten her head-to-head competition in the ratings every week for the past year, so the network should compensate her not for being *on par* with the other network personalities, but for being far above them in every demo. She also wanted to mention how inappropriate it was for these two pompous egomaniacs to isolate her out on the beach and use their positions of power to intimidate her into negotiating a contract without her agent being present. But she swallowed her urges and offered a fake smile that told them without words what she thought of the offer.

"Like I said, I promise to take a hard look at the contract this week, now that I have a bit of free time. And Dwight will get back to you right away with our thoughts."

"You do that," David said. "We look forward to hearing your thoughts. *American Events* is on hiatus for summer, but we can't allow the show to be in limbo for too long. *American Events* finished *first* in the ratings, and we want to pick up in the fall exactly where we left off. If for any reason you decide not to be part of that effort, we'd like enough time to choose your successor."

"The list is long," Mosley said. "Of potential suitors. *American Events* has the ability to make a star out of anyone who helms it. If you decide to part ways, the network would appreciate some time to prep the new host on exactly what leading *AE* requires."

She wanted badly to call their bluff. Replacing Avery now, after the show's most successful season, would be suicide. But she played along.

"I'll call Dwight in the morning," she said. "We'll get right on it."

Both men nodded as if the conversation had gone exactly as planned, then turned in the sand and headed back toward the house. It took Avery a couple of minutes to stop shaking after they were gone. Finally, she walked up the beach and across the gangplank. The remnants of sunset cast her shadow in a thin silhouette in front of her as she walked. The breeze was fresh and cool and made her realize how much she had been sweating. When she made it to the patio, she slipped her feet back into her high heels and walked along the side of the pool, which was glowing red from underwater lights, past tiki torches that lined the perimeter of the patio, and around propane fire-pit tables that gave off enough heat to hold off the chill of the ocean breeze. Servers pushed carts that held the evening's feast—roasted duck with mixed vegetables—and began serving dinner. Just as Avery took her assigned seat, Mosley Germaine stood from his throne at the head of the table and used a fork to lightly tap his wineglass and capture everyone's attention.

"I'd like to formally welcome everyone to this magnificent evening. We have all gathered here to celebrate our collective success as the cable news leader for the eleventh straight year. None of us alone are responsible for such a splendid accomplishment, and none of us alone can take credit. It was, and will continue to be, a group effort."

He raised his glass. "To past accomplishments and future success."

Everyone joined him.

"*Cheers!*"

Avery reached for the champagne flute in front of her, raised it quickly, and then took a long swallow, breaking her one-drink rule. Her strategy had already gone to hell. What was the point of staying sober?

CHAPTER 5

Coronado, CA
Tuesday, June 15, 2021

"Seven-fifty a year, for four years. That's the new offer. It includes a fifth-year option based on ratings during the final year of the contract. Incentives for reaching benchmarks in certain demos will be included as year-end bonuses."

"Seven-fifty?" Avery asked. "That's what they came back with? It's still low, Dwight."

"They came up from six-fifty, Avery. Three million over four years is a solid offer," Dwight Corey said. "As your agent, I strongly advise that you take the money and run."

It was a comfortable seventy-two degrees in Coronado, California, where the infamous Navy SEAL obstacle course was located. The track stood in all its glory in front of them. Avery had kept in touch with the SEAL who consulted on the minivan episode and, after hearing about the rigors of the SEAL program, Avery hatched the idea of giving her audience a front row look at the life of a Navy SEAL, from recruitment to Hell Week to the six-month BUDs training program. Others had produced similar exposés, but Avery had ideas about how she could put a different spin on hers.

She would attempt to complete some of the benchmarks the highly trained warriors were required to overcome before they were christened as members of the elite Special Forces group. She would jump into a pool with her arms bound behind her back and try to survive for sixty minutes, as every SEAL had done. She would brave the icy ocean waters and take the notorious night swim with the sharks. The Navy SEAL obstacle course was considered one of the hardest in the world, and Avery thought it was a good place to start.

Avery had worked her contact and arranged this morning's abbreviated test run through the course. Waivers were signed and confidentiality papers drawn up. If she managed to get the concept green-lighted, sometime during the next season of *American Events*, Avery would attempt to run the entire course, or as much of it as was physically possible, while cameras rolled. She would wear combat boots and fatigues if she ever reached that point, but for today's practice run Avery wore sport shorts and a spandex athletic tank top, short ankle socks and Nike running shoes. Her agent, on the other hand, was impeccably dressed in a beige Armani suit with the coat open but his vest buttoned and his tie tight at his neck. The morning sun glistened the beads of perspiration on his forehead and reflected off his aviator sunglasses.

"What are you, Dwight? Six-five, two-twenty?"

"Six-six, two-forty."

"I'm five-ten and . . . well, considerably less than that. Take that snazzy suit off and run this track with me."

"Not a chance. We need to figure out your contract before they pull the offer."

"Run this track with me and then I'll consider this terrible offer you've negotiated."

Ten days had passed since Avery went face to face with Mosley Germaine and David Hillary on the beach. Since then, hard negotiating had taken place.

"It's a good deal, Avery. They offered, we countered, and

now they've come back somewhere in the middle. It shows their commitment to you."

"They did not come back in the middle. They barely budged." Avery bent at the waist to stretch her hamstrings. "Mack Carter was making eight million dollars a year hosting *American Events*, and my ratings are *better* than his."

"Mack hosted the show for years. Hell, he practically created it. There *was* no *American Events* before Mack Carter. At least not the *American Events* that we all know today. And he certainly didn't make eight million during his second year as host."

"Ratings and revenue trump years of service, and you know it, Dwight. This is a lowball offer that would lock me in during what should be the most productive years of my career."

"You're young. You have decades of prime years in front of you. Avery, listen to me carefully. We can't demand Mack Carter money. He was an anomaly. Networks don't base offers on outliers, they base them on averages. This is in line with other newsmagazine show hosts."

"My *average* ratings are higher than any of my competitors."

Avery straightened and then bent sideways, reaching her arm across the side of her face to stretch her obliques.

"The show supported Mack's salary for many years," she said. "Today, ad revenue is higher with me hosting. Twelve percent higher, in fact, but they want to pay me a fraction of what they paid Mack. Do they think I'm naive, or just really bad at math? Or is it because I'm a woman?"

Avery stood up and looked at her agent.

"My last episode killed. The ratings were off the charts in every demo. We ended the season on a high note, and we should strike while the iron's hot. We have everything in our corner, all the bargaining chips."

"Oh, you mean the episode when you allowed your insane producer to drop you to the bottom of a swimming pool in a *minivan*? That's called a sweeps week stunt, and I forbid you from ever doing anything like it again. Keep pulling stunts like that and you won't have *any* years in front of you— prime or otherwise."

"It's good to know you care so much, Dwight. I like this softer side of you, but I prefer the ruthless, deal-making agent who's always had my back. Especially when you're negotiating the most important contract of my career."

"The network is not going to base your contract on sweeps week."

"I'm not asking them to base it on sweeps. I'm asking them to base it on the entire last season. The numbers speak for themselves, from ratings to revenue."

Over the past year, Avery had done a redesign of the classic newsmagazine show. The biggest difference between Avery and her competition? She never touched politics. The talking heads had that angle covered, and Avery didn't have the stomach for it. She lightly covered current events and performed the obligatory interview with dignitaries when the present environment demanded it. But she allowed her co-anchors to cover the hard news of the day while Avery took on society's nonpolitical topics. She had parlayed a journalism major into a law degree, and they each served her well in her role on *American Events*. Avery had a knack for sniffing out the truth when looking into a true-crime story, and the legal smarts to know when to hand her findings over to the authorities. One of her most-watched exposés covered the details of a missing toddler from Florida. Avery's investigation—which included interviews with the parents, a deep forensic analysis of the case report, and the discovery of new information provided by the father— uncovered disturbing evidence that suggested the child had drowned while under the supervision of her grandmother, who then hid the child's body in a shed behind her home. So startling were Avery's discoveries and so vetted were her sources that the authorities took notice and reopened the case. *American Events* cameras rolled when police showed up at the grandmother's house with search warrants and confirmed the tragic findings.

Over the past year her popular true-crime specials were legend, and her stories of hope and survival—from sinking a minivan into a pool in order to demonstrate how to escape, to jumping from an airplane to reveal the best way to recover from a failed parachute—drew viewers from all walks of life. Simply put, Avery Mason was redefining newsmagazine television and others were scrambling to keep up.

Her first contract with HAP News was a modest two-year deal that named her as a contributor to *American Events*. It allowed Avery to host several segments each season and occasionally fill in for Mack Carter when he took vacation time. Avery used those introductory years to get her feet wet and learn the business. Her rising popularity soon brought a more substantial contract that named her co-host of *American Events*. Mack Carter was the star, but Avery was earning a name for herself and finding an audience. When Mack died—a shocking event that stunned the nation—the network restructured Avery's contract into a lucrative one-year deal that paid her half a million dollars as they scrambled for a permanent host. The future of *AE* was uncertain, and in that moment, Avery was an experiment. She was inexperienced and unproven. She was young and untested. She was, everyone believed, a temporary fix. But Avery Mason had proven them all wrong. She rose to the challenge and never balked.

A year later, she now boasted an impressive record of success during her stint as the face of *American Events*. She was no longer the new girl on the block. She was no longer hoping to break through and find an audience. She had found one, and they were devoted. She was established, she was polished, and she planned to etch her legacy into the framework of the network. Katie Couric-style. Diane Sawyer-esque. But only if she stayed strong during these negotiations and showed no sign of weakness. And, Avery was well aware, if she managed to keep her past from ruining it all. Because if there was one thing that spurred the public's interest even more than watching the birth of a young starlet rising to fame, it was watching them fall from grace. Schadenfreude had become the new American pastime.

Avery walked over to Dwight. "I'm coming off a contract that by any measure was a bargain for HAP News. The bottom line is that with me as host *American Events* brought in revenues that were higher than any other show the network produced, and for the last year I've been one of the lowest paid anchors. David Hillary has made a killing off me. Now it's time for him to pay me."

Dwight took a deep breath. "Give me a number."

"Seven figures."

Dwight ran a hand over his bald head.

"It's not an outrageous ask," Avery said. "Not if you look at the numbers. And not just my numbers—ratings are up for the entire Friday night lineup because viewers stick around after *AE* is over."

"If I go back to them with a counter that high, they're going to want to know what they're paying for."

"They're paying for me, and the audience I bring with me."

"Content, my young and indestructible warrior. They're going to ask what sort of *content* you have planned for the fall. You know, your *second* full season." Dwight spread his hands and looked around. "A rehash of the Navy SEAL program is not going to cut it."

"This is just for fun. And I'm going to do a lot more than rehash the SEAL program. I'm going to immerse myself in it. But that's for later next year. For this coming fall, I'm sniffing a story that's coming out of New York. It has to do with 9/11 and the timing is uncanny."

"Give me some details. I'll need ammunition if you're sending me back to the table."

"The medical examiner in New York just identified the remains of a victim who died in the World Trade Center attack. Twenty years later and they are still identifying victims. I'm heading to New York to look into the story."

"Mason! You're up. Let's move!" a Navy commander yelled from the obstacle course starting line.

"Gotta run, D. Talk to Germaine and Hillary. Show them the numbers and remind them what a bargain I've been for the last year."

Avery hustled to the starting line, got into her ready position, and took off toward the rope wall. She grabbed the knotted line and started her ascent.

"Shit," Dwight said as he pulled his phone from the breast pocket of his unwrinkled suit.

CHAPTER 6

Negril, Jamaica
Tuesday, June 15, 2021

Walt Jenkins rented a lonely house in the forested region between Negril and West End. A ten-minute drive to the east took him into the heart of Negril and the inlands of Jamaica, far from the white sand beaches that encircled the island and the mythical resorts that decorated their shores. The interior of Jamaica was less glamorous. The blue and pink and yellow homes shed their paint, dogs wandered through the streets, and a population worked to survive. But it was a kind populace, one that welcomed the American who had moved to their land to get away from some unspoken problem back home. The locals never asked Walt what he was running from. Love or the law, his Jamaican friends liked to say, were man's only two problems in this world. But Walt had come to the right place, they told him. On this island there were "no problems, mon." For three years Walt had tried to buy into that philosophy. The rum helped.

A thirty-minute drive to the west took him to the cliffs of West End, and to more tourists than he cared to see in a lifetime. But there was an establishment there called Rick's Café and it was the only place Walt could find Hampden Estate rum—other than visiting the distillery itself, a massive compound located in Trelawny where the rum was distilled in giant pot stills. Walt had visited the distillery several times and had become close friends with the owner. His fondness for the rum made him trek to Rick's Café a couple of times each week when he had a taste for the good stuff.

The ice rattled in his glass as Walt walked to the front porch of his house. He sat in the rocker and stared out at the horizon. It had been his nightly ritual for as long as he'd been here in Jamaica. Situated deep in the forests of Negril, the sunsets from his front porch were not as spectacular as when he ventured to the coast, but they were still worthy of thirty minutes of quiet solitude. Instead of sinking into the Atlantic, here on his porch the sun simply dipped beneath the branches of palm trees and mangroves, silhouetting them black against the cherry-stained sky.

He sipped rum until the sun was gone and the stars took over the sky. It was quiet here, very different from his old life back in New York. The occasional bark from a stray dog replaced the constant blaring of horns, and he had never once been awakened by the screaming siren of an ambulance or fire truck while here in Jamaica. During his first week at the house, one of those strays had wandered onto Walt's porch and sat down next to the rocker. Walt scratched behind the dog's ear and brought him a bowl of water and beef jerky. The dog never left. Walt named him Bureau and a friendship was born.

Bureau sat at Walt's feet now as he clicked on the porch light and pulled the book he was reading onto his lap. There was a television in the house, but it picked up only local stations and offered little in the way of sports. He'd turned it on once during his first week in Jamaica but hadn't bothered with it since. Three years later, he wasn't sure it still worked. He read the local paper, and followed the Yankees and other events related to home on his iPhone. It was a device meant for communication, but Walt couldn't remember the last time he'd used it to place a call. It had been longer yet since the damn thing had rung.

He took another sip of rum and opened his book, the latest John Grisham he'd been using as a distraction from thinking too much about his upcoming trip. As soon as he opened the book, though, his self-sabotaging ways prevented the diversion he was hoping to find in the pages. The chapter where he'd left off was kept by an American Airlines reservation he had printed the day before. He was headed back to New York, and the sight of the reservation stirred anxiety in his chest. He took another sip of rum, his self-prescribed antidote to such uneasiness, while cursing the subliminal workings of his brain that had caused him to place the ticket in a spot where he'd never miss it, and admiring the move at the same time. In his previous life he was a surveillance agent with the FBI. He worked on the fringes, never in the spotlight, and his actions had always been hidden and inconspicuous. He was glad to know that this many years removed from the Bureau he hadn't lost his touch, even if tonight he was his own target.

He moved the reservation to the back of the book and began reading. The words, though, were lost on him. While his eyes blindly skimmed the pages, his mind was already running through the details of his upcoming trip, what he would say, and how he would handle seeing her again after so long.

Love or the law, man's only two problems in this world.

CHAPTER 7

Los Angeles, CA
Wednesday, June 16, 2021

The red Range Rover was the perfect cruising vehicle for Avery's cross-country journey. With the cruise control pegged at eighty mph and nothing in front of her but open road and an entire country to conquer, the Range Rover nearly drove itself. She'd purchased it a year ago after signing on as temporary host of *American Events*. It was the first time in her adult life that Avery Mason had made any real money of her own. She'd spent an obnoxious amount of money for four wheels and a souped-up engine, but there was some part of her psyche—perhaps the unbreakable link to her past life—that made it an easy purchase. Maybe she had more of her father's blood in her than she cared to admit. The difference, Avery never stopped reminding herself, was that her status in the world had been earned honestly, and legally. The same certainly could not be said of her father.

She was headed to New York by way of Wisconsin, a journey that would cover more than three thousand miles. The airlines were faster and easier but were out of the question.

As was rail travel or the thought of renting a car to avoid putting thousands of miles on her Range Rover. Airline reservations, train tickets, and rental car receipts left paper and digital trails. Avery wanted to make as few footprints as possible while she tiptoed across the country. She had business in New York and would do her best to conduct it under the radar. No one was watching her, she had convinced herself, and hitting the road rather than taking to the air was pure paranoia. Still, the fewer tracks she left, the better.

On Wednesday morning, she drove out of Los Angeles via the 605 and hooked up with Interstate 15 where she stayed for ten straight hours, less two bathroom breaks. She jumped onto I-70 and arrived in Grand Junction, Colorado, just as the last tussles of sunlight burned on the horizon. She found a Hyatt and paid cash for a single night. When she laid her head on the pillow she could still feel the smooth vibration from her hours on the road. She closed her eyes and hoped for sleep, always an elusive item during her summer treks. Like clockwork, memories of her family pushed themselves to the forefront of her mind during her cross-country trips. How could they not? Her family was what she had run from. Her family was what she was hiding.

During the rest of the year, Avery was a sound sleeper who never remembered her dreams. But each summer when she headed back to her past, her dreams were vivid and wild. They mostly alternated between her mother and father—a dead mother and a convict for a father. She loved her mother with all her heart, and had once loved her father the same way. But that love had been tainted by her father's betrayal, and in its wake was a combination of hatred and scorn for the man Avery had once considered her hero. Tonight, though, holed up in a hotel somewhere near the Rockies, her parents were absent from her dreams. When sleep came to her, so too did memories of her brother.

The Oyster 625 weighed in at seventy thousand pounds and measured sixty-four feet in length. A blue water cruiser capable of handling the rough seas off the coast of New York, the sailboat was big, sturdy, and expensive. With a price tag north of $3 million, it was an obnoxious gift from her father for her twenty-first birthday. Designed to accommodate a racing crew of eight, the boat was also crafted for leisurely outings that could be handled by a pair of accomplished sailors, which Avery and Chris-topher were. Yet, two hours after Claire-Voyance *left the marina, the sea churned with angry waves that crested at four feet and crashed over the sides of the boat. On down-swings, the waves seemed to swallow the bow. The rain came in dense sheets that cut visibility to next to nothing.*

They'd brought down the sails and the engine was fighting against the waves and the currents. The marina was more than two miles away and only choppy water and black skies were visible. The ocean lifted the magnifi-cent boat into the air and dropped it like a toy into the crashing waves. Avery felt the Oyster pulling to the star-board side and she had trouble reining it in. The wheel wanted to twist clockwise and she fought to keep her west-ward course. The big boat, however, was pulling too hard. Something was wrong. Then she noticed the heel. No, not a heel but a dip. The bow was inching downward, as if ready to dive into the sea. She thought it was a swell that had dipped the front of the boat, but when it didn't recover she knew it was sinking.

She lifted the cover of the DSC—digital selective call-ing—button and pressed it, sending a distress signal to the Coast Guard telling them the name of the vessel and her exact location in longitude and latitude. For good measure, and because she was scared to death, she picked up the transmitter and placed it to her lips.

"Mayday, mayday, mayday. This is Claire-Voyance. *Mayday, mayday, mayday."*

The squawk of the voice was loud and static filled, yet barely audible over the rain and wind.

"Go ahead, Claire-Voyance, *this is the Coast Guard. We have your location and are dispatching a crew. What's your situation?"*

"We're an Oyster 625 in heavy rain and high winds. Four- to six-foot white caps and taking on water."

"Roger that, Claire-Voyance. *How many onboard?"*

"Two," she yelled over the roar of the waves. *"We're in a squall and taking on water. We're heavily pitched to the starboard side."*

"What's your timeframe, Claire-Voyance*?"*

"I'm not sure," she said, as a wave crashed down over the bow of the boat. *"My brother went below deck to find the source of the breach. To see if he could contain it."*

"Tell your brother to come above board. We'll stay with you until our crew arrives."

"We won't have time," Avery said as another wave engulfed the bow. *"We're capsizing."*

Avery bolted up in bed before she knew she was awake. It was her normal reaction to the recurrent dream, and she had determined it was a defense mechanism. Jolt herself awake so she didn't have to relive the image of the Oyster's bow dipping below the surface and then twisting vertically before spearing to the bottom of the ocean. Wake herself before her mind replayed her battle with the sea as she fought against the six-foot waves that did their best to drown her.

She lay back in bed and sunk her head into the pillow, pushing away all the confusing thoughts that hid in the shadows of her mind and waited to surface each summer when Avery made her trip home. She couldn't allow those thoughts to distract her from what she needed to do. She had the summer to tie up the frayed and loose ends of her family's saga. What happened after that would be out of her control. If, at that point, the floodgates opened and all the sordid details of her past spilled forth, at least she would have done her best for the ones she loved.

CHAPTER 8

Sister Bay, WI
Friday, June 18, 2021

Avery was back on the road by 6 A.M. the following morning with a tall coffee in the console—two creams, two sugars—smooth reggae on the radio, and open road in front of her. East of Denver she slipped onto I-80 where she'd stay for two days. Lincoln, Nebraska, was her second overnight. On Friday morning, she crossed the entire state of Iowa before finding the Wisconsin boarder. She headed northeast, conquering the state on a diagonal track. White cedar and jack pines soon dominated the landscape as far as the eye could see. The lodge pole pines reminded her of her teenage years and the summers she spent in this part of the country.

By 3:30 p.m. Friday afternoon she made it to the southern edge of the thumb of the Door County peninsula. She drove north on Highway 42 and followed the two-lane road for forty miles. The shores of Lake Michigan's Green Bay were to the west as she passed through the towns of Egg Harbor and Fish Creek. Eagle Harbor glistened in the afternoon sun as she navigated through the busy town of Ephraim. The red-striped awning of Wilson's ice cream parlor filled her mind with memories of long, hot summers as a teenager—the best of her life.

Toward the tip of the peninsula Avery found Sister Bay, Wisconsin, the town where she had spent every summer of her childhood. Avery's parents had shipped her from Manhattan to Wisconsin, where she spent the summer, starting in the sixth grade, along with other wealthy kids from around the country, at Connie Clarkson's School of Sailing. Eighty percent of the kids at the summer camp came from the Midwest. The rest traveled from the West and East Coasts and were kids whose parents were hungry for them to learn to sail at one of the most prestigious and sought-after institutions in the country.

Avery's parents had done the same for her older brother, Christopher, whose return home at the end of every summer came with grand tales of life on the water, harnessing the Lake Michigan winds, and gliding through Green Bay. The names and places became legend to Avery. Washington Island, Rock Island, St. Martin Island, Summer Island, Big Bay de Noc, and Peninsula Point Lighthouse. Avery couldn't wait for her turn. When it finally came, she seized the opportunity. By the time Avery was in eighth grade she could manage a twenty-two-foot schooner by herself. During high school, Avery returned to Sister Bay each summer as a sailing instructor—a position typically reserved for college students but one Avery earned from her advanced skills on the water. At seventeen she was a more polished sailor than any of the college-aged kids who taught at the school, and she could give many of the adults a run for their money. During college her summers were spent running Connie's school as the chief instructor. Avery owed her work ethic and indomitable spirit to the summers spent in Sister Bay, and specifically to Connie Clarkson, the owner of the sailing school and Avery's mentor.

As she navigated the last mile of her journey, Avery's thoughts shifted from those wonderful summers of her youth to the troubled times of recent. Things were easier as a kid, when all she cared about was being on the water and harnessing the wind. Things were easier then, before she learned that everything in her life was a fraud.

She pulled the Range Rover through the long, canopied drive that led to the parking lot of Connie's sailing school. Sitting on ten acres, the property was forested and nestled along the bay. Twelve Northwoods-styled cabins were situated around the property to house thirty-two students each summer. Avery parked and stared out at the waters of Lake Michigan. A dozen boats were moored at the dock, with two lifts anchored in place to pull the skiffs from the water. In the middle of June the place was busy with students and instructors. Avery allowed the flood of emotions—from her time here as a young woman, to her relationship with Connie Clarkson, to the memories of her brother, and to the betrayal and destruction her father's lies had caused—to overwhelm her.

She didn't bother to camouflage her red-rimmed eyes or smeared makeup before she crossed the parking lot and walked up the steps of the main house. She knocked twice and waited. A minute later, Connie Clarkson answered. A smile came to the woman's face. They embraced like mother and daughter.

"Claire," Connie said into her ear. "I'm so glad you made it."

CHAPTER 9

Manhattan, NY
Friday, June 18, 2021

It had been three years since Walt Jenkins left New York; 1,140 days since he exchanged the hustle and bustle, the congested streets, and smog-filled air for the quiet tranquility of Jamaica. The time had passed in random stretches of achingly slow weeks and blink-of-the-eye months. By any measure he was doing better today than when he had left. Not fully back to where he had been, but fixed to whatever degree that time heals all wounds, both physical and emotional. He was back in New York for just one night, the same night for which he had returned each of the past three years. Keeping with the tradition of his life, Walt's return to New York was counterproductive at best, blatantly destructive at worst. He was too smart to believe anything good would come from this night, but too stupid to stay away.

As June approached and the annual survivors meeting crept closer, Walt found himself checking airfare. He returned each year for the annual meeting, selfishly took from the participants whatever spiritual enlightenment he needed to make it another year, and then hopped on a plane back to Jamaica where he drank rum in quiet isolation and tried to undo the damage the trip had caused. It was no way to exist and could not continue. Yet here he was again, caught in a downward spiral from which he could not escape. Something needed to change or he'd swirl down the drain of life and never be seen again. He'd been on the brink with alcohol before the Bureau fired him—*retired* him, he corrected himself, with his full pension. That was three years ago, and he definitely overindulged now. He hadn't talked with his parents or siblings in three years, save for a phone call at Christmas. He'd lost just about every friend he'd ever made. The reason behind it all was a woman. The very one he went to New York to see each year. Walt Jenkins gave *self-sabotage* new meaning.

The New York chapter of Trauma Survivors held its reunion each June in Ascent Lounge of the Time Warner building in Manhattan. It was an annual gathering of trauma victims who had miraculously beaten the odds to cheat death and come out on the other side of life. Alive, yes. But different from the people they had once been. The night consisted of speeches and awards, guests of honor and distinguished charter members, old stories and new. An entire portion of the night was reserved for honoring the doctors and nurses, EMTs and firefighters, and other first responders whose quick thinking and skill had saved every life of every survivor present.

Present this evening were survivors of every kind: A woman who was the only one to walk away from a plane crash that killed eighty-two other passengers; a man who had jumped from a burning car just before it exploded as it crashed down a mountainside; a hiker who had endured two weeks in the wilderness with no food and little water; a motorcyclist who had no earthly reason for walking away from the crash that turned his bike into a jagged ball of steel; and Walt Jenkins, the federal agent who had survived two bullets to the torso— one that tore his neck to pieces, the other that pierced his heart. Ninety-nine times out of one hundred, his trauma surgeon told him, such gunshot wounds were fatal.

In addition to the survivors, the guest list included family members who had lost loved ones to the same trauma the other guests had survived. The families of the victims of that plane crash that killed all but one of the passengers. The parents of the drunken teenager who had died during the auto accident that sent the man's burning car over the cliff. The sister of the man who did not make it out of the wilderness with his hiking partner. The truck driver whose cab had been the backstop for the sliding motor-cycle. Walt returned to New York each year to see one family member in particular.

This far removed from his former occupation in the FBI, Walt owned just one suit. Formal attire was not required for his new life in Jamaica, and he had trashed every sport coat and tie he owned before he made the move years earlier. Now he pulled the lapels down tightly on his shoulders, straightened his tie, and took a deep breath before he pulled open the heavy doors of the Ascent Lounge. He made a beeline for the bar.

"What kind of rum do you have?" he asked the bartender.

The young man slid a menu across the bar. Walt ran his finger down the surprisingly large selection of rum and chose a Mount Gay 1703. The bartender poured it on the rocks and served it in a bottom-heavy tumbler, which felt perfectly balanced in his hand when Walt lifted it to his lips. His pension was not fat enough to afford Mount Gay, and ordering rum he couldn't afford always stirred anxiety in his gut. Until he took the first sip. With drink in hand he leaned against the rail of the bar and surveyed the room. It was still early. The presentations and speeches had not yet started. He wanted a drink or two in him before he came face to face with her. As he swallowed his second sip of rum, he felt a light hand on his shoulder.

"Walt," a woman said.

Walt knew the voice immediately. Dr. Eleanor Marshfield was the trauma surgeon who had sewn him back up. He turned with a smile.

"No surprise that I found you at the bar," Dr. Marshfield said.

Walt offered a pained look on his face, then held up his rum. "Guilty as charged. Can I buy you one?"

"No, thank you. I'm on call."

Walt nodded. The woman spent her life waiting for tragedies—car accidents and gunshot wounds. It was a hell of a way to live, but Walt was glad for her calling. She had saved his life.

"How have you been, Walt?"

"Good." Walt bobbled his head up and down. "*Pretty* good."

"How's work?"

"I'm . . . not working anymore."

Dr. Marshfield raised her eyebrows and wrinkled her forehead. "I thought that was only a temporary thing."

Walt smiled. "Me too. But I guess there's an unwritten rule in the FBI that after an agent takes two bullets through the heart, his services are no longer required."

"It was just one through the heart. The other was through your neck. I'm good, but I'm not *that* good."

"Thanks for the correction."

"What's been occupying your free time as a retired man?"

Rum, surf, guilt, and regret.

"I haven't quite figured out the retirement thing yet," he finally said. "But I'm working on it."

"You're young. You've got your whole life in front of you."

Walt didn't bother mentioning that that was exactly what he was worried about.

Dr. Marshfield's phone buzzed and she looked at the screen. "I was hoping to stay longer. I've only spoken to a few of my past patients, but I've got to run over to the hospital. It was great seeing you, Walt. I'm glad you're doing well."

"Thanks, Doc. I'm glad you found me."

She smiled. "See you next year?"

"If I'm still alive."

"You will be. Just don't run into any more bullets. And maybe take it easy on the alcohol."

He watched her leave and took a sip of rum before he returned to scanning the crowd. He spent thirty minutes looking for her, his eyes fooling him a number of times—thinking he'd spotted her only to be disappointed when the woman turned, allowing Walt to see the face of a stranger. He ordered another rum.

"Walt. Freakin'. Jenkins!"

Walt looked to his left. The face that materialized was from his distant past. Scott Sherwood was his former staff chief when he was working for the New York State Bureau of Criminal Investigation back in the nineties.

"Scott?" Walt shook his head and smiled. "What the hell are you doing here?"

"I came with a friend. She said she needed moral support, but since the moment we walked through the door she's been talking with the doctors and nurses who helped her. I was about to take off when I thought I recognized my old friend at the bar. Damn! How long has it been?"

"I don't know. Twenty years?"

"Has it been that long?" Scott shook his head. "Where does it go?"

"You tell me."

"What have you been doing for the last few years? I ask around about my old friend Walt Jenkins, but nobody knows a thing?"

"Yeah, I've been out of the loop. I had to ditch New York to get myself straight. Never really found my way back."

"You know I reached out a few times after you . . . you know. After you were shot."

"I did know that, Scott, and thank you. I'm sorry I never got back to you. That was a weird time for me. Shit, I never got back to a lot of people. But I knew you had called. It meant a lot to me. I'm a shit for not letting you know."

"No," Scott said, waving him off. "I can only imagine what you were going through. I just wanted you to know that I heard about your situation and had you on my mind, that's all. Everyone back at BCI was thinking about you."

Walt pointed at the bar behind him. "Let me buy you a drink?"

Scott nodded. "Sure. Beefeater and tonic."

Walt ordered from the bartender and handed Scott his drink.

"To old friends," Scott said, taking his glass and tipping it toward Walt.

Walt smiled. "Old friends."

"So what *have* you been up to? God knows I've asked enough people. Nobody knows what happened to you."

Walt smiled. "Nothing exciting. I had to get out of town for a while, so I did."

"Where'd you go?"

Walt paused before answering. "Uh, I actually headed to Jamaica. I thought it would be for a month or two. Turns out, I never came back."

"Jamaica?"

Walt nodded. "Negril, on the West End."

"I wouldn't know Jamaica from Aruba. And what? You're going to sit on a beach the rest of your life?"

"Not really sure. The Bureau gave me a nice pension, and I don't have any definitive plans at the moment."

"Sounds like life is good. I'm glad to see you doing well, Walt."

Walt smiled and nodded again. Over Scott Sherwood's shoulder and through the crowd, he finally spotted her. He hadn't been looking, yet somehow his gaze was drawn to her. She was talking to someone, and laughing in a way that brought comfort to his heart. A heart that literally ached from time to time—mostly from the scar tissue that had formed, but sometimes, he was sure, because he missed her so much.

"Scott," Walt said, taking his gaze off her to look at his old friend. "It was really good seeing you, buddy. I don't mean to cut you off, but I've got to talk with someone I just noticed was here."

"Of course. Thanks for the drink. Good seeing you, too. Jamaica, huh?"

Walt smiled. "Come down sometime. I've got an extra room."

"You serious?"

Walt glanced back into the crowd, sensing an urgency to speak with her. As if another moment's delay would cause him to miss his chance. He looked back at Scott Sherwood.

"Of course I'm serious."

Scott set his drink on the bar and reached for his phone. "Let me get your number. Maybe I'll call you to take you up on the offer."

Walt smiled impatiently. He rattled off his cell phone number.

"You better answer when I call."

Walt slapped his friend on the shoulder. "You bet. Good to see you, Scott."

Walt turned and made his way through the crowd. She seemed to sense his presence because she turned just as he was approaching. Immediately, she smiled. They stared at each other for a moment; everyone else in the room disappeared. So much was spoken between them without either saying a word.

Finally, she reached out and put her arms around his neck.

Walt wrapped her in a tight hug.

"Hi, Meghan."

"My God, it's good to see you," she whispered in his ear.

There were a thousand things Walt wanted to say. A thousand things he had rehearsed. Things he had thought about every day during the year that had passed since he had last seen her. That he loved her as much now as he did three years ago. That he missed her in a way he had never missed another person. That if the universe were a less cruel place, they'd have met each other earlier in life. That he hadn't left because his love for her had faded, but because it was easier to be miserable living on an island in the Caribbean than in the same city as the woman he loved but couldn't be with.

Walt said none of those things, though. He just closed his eyes and held her tight, feeling her heart thud against his own.

CHAPTER 10

Sister Bay, WI
Friday, June 18, 2021

It had been years since anyone called her Claire. No one else, in fact, referred to her today as anything other than Avery Mason. She wondered if it was really possible to erase a past and become someone else. Childhood memories rooted deeply in her subconscious told her that it was not. No matter how many years passed, some part of her would always be Claire Montgomery. The part of her that was tethered to Connie Clarkson had no other identity.

Born Claire Avery Montgomery, she had not legally changed her name to Avery Mason, but had used the moniker in the byline of her first article for the *LA Times* when she was twenty-eight years old. It stuck. Not coincidentally, it was the same year her father was indicted for one of the largest Ponzi schemes in American history. The name change was a strategic move made after she graduated law school and tried to escape her family's legacy. Being the daughter of Garth Montgomery had ended her legal career before it started. No one would trust the daughter of one of America's greatest thieves to honestly pursue criminals, so she hadn't tried. With a useless law degree and a family lineage she was trying to expunge, she fled New York and landed in Southern California. She fell back on her undergraduate degree in journalism to secure a job as a beat writer for the *Los Angeles Times*. It paid little and was a far cry from the life she had left behind. Once the daughter of a billionaire and the recipient of a trust fund meant to provide a lifetime of financial independence, she landed in LA and for the first time in her life needed to fend for herself.

Soon after starting at the *Times*, she stumbled across the story of the missing Florida toddler. The story was picked up nationally, and her investigation gained the attention of Mack Carter. She, as Avery Mason, was asked to appear as a guest on *American Events* to tell the story, which led to a three-part special. The final two-hour episode included the dramatic footage of Avery, followed by *American Events* cameras, accompanying the police when they made their disturbing discovery in a shed behind the grandmother's home. Mack Carter had been so impressed with Avery's investigative instincts that he asked her back on the show several times that year. She was just twenty-nine years old at the time. The frequent guest spots led to a more permanent role as a regular contributor. Her ratings proved the young journalist popular. After two years as a contributor, she was asked to join the show permanently as co-host. When Mack Carter died she found herself in the unlikely position as the new face of one of America's longest running newsmagazine shows. On the surface, Avery Mason was a young, successful journalist with her entire career in front of her. Inside, she was a nervous wreck that the attention would shine a spotlight on her past and link her to Garth Montgomery—her father, the Thief of Manhattan.

Throughout the 1990s and 2000s the Montgomery family

had been a symbol of the American Dream—a hardworking family who had reached the upper echelons of society through grit and determination. Garth Montgomery founded Montgomery Investment Services in 1986, a New York–based hedge fund that offered security brokerage and investment advisory services to banks, financial institutions, and high net worth individuals. After three decades of managing the portfolios of some of the country's wealthiest people, advising some of the world's largest corporations, overseeing retirement funds for America's biggest unions, and controlling the endowments of influential universities, the firm had $50 billion in assets under management. It looked like a well-managed global fund making millions for its clients. In reality, it was a massive Ponzi scheme that paid long-term investors outrageous returns generated from new investors' deposits. A house of cards waiting to fall, it finally did, and in stunning fashion.

Forensic accountants determined that more than $30 billion had been fraudulently obtained and squandered on Garth Montgomery's jet-setting lifestyle. The rest of the company's "assets" were make believe—the books were so cooked they nearly incinerated when the feds finally got their hands on them. The federal indictments came the summer after Claire Montgomery graduated law school, and she still held vivid memories of federal agents crashing through the front door of her family's Manhattan penthouse, pulling her father from bed in his pajamas, and walking him in handcuffs to the waiting squad car parked in front of the building. The perp walk had been seen the world over. Photos of it were splashed on the front page of every newspaper, and video footage led every news program. Type the name *Garth Montgomery* into any search engine and the first image that popped up was her father, pajama-clad with hands cuffed behind his back and a score of federal agents leading him from the building.

Despite that she had been warned of the details, she was still shocked by the enormity of the situation when the specifics of House of Cards—the FBI's name for the operation that brought down Montgomery Investment Services—became public. It was like watching a horror movie that starred her father as the villain. If the allegations were true, and she knew they were, it meant that her father had defrauded thousands of people out of their life savings, many blue-collar workers out of their retirements, and universities out of decades of endowment contributions. The allegations meant the Montgomery family was a mirage, both morally and materially. Everything they owned was contaminated by greed and deceit—the penthouse, the Hamptons mansion, the Aspen villa, the beachfront condo on St. Barts, the cars, the jet, her trust fund. Even the *Claire-Voyance*, her majestic sailboat that had sunk the previous summer, had come from ill-gotten money. But it wasn't just the *things* that were an illusion, it was the lie that they were ever a happy family.

Perhaps worse than the financial fraud was the personal deceit that came to light in the wake of her father's conviction. Garth Montgomery's mistress was discovered. A forty-year-old woman her father had been sleeping with for more than a decade, her entire lifestyle had been financed by Garth Montgomery and the money he stole. The affair dated back to Avery's teenage years, and all at once the late nights her father constantly worked and the frequent business trips made sense. Even the idea that Avery and her brother had been shipped off to Wisconsin each summer had felt tainted by deceit. The revelation of her father's dual life had cut deeper than knowing her whole life had been a fantasy. The discovery wrecked her mother—a complete deconstruction of the life she believed she had built with the man she loved. A heart attack claimed Annette Montgomery when she was just sixty-two years old, a mere eight months after federal agents hauled her husband from bed in the early dawn hours. Despite an autopsy revealing chronic and undetected coronary artery disease, Avery couldn't get past the idea that her father's betrayal had been the real cause of death. It was this festering thought that continued to fuel the disgust she felt toward her father. Though her mother's passing had been another tragedy to bear, there was some sense of peace knowing her mother would not have to endure the stigma that came with being the wife of one of the most hated men in America.

Anguish and anger eventually gave way to clarity. The life Claire Montgomery had lived for twenty-eight years was over. Survival would come only from reinventing herself. So she did, and Avery Mason was born.

CHAPTER 11

Sister Bay, WI
Saturday, June 19, 2021

Avery spent the evening at Connie Clarkson's home drinking wine and catching up. Earlier in the day she toured the campus, visited the cabin where she used to stay each summer, walked the docks, and spoke with the students who were spending the summer. In the evening, she and Connie shared stories and life's highlights since they had last seen each other the year before. Avery asked about the school. Enrollment was full and the waitlist was long. The school would survive. Connie would make it. Things were not the same today as they had once been, but Connie was managing. If the woman held a grudge about what had happened, she had never shown it.

It was, of course, Connie's connection to the Montgomery children and the many summers they spent in Sister Bay that allowed Garth Montgomery to approach her with an investment opportunity. Connie was hesitant at first to become so intimately connected in business to the father of two of her former students, but eventually gave in to the smooth-talking financial wizard. There were too many benefits of investing with such a storied firm for Connie to decline. Garth Montgomery promised to work tirelessly for her and capture the returns that were so common at Montgomery Investment Services. The firm had strict rules about minimum investments, but Mr. Montgomery was willing to waive the rules for such a close family friend. Connie had socked away $2 million over the course of her life, and handed every penny over to Avery's father. He promised to double it in five years.

The feds knocked on the front doors of Montgomery Investment Services a year later. Search warrants followed, as did freezing of accounts and seizure of assets. When the dust settled, along with every other client of Garth Montgomery, Connie Clarkson learned that her money was gone. Detailed accounting showed that it had been paid to long-term investors who were due outrageous returns the fund could not legitimately cover. Some of it was surely squandered on the lavish lifestyle of a billionaire who had robbed his way to the American Dream. Garth Montgomery had promised Connie everything and left her with nothing.

Their conversation eventually moved away from Garth Montgomery and settled on the death of Avery's mother. Connie was Avery's surrogate mother, so it was natural for Avery to pour out her heart to this woman. And then, as always, talk moved to Avery's brother. Christopher had been, after all, Connie's most cherished student over the years.

It was only later that night, after Avery was tucked quietly into Connie's guest room, that her thoughts returned to her father. Despite the prosecution's argument that Garth Montgomery was the very definition of a flight risk, he had disappeared after posting bail. The feds suspected he hadn't gotten far, having surrendered his passport, and with all of his assets frozen. Mexico, likely, but South America couldn't be ruled out. Although sightings had been reported as far as Europe and Australia. The only thing they knew for certain was that he had gotten far enough to stay hidden for the past three and a half years.

The feds had spoken to Avery multiple times over those years, and questioned her about her father's whereabouts. She always told them the same thing: she had no idea where her father was hiding, had no interest in finding him, and was happy he was gone. It had always been the truth. Then the postcard arrived and changed everything.

On Sunday morning Avery and Connie took a sail aboard the Moorings 35.2 that was moored at Connie's dock. Avery knew the boat, built by Beneteau, was sturdy, well designed, and expertly crafted. It didn't stop her from meticulously inspecting every detail. By seven in the morning they were on an even heel with Connie at the helm. Even after losing her life's savings, Connie Clarkson's passion never faded. The woman lived to sail. Avery owned a thirty-five-foot Catalina that she docked in Santa Monica and sailed nearly every weekend. Despite this, she took instruction from her old mentor as if she hadn't sailed in years. They made it to Washington Island before turning back. The spinnaker flapped wildly as they came about, and then filled again as they reached a close-hauled course on their new tack. As the boat dug into a fifteen-degree heel, they both sat back and enjoyed the ride. Over the last few years, Avery had seen pain and disappointment affect Connie in unmistakable ways. But today, as she sat at the helm of this particular sailboat, Avery saw the sparkle she remembered from her teenage years return to Connie's eyes.

By afternoon Avery was back in her Range Rover and on the road again, eyes red rimmed and burning from her goodbye. Five hours later she fought traffic on the Dan Ryan Expressway as she battled through Chicago. It was dark by the time she made it across Indiana and into Ohio and started looking for a hotel. The first stop of her journey was behind her—the annual pilgrimage to Connie Clarkson's home. Avery had another full day of driving before she would reach New York. There, she would chase the story of a 9/11 victim identified twenty years after the Twin Towers fell. But really, she would be chasing something else.

As she drove, the postcard sat on the passenger seat. It carried an image of a wooden cabin surrounded by the leaves of autumn. On the back was handwriting Avery had recognized the moment she pulled it from her mailbox. She had ripped up the card when she realized whom it was from. Later, though, the untamable lure of unconditional love found her, and the natural bond that ties daughters to their fathers emerged and forced her to tape the pieces back together and read her father's words. It did not take long to dawn on her that her father hadn't sent the card because he missed her. He hadn't sent it to acknowledge his wife's passing. He sent it because he needed help.

Getting in touch with her father would be dangerous. Offering assistance of any kind would be outright stupid. She had nothing to gain from doing so, but everything to lose. Still, she couldn't stop looking at the numbers her father had written along the bottom of the card.

777

She knew what they meant, and had tried hard to ignore them. The federal agents who had asked Avery questions about her father's whereabouts had it wrong. He was not in Mexico or South America. He hadn't made it as far as Europe or Australia. He was right here in the United States, and Avery knew exactly where.

CHAPTER 12

Manhattan, NY
Tuesday, June 22, 2021

Exhausted from her week of travel, and drained from the emotional upheaval of seeing Connie Clarkson, Avery had taken the day to decompress. But now, feeling rejuvenated, she needed the distraction of her work to clear her mind. She came to New York to gather information. She came to chase a story. Her meeting tonight was meant to test the strength of that story. Avery believed that the identification of a 9/11 victim twenty years after the towers fell was fascinating. If the details turned out to be as interesting as they sounded, Avery would pitch the idea to her producers and get the network to greenlight formal recorded interviews for production in the fall to coincide with the twenty-year anniversary of 9/11.

In the evening, she took a long, hot shower, put herself together, and rode the elevator to the lobby where she hailed a cab to Kips Bay. The taxi crawled through Manhattan traffic until the driver pulled to the curb outside Cask Bar. Avery paid the fare, crossed the sidewalk, and entered the tavern.

Inside, she took a seat at the long mahogany bar and ordered a Tito's and soda. She checked her watch, 7:30 p.m., and kept an eye on the door. Halfway through her cocktail, Avery spotted a tall woman stride through the door and immediately recognized her.

Dr. Livia Cutty had completed her residency and fellowship in North Carolina before taking over the Office of the Chief Medical Examiner in New York. Her time in North Carolina had been punctuated by her involvement in a disturbing case of missing women from bordering states, and the evidence she discovered that helped break the case. After she came to New York, she was linked to one of the most-watched true-crime documentaries in television history when her expertise in forensic pathology helped successfully solve the case of an American medical student who had been killed in the Caribbean. Her exposure in both cases attracted worldwide attention. Both criminal defense attorneys and prosecutors alike sought Livia Cutty's expertise as a high-profile forensic pathologist. She was a medical consultant for NBC and HAP News, and Avery had worked with her on a number of occasions over the past few years when her true-crime specials required the knowledge of a leading pathologist. Avery had reached out to discuss the recent discovery her office had made—the first successful identification of a 9/11 victim in years.

"Livia, thanks so much for this," Avery said as Livia walked up to the bar.

"Are you kidding me? When Avery Mason calls, I'm interested. What are you doing in New York?"

"I'm on summer sabbatical, but when this news broke I knew I had to talk with you to get the details."

"Happy to help any way I can."

They sat on adjacent stools and Livia ordered a white wine.

"I'm fascinated with the discovery your office recently made," Avery said. "I'd love to get some details about it. I'm hoping to feature the process and the discovery on my show in the fall. The timing is eerie."

"It is," Livia said. "Twenty years later and we're still identifying victims from the World Trade Center. It's mind numbing."

"I'm curious how that's even possible. Tell me about it."

"Well, I obviously wasn't the ME in New York during 9/11. But I've heard stories from folks who were on the frontlines. Some of them are still part of the office today. It was horrific, as you might imagine. When the towers fell, the loss of life was not only tragic, but destructive. Gruesome, even. There were very few fully intact bodies recovered from the rubble. Mostly what was found were body parts. It made identifying the victims a monumental challenge. Many recovered body parts were too badly damaged to match them together, so each one had to be identified. Since many of the bodies were catastrophically burned, the usual methods of identification—finding a tattoo or a birthmark or other distinguishing characteristics—were impossible. Instead, we had to rely on DNA. Dental records helped in some cases. But relying on dental ID and DNA analysis had its limitations. Those methods are reliant on the families delivering dental records and DNA samples of their loved ones to the medical examiner's office. As we sit here tonight, there are over twenty thousand pieces of remains, mostly bone fragments, that have yet to be identified. We've extracted DNA from a portion of those remains but we have nothing to match it to."

"Because families never provided a reference DNA sample?"

"Correct."

"And the rest of the twenty thousand remains?"

"Until recently," Livia said, "we had no way of extracting DNA from them. And remember, we're talking about thousands of bone fragments. The math is simple. Just fewer than three thousand people died when the towers collapsed. We have over twenty thousand specimens to ID. Many of those specimens belong to the same victim. Occasionally, we extract DNA from bone and realize the remains belong to an already identified victim. We check it off the list and move on. But many of the bone fragments were burned so badly that nearly all of the DNA was destroyed."

"Until you developed this new technology."

"Correct. And I wish I could take credit for developing it, but I can't. I'm only peripherally involved in the identification process. That's handled by Dr. Arthur Trudeau who, along with his team of scientists and technicians, works tirelessly each day on the 9/11 project."

"Tell me about the process. Again, I hope to come back later in the summer and formally interview you on camera. Dr. Trudeau, as well."

Livia nodded. "That could certainly be arranged. I, too, find it fascinating. Here's how it works. Typically, extracting DNA from bone is straightforward. A scraping is taken from the bone's surface to obtain bone cells. DNA is then extracted from those cells using EDTA and proteinase K, which are enzymes that break down the cell wall and allow the DNA to spill out. If you want to get into the weeds on the chemistry of how it works, I'm happy to."

Avery shook her head. "No thanks. We'll find a way to more easily explain the process when we get to that point. For now, I'll take your word for it. It's a simple process if you say so."

Livia offered a smile. "It's the classic method, or the gold standard. Performed every day at crime labs across the country. But most of the bone harvested from Ground Zero was too badly burned to extract DNA from the surface. Remember, the jet fuel burned at two thousand degrees for more than one hundred hours. Some of the bodies were likely incinerated completely to ash. But the remains that *were* found were brought to the New York ME's office for identification. The remains that could not be immediately identified were stored and preserved for later analysis. That analysis has been ongoing for years and is still happening today, twenty years later. This latest identification came from a new process of pulverizing the bone nearly to ash, and then taking the residue from the innermost aspect of the bone, the area that was furthest from the damaging flames, and extracting DNA from the cells we find there. It's proven to be quite effective. We're optimistic that many more IDs will follow."

"Fascinating," Avery said. "And the family of the victim who was identified? How is the discovery presented to them?"

"There's a protocol in place for every family that has provided us with DNA samples. First a phone call is made, and then an in-person visit is scheduled."

"Do you make the visits?"

"No. That's left for Dr. Trudeau."

"The most recent identification. It was of a woman named Victoria Ford," Avery said. "Can you tell me anything about her or her family?"

"I only know as much as Dr. Trudeau told me. The victim's parents are no longer living. She was married but had no children. Her husband has remarried, so her sister was the next of kin. That was who Dr. Trudeau met with."

"Do you have a name? Of the victim's sister?"

Livia nodded. "Her name has been released, so I'm able to provide it. Emma Kind. She lives here in New York. Out a ways, I believe. Near the Catskill Mountains."

"Okay," Avery said. "So you'd be willing to welcome my production team into your crime lab later this summer?"

"I'd be happy to give you a grand tour of the world's largest crime lab, as well as the bone-processing lab where this recent identification was made."

"Excellent. I'll get some dates scheduled and be in touch."

"Great seeing you, Avery."

"You too, Livia. Thanks again."

"I saw your minivan episode, by the way. That was wild."

"Thanks. It was a little ostentatious, but ratings rule my world. This story, though, the 9/11 victim being identified, I think it has the power to draw a huge audience but in a more personal way. We're all connected in different ways to 9/11. We all remember where we were when we watched the scene unfold on television. I want to do this story the right way."

"I know you will. What's next?"

Avery shrugged. "I'm off to the Catskills to find Emma Kind and see if she's willing to talk about her sister."

Avery spent the following day making phone calls and rattling cages, utilizing every contact she had to track down people who knew Victoria Ford. She had no idea her presence in New York, or her interest in Victoria Ford, would draw so much attention.

CHAPTER 13

Negril, Jamaica
Wednesday, June 23, 2021

Rick's Café was a popular bar built into the cliffs on Jamaica's West End. This afternoon, like every other day of the year, it was populated by throngs of bathing-suit-clad tourists slurping fruity cocktails and staring off into the Caribbean Sea. The tiered outdoor seating area was located at the cliff's edge where patrons sat forty feet above the turquoise water, separated from the cliff's sheer drop-off by a waist-high stone wall. Stairs etched in the rocks provided access to lower levels, where circular umbrellas dotted the patios and provided shade to sunburned vacationers lunching at the café. A cove carved its way into the rocks and provided access to catamarans that sailed up to the trendy destination and allowed their occupants to jump ship—which was usually done via a drunken trip down the stern-side waterslide that spat tourists into the ocean. Ladders draped the sides of the cliffs and led thirsty patrons to the café's outdoor bar.

Walt Jenkins sat at the corner of the bar, shaded by fronds of a palm tree, and stared out at the ocean. A Hampden Estates rum rested on the bar in front of him, the slow-melting ice mellowing the 120-proof spirit. Still reeling from his trip to New York, where he came face to face with the woman he loved, Walt hadn't been shy over the last few days about his admiration for single-batch Jamaican rum. He didn't smoke pot, as so many of his friends here on the island did, and he had never ingested a pill stronger than ibuprofen. Rum was his cure-all antidote to anything life threw at him. He drank it in good times and bad, and it affected him differently in each circumstance. This time around, however, despite his best efforts, the rum was not providing its usual soothing balm.

Meghan Cobb remained on his mind. Despite the fact that he still loved her, Walt knew he couldn't be around her for the simple fact that some part of him hated her, too. He took a sip of the Hampden Estate, stared out at the ocean, and cursed the universe like he always did in the days following his return from New York. Then he allowed his mind to drift back to the day he met her.

> *In his forties, twice divorced and with no kids, Walt Jenkins had stopped looking for the perfect life to suddenly appear before him. He was more than a decade into his FBI career, content with his status in the world, and approaching the middle of his life and carrying the normal regrets of a man who had never had children and now found himself mostly alone. These were his thoughts as he drove through the Adirondack Mountains. He had tacked a couple of vacation days onto either side of the long Fourth of July weekend, rented a cabin in the hills, and had been enjoying a few days of quiet isolation. He was headed into town to pick up a steak and replenish his beer when he saw the SUV on the shoulder. An obvious tilt to the passenger side suggested a flat tire.*
> *Although Walt had been an FBI agent far longer than he was*

*ever a patrolman, his inner psyche would forever carry a sense
of obligation when he saw a disabled vehicle.*

*The SUV had pulled onto the shoulder but was perilously
parked just beyond a bend in the road where reckless drivers
might not see it as they screamed around the corner. Walt
pulled over and kept a good distance between the two cars so
that his was visible to passing traffic. He turned on his haz-
ards, climbed from behind the wheel, and walked toward the
SUV, making sure to offer a wide berth. The last thing he
wanted was to frighten the woman behind the wheel, who was
stranded and alone on an isolated mountain road.*

*He waved from several feet away. The window came down
and Walt saw an attractive woman smile nervously.*

"Flat tire?" he asked.

The woman nodded. "I'm trying to get a hold of Triple A."

*"It'll take me fifteen minutes to get your spare on. Twenty
at most."*

*"Thank you," the woman said, still with her phone to her
ear. "I'm already in the queue."*

Walt sensed her trepidation.

*"Years ago I used to be a police officer, so I've changed a lot
of tires in my day. If you'd rather wait for Triple A, I'm happy
to head back to my car and wait there to make sure they
arrive. But way out here in the mountains on a holiday weekend, you're likely looking at an hour or two wait until they
dispatch someone."*

*Walt pulled his wallet from his pocket and showed the
woman his identification.*

"FBI?"

*He smiled. "I'm a field agent in New York. Walt Jenkins."
He extended his hand.*

*The woman reached through the open window. "Meghan
Cobb." She smiled nervously. "Fifteen minutes?"*

"Maybe twenty, but it won't be a problem."

A few minutes later, the jack tilted the car at an oblique angle. Walt was on his knees changing the tire. They talked the entire time, and then for thirty minutes more after the spare was in place. A getaway meant to be spent alone was instead spent with Meghan Cobb. She was untangling herself from a nasty relationship. He was three months post-divorce. By any stretch of the imagination, their relationship should have been a rebound for both of them. Instead, over the next year they fell in love. And then, on a hot summer night, just after his forty-fifth birthday, Walt was shot when he and his partner were on a routine surveillance operation. The bullets that found him had taken fortuitous paths through his body. The first entered through his sternum, exited through his scapula, and pierced his heart in between, miraculously missing his aorta. The second passed through his neck and had just as miraculously missed his spinal cord. No miracles, however, had been bestowed on his partner, who was sitting next to Walt in the unmarked car. The bullets that ravaged Jason Snyder's body had found major organs and vessels. He was dead before the ambulance arrived.

After that, Walt learned what true loneliness felt like.

In the aftermath of his partner's death, a shitstorm descended, the likes of which Walt had never before experienced, and Meghan Cobb was in the middle of it. To remedy the situation, Walt agreed to early retirement, secured his pension, and headed to the Caribbean where he limited his contact with Meghan to once a year—one night each June when he returned to New York to attend the annual survivors meeting. In the days leading up to the event he battled a combination of excitement and fear. In the days after, he suffered buyer's remorse over what he'd gotten out of the trip and always wished for a do-over. He wished he had found the courage to confront her about her lies. He wished he had found the strength to express his anger about being placed in such a precarious position.

The regret passed. It always did. Then, just one dominant emotion lingered. At the bottom of every glass of rum, he found guilt. It was a dangerous spiral, and Walt Jenkins had no idea how to pull out of it.

CHAPTER 14

Negril, Jamaica
Wednesday, June 23, 2021

He took another sip of the Hampden Estates and enjoyed the sweet burn at the back of his throat. A big catamaran crept into the cove. Drunken tourists dove into the blue waters and swam toward Rick's Cafe. Like ants emerging from a hill, the red-shouldered, paled-faced travelers climbed the ladders and materialized from the rocks below to swarm the bar. Some staggered after having chugged too much rum punch on the sail over from the all-inclusives in Negril. The herd barked orders to the bartender as Peter Tosh and Bob Marley blared from overhead speakers.

"Rum Runner."

"Red Stripe."

"Jamaican Breeze."

Walt lifted his glass from the bar, slipped off his stool, and made his way through the crowd and out onto the cliff-side patio. A table for two was free and he took a seat. He wanted time to enjoy the sun and the view, to sip his rum and allow it to work its magic, but the arrival of a catamaran was usually his signal to head home. Off to his left, a local cliff diver climbed to the top of a birch tree whose limbs stretched over the edge of the bluff. A platform had been built tree-house-style into the limbs and allowed the climber to stand nearly one hundred feet above the cove. Everyone stopped drinking and craned their necks to watch his progress, cameras and cell phones trained on him. The reggae music quieted when the man sat down with his legs straddling the wooden plat-form and swinging in the afternoon breeze, teasing his audi-ence and making them wait for his impending dive.

With everyone preoccupied and staring up the cliff, a man slipped into the seat across from Walt. When Walt noticed him, they both smiled.

"What an entrance," Walt said. "Very Jack Ryan of you."

"Sitting down with an old friend is considered a form of espionage?" the man asked.

"It is when you sneak up on me in the middle of no-where." Walt laughed. "James fucking Oliver. What the *hell* are you doing in Jamaica?"

"I've been looking for you for some time, and a little bird told me where you've been hiding."

So far this afternoon, Walt had barely sipped two ounces of rum. His mind was clear, not yet clouded the way it had been for the last few days since leaving New York. He was thinking lucidly, and the sight of his old FBI boss caused the neurons of his mind to fire like they used to when he was ac-tive in the Bureau. An eighteen-year veteran, Walt's reaction to, and analysis of, all circumstances was shaped by Oliver's training and experience. Three years removed from the Bu-reau, those old senses had dulled a bit. The sight of his old supervisor, however, brought Walt's training and instincts flooding back to him. He had been careful over the last cou-ple of years not to tell people where he was staying. Only his parents and siblings knew he was renting a house in Jamaica with no plans of returning to the States. And not even his family knew that Walt's original visa had been parlayed into dual citizenship. He had been especially careful to avoid telling any of his old FBI buddies where he was hiding. There were many reasons for his recluse nature, but mostly it was because in the wake of the shooting, and the scandal that broke afterward, Walt had become unwelcomed within the Federal Bureau of Investigation. He had hoped time would solve that issue, but three years hadn't put a dent into restoring his reputation in the eyes of his former colleagues.

As Walt stared at his old Bureau boss now, two things occurred to him. First, Scott Sherwood—his old station chief from when Walt was a young detective in New York State, and whom Walt had *accidentally* run into at the survivors meeting—was the one who ratted out his location. It was suddenly obvious why Scott had insisted so strongly on exchanging contact information. Second, if James Oliver had gone to the trouble of planting Scott Sherwood at the survivors meeting to pin down Walt's whereabouts, he sure as shit wanted something. And if the Bureau wanted something from him three years after they forced his retirement, it was nothing good.

"Let me guess," Walt said. "That little bird was a shithead named Scott Sherwood."

"You always were the sharpest agent I had. I see nothing's changed."

"A lot's changed, Jim."

Jim Oliver looked around Rick's Café. "That's for damn sure." He pointed at Walt's glass of rum. "But some things have stayed the same."

"Old habits die hard. Can I get you one?"

Oliver shrugged. "When in Rome."

Walt waved over the waitress. "Two more, please. Hampden Estates overproof on the rocks."

"No problem," the waitress said in a pleasant Jamaican accent.

As she walked toward the bar, Walt looked back at Oliver. "This shit's expensive. I assume the Bureau's picking up the tab?"

"Why would you assume that?"

"Because if you're sitting in front of me at a cliff-side tavern in Negril, Jamaica, the Bureau wants something. And if this is an official meeting, the agency can pick up the tab."

Oliver shrugged again. "Why not. It's the least we can do."

A collected gasp came from the crowd as the cliff diver stood up on the platform perched high in the birch tree. With his legs tight together, he puffed out his chest and extended his arms straight out to his side, crucifix style. Then he bent at the knees and jumped. His body rotated in a slow backward somersault as he jetted toward the water, taking a full two seconds to cover the one-hundred-foot jump before landing feet first and disappearing into the cobalt water, barely producing a splash in the process. The crowd erupted in cheers.

"I must admit," Oliver said, taking his gaze off the action and looking back at Walt, "retirement sure sounds good at the moment."

"*Forced* retirement. Remember? You made me quit. But it's grown on me. And, Jim, I'm really happy here all by my lonesome."

"Come on, Walt. A forty-something-year-old guy, in the prime of his life, day drinking by himself at a bar in *Jamaica*? You're not happy, you're a goddamn cliché."

"Whatever you think about me, just know this: I'm not interested."

"Is that any way to treat your old boss? I came all the way down here to see my friend and have a chat."

"That's exactly what's worrying me."

The waitress delivered their drinks and Oliver raised his glass.

"To old friends?"

Walt hesitated a moment, and then shook his head and exhaled a lungful of pent-up anxiety. "Goddamn, Jim. It's good to see you."

"You too, pal."

They touched glasses and each took a sip of rum.

"Now stop screwing around and tell me what you want."

Oliver's expression went stoic. "It has to do with a case you investigated. We need some help."

"I didn't investigate cases for the FBI. I gathered intel."

"It's a case from before you joined the Bureau."

"*Before* I joined the Bureau? We're going back a ways, my friend."

Oliver nodded. "Twenty years."

Walt squinted his eyes. "Which case?"

"Cameron Young."

"Wow. Now there's a blast from the past."

"So you remember it?"

"Of course I do. It was my first homicide—wealthy novelist found hanging naked from his balcony in the Catskills. The image is still burned into my memory."

In addition to the crime scene, Walt remembered other things about the case, too. He had started his career in law enforcement as a cop in New York State's Bureau of Criminal Investigation before working his way up to the detective squad at the ripe age of twenty-eight. The murder of Cameron Young was his first solo case. Because the victim was a high-profile writer, Walt's first investigation had been conducted under the hot lens of the media. Every discovery had been made public, and his margin of error was narrow. He knew from the outset that he could make no mistakes. And he hadn't. He conducted a meticulous investigation and gathered his evidence by the book and with no corners cut. The shortcuts came from those above him.

But it was not Walt's job to build the prosecution's case, only to gather the evidence and turn it over to the DA's office. And he had. All his ducks had been arranged in a neat row, the DA had convened a grand jury, and the indictment of Victoria Ford was imminent. Then 9/11 came and the case fizzled and disappeared. Afterward, Walt heard rumors about the district attorney and the manipulation of evidence. When he searched for specifics, he found only resistance and dead ends. A year later, the FBI recruited him to fill one of the many holes in counterterrorism. He forgot about the Cameron Young case and gave up detective work to chase terrorists.

"I'm usually pretty good at recognizing angles," Walt said. "But hell if I can figure out why the FBI would be interested in a homicide from twenty years ago."

"Something's come up and we need your help. Your involvement in the Cameron Young case might provide perfect cover."

"Cover for what?"

"Ever heard of a woman named Avery Mason?"

Walt's eyebrows pinched together. "The *American Events* lady? Of course. It's the only television show I watch down here. I stream it on my tablet."

"Her birth name is Claire Avery Montgomery. She changed it to Avery Mason when she landed in LA."

Walt shrugged. "Don't a lot of Hollywood types change their name?"

"Maybe. But Avery Mason's name change has nothing to do with Hollywood and everything to do with heritage. Do you know who Garth Montgomery is?"

"The Ponzi scheme cheat?"

"That's him."

"Didn't he steal something like ten billion dollars from investors?"

"Try fifty. He convinced giant corporations to invest in his hedge fund on the strength of its returns. But the books were cooked. Feds caught on and made their move. To stay out of prison he offered to testify against his partners. Then he disappeared. No one's seen him since."

"What's this got to do with the *American Events* lady?"

"She's Garth Montgomery's daughter, and she's done a magnificent job of hiding in plain sight. None of the millions of people who tune in to her show know her real identity. But we do, and we've been watching her for some time now. We believe she knows where her father's hiding, and we think she's been aiding and abetting him."

Walt slowly nodded. "I'm still not making the connection to the Cameron Young case."

"There's been a development in the case. Remember the name of the woman who killed him?"

"Victoria Ford," he said. "What's the development?"

"About a month ago, the medical examiner's office in New York made a positive ID on remains found at Ground Zero. They belonged to Victoria Ford, and that's where you come in, my friend."

Walt leaned closer to his old boss. "I'm listening."

"Avery Mason is snooping around New York, hoping to put together a story about a 9/11 victim identified twenty years after the towers came down. It won't be long before she learns about Victoria Ford's history and the crime she was accused of. If you've seen her television show, you know she won't stop at Victoria Ford's story. She'll want to know all about Cameron Young's murder. It's not a stretch to suspect that Ms. Mason will become very interested in that old investigation. It's her forte. And Cameron Young's story involves a young detective named Walt Jenkins."

Jim Oliver smiled and took a sip of rum, making Walt wait a moment before he continued.

"Avery Mason is going to want to speak with that detective and find out everything he remembers about the case. We need you to get on a plane and head back to New York to get yourself reacquainted with the Cameron Young case."

Walt, still leaning across the table, slowly raised his eyebrows. "And then do . . . what?"

"Wait for Avery Mason to reach out to you. When she does, we need you to help her with the case. She'll want to retell the Cameron Young story. It was full of sex and betrayal, which is television gold. Work with her. Give her whatever she needs. And in the process, we hope you can uncover any details about where her father is hiding."

"How am I supposed to do that?"

"Get close to her. She's in New York for a reason other than the Victoria Ford story. We think she's about to help her father somehow, or at the very least make contact with him. If you're close to her, even if you're just *around* her, you might learn something that will help us."

Walt sat back and shook his head. "Does this little sting you have planned come from the higher-ups? It sounds sanctimonious and desperate."

"A sting? That's a little dramatic. This is simply an intelligence-gathering operation, just like the old days."

"Does it come from the top, Jim?"

"It's my idea, so it comes from me. If you're asking if it's legit, the answer is yes. The brass are onboard because we're stumped on this Garth Montgomery problem and it makes us look bad. House of Cards was a two-year operation that cost the taxpayers millions, and we somehow allowed the main target to slip through our fingers *after* we apprehended him. This is the end of the road for me, Walt. My entire career will be defined by what happens with Garth Montgomery. I'll either be the comeback kid, or the loser."

Oliver leaned closer to Walt. "Simply stated, I *have* to find this son of a bitch. In order to find him, we have to get creative. This is as creative as I get. So yes, everyone is onboard, but I pushed to get them there. I need your help, Walt. You'd be back on the payroll for as long as it takes."

There was a long pause as Walt digested the offer. He'd been looking for something to pull him out of the downward spiral he was trapped in. He never imagined help would come from his former employer. And he had no idea it would involve a case from his distant past.

"What do you say, Walt? Retirement never suited you. We both know that."

Walt looked back at Jim Oliver, paused briefly, and then nodded.

"Excellent." Oliver held up his nearly empty glass of rum. "Now, I'll need another one of these before I get into the details."

Walt stared at his former boss for a long moment. Finally, he raised his hand and flagged down the pretty waitress with the sweet Jamaican accent. For the rest of the afternoon, and deep into the evening, he listened to Jim Oliver describe the operation that would pull him back to New York. He did his best to drown his doubt in rum.

PART II

Fate

CHAPTER 15

Catskill Mountains, NY
Friday, June 25, 2021

The house was nestled somewhere in the foothills of the Catskill Mountains. Avery sat behind the wheel of the Range Rover as she cruised the two-lane mountain roads flanked on each side by thickets of forest. The drive was peaceful, with only the occasional car passing in the opposite direction. An hour and a half after she left the city, she turned into the drive of Emma Kind's home. It was a cute Victorian with a wraparound front porch and a score of potted hibiscus hanging in long lines from the eaves. Even before Avery turned off the ignition, a round woman with graying hair walked through the screen door and stood on the porch. She looked to be in her sixties. She smiled from behind wire-framed glasses and lifted her hand in an amicable wave. The gesture prompted Avery to do the same from the front seat.

"You have *got* to be kidding me," the woman said as Avery climbed from her car. "Avery Mason, in my front yard."

Avery smiled as she walked toward the porch. When Avery had called earlier in the week, she'd heard more than a little skepticism in Emma Kind's voice about whether she was really speaking with Avery Mason, the host of *American Events*.

"This is too much," the woman said. "I told you I wouldn't believe it until I saw it, and now I'm seeing it."

"Your house is gorgeous," Avery said when she reached the bottom of the porch steps.

"Thank you. Come inside, please."

She climbed the front steps. "Avery Mason."

The woman shook her hand emphatically. "Emma Kind. This is really just too much. Come on in."

Avery followed Emma inside. The interior of the house was as quaint—a mixture of classic Victorian with a woodsy vibe. Sturdy oak beams lined the pitched ceilings, cherry-oak wood floors shined with the afternoon sun, and ornate moldings outlined the entryways.

"What can I get you to drink?" Emma asked. "Tea, water, coffee?"

"Oh, I'm okay. Thank you, though."

Emma opened the fridge and pulled out a bottle of chardonnay. "Avery Mason is standing in my kitchen, so I'm having a glass of wine. Would you like to join me?"

"I suppose it would be impolite to say no twice."

Emma smiled and removed two wineglasses from the cabinet. They headed to the back where they sat in the shade of a large patio umbrella and stared off to the mountain peaks in the distance. Emma poured two glasses of chardonnay.

"Thanks for meeting with me," Avery said, taking a sip of wine. "I'm sure it's not easy to talk about your sister, even this many years later."

Emma pulled her gaze from the mountains and looked at Avery with a smile. "Even after twenty years I still miss her."

"Victoria was your younger sister?"

Emma nodded. "By five years. She was thirty-five when she was taken from this world." Emma raised her eyebrows and shook her head. "Hard to believe she'd be fifty-five today. There's just no way for me to picture my baby sister in her midfifties. You know, when a loved one dies young your perception of them is placed in a time capsule. You're only able to remember them as they were then, not as they would be today. Victoria was so young and healthy, full of life. To me she will forever be that vibrant young woman. It's the only way I'll ever know her."

"Does the news of finally identifying Victoria's remains bring closure for you?"

Emma took a sip of wine. "In a way, I suppose. But not the type I'm looking for."

"What kind is that?"

Emma blinked and studied Avery for a moment, a look of curiosity coming over her. "Do you know much about Victoria?"

"Not much. Only that she died on 9/11 and her remains were just identified by the medical examiner's office. I was hoping you could tell me about her."

"Yes, of course. And I *have* waited twenty years to finally put my sister to rest. Maybe that'll be possible now, but I doubt I'll be able to do it properly."

"You mean with a funeral?"

Emma smiled in a way that made Avery feel as if she were missing something.

"You really don't know about Victoria's past, do you?"

"No," Avery said. "That's why I'm here."

Emma shifted her gaze back to the panoramic view and took another sip of wine. "My sister was involved in a murder investigation prior to her death. It was a great, big, sensationalized case around here. An awful case, gruesome in its nature and filled with perverted sex. The media and the police painted Victoria out to be a monster."

Avery sat up taller in her chair. "Victoria was involved in the investigation, meaning . . . ?"

"Meaning they said my baby sister was a killer. Something

I know without doubt is false. So until I find a way to come to terms with that, I'll never be able to properly put Victoria to rest."

Avery had come out to the country looking for a feel-good story about a woman finding closure twenty years after her sister was killed on 9/11. Instead, she'd stumbled onto a twenty-year-old murder investigation. Her mind buzzed with possibility, and the curiosity center of her brain ached for every detail.

"Would you tell me about it?" Avery asked, trying not to sound too eager.

Emma nodded. "That's what the wine is for."

CHAPTER 16

Shandaken, NY
Friday, June 25, 2021

Walt Jenkins's plane landed the day before. Had he not recently come to the realization that his life was in a downward spiral, he might have passed on Jim Oliver's offer. But Walt was looking for an opportunity to stop running, and perhaps he'd found it. The Bureau put him up in a suite at the Grand Hyatt in Midtown. It took Walt just over an hour to make the trip out to the country. The Bureau of Criminal Investigation branch of the New York State Police was an investigative division of plainclothes detectives that, for the most part, assisted local law enforcement that lacked the investigative resources needed for major crimes. The 2001 murder of Cameron Young in the Catskill Mountains, near the town of Shandaken, had certainly been an example of a county police department caught off guard. The community consisted of wealthy individuals who owned second homes in the area and spent long weekends and holidays in the town. Before Cameron Young had been found hanging from his balcony, there hadn't been a homicide in the area in four decades.

The Shandaken Police Department was not prepared for the murder, and the chief had quickly called the state authorities for help. Walt had been assigned to the case. At twenty-eight years old, he had been the youngest detective in the BCI. The older cops in Shandaken had not been happy to see him pull up to the crime scene. Their sentiment, Walt knew, was that if they wanted a kid's advice on how to handle a homicide they'd ask their own teenagers. But Walt had been undeterred by the cold reception and worked hard to win them over. He was careful to include the police chief in every decision, despite that, once invited, the BCI had full jurisdiction. When the name of the victim leaked—Cameron Young, a well-known novelist—the media took notice. When details about the gruesome nature of the crime were disclosed, as well as the links to sexual deviance, the media sunk its teeth into the story. To keep jurisdictional peace, Walt named the chief as official spokesman and invited him to speak at each press conference. When the cameras rolled, it was not Walt Jenkins revealing the details of the case and answering questions from the press, but Chief Dale Richards. Walt worked in the background. He was happy to stay out of the spotlight and concentrate on piecing the evidence together.

Now, on Friday afternoon, Walt pulled the nondescript government car—on loan from the New York office of the Federal Bureau of Investigation—into the small parking lot of the Shandaken Police Station. Because Chief Richards had been the front man of the Cameron Young investigation, the case files resided at the Shandaken police headquarters. Twenty years later, Walt hoped they still existed.

He walked across the parking lot and entered through the front door. As soon as he opened the door, Dale Richards stuck a cup of coffee toward him with a thick hand and a huge smile.

"Walt Jenkins, a man I thought I'd never see again."

Walt offered a smile. "Dale, good to see you. It's been a while."

"Twenty years," Dale said.

Those years had not been kind to Dale Richards. The man had gained what Walt conservatively estimated to be one hundred pounds. He wore a short-sleeve golf shirt that wrapped tightly around the man's midsection, stretching the microfibers to maximum capacity. Dale's neck sagged at his chin and tapered like a turkey's wattle into the man's chest. Twenty years earlier, Dale sported dark hair combed straight back and held in place with product, revealing then the man's receding hairline. The retreat had never ended and now only a thin apron of hair remained, wrapping around the base of his skull.

"Damn," Dale said. "You look like you haven't aged a day since we worked together. Still got that baby face."

"Thanks. You're looking good."

"I see you haven't lost your politeness. Listen, I'm not turning any heads, but I *feel* good. Doctor keeps telling me to lose weight or I'll die early. But I'd rather be fat and happy than skinny and miserable. And I can still kick the crap out of most of the young punks that come through this place thinking they're going to be the next top cop."

"I don't doubt that."

"I was shocked to get your call, Walt. The Cameron Young case was a long time ago."

"Were you able to find anything?"

"Not yet, but I've narrowed it down," Dale said. "Follow me."

Walt took a sip of the coffee, winced as he swallowed it, and followed Dale Richards to the basement of the small police department. It took an hour of rummaging before they found it—a single cardboard box on a shelf with a thousand others. It was marked *Cameron Young, 2001*. Dale pulled it off the shelf, blew away a thick layer of dust, and handed it to Walt.

"I knew it was down here."

"Thanks, Dale. You're a lifesaver."

"What's the interest?"

"You remember Victoria Ford?" Walt asked.

"Of course."

"Her remains were just identified by the OCME in New York."

"Get outta here."

"For real. We got word that there might be renewed interest in the old case, so I thought I'd refresh myself with the details."

"Everything should be in there. Everything we had, anyway."

"Can I get this back to you in a week or so?"

Dale shrugged. "Case has been closed for twenty years. Keep it as long as you'd like."

Three hours later, Walt was perched on the queen bed of his hotel room with pages of the Cameron Young file around him. On the way back to the city he had stopped at a liquor store and found a bottle of Richland single estate rum. It wasn't his preference, but it would do. For the first time in a while, he wasn't looking for the rum to carry his problems away. Today, as he read the old case file, he was interested only in getting reacquainted with the players involved in the Cameron Young investigation. If he was going to meet Avery Mason and discuss the case with her, he needed to remember every detail. But there was another reason for Walt's anxiousness to revisit the Cameron Young case. Despite what Dale Richards had claimed, Walt knew better. The case had been abandoned, but it had never been formally closed.

THE CAMERON YOUNG INVESTIGATION

Planted on a five-acre clearing in the foothills of the Catskill Mountains, the main house was a grand log-style design by Murray Arnott. Built from Alaskan timber, the exterior featured a colossal A-frame grand gallery reminiscent of a Vail skiing lodge with dual windows angling into the peak and providing views of the mountains. To each side of the steeply angled roof, the home carried on in rustic extensions of horizontal logs that made up the bedrooms on one side and the recreation area on the other. The interior featured formal dining and living rooms, a home theater, an ornate library, and five bedrooms—each with private bath. The open floor plan centered around an impressive stone fireplace that climbed up to the vaulted ceiling. Twenty-foot windows offered endless views of the Catskill Mountains. The kitchen was mahogany and stainless steel, with sturdy wooden beams shooting up the pitched ceiling. A sweeping wooden staircase off the back patio led down to a pool, which was still covered this early in spring. Twin creeks ran on either side of the property and offered the constant rhythm of babbling water that shut out the rest of the world. A bridge arched over one of the creeks and led to the small studio the owner used for quiet days writing his novels.

Unseen and private, other large homes populated the buttes of the Catskills. They belonged to the rich, and sometimes famous. Cameron and Tessa Young had purchased the log-style home three years earlier when Cameron's third novel found the *New York Times* list and stayed there for a year, selling over a million copies. His first two novels had earned him a nice living, but the third set him apart. And the two that followed put him into an elite class of novelists. His books had taken off around the world and the Youngs were enjoying their financial success. Years before they had used Cameron's second advance as a down payment on the Catskills home. His last royalty check wiped out the mortgage. By all measures, Tessa and Cameron Young were living large.

Tessa was a professor of English literature at Columbia University, where she taught comparative literature and dissected some of the greatest works bound between two covers. The irony that this distinguished professor's husband struck gold writing lowbrow commercial fiction was not lost on either of them. She endured her husband's writing because it supported their lifestyle, but regarded it for what it was—spectacularly successful garbage.

On the back patio, four Adirondack chairs were positioned around the fire pit. Tessa and Cameron sat in the chairs and watched the bruised-color sky of evening silhouette the mountains. The fire offered enough warmth to stave off the chill that came as the sun sunk below the mountain peaks. They were enjoying drinks with their friends, Jasper and Victoria Ford. Jasper was the realtor who had found the home, negotiated the price, and brokered the deal. To celebrate the purchase, Cameron and Tessa had invited Jasper and his wife out for a sail. The four had become fast friends. Over the past three years, Jasper and Victoria had been on countless sailing excursions with the Youngs, who were avid sailors, and the four had even vacationed together in the British Virgin Islands.

"Cameron," Jasper said. "Your latest releases this summer?"

"June," Cameron said. "I'll be touring for three weeks. Starting on the West Coast and hitting fifteen cities on the way home. I'll be back just before the Fourth of July." He pointed to his studio across the creek. "Then I'll be back in the lab trying to hit my deadline for next year's release."

"I don't know how you do it," Victoria said. "I just can't get the words out as fast as you. I wish I had the discipline."

Victoria was a financial planner for a midsized firm, but harbored a passion to write novels herself. Over the course of their friendship this secret had come to light. Cameron offered advice and had pulled all the publishing strings he could to help Victoria with her writing.

"Deadlines are very effective motivators. And from what little you've shared, it sounds like you're quite a prolific writer yourself."

"What's the saying?" Victoria asked. "If a tree falls in the forest but no one is there to hear it, does it make a sound? In publishing, if you write a book and no one reads it . . . are you really a writer?"

"Of course you are," Cameron said, with a soft encouragement to his voice. "A writer is someone who writes, not just someone who sells published books. I'm dying to hear about your manuscript. When can I read it?"

"Oh, Lord, never," Victoria said.

"She won't even let *me* read it," Jasper said. "We've been married eight years and I've never read a sentence from any of her manuscripts. How many is it now? Five or six, at least."

"Five," Victoria said. "And even with Cameron's recommendation, his literary agency rejected my query. To date, over one hundred literary agents and editors have politely declined my work. The last thing I'm going to do is let my husband or friends read my manuscripts when I can't even find an agent to represent me."

"It's all subjective," Cameron said. "What one agent hates, another loves. Don't give up, Victoria."

"Timing too." This was from Tessa, who put her hand out to rub Victoria's knee. "The market might not be ready for your stories now, but someday it will."

"Okay." Victoria raised her hands in surrender. "Let's change the subject."

She reached into the ice bucket and pulled out a bottle of wine. "This is a Happy Canyon Blanc from Santa Ynez Valley. Jasper and I picked it up on our vacation last fall." Victoria poured everyone's glass full.

"To friends," she said. "And, to Cameron's new book coming out this summer."

The four friends reached their glasses together and touched them lightly.

Cameron looked at Victoria. "To literature, in all its shapes and sizes."

CHAPTER 17
Manhattan, NY
Friday, June 25, 2021

Walt lay on the hotel bed with one arm behind his head and the other holding pages from the Cameron Young file. He'd been reading for an hour, and the details of the case and its players were coming back to him. He put the pages down and reached for the glass of rum on the nightstand. He took a long swallow, knowing he'd need the rum to get him through the pages he was about to read. His stint at the FBI never brought him face to face with murder and death the way his time as a homicide detective had. It was something he didn't miss. But today he would venture back to that time. He set the glass back on the nightstand and began reading the autopsy report.

THE CAMERON YOUNG INVESTIGATION

Cameron Young's body, after technicians had lowered him from the balcony, was transferred to the New York State medical examiner's office. Dr. Jarrod Lockard was tasked with the postmortem. Medical examiners and coroners had always been a peculiar lot to Walt. Outliers who took such a road less traveled in life that it literally led them to death. Being able to dissect the human body, Walt believed, had to come with some glitch in the psyche. Dr. Lockard was nicknamed the Wizard for his abilities to conjure every clue left behind by the bodies that came through his morgue. Jarrod Lockard was so much a genius in this particular niche that other aspects of life had gone unattended—like personal hygiene and appearance, as well as any effort to display the slightest hint of social awareness. Walt wondered if examining the dead had taken its toll on Dr. Lockard, as if each trip into the body of the deceased pulled the man further from life. Not so much toward death, but rather to some in-between place that left him alienated from the living and only able to associate with the corpses that filled his days.

Despite having just turned fifty, Dr. Lockard's hair was bone white and made up of wild knots that hadn't seen a

comb in years. A few particularly enthusiastic strands
stood out from the rest and appeared to carry an electric
current. Combined with eyes set so deep in their sockets
that the man needed to strain his forehead to keep his eyelids open, Dr. Lockard offered a perpetual look of surprise
reminiscent of Doc Brown from *Back to the Future.*

"Come in," the doctor said when Walt knocked on the
door to his office.

Walt walked into the office. "Doc," he said, extending his
hand and doing his best not to look as nervous as he felt.
Why Doc Lockard put the fear of God into every detective
at the BCI was a mystery none of Walt's colleagues
attempted to explain.

"Thanks for getting on top of this so quickly," Walt said.

Dr. Lockard offered a limp handshake that felt like poorly
kneaded dough, and a stoic expression that was neither
welcoming nor dismissive. He pointed at the chair in front
of his desk. "You've got an interesting one here. Have a
seat. There's a lot to discuss."

Dr. Lockard poured coffee into two Styrofoam cups and
handed one to Walt. The doctor sat behind his desk and
pulled a file folder in front of him.

"Cameron Young," he said, opening the file and paging
through his notes. "You ever read any of his books?"

Walt shook his head. "I've never found much time to
read fiction."

"Damn shame. I was a big fan of his. Thrillers. Good
stuff."

A quick image flashed in Walt's mind of Jarrod Lockard
reading by candlelight as he ate chicken wings and flipped
pages, leaving greasy fingerprints behind.

The doctor pulled out a photo of Cameron Young's
naked body lying on the autopsy table. The Y incision ran
from his shoulders to his pelvis and was closed by thick su-

tures that dimpled the pale skin. Doc Lockard slid the photo across the desk.

"I wish I could tell you the postmortem was routine. Unfortunately, it was anything but. Here's what I've got for you. External exam showed extensive ligature damage to the victim's neck consistent with a long drop hanging. His neck was broken at the fourth cervical vertebrae, which was subsequently displaced anteriorly, shearing the spinal cord. The victim fell eight and one-half feet from the second story balcony before the rope stopped his descent, producing approximately one thousand pounds of pressure on his neck. Another foot or two, and he might have been decapitated."

Walt nodded slowly, examining the gruesome picture as if there was something to be gleaned from it. Finally, he slid the photo back to Dr. Lockard. "Sounds pretty clear cut to me, Doc."

"On the surface. But it gets messy when we take a closer look at the neck anatomy. Do you know the difference between long drop and short drop hangings?"

"Long drops are what you just described. Vic drops from a certain height and the sudden deceleration from the noose breaks the neck. Like the hangings from the medieval times, and the crap they're still pulling off in Iran. Death comes immediately. Short drops are when the vic slowly lowers himself into a hanging position and eventually dies from traditional strangulation."

"Impressive, Detective. You're correct on all counts. A couple other details that are pertinent: In short drop cases, the ligature trauma to the neck is less extensive. The noose slowly tightens and prevents oxygen from getting to the brain. Stay in that position long enough, and the brain stops telling the lungs to breathe. Or, if the noose is tight enough to constrict the trachea it prevents inhalation.

Either way, the resultant cause of death is asphyxiation. In long drops, conversely, death comes from severing of the spinal cord. This is especially true if the position of the noose's knot is under the chin, as it was in Mr. Young's case. The sudden jolt of the rope running out of slack causes hyperextension of the neck and the consequent anterior displacement of the vertebrae. The problem I'm having with the postmortem in Mr. Young's case is that he showed signs of both short and long drop hangings."

The doctor slid another photo across the desk. This one was a close-up of Cameron Young's neck.

"See here? A band of ecchymosis runs around the neck, *above* the ligature laceration produced from the long drop, suggesting that the rope had been slowly tightened for some period of time antemortem, or *prior* to him suffering the long drop trauma. Congestion in the lungs, as well as petechiae of the cheeks and mucosal lining of the mouth, support this conclusion. Subconjunctival hemorrhages paint a textbook picture of a slow oxygen deprivation coupled with increased venous pressure in the head."

"English, Doc?"

"He was choked to death slowly *before* someone threw him over the balcony."

Walt turned his head slightly to the side as he digested the doctor's words. "He was dead *before* he went over the balcony?"

"Correct. The long drop trauma came postmortem. This conclusion is supported by the amount of blood produced from the ligature wound. In addition to the vertebra shearing the spinal cord, his left carotid artery was severed. If this had occurred at the time of death, I would expect to find arterial spray from the last few beats of the heart. But the blood pattern and loss were consistent with leakage of residual blood that had pooled in the vessel, rather than propulsion from a vessel under pressure."

Walt ran the back of his hand over the stubble of his cheek as he considered the doctor's findings. As he was thinking, Dr. Lockard moved the photo of Cameron Young's neck to the side and slid another in its place.

"I've got a theory about the neck wounds."

The new photo was of Cameron Young's backside as he lay facedown on the autopsy table.

"Look here." Dr. Lockard pointed at the photo. "The lateral side of each buttock showed signs of trauma—thin welt marks. Similar marks were noted on the chest and upper arms. Any guesses what these marks are?"

"I saw those when he was hanging from the balcony. I figured they were made by a whip."

"You're impressing me this afternoon, Detective. The marks are from a leather flogger whip. S and M stuff. Pretty brutal, too, from the appearance of the welts. And I believe this finding goes hand in hand with the slow drop trauma to the neck."

Walt shook his head. "I'm not following you."

"I suspect Mr. Young was reaching sexual gratification while being choked."

"Autoerotic asphyxiation gone wrong?"

Dr. Lockard shook his head. "*Erotic* asphyxiation, yes, but there was nothing *auto* about it."

Dr. Lockard pulled another photo from his file and again slid it in front of Walt. It was a tight shot of Cameron Young's penis. Without moving his head, Walt shifted his gaze from the photo to Doc Lockard and raised his eyebrows.

"Why am I looking at this, Doc?"

"Based on engorged blood vessels in the shaft of the penis and superficial abrasions on the epidermis, Mr. Young had been fellated shortly before he died."

Walt shook his head. "Someone blew him?"

"Crude language, Detective. But, yes. Just *prior* to death, someone used oral stimulation to bring Mr. Young to the edge of climax. The corpus cavernosum was swollen, but the vas deferens was free of sperm and the seminal vesicle had not released its collection of semen."

"Doc, just get to the point," Walt said, sliding the photo back across the desk.

"My examination suggests that someone performed oral sex on Mr. Young, bringing him to the edge of climax, but before he ejaculated the rope around his neck caused him to stop breathing."

"Christ. You got all that from an autopsy?"

"Each body tells a story, Detective."

The Wizard had been busy, Walt thought as he ran a hand through his hair and sat back in his chair.

"From what you see," Walt asked, "he was a willing participant in whatever the hell went on?"

"Perhaps right up until the end. There were heavy amounts of the victim's own skin cells under his fingernails, suggesting that he clawed at the rope around his neck before he died. I noted scratch marks on the neck above the ligature wounds."

"So he panicked at the end and tried to take the pressure off his neck, but was too late."

"Correct."

"And no chance this was a suicide, as some defense attorney will surely claim?"

"Definitely not."

Dr. Lockard pulled another photo from the file and continued.

"The rope used to strangle Mr. Young was jute rope, which we commonly see in S and M bondage. High friction, low stretch." Dr. Lockard pushed the photo across the desk. "The same rope was used to bind his hands and wrists. Two important points here. Let's talk about the knots that bound the victim's hands first. As you know, some suicide victims secure their own hands behind their backs to prevent saving themselves if they have second thoughts."

Walt nodded. "The voice of insanity safeguarding against the voice of reason."

"In this case, it's clear that someone *else* bound Mr. Young's hands."

Dr. Lockard pulled two more photos from the file. The first was of Cameron Young still hanging from the balcony, a close-up of his bound hands held together with rope stretched tight by rigor mortis. The second photo, taken at the morgue after rigor had softened, was of the knot.

"The knots used to bind Mr. Young's hands were not the type seen in suicides. You see here?" Dr. Lockard pointed at the photo. "For a suicide victim to bind his own hands together, he has to use some sort of slipknot. Sink your hands into loose knots, pull your arms apart, the knots tighten. That's the only way to do it. These were not slip-knots. They were tightly bound knots. Doing some research, I believe they are alpine butterfly knots. This is outside my area of expertise, but it looks like the knots are commonly used in mountain climbing, and require two hands to complete. It's impossible to tie two alpine butterfly knots this close together and step through them to get your hands behind your back. And it's clearly impossible to have tied them blindly behind one's back."

"So someone else tied him up?"

"Correct."

Walt gathered all the photos, tapped them a few times on the desk to organize the stack, and then placed them facedown to the side.

"So Cameron Young was getting his rocks off during a

sordid S and M evening. Based on the extensive whip marks on his back and thighs, it was a violent night of games. Part of the foreplay included a rope being tied around his neck. The rope was tightened to some degree for added eroticism while someone simultaneously performed oral sex on him. The rope became too tight and he died before he reached climax. His partner panicked, tied the end of a long length of rope to the heaviest thing they could find, which ended up being the safe in the closet, and then tossed him over the balcony to make it look like suicide. Do I have your theory correct?"

"That's a pretty clean summary of my examination. Have any suspects?"

Walt stood up. "I'm working on it. Thanks, Doc."

CHAPTER 18

Manhattan, NY
Friday, June 25, 2021

Jim Oliver had set him up in a suite at the Grand Hyatt and Walt was happy to be free from the claustrophobia that surely would have come from a single room. After remembering Dr. Lockard, with his beady eyes and unkempt hair, as well as the vivid image the doctor had painted of Cameron Young's last night, Walt needed a little space to move around and shake the restlessness from his limbs. Even twenty years later, the doctor had the ability to unnerve him. Walt walked from the bedroom to the minibar and poured two more fingers of rum. He sat down at the desk in the main living area where more pages from the file waited. They were transcripts of his first interview with Tessa Young, the victim's wife.

THE CAMERON YOUNG INVESTIGATION

They were back in the Catskills for a long weekend, gathered around the stone patio out back, with the sweeping staircase leading down to the pool and with the mountains sprawled along the horizon. It was a beautiful summer afternoon. They had spent the morning on the Youngs' sailboat, and now a bottle of sauvignon blanc stood in the middle of the table and each of their glasses was full.

Victoria took a sip of wine. Tessa spun her wineglass but hadn't tasted it yet.

"I saw the *Times* reviewed your book," Victoria said to Cameron. "Impressive review."

"For once," Cameron said. "They usually rip me apart. Cardboard characters, thinly plotted storyline, trying but failing to be clever, nothing but a beach read, and on and on. I've heard all the insults over the years, but this time they actually liked it. It's a miracle."

"How was the tour?" Jasper asked.

"Tiring. But it was great getting out there and meeting the readers, though I'm happy to be home, and looking forward to a less hectic summer. I've got to deliver a manuscript in the fall and I plan to use the summer to wrap things up."

"Victoria, maybe Cameron will let you borrow the hut to get some writing done," Tessa said, pointing over at Cameron's writing studio, which sat on the other side of the babbling creek.

At eight hundred square feet, it was a mini replica of the main house.

Cameron shook his head. "Sorry. That's all mine. No one's allowed in there beside me and my muse."

"He's selfish that way," Tessa said.

"Not selfish, just superstitious. It's worked so far and I'm not going to mess with it. Once I cross that bridge, something clicks in my head and I don't walk *back* over it until I reach my writing goal for the day."

"It's an obnoxious man cave, and I sometimes wonder what goes on in there. But since I'm not allowed inside, I guess I'll never know." Tessa waved off her husband and stood from the patio table. "I have cheese and crackers inside."

"I'll help you," Victoria said.

Once inside, Victoria took Tessa by the elbow and led her into the hallway so they were out of view from the patio.

"You're not drinking," Victoria said.

"You mean the wine?"

"Yes, Tessa. I mean the wine. You're not drinking it."

Tessa shook her head. "I'm just taking it easy. It's two in the afternoon and I'm exhausted from our sail this morning."

"You're pregnant."

"What?"

"Are you?"

There was a long pause. Finally, Tessa smiled. "I'm not sure. I might be."

"Oh my God! Why didn't you tell me?"

"There's nothing to tell. Cameron and I are trying, that's

all. I didn't think it would happen so quickly. And I'm not even sure yet. I'm just late. But I don't want to drink just in case." Tessa smiled again. "I'll probably take a test next week. Don't say anything."

"I won't say a word," Victoria said. She pulled Tessa into a tight, rigid hug.

That evening, Jasper ran to the market for steaks. Tessa slept soundly in a lounge chair on the patio. Cameron came down the stairs and Victoria met him in the hallway where Tessa had spilled her secret earlier in the afternoon.

"You're a bastard!" Victoria said, bringing her hand up and slapping him sharply across the face.

"What the hell?" Cameron grabbed her wrist.

"She's pregnant?"

"What?"

"Tessa is pregnant?"

"No."

"You're *trying*. She told me all about it.*"

"Lower your voice! You want her to wake up?"

"I don't give a *shit*. You're a bastard!"

She tried to slap him with her other hand, but Cameron grabbed that wrist as well.

"Stop it," he said, fighting to subdue her as she flailed against his grip.

"You told me you weren't sleeping with her," Victoria said.

"She initiated it. What was I supposed to do? Tell my wife I've taken a vow of celibacy?"

"So what's happening here? You're trying to get your wife pregnant? The woman you promised me you're about to divorce, you're now trying to impregnate?"

"You're being irrational. It was the first time we've slept together in months."

Victoria clenched her teeth together. "You made me get

a goddamn abortion, Cameron. I aborted our baby because you convinced me the timing was not right. That it was too soon and that it would blow up our lives. Do you remember this?"

"Of course I remember."

"But the timing is right with Tessa? You're a fucking monster! And a goddamn liar!"

He put his face in front of hers, so their lips were just inches apart. "You know I love you. And you know I want to be with you."

"Then why aren't you?"

"What do you suggest I do? Walk out there right now and tell Tessa I want a divorce? Wait for Jasper to get home so we can all have a discussion over dinner about our affair, about how we've fallen in love and that we plan to leave them?"

"We'll have to have that discussion at some point."

"I know that. But I'd say over the Fourth of July while we're all staying together is not the right time."

There was a pause while Victoria looked down at the floor. "Is she really not allowed into your studio?"

"Hell no," Cameron said, lowering himself so that he could look up into her averted eyes. "The studio is just for us. You can use it whenever you want. I love watching you write in there."

Victoria kept her gaze focused on the floor, trying her best not to look into his eyes.

"Sooner or later," Cameron said, "you're going to have to let me read one of your manuscripts."

He stood up taller and she allowed her gaze to follow him. Their mouths came together in a passionate kiss. He pushed her against the wall, and his hands cupped the back of her shorts. She bit his bottom lip and for a moment worried that things would go too far while they stood in the hallway, just a few paces from where Tessa slept on the patio chair. Just then, while tangled together, the patio door slid open and Tessa stepped into the kitchen. At the same moment, the alarm on the front door chimed as Jasper returned from the market. In a panic, Victoria pulled roughly out of the kiss and pushed Cameron's body away from her as she twisted into the bathroom, locking the door behind her. Cameron ran a hand through his hair, collected his breath, and walked into the kitchen.

"You shouldn't have let me fall asleep," Tessa said, patting her cheek with the palm of her hand. "I think my face is sunburned."

"Sorry, hon," Cameron said, clearing his throat. "You looked so peaceful, I didn't want to wake you."

Jasper walked into the kitchen holding a paper bag from the butcher. "Four rib eyes, thick cut. Plus asparagus and portabellas."

"Good man," Cameron said, forcing a smile.

Jasper looked at him with a thick crease cutting between his eyebrows. "What happened to your lip?"

Cameron reached up and touched his lower lip, still feeling Victoria's teeth. When he pulled his hand away, his fingers were smeared with blood.

"Oh." He swiped his tongue over his lower lip and wiped away the blood with the back of his hand. "I must have bitten it."

"You nearly bit it *off*. Better put some ice on that bad boy," Jasper said as he placed the steaks on the kitchen counter. "I'll season these so they're ready for tonight."

"Good idea," Tessa said, keeping her face stoic and her gaze leveled on her husband as she walked to the freezer, removed an ice cube, and handed it to him. "For your lip."

CHAPTER 19
Manhattan, NY
Friday, June 25, 2021

Walt took another sip of rum and quickly turned the page. He was amazed at how quickly the details of the investigation were coming back to him. He realized that the memories had not so much faded and disappeared, but had instead been warehoused. Stored away and slowly covered by the dust of life—the accumulation of years and the distractions that accompanied them. But as he flipped through the pages of the file now, he was transformed back into that twenty-eight-year-old kid who had found himself in the middle of a homicide investigation that was about to capture the attention of the nation.

THE CAMERON YOUNG INVESTIGATION

Walt finished his second walk-through of the big house in the Catskill Mountains and started his long drive back to the city. He worked through what he knew so far. The community he was leaving was quiet, calm, and tranquil. People there were wealthy. People there knew each other. Crime was uncommon. There was little chance Cameron Young had been killed randomly. There was little chance the man did not know his killer.

As he drove, Walt reviewed what he had learned in the last twenty-four hours about the art of deviant sex, having brought himself up to speed on the nuances of BDSM sex during a two-in-the-morning Internet binge the previous night. He cringed at the thought of anyone looking through his browser history. BDSM—bondage/dominance/sadism/masochism—was aggressive, often rough and painful sex between two consenting adults that included a wide variety of props and toys. *Consenting* was a buzzword Walt had seen in just about every article he read, although he wondered how consenting Cameron Young had been the night he died. Something dark and dangerous had taken place in that bedroom.

The analysis of the blood found on the carpeting of the

closet, as well as the urine in the toilet, was being expedited so it could be compared against DNA samples Walt would soon collect from potential suspects. Similarly, the fingerprints lifted from the kitchen knife and the wineglass left on the nightstand would also be compared against prints Walt would obtain. After his initial interview, Walt decided the first samples he would ask for would be from Cameron Young's wife.

Walt drove his unmarked squad car across the George Washington Bridge. He fought stagnant Manhattan traffic until he found a mostly legal parking spot in the West Seventies neighborhood on the Upper West Side. The Youngs' Manhattan residence was a two-bedroom ground-floor apartment on Seventy-Sixth Street. Walt shrugged his suit coat onto his shoulders and adjusted his cuffs as he walked to the front door and rang the bell. Tessa Young answered. Her eyes were red-rimmed and wet, her nose chafed and raw.

"Mrs. Young. Thanks for agreeing to speak with me again. I know you're having a hard time, but I'd like to bring you up to speed on what I've learned."

Tessa nodded, ran the back of her hand across her nose, and allowed Walt to enter her home. He followed her to the kitchen and accepted Tessa's offer of coffee. She poured two cups and they sat at the kitchen table.

"Again, I'm sorry to give you no space during this difficult time, but my job is to figure out what happened to your husband, and to do it as quickly as possible. To that end, I need to ask some pointed questions."

Tessa nodded again. "I understand."

"Cameron was at your vacation home in the Catskills when he was killed. When was the last time you were at the house?"

"Over the Fourth of July."

Walt pulled out his notepad. "Was it just you and your husband?"

"No, we were there with friends."

"Can you provide names?"

"Jasper and Victoria Ford."

"Good friends of yours?"

Tessa nodded, but Walt saw something change in her demeanor. "Jasper sold us our house in the Catskills. He was the realtor who brokered the deal. We invited him and his wife out for a sail to celebrate. We've been friends since then."

"So, you've been friends for a couple of years or so?"

Tessa nodded. "Three."

"You were last at the house over the Fourth, but not on July fourteenth or fifteenth, when your husband was killed?"

"No."

"Was it common for your husband to go to the vacation house without you?"

"Yes. He was finishing a manuscript and often went to the mountains for quiet. He has a writing studio there, next to the house."

Walt had been through Cameron Young's work space, a small structure that stood across the creek on the north side of the home. It was a small replica of the A-frame log house, and was made up of a writing desk and computer on one side and a wood-burning fireplace and recliner on the other. A minibar stood in the corner and sported both a coffeemaker for mornings and a small collection of spirits for afternoon or evening. If Walt had a creative bone in his body, he would have marveled at the tranquil setting that had produced a string of best sellers over the last few years. But Walt Jenkins wasn't creative, he was analytical. He took a clinical approach to the space and tried to learn if the writing studio offered any clues to what had happened to Cameron Young.

"When your husband went out to the Catskills, how long would he stay?"

"Depends on how far behind he was on a deadline. A day or two, usually. He didn't always go alone. Sometimes I went with him. He has his studio, I have my office in the main house where I did my own work."

"So you each had your own private work space?"

Tessa nodded.

"Were you and Cameron getting along?"

There was a pause. "Sometimes."

Walt nodded. "How would you describe your marriage?"

"My marriage?"

"Yes. Were there problems in the marriage?"

"There're problems in every marriage."

"But specifically with yours, Mrs. Young."

Tessa shrugged. "Sure. We had lots of problems."

"Can you describe them?"

Another pause. "If you're asking if we were happily married, I'd say no. We'd been having problems for years but were trying to make it work."

"Were you having financial problems?"

"Excuse me?"

"Money issues are a common source of struggles within a marriage, so I'm asking if you had any issues with money."

"No, money was not a problem. Cameron's books, for the last couple of years, were quite successful. We don't have any debt, besides the mortgage on this apartment. The house in the Catskills is paid off. We have plenty of money saved."

"When you say *plenty* . . . ?"

Tessa shook her head as she calculated. "Three million.

Maybe more. Cameron handled the finances. I see the balance once a year when I sign the tax returns."

"Was the money in a joint account?"

"Yes, Detective. I could get my hands on all the money I ever needed at any time. I certainly wouldn't have to kill my husband for it."

Walt made a note on his pad.

"Did your husband have a life insurance policy?"

"We both do. We took them out just after we married. Million-dollar policies on each of us."

Tessa Young's tone regarding the millions of dollars she and her husband were worth was so matter-of-fact that Walt didn't know what to make of it. She was either a damn good actress or she had nothing to hide.

"You are a professor, is that correct, Mrs. Young?"

"Yes."

"Would you say that most of your income came from your husband?"

"I make a hundred and fifty thousand dollars a year as a professor at Columbia University. But yes, our income came mostly from my husband."

Walt made a few notes in his book, and then looked up from the page and made eye contact with Cameron Young's widow.

"Some of this will be difficult to hear, and may be uncomfortable to discuss, but I need to ask."

Tessa waited, and finally nodded.

"Your husband was gagged, Mrs. Young, with what is called a ball gag. It's a bondage device used in S and M sex."

Tessa Young said nothing, just held Walt's stare.

"Did you and your husband engage in sexual behavior that included bondage?"

"For Christ's sake, no!"

Walt paused.

"Your husband was bound with rope also commonly used in S and M sex. Do you possess any of that rope?"

"Of course not."

"Would you allow me to look around your home?"

"My lawyer would tell me to let you look anywhere you wish, but would insist on a search warrant."

Walt removed a slip of paper from his folder. "I'd never ask without one."

"Look for whatever you want, Detective. Go through my drawers and take samples of my underwear, or whatever perverted thing you have on your mind."

Walt continued undeterred. "We found blood, urine, and fingerprints in the bedroom of your Catskills home. It will be important to know which ones belong to you, as I'm sure your fingerprints will be found in the bedroom of the home you own. Are you willing to provide fingerprint samples and allow my technicians to swab your cheek for DNA analysis?"

"Am I a suspect in my husband's murder, Detective Jenkins?"

Walt pursed his lips and opened his palms. "I'm collecting information at this point, Mrs. Young. With any homicide, I ask for samples from the spouse. It's just part of the process."

"You look like you just graduated high school. How many homicides could you possibly have worked before this one?"

Walt kept a stoic expression on his face and did not indulge her with an answer.

Tessa finally nodded. "Of course. I'll give you whatever you need."

"I'll arrange it for this afternoon."

She nodded. Walt went back to his notepad.

"When you say you and your husband were trying to make your marriage work, what does that mean?"

"It means we were trying not to get a divorce."

Walt waited.

"I'm pregnant," Tessa finally said, as if admitting to a crime. "We thought if we had a child together, it would fix things. At least that's what *I* thought."

Walt closed his eyes a moment. He had perhaps pushed too hard. Still, he noted her pregnancy in his book and then stood.

"I'm sorry to make you talk about all this. I'm just trying to figure out who killed your husband."

Tessa put a hand over her forehead, as if fighting off a migraine. Walt's phone rang. It was headquarters calling.

"Excuse me," he said, as he turned and answered. "Jenkins."

"Hey, Walt, it's Ken Schuster."

Schuster was the lead crime scene technician assigned to the Young case.

"What's happening, Ken?"

"I was categorizing evidence we collected from the Catskills mansion. There's something here you need to see."

Walt walked out of the kitchen, through the hallway, and into the foyer where his conversation wouldn't be overheard.

"I'm at the Youngs' residence now, speaking with the wife. I'm about to search the property."

"You're going to want to see this. Stat."

"What is it?"

"We found a thumb drive in the desk drawer of the office. There's a video on it."

"What sort of video?"

"Ah, well . . . it looks like a homemade sex tape."

Walt glanced back into the kitchen. His mind flashed back to moments earlier when Tessa Young described her and her husband's separate work spaces. The studio was *His*. The office in the main house was *Hers*.

"Who's on the video?"

"Cameron Young and a woman."

Walt lowered his voice further. "His wife?"

"Nope."

"I'll be right there."

Walt raced back to the BCI headquarters after his brief interview with Tessa Young and an even shorter search of her home. Now he sat in front of the iMac with Ken Schuster and watched the footage unfold on the monitor. Cameron Young was naked and in a compromised position, bent over an apparatus Walt recognized from his late night research.

"I mean, look at this shit. What the hell *is* that thing?" Ken asked.

"A spanking horse," Walt said matter-of-factly. "Or sometimes referred to as a boarding horse."

Ken slowly turned away from the monitor and gave Walt a sideways glance.

"Research," Walt said, pointing at the screen to get Ken's gaze off him.

When a participant lay facedown on the apparatus, it exposed one's buttocks to maximum punishment or pleasure. The video played for nearly one minute, Cameron Young's backside on full display. Walt recognized the background in the video and realized it had been filmed in Cameron Young's writing studio, although the shot was somewhat off center. It looked as though the camera had shifted and now the action took place to the left side of the screen.

"Anything on here other than this guy's ass?"

Ken pointed at the timer on the bottom right of the screen and raised three fingers to start the countdown. *Three, two, one*. As soon as Ken lowered his third finger, a loud *smack* came from the computer speakers. Walt startled, nearly as much as Cameron Young's body recoiled, as the multi-threaded whip lashed across his buttocks. The smacking noise came again with a second lashing.

"Jesus Christ."

"Oh, it's wild stuff all right," Ken said.

The *thwack* came a third time.

"I don't think I can watch this," Walt said.

"You'd better."

A muffled female voice could be heard from off screen, but her exact words were too difficult to make out, as if the camera's microphone was not working properly.

"Whose voice was that?" Walt asked.

Ken pointed at the screen, never taking his eyes off the action. Finally, the backside of the woman came into view. Only her lower back, buttocks, and legs were visible because of the amateurish nature of the video and the off-centered angle. Soon though, the woman kept walking and came into full view. Dressed in black dominatrix leather, studded wristbands, and a choke collar with silver spikes pinched around her neck, the woman walked past Cameron Young's exposed buttocks and to the far end of the shot. The whip hung perilously from her right hand. When she turned to face the camera Ken paused the video, capturing her image clearly.

"Who is it?" Walt asked.

"Victoria Ford. Tessa Young's best friend."

Walt stood. "You sure about the ID?"

"Positive."

"Anything else on there I need to see?"

"If you haven't enjoyed it thus far, I'm pretty sure you won't like the rest of it."

"Mark that as evidence, and protect the shit out of it. Document a clear chain of custody."

"You got it, boss."

Walt hurried back to his office to find out everything he could about the woman named Victoria Ford.

CHAPTER 20

Catskill Mountains, NY
Friday, June 25, 2021

The bottle of chardonnay was empty by the time Emma finished telling Avery about the murder investigation her sister had been involved in at the time of her death. Avery had driven to the Catskills to interview Emma Kind about the recent identification of Victoria Ford's remains and to determine if there was enough there on which to base an *American Events* feature. The idea that she had stumbled onto the story of a grisly murder had her mind churning with ideas about the special she could put together with the details of this case.

Avery's head swam with a comfortable wine buzz, but she didn't protest when Emma emerged from the house with a second bottle. Avery wanted to know everything about Emma's long dead sister and the crime she was accused of. Another bottle of wine seemed like the perfect conduit to keep Emma talking. Besides, Avery was fascinated with the ancient artifact Emma had carried from the house along with the second bottle of wine. She recognized it as a telephone answering machine straight from the nineties, and now it sat in the middle of the patio table. Emma had excused herself in the middle of the story about Victoria to rummage through the house. It had been quite a production for Emma to salvage the answering machine from the storage room. It was an even greater one to resuscitate it. A relic from the past, the machine required both batteries and an electrical outlet to bring it to life. All the time, Avery sipped chardonnay and tried to control the suspense of what waited on the machine. Now, an extension cord ran from the kitchen outlet, through the patio doors, and to the table where the machine sat. Triple A batteries ignited the indicator light on the surface. The machine was, indeed, alive and well.

"At first," Emma said, "the news was just that a wealthy novelist had been killed in the Catskills. Then rumors of an affair came out. When Victoria was connected to the murder, I didn't believe it. I wouldn't, in fact, until that awful video was leaked and Victoria became the center of the story. The press were like rabid animals. Reporters waited for her in the lobby of her office building, and outside her apartment. The video was everywhere. There was no social media back then, but the Internet was just sprouting its wings. The image of Victoria in that dominatrix outfit made it onto every news program and into every newspaper. The video was downloaded thousands of times and watched endlessly in every home whose owners held voyeuristic tendencies. The news media salivated over every detail. For a short time, S and M and bondage became daily headlines and utterances of news anchors around the country."

Avery was in junior high at the time, but even now vaguely remembered the stir the video had caused. It was difficult for her to believe that two decades later she had stumbled onto the story. Avery understood why the media took such intense interest back then. The headlines would have been like giant meat hooks on which to capture an audience, move news-papers, and sell advertising spots. Not only twenty years ago, she thought, but today as well. Avery imagined her own headlines for *American Events*. The remains of a 9/11 victim identified twenty years after the towers fell, a woman at the center of a sensational murder investigation involving a pop-ular novelist, and a torrid tale of sex and betrayal. The possi-bilities were endless. The crime scene details would likely be shocking and were sure to tap into the morbid fascination of the *American Events* true-crime fans. Avery wondered if she could get her hands on the crime scene photos and other specifics from the investigation. Or even, she allowed herself to imagine, edited snippets of the sex tape.

"In the weeks leading to September eleventh, one piece of bad news after another trickled in," Emma said. "The evi-dence started to pile up, and I couldn't believe what I was seeing on the nightly news. A length of rope was discovered in Victoria's car that police said matched the rope around Cameron Young's neck. The whole damn crime scene was apparently covered in Victoria's fingerprints and DNA. Her urine was recovered from the bathroom toilet and her blood was found in the master bedroom."

Avery's chardonnay-clouded mind raced. She was still working angles in her mind about how to obtain footage of that homemade sex video. But she needed more than that. She needed access to the case file and the intimate details about the investigation. She thought for a moment about the channels she could peruse to obtain such details. Finally, she brought her thoughts back to the present and pointed at the answering machine.

"What does the answering machine have to do with all of it?"

Emma took a sip of wine to steady herself. "Victoria called me that day."

"What day?"

"September eleventh. After the first plane struck the North Tower. She called to tell me she was trapped. She called to . . . to say good-bye."

Avery slowly put down her wineglass. "Oh, Emma, that's awful. And you kept the message all these years?"

"Yes. But not for that reason. Not because it was Victoria saying good-bye. She told me something else that day. I want you to hear it."

Avery waited, not blinking and barely breathing. The wine buzz was simultaneously interfering with, and facilitating, her concentration. Slowly, Emma reached over to the answering machine and pressed the *play* button. There were a few seconds of static before a voice was heard.

"Emma!"

The voice of Victoria Ford was amazingly clear as it echoed from the twenty-year-old machine.

"If you're there, pick up the phone!"

There was a long pause as Victoria waited for her sister to respond to her desperate plea. Avery shifted her gaze from the machine to Emma, but Emma had her eyes closed. Avery wondered how many times the woman had listened to this recording over the last twenty years. In the background of the recording, Avery heard yelling and crying and general chaos.

> *"Emma, I'm in the city . . . at the World Trade Center. Something's happened. There was an explosion and people are saying a plane hit the building. I'm in the North Tower and . . . I think we're trapped. There's a fire on the floors below us that is prevent-*

ing us from getting to the ground floor. We're all
heading up to the roof. There will be helicopters,
some are saying, to rescue us. I don't know if I
believe it, but I'm following the crowd. There's
nowhere else to go. I love you! Tell Mom and Dad I
love them, too. I'll call again when I know what's
happening. Bye for now."

Emma pressed a button to stop the recorder. She looked up
to Avery, who had tears in her eyes.

"Emma, that's . . . tragic. I'm so sorry. It must be horrible
to . . . have that tape. To have that reminder."

"There's more," Emma said. "Another message. And
that's what I really want you to hear."

Emma took a deep breath and another sip of wine before
starting the answering machine again.

"Emma, it's me. Umm . . . listen. I'm hearing some
crazy things right now. It's all very chaotic and I
don't know what to believe. Terrorists and airplanes.
There was another explosion and people are saying a
second plane hit the tower. Or the South Tower. I
don't . . . there's nowhere for us to go. The door to
the roof was locked, so we're going to try to go down
again. Someone said they know a different stairwell
that might be open. So . . . I'm going now. But . . ."

A long pause hollowed the air on the patio and Avery noticed she had stopped breathing. She was leaning closer to
the answering machine, waiting for Victoria Ford's next
words. There was a softness to this recording that was not
present in the first. A lack of background noise and absence
of the chaos that had been present in the first recording lent

a stillness to this message that gave Avery the impression that not only Victoria Ford, but the building itself had given in to its fate. Victoria's voice finally came.

"Everything that's happening with me. Everything with the investigation. Please know . . . It's important to me that you know . . . I didn't do the things they've accused me of. I loved Cameron, that much is true. But I didn't kill him. You know me, Em. You know I'm not capable of that. They said they found my blood and urine at the scene. But that can't be true. None of it can be true. Please believe me. If I . . . Emma, if I'm not able to get out of this building . . . Please believe that I'm innocent. Please . . ."

Avery waited through several seconds of silence. For a moment she thought the recording was finished, but Emma made no move to stop the machine. Finally, Victoria Ford's voice came back to them one last time.

"Find a way, Em. Find a way to prove it. Please? Just find a way to prove to the world that I'm not the monster they've painted me to be. I've gotta go now. I love you."

Emma reached to the center of the table and stopped the recording. She looked up at Avery.

"So there you have it. My sister's dying request was for me to prove her innocence. I've tried for twenty years but have made little progress. The people who were involved with the case back then, like the rest of the world, became overwhelmed by the aftermath of 9/11. When things returned to some state of normal, my sister and the case against her was packed away. The matter was considered finished. I tried to keep the investigation going, knowing that the things they claimed my sister did could not be true. But no one wanted to hear from me. No one wanted to talk to me. No one cared."

"I care," Avery said.

She had not simply found a story that would stand out from the fall lineup of exposés commemorating the twenty-year anniversary of 9/11, she had found a mystery. She had traveled across the country for another, perhaps more important, reason. She was using the identification of Victoria Ford's remains as cover to hide the real purpose of her presence in New York, which was to finish the business of the Montgomery family for good. But somehow, without looking for it, Avery found herself in the middle of the Catskill Mountains with an afternoon wine buzz and staring at a big, fat ratings giant of a mystery.

"I'm a big believer in fate," Emma said. "Everything happens for a reason. I believe fate brought you to my doorstep. Victoria asked me to clear her name. She didn't want to be remembered as a killer. Over the years, I haven't had much success in disproving any part of the case against Victoria. The blood, the urine, or any of the other evidence. But I haven't had much help either. Maybe that's about to change? With your help . . . I mean together, maybe you and I will have better luck. The same way that Victoria will always be that young and healthy woman in my mind, she will always be innocent to me, as well. So when you asked if finally identifying my sister's remains brings me closure . . . perhaps a bit. But the only thing that will bring me *peace* is finally proving that my baby sister never killed anyone. Will you help me?"

Avery's agent had asked for details about the content Avery planned to bring to the upcoming season of *American*

Events. Dwight Corey had asked for ammunition before he went back to the negotiating table. She had just stumbled into a munitions factory.

"Will you help me?" Emma asked again.

Avery slowly nodded. "I will."

PART III

Deception

CHAPTER 21

Manhattan, NY
Monday, June 28, 2021

"Where?" Dwight Corey asked.

Avery sat at Jacques, the bar at the Lowell Hotel, and used the straw to stir the ice in her Tito's and soda. It had been three days since her drunken afternoon with Emma Kind, when two bottles of chardonnay had accompanied some startling revelations about Victoria Ford.

"New York," Avery said.

"What are you doing in New York?"

"Chasing a story."

"Well, your timing is for shit. Mosley Germaine wants to meet to discuss your contract. He's left a string of messages for me to call him back."

"Did they come up from seven-fifty?"

"They're holding firm, but they want to talk incentives and perks."

"I'm not talking incentives and perks until the base is set. Did you get my e-mail?"

Avery had sent her agent an e-mail detailing the salaries of newsmagazine hosts for the past twenty years, adjusted for inflation and according to ratings. The spreadsheet included the hosts of *Dateline*, *20/20*, *48 Hours*, and *60 Minutes* coupled with the Nielsen ratings for each. According to the models Avery compiled, pitting her ratings against the competition, $750,000 per year would be grossly underpaying her.

"Avery," Dwight said with more than a bit of skepticism in his voice. "Are you in New York taking meetings with other networks?"

"Hell no. I'd never take a meeting without my intimidating-as-hell six-foot-six agent, in his impeccable suit and with his flawlessly manicured nails, standing next to me. I'm starting to question your negotiating skills, but you still scare the hell out of most people. I'm in New York chasing a story, that's all."

"We need to talk about Germaine's offer."

"Not until he's serious about what he's offering. Listen, you told me to find you some content for next season. I've found it."

"Okay," Dwight said. There was a long pause before he spoke again in a dejected tone. "Give me the thirty-second recap of this story that sent you to New York. Go."

"The remains of a 9/11 victim were recently identified using new DNA technology at the New York medical examiner's office. I spoke with the ME, Dr. Livia Cutty, and she's willing to give me an inside look into the new technique, which she feels is a significant breakthrough to IDing the twenty thousand unidentified 9/11 remains that are still stored in the crime lab."

"Sounds interesting, and the timing works for this fall. But I'm not sure it's feature-film interesting."

"I'm just getting started. I tracked down Emma Kind, the sister of the woman who was just identified. I was looking for a personal side to the story. Something that had a chance to stand out this fall when everyone else will be doing stories about the twenty-year anniversary of 9/11. Then I learned that the identified remains belonged to a woman who happened to be facing indictment for murder. When she died, Victoria Ford was about to go on trial for the murder of her married lover—a wealthy novelist named Cameron Young."

"Wait a minute," Dwight said. "Why do I know that name?"

"Because in the nineties he wrote a string of best-selling thrillers. From the research I did over the weekend, he was very popular. His books were number one on all the lists and sold all over the world. Millions of copies. His death was a big story at the time. And then, just as this juicy murder investigation was becoming the focus of the nation, it got overshadowed."

"By September eleventh."

"Exactly. Most everyone forgot about Cameron Young and the mistress who killed him, and understandably turned their attention to the new and real threat of terrorism coming to our shores."

"Okay," Dwight said, in a slow drawl. "So what's your angle? The remains of the latest 9/11 victim belonged to a convicted killer? Not sure that's exactly a feel-good story for the twenty-year anniversary."

"Forget about the feel-good stuff. Forget about commemorating the twenty-year anniversary of 9/11. That's just the hook. I plan to look into the murder of Cameron Young. This is a true-crime story that will blow away anything I've covered before."

"I'm not following you. The case was open and shut, was it not?"

"Not necessarily. Emma Kind tells a compelling story about her sister. Victoria Ford might be guilty as sin, but something tells me there's more to the story. Something makes me want to dig into the details. In just a couple of days I've turned over a ton of information about the case, and I haven't even talked with anyone directly tied to the investigation yet. But Emma is helping me on that front. She gave me a list of all the people who were in her sister's life. I'm tracking down Victoria Ford's widower. I'm going to speak with her friends. Her family. The attorney who represented her. I'm trying to get in touch with the detective who investigated the case. I've reached out to the authorities and they're getting back to me. I'll also reach out to Cameron Young's family. There're a lot of angles here, Dwight. The murder itself was bizarre—an S and M bondage scene that included the victim hanging from the balcony of his mansion. Oh, and there's a homemade sex tape out there somewhere."

"Christ. Okay, slow down. I'm not sure this is the best use of your time right now, while we're in the middle of negotiating your contract."

"It sure as hell is. I'm putting my foot on the accelerator. I'm going to research this murder and see if there is any way the cops pinned this on the wrong person, as Emma Kind believes is the case. If I find any evidence to that end, I'm going to gather it all and put together a stunning exposé about the latest 9/11 victim to be identified, one who happened to be wrongly accused before she died."

"What if all you find is that she was guilty as charged?"

"Then it's *still* an interesting story. Because it's with good reason that Emma Kind believes her sister was innocent."

There was silence on the line between them.

"You know, Avery, while you're running around New York City, Germaine could rescind the offer at any moment and go with someone else. Are you willing to risk that?"

"She has a recording," Avery said.

"Who?"

"Emma Kind."

"What sort of recording?"

"An answering machine recording of her sister from the morning of 9/11. After Victoria learned that she was trapped in the North Tower, she called her sister. The recording was made just before the tower collapsed."

"Shit," Dwight said in a disgusted tone.

"What?"

Avery heard him take a deep breath and slowly exhale it.

"You're starting to pique my interest. Go."

"On the recording, Victoria Ford claims to be innocent. She tells Emma there's no way she's capable of killing anyone, and she asks her sister to prove as much in the event Victoria doesn't make it out of the North Tower."

"You can *get* that recording?"

"I already have it."

"You have it in your possession? With this woman's permission to play it to millions of viewers?"

"Absolutely. Emma and I are best friends after a couple bottles of wine on her back porch. She gave me the answering machine so I could review every detail of the recording. She'll give me all the help I need as long as I agree to help clear her sister's name."

"Out of all the crazy ideas you've come up with over the last couple of years, this one might actually have some shoulders."

"Oh, it's got shoulders. Big, broad, bowling ball shoulders that would make even Dwight Corey envious. And I plan to ride them all summer long until I find the truth."

"You sound excited."

"I'm on the road, I'm on my own, and I'm in the trenches. I'm feeling good about this one, Dwight."

"I'll stall Germaine for another week or two. Keep me posted."

Avery smiled. "Always."

CHAPTER 22

Manhattan, NY
Tuesday, June 29, 2021

A very walked from her hotel lobby. The contrast to suburban Los Angeles was always startling when she returned to Manhattan. Her two-bedroom condo on the twelfth story of the Ocean Towers high-rise in Santa Monica offered forever views of the Pacific Ocean and long stretches of welcoming beach to the north and south. Everything in Santa Monica was low and spaced out. Here in Manhattan, it was all stacked high and compressed, the infrastructure designed to pack people tightly on top of each other. It was a nice change of pace while she chased her story, but not somewhere she ever wanted to live again. She'd spent her childhood in this city, but had longed to get away from the congestion ever since that first summer her parents sent her to Connie Clarkson's sailing camp in Sister Bay, Wisconsin. Avery hadn't expected to drift as far as the West Coast, but now that she had lived there for a number of years, she couldn't consider setting up camp anywhere else.

The sights and smells of her childhood stomping grounds produced the normal nostalgia, but something else, too. So many bad things had happened in this city. So many things Avery wanted to forget. Things that had turned her life upside down, chased her away, and forced her to become someone new. Returning always dredged up memories that muddied the waters of her life. Only time had the ability to settle and calm them. Of course, the solution to this regular stirring up of bad memories would be to stop coming back to New York. But more than a few things continued to pull her back to this hallowed place. The first was the memory of the last time she had been out on the water in her Oyster 625.

She walked down the stairs of Penn Station and pushed through a turnstile to the subway. She settled into a seat near the rear of the subway car and rode in quiet contemplation until she exited at Chambers Street. She walked with afternoon commuters for several blocks, heading south until she found Vesey Street, where she eventually wound her way west to North Cove Marina. All of her senses bombarded her—the smells and the sounds and the images—and conspired to collapse time and erase the years that had passed since she was last here. It was the summer before her third year of law school. Her parents had gone to the house in the Hamptons for a long weekend, and Avery and Christopher were due to join them the following day. In the meantime, the Oyster 625 was theirs for the taking.

As Avery looked out at the marina and the boats, she thought of Christopher and that summer morning. They knew a storm was brewing out in the Atlantic. They knew they would run into weather. They knew it would be dangerous. They knew it was a bad idea to take the Oyster out that day. But still, Avery climbed aboard and motored out of the marina.

She walked down the long dock now, a slow stroll that took her back in time until she stopped at the slip where the *Claire-Voyance* once rested. In its place was some other boat owned by some other family. Avery closed her eyes as memories ran through her mind of whitecapped waves crashing over the bow. She squeezed her eyelids tight as she thought of the sheets of rain that turned day into night, and of the bow as it slipped under the surface of the ocean. A shiver found her shoulders when she remembered climbing over the railing and jumping into the cold, turbulent waters where the waves crashed over her head. Pressing her fingers into her temples, she tried but failed to dull the image of the sailboat's stern rising into the air, not unlike the image in *Titanic*, before it speared to the bottom of the ocean. Her life vest had just barely kept her alive until the Coast Guard found her.

But the memory of the last time she had sailed the *Claire-Voyance,* and what that final voyage meant for her brother, were not the only things that continued to bring Avery back to New York. She walked back up the dock and pulled from her purse the postcard that had arrived in her mailbox months earlier. She studied the image of the wooded cabin on the front and then turned the card over to read the message written there.

> *To the one-and-only Claire-Voyant,*
> *Just hanging out and watching the Events of*
> *America. Could use some company.*

On the bottom right corner of the card, Avery saw the numbers again.

777

Could she really do it? She had come all the way across the country for a reason, but could she really go through with it? Avery knew that she held his life in her hands, and that the decisions she made while in New York could secure his freedom, or strip it from him.

CHAPTER 23

Manhattan, NY
Tuesday, June 29, 2021

She left the marina and started her way east. Walking the streets of her childhood city this afternoon made Avery realize how far she had come since she'd thrown shovelfuls of dirt over her old identity and fled to Los Angeles. The plan had been to never look back, but Avery had failed miserably at that. She checked the rearview mirror of her life so often it was a wonder she hadn't caused a head-on collision. But her success at *American Events* had provided stretches during which she forgot about this city and its secrets. This year's journey, and all she had planned, would perhaps provide the clean slate she was searching for.

It took over an hour to walk back to Midtown, but she needed the time and the solitude to clear her mind of the memories stirred up from her visit to North Cove Marina. It was almost six in the evening when she walked over to Seventh Avenue and turned on West Forty-Seventh Street. She found THE RUM HOUSE painted on the front window of the establishment, pulled open the door, and walked inside. Avery spotted him before he noticed her. Sitting on a stool, his right hand twisted a tumbler on the bar in front of him while his left hand rubbed a spot in the middle of his chest. Avery's research told her that this man had been just twenty-eight years old when he ran the Cameron Young investigation. That put him in his forties today, but from this distance and with the shadowed lighting of the bar darkening his features, he looked younger. On second glance, as she approached, Avery thought she had the wrong man. But no, she was looking at detective Walt Jenkins. He just didn't look much different than the photos she had seen of him from 2001, when his face appeared in the newspaper articles she had read and the archived footage of press conferences she had watched online. He could pass for his midthirties and had the sort of appearance that made Daniel Craig attractive—short-cropped hair blended into tight sideburns, smile lines that bracketed his lips, which were creased now as he considered his drink, and the early presence of crow's feet at the corners of his eyes. He looked up from his drink as Avery walked up. When they made eye contact, she saw that his irises were a sort of ice blue that on first glance could be mistaken for gray.

Avery sensed that he recognized her. Celebrity had never been something she sought, quite the contrary since she fled New York City. But fame had somehow found her. Millions tuned in to *American Events* each week, so it was inevitable that she was often recognized. Walt Jenkins lifted his chin, which Avery noticed was cleft in the middle, and offered a smile. His teeth were straight and white and contrasted against his tanned complexion. Avery reached out her hand.

"Detective Jenkins?" she said.

He raised an eyebrow as he shook her hand. "Now that sounds strange. I haven't been called Detective for years. Walt Jenkins."

"Hi, Walt. Avery Mason. I read that you're retired, which

is hard to believe. You don't look old enough. I mean, you don't come off as a retiree."

"I'm not a card-carrying member of AARP just yet, but I am most definitely retired from detective work. For many, many years now."

"With the NYPD?"

"No, I was never with NYPD. Back when I was a cop, I worked for New York State and the Bureau of Criminal Investigation."

"Yes, your work at the BCI—that's what I was hoping to pick your brain about."

"Sure thing. Have a seat. Can I buy you a drink?"

Avery sat on the stool next to him and pointed at his drink. "What is that, bourbon?"

"Rum."

"Rum?"

"The place *is* called the Rum House."

"On the rocks?"

"It's how good rum is meant to be enjoyed. Not ruined by mixing it with soda or Red Bull or whatever the hell the kids are doing these days. Can I entice you?"

"I'm a Tito's and soda gal, if they even serve vodka at a rum bar."

Avery waved down the bartender, who mixed the drink in record time and set it in front of her.

"So what's your background?" Avery asked. "You made detective at twenty-eight and retired early?"

"Not exactly. After my stint with the BCI I actually moved on to the FBI."

Avery had lifted her glass to take a sip but paused, with the rim of the glass an inch from her lips, at the mention of the FBI. Finally, she took a long swallow of vodka, shaking her head as she replaced her drink on the bar.

"How did I not know that?"

"You tell me. You're the investigative journalist."

Avery tried to process the idea that she was sitting in a bar with a member of the FBI, an agency that had a vested interest in her family.

"In your defense," Walt said, breaking the silence, "my Bureau career was not what you'd call *distinguished*. It's easy to miss. I basically pushed papers for a few years after 9/11 and I'm still not sure any of my efforts advanced the war on terror. Then I transferred to surveillance where I spent the remainder of my career."

Surveillance, Avery thought. Not *white-collar.*

"So how did you manage to retire in your forties? Put your twenty in, and live happily ever after?"

"Not quite. I was injured on the job and was politely asked to step aside. I politely did."

"Really. And now what?"

"I'm renting a house in Jamaica where I've spent the last few years. I try to come back to New York only when necessary. This city holds some tough memories and coming back always stirs them up."

Avery thought of her afternoon, her trip to the marina, and her long walk through the streets of Manhattan where she tried to settle her own troubling memories. She had done her best to distance herself from the Montgomery family wounds, at least to hide from them. Specifically, she had tried to escape her connection to the Thief of Manhattan, as her father was known in the press. Her father's infamy was why she had an uneasy feeling as she sat next to a former FBI agent, and her torrid past explained why she was thrown off by her attraction to Walt Jenkins. The battle that waged between her former and current selves was all consuming. It dominated both her professional and private life. It had prevented Avery from having a meaningful relationship with a man for the past many years. Her last serious relationship had been with a fellow student during her second year of law school. She ended things when the truth about her father's firm began to trickle out to the public and the ramifications reared their ugly heads. She knew the years spent learning the law were as wasted as if she had spent them in a crack house. No law firm or municipality would hire Garth Montgomery's daughter to put criminals behind bars. The irony would be too great for even the dysfunctional political system of the United States to swallow.

Her storied history explained why Avery was thirty-two years old and had never been in love. Relationships were tricky. *Real* relationships—ones that went further than a couple of months of off-and-on dating. Because beyond that point things became confusing with men. She didn't quite know where her life as Avery Mason started and that of Claire Montgomery ended. Those dual personalities over-lapped in ways that made honesty a monumental challenge. Her mind had attempted many times to navigate the serpentine roads that made up the early conversations at the start of a relationship, when both parties shared stories about their pasts, about their childhoods, about their parents and siblings. For Claire Montgomery, the canvas of her past was splattered with the drippings of a frantic artist gone mad. For Avery Mason, that canvas was blank. That both identities were forever bound by a hatred toward the father who betrayed his family complicated matters. That she couldn't stop herself from loving the son of a bitch only made things more confusing. Put it all together and it was not hard to see why Avery welcomed men into her life—and specifically into her bed—with great trepidation.

She snapped herself back from her thoughts.

"You were in Jamaica when I called?"

Walt nodded. "I was."

"What's in Jamaica?"

"Some really good rum and a dog named Bureau."

"Who's taking care of the dog?"

"He can take care of himself, mostly. He used to be a stray, but I've turned him soft. A friend is watching him while I'm gone," Walt said.

Avery pointed at the bar and cocked her head. "Now the rum makes sense. And the tan. I'm honored you came back to the States on my request."

"I'm a big fan of *American Events*. When I heard Avery Mason was trying to track me down, my interest was piqued. So tell me, what's on your mind?"

"Cameron Young."

"That much I know. What about him?"

"I've been looking into his death and the murder investigation that surrounded it. I'm considering revisiting the case as a potential feature on *American Events*. Taking a hard look at the case and retelling the story for one of my true-crime specials. Since you were the lead detective, I thought you'd be a good place to start."

Walt nodded. "The Cameron Young case checks all the boxes for a sensationalized exposé on a newsmagazine show, that's for sure."

"It does," Avery admitted.

"Wealthy novelist."

Avery nodded. "Gruesome crime scene."

"Sex," Walt said with raised eyebrows. "And kinky sex at that."

"Yes, crazy S and M stuff from what I've read. Plus betrayal."

"Lots of that."

"And now, the identification of Victoria Ford's remains twenty years after 9/11."

Walt raised his glass of rum. "Shit, I'd tune in for that."

Avery laughed. "Thanks, I'll count you as a devoted fan if

I ever get this project off the ground. But honestly, I'm look-ing to do more than just *retell* the case."

"Yeah? What do you have in mind?"

She paused to take a sip of vodka, knowing her next com-ment would not be well received. "I'm looking to tell a dif-ferent story. One that's less focused on the wealthy writer who was killed and more dedicated to the woman accused of killing him."

"In what way?"

Avery paused for another moment.

"Is there any way . . . the BCI could have gotten it wrong about Victoria Ford?"

She watched Walt Jenkins consider the question while he spun his glass in the thin puddle of condensation that had formed on the mahogany bar. He lifted the tumbler and took a sip, then looked at her with a straight face.

"No."

Avery squinted her eyes. "Just like that? No way there could be another theory? The crime happened twenty years ago. Do you remember all the details from so long ago?"

"Of course not. But since you called, I've taken some time to review the case and refresh my memory. The case against Victoria Ford was airtight. It had to be, due to the media cov-erage at the time. It wasn't circumstantial. It wasn't specula-tive. It was based on physical evidence collected from the scene—DNA, fingerprints, a really damning video, and much more. It was a slam-dunk. If you sift back through the details of the case, you'll see what I'm talking about."

"Okay," Avery said, nodding her head. "That's what I was hoping to do. Would you be willing to sift through those de-tails with me? Take a deep dive back into the case so I can piece together how you came to suspect Victoria Ford as Cameron Young's killer?"

Walt pouted his lower lip and nodded. "That's why I'm

here. I still know people at the BCI, and I took the last couple of days to review the case. Crime scene photos, logged evidence, interview transcripts, recordings and videos of the intake interviews and follow-ups. There are thousands of pages of reports, warrants, phone records, e-mails. Plus, all the evidence collected."

"That's exactly what I'm looking for."

"I'd have to check with the bureaucrats to make sure they don't mind a journalist viewing the file, but this many years later I don't think it'll be an issue. If I get the okay, I'd be happy to share it all with you."

Now Walt paused.

"But to what end? So you can twist things around and convince a few skeptics that Victoria Ford might have been innocent? Turn her into the victim, falsely accused and all the crap true-crime documentaries push these days? Then tie that speculation in with her remains having just been ID'd?"

Avery took another sip of vodka, buying time to collect her thoughts and organize a pitch.

"I originally came out here from LA because I wanted to do a story on the latest 9/11 victim whose remains had been identified. That victim turned out to be Victoria Ford. I wanted to come out here and learn about the new technique used in the identification process, and maybe speak with Victoria's family, which I did. I met her sister, and she tells a pretty compelling story about Victoria."

"Let me guess. She believes her sister was innocent and there's no way she could have killed someone."

Avery nodded. "Yeah, something like that."

"Do you have siblings?"

Avery paused, glancing at the cubes in her vodka briefly before looking back at Walt Jenkins. This, right here, was why it was so difficult to meet new people—figuring out how much of the truth to reveal about herself, and how much to hide. Every detail she offered was a trail to her past.

"I had a brother," she finally said. "He died."

"Sorry. Not a great example."

"No, that came out the wrong way. God, I'm an idiot. I didn't mean to be so blunt about it."

There was a short pause that reset the conversation.

"Let me try again," Walt said. "Think of your best friend. If she were convicted of murder, would you believe she was guilty?"

"Absolutely. She can be a vindictive bitch."

Walt laughed. "You're not making this easy for me."

"I understand your point. No sibling is willing to believe their sister killed someone."

At first, Avery hadn't believed her father was one of the biggest white-collar criminals in American history. But in the face of overwhelming evidence, she had no choice. Yet, there was still some part of her that held on to the ideal perception of her father, back from before he detonated his family and collapsed all of their lives.

"Most family members respond with denial," Walt said. "Even when presented with undeniable evidence. There are killers on death row whose mothers and fathers and sisters and brothers believe are innocent. They believe this despite the guy's own confession. Despite the guy's remorse. Family members have an impossible time imagining their loved ones as killers. So I have no doubt that Victoria Ford's sister believes she's innocent. But a review of the case will prove otherwise. In the end, evidence doesn't care about your feelings."

Avery was tempted to mention the recording she had heard of Victoria Ford pleading for Emma to clear her name after she realized her fate in the North Tower. Avery believed the earnest tone to Victoria's appeal would be a worthy adversary if pitted against even the most overwhelming evidence. If not in an actual courtroom, then at least in the court of public opinion. And that arena was all Avery cared about as she considered the Victoria Ford project and how it pertained to *American Events*.

There would be a time to share the recording on Emma Kind's answering machine. There would be time to develop the narrative of the story she hoped to tell. But Avery needed information first. She was on the hunt for material, foraging for the long winter—the metaphor she and her team used to describe the process of building a story. Gather all the information you can find and then pare it down to the essentials. She was uncertain exactly what that story would look like, if it would work, and whether Walt Jenkins would play a significant role in building the story or be the wrecking ball that toppled it. Until she knew, Avery would keep Emma Kind's answering machine to herself.

"Let's start there," Avery said. "With the evidence. I'd love to review the case with you so you can show me where that evidence led you."

"It led me straight to Victoria Ford. But fair enough. Give me a day to make some calls and get my notes organized?"

"Absolutely. You still have my number?"

"Yeah," Walt said.

Avery reached into her purse to pay her bar tab.

"It's on me," Walt said.

"I made you come all the way from Jamaica. The least I can do is buy you a drink."

Avery dropped money next to her glass and slipped off her stool before heading out of the bar.

CHAPTER 24

Manhattan, NY
Tuesday, June 29, 2021

Walt Jenkins watched the tall, attractive journalist he'd seen a thousand times on television walk out of the Rum House. It had been a week since his old Bureau boss tracked him down at a cliff-side café in Jamaica, and here he was now, sitting in a dark bar in Manhattan. The contrast was startling. After just three years in Negril Walt realized how accustomed he'd become to island life and how far removed he was from his time as a surveillance officer. But still he found himself laying the groundwork, brick by brick, like he'd done so many times before, not sure where he was headed or what the next piece of road looked like.

The plan was to be up-front and honest about his past if Avery Mason broached the subject. She was an investigative journalist, and attempting to hide anything about his career in the Bureau would be a mistake. It seemed to rattle her just momentarily when he mentioned his past connection with the FBI, but she brushed it off quickly. He was certain she would spend the time between now and the next time they met looking into his story. It would all check out. The only thing he hadn't mentioned was that he was back on the FBI's payroll. Jim Oliver had been careful to explain that they were paying Walt as an independent consultant, and not refitting him with his old title of *special agent*. If Avery Mason got nervous and started snooping, Oliver wanted Walt's connection to the Bureau to end where it had three years ago—retired in good standing and with full pension.

He took a sip of rum, a Samaroli Jamaican Rhapsody that was too big for his wallet. Thankfully, the government was picking up the tab. He rubbed the scar on his sternum, like he'd been doing thirty minutes earlier while he waited for Avery to arrive. The scar still bothered him from time to time, producing a gnawing itch that drove him mad. The doctors promised it would eventually fade, but warned that until it did he should work to identify the triggers that brought on the symptoms and do his best to avoid them. As Walt sat at the Rum House in Times Square he realized that the last time the scar bothered him was a couple weeks earlier when he sat on his front porch pretending to read a John Grisham novel but really contemplating his upcoming trip to New York for the survivors meeting. Was the city itself a trigger, or all the baggage that waited here?

He finished his rum with a final tilt of the glass. This city held the mistakes and pains of his past, and he believed, like most, that to overcome those mistakes and ease the pain he needed to run from them. But that wasn't true. To make things right, he needed to face things head-on. As he was settling on the best way to do that, out of thin air an operation had developed. His first in years. It was an opportunity to pick himself up, dust himself off, and get back in the saddle. Whether it was an opportunity to put his past behind him or an exercise in procrastination, he hadn't figured out yet.

He waited another minute and then strolled out of the bar to keep tabs on his new subject—a woman who happened to be one of the most popular television journalists working today. If he hadn't been making a concerted effort to limit his alcohol intake, he might have thought the rum was getting to him.

CHAPTER 25

Manhattan, NY
Wednesday, June 30, 2021

The following morning, Avery was up early. Dressed in skinny jeans and comfortable walking shoes, she tucked her purse tight to her side, adjusted her Prada sunglasses, walked out of the lobby of her hotel, and headed toward the nearest subway hub. She took the F train from Midtown to Brooklyn, riding for thirty minutes until she exited at Fourth Avenue in the Park Slope neighborhood. She'd planned her route the night before and could practically close her eyes and find her way. Still, she pulled the small piece of paper from her purse as she walked and looked at the address one more time. The brownstone was six blocks from the train. She tried to control her nerves as she walked. She eventually turned on Sixteenth Avenue, where halfway down the street, she found the address. Climbing the front porch steps, she rang the bell and clutched her purse to her side as if she was worried she may be mugged.

The front door opened and a man stood in pajama pants and a white ribbed shirt under a long bathrobe. His hair was greasy, an unlit cigarette dangled from his lips, and the fingers of his right hand curled around the handle of a coffee cup. Tiny oval glasses, the lenses of which were streaked and dirty, shielded his eyes.

"Five hundred," the man said in a German accent that had been Americanized over the years and then tainted further by his time in Brooklyn.

"I'm sorry?" Avery said, confused by the random statement.

"Five hundred," he said again, the mumble making the cigarette flutter between his lips.

Avery raised her eyebrows, took a conspicuous look up and down the street. "Are we going to do this on your front stoop?"

"Five hundred gets you inside. *Then* we talk."

Avery nodded, reached into her purse, and produced five crisp hundred-dollar bills. The man snatched the cash out of her hands like a hungry dog nipping a treat from its owner's fingers, stepped to the side, and pushed the front door the rest of the way open. Avery walked inside as a cool prickle of apprehension moved in a slow wave across the back of her neck. The man pointed to a worn couch as he headed to a safe that stood against the far wall. He hunched in front of it, spun the dial, and pulled the door open. Depositing the cash inside, he removed a folder and slammed the safe door shut. The man turned around and sat in a side chair, placing his coffee cup on the table in front of him.

Avery hadn't moved from her spot just inside the front door. The man looked at her with a confused expression. He pushed the petite glasses up the bridge of his nose.

"Sit," he said. "I don't bite."

Avery walked to the couch and sat down.

"I'm André," the man said. "I hear we have a mutual friend?"

Avery nodded. "That's why I'm here."

"So here's how this works. Passports are difficult. Not impossible, but difficult. At least, if you want them done right. You want something . . ." He waved his hands, searching for the correct English word. "Shit." He shrugged his shoulder. "You go anywhere. You want something good, you come to André. That's why my price is my price. So I'm going to ask, even though I know the answer due to our mutual friend's . . . *background*, I guess you'd say. But there's a lot of work involved for me producing a believable passport. Some liability, too. So, I must ask, can you afford?"

"Yes," Avery said without hesitation.

This man charged $5,000 to produce a single American passport. Legitimate, believable passports that would, André claimed, pass scrutiny by any customs agent on the planet. Of course, the validity of that claim could only be proven in practice. It could only be confirmed when the one using the passport handed it to a customs agent as they tried to enter another country. At that moment, André's claim would be either true or false. At that moment it would also be too late to complain if things went wrong. If some sensor beeped when the document was scanned, and some warning was triggered, their "mutual friend" was shit out of luck.

"I figured the price was not an issue," André said. "Now, timing. When do you need this?"

"As soon as possible."

André held out his hand and twitched his index finger. "Give me the photo. Let me see what I'm working with."

Avery produced the photo from her purse and handed it to André, who opened the folder he had taken from the safe and laid the image onto a template to check the dimensions.

"Good quality. Right size." He nodded his head as he analyzed the photo. "Okay, this'll take me a week. I'll need twenty-five hundred now, twenty-five hundred when I'm done."

"And the five hundred I just gave you?"

"I told you, that got you in the door."

Avery was in no position to haggle. She produced another envelope from her purse and handed it across the coffee table. André quickly fingered the cash to make sure the count was correct. He stood and walked back to the front door, his silk bathrobe swirling like a cape behind him. He peered through the peephole and then opened the door.

"Out you go," he said. "Come back in a week."

CHAPTER 26

Brooklyn, NY
Wednesday, June 30, 2021

Fresh arrangements and bouquets decorated the sidewalk outside the florist. She smelled the hand-tied sunflowers and the amaryllis with baby's breath as she pulled open the door. Inside, the sweet aroma was even stronger. The scents captured her attention and distracted her from the worry that had settled in since she left the brownstone. Not for the first time, Avery wondered what the hell she had gotten herself into. She was risking everything to pull this off, and the more she allowed the rational half of her mind to consider the possibility of this plan working, the more she worried that her Achilles' heel—unconditional love—was going to bring her down like the rest of the Montgomery family members. But that unconditional love had forced her to come this far. She knew she could not simply turn it off.

She spent ten minutes in the flower shop, a reprieve where she took in the syrupy scents and admired the arrangements. She finally made her selection, paid at the register, and carried the bouquet of roses out the door. The air was damp with humidity and the sun was warm on this cloudless summer morning. She walked for ten minutes until she came to the entrance of Green-Wood Cemetery. Meandering paths cut through the hills beyond the gate, and the occasional gaudy mausoleum stood out among the headstones that dotted the landscape. Avery walked along the familiar trail until she came to the Plot, as she had come to know it in her mind. It took another minute to gather the courage to approach it. She had traveled three thousand miles—hard, fatiguing miles that took her from one end of the country to the other, making a heart-wrenching stop to see Connie Clarkson along the way, a woman who had been devastated by the Montgomery family—and yet, these last few steps were the hardest part of the journey.

This many years later, it was still a challenge to stare down at a gravestone. It was so nonsensical she could barely read the name it held. She should have cried, but she didn't. That part of her brain could no longer be triggered. This yearly voyage had become more business than ritual, and mostly she felt the need to get it over with. She stood over the grave for a minute or two before she finally crouched down and rubbed her hand over the front of the tombstone.

She remembered again the day her older brother insisted she take the boat out while storm clouds grew thunderous on the horizon. "Goddamn you, Christopher," she whispered to her brother's headstone. Then she stood, took a couple of steps to her right, and laid the bouquet of flowers on the neighboring grave.

"Love you, Mom," Avery said, before turning and walking back the way she'd come.

Walt Jenkins was rusty after his three-year sabbatical. There was an art to following someone, be it on foot or in a car, and to do it well required practice and maintenance. The only things Walt had followed over the last three years were the Yankees and the progress of a barrel of Hampden Estate Jamaican rum on which he had purchased futures. It was the local rum distillery about an hour from his house in Negril. The thought reminded him that he needed to check the last time the barrel had been racked. He shook his head and pushed the thought to the side—stray thoughts did not serve a surveillance specialist well, another indication he'd been away too long.

Earlier he had allowed a few morning commuters to exit the train after Avery Mason in order to keep a good pocket of people between him and her. He'd taken down the address of the brownstone she visited, stood down the block when she entered the flower shop, and took his time following her into the cemetery after she walked through the gates. Now, as she hurried away from the grave site where she had spent the last few minutes, Walt was less interested in following her. After she disappeared over a hill, he strolled to the plot where she had left a bouquet of flowers. Crouching down, he read the headstone. Finally, he reached into his pocket, grabbed his phone, and dialed Jim Oliver's number. It was strange to call his old FBI boss after so many years.

"Oliver," the voice said over the phone.

"She left her hotel this morning. I followed her to a brownstone in Brooklyn."

"Address?"

Walt read the address from a slip of paper he had scrawled it on. "From the brownstone, she headed to Green-Wood Cemetery."

"Yep," Oliver said. "She goes there every year."

CHAPTER 27
North Carolina
Wednesday, June 30, 2021

Nestled in the foothills of the Blue Ridge Mountains and sporting six bedrooms, eight thousand square feet, and majestic views of iconic Lake Norman, the house was one of the most well-known properties in the area. Recently renovated, it was featured in *Architectural Digest* and had graced the pages of *Magnolia Journal*. Originally purchased for $6 million, if sold today it would snag twice that much. A Cadillac Escalade pulled through the front gates and parked in the circular cobblestone drive. Its passengers included the editor-in-chief of Hemingway Publishing, the largest publishing house in the world, as well as the company's chief executive officer. They each had one goal today: lock their largest-selling author into a multiyear deal that guaranteed her novels would continue their mind-blowing run with Hemingway for the foreseeable future.

The first Natalie Ratcliff book, *Baggage,* hit shelves in 2005. Hemingway Publishing put out a modest initial press run for the debut, but threw a weighty promotional campaign behind the book. A quirky mystery featuring Peg Perugo—an out-of-work, heavy with *Baggage* female protagonist who finds love in all the wrong places as she stumbles her way through criminal investigations before nabbing the bad guy—*Baggage* found an audience. Natalie Ratcliff's debut became a word-of-mouth publishing phenomenon, and six weeks after it was published the book found the best-seller list. Three weeks later it made it to the top. Foreign rights poured in and the book marched around the world, climbing best-seller lists in every country where it was published. It sold a staggering eight million copies, and made Natalie Ratcliff (and Peg Perugo) a household name. The only book mighty enough to knock *Baggage* from the top of the *New York Times* list was its sequel, *Hard Knox*, which went on to sell eleven million copies. Natalie Ratcliff, once an emergency room physician, quickly grew bored of medicine and waiting rooms filled with sick patients. Concentrating on writing, Natalie pumped out one novel a year and became the best-selling fiction author of the decade. Today, over one hundred million Peg Perugo novels had sold worldwide.

Natalie was spending the summer finishing her sixteenth manuscript, the final in a three-book deal with Hemingway Publishing. Each time Natalie neared the end of a contract, publishers made pitches to Natalie's literary agent about why she should leave Hemingway and publish with their imprint. Hence, the Escalade parked in front of the Lake Norman mansion. Hemingway Publishing had no intention of letting their top-selling author slip through their fingers. Hemingway had discovered Natalie Ratcliff and her peculiar but lovable protagonist, and Hemingway planned to keep them both. The Escalade may as well have been a Brinks truck.

Kenny Arnett had been the CEO of Hemingway Publishing for more than a decade and had an impressive knack for retaining his A-list authors. Diane Goldstein had edited every Natalie Ratcliff book ever published and felt that she knew Peg Perugo personally. Years before, Diane had taken a chance on *Baggage* after several other houses passed. Many industry insiders scoffed when Hemingway offered $2 million for Natalie Ratcliff's third and fourth books, believing Peg Perugo had run her course and that the follow-ups would go the way of many overpriced genre books—big price tag and little return. In retrospect, $2 million turned out to be a bargain for what the books returned. Fifteen books later, Peg Perugo was an unstoppable force with a massive following who loved her flawed personality, her padded midsection, and her ability to outsmart—by accident or otherwise—the baddest of the bad guys.

Kenny stood on the front porch and rang the bell. Diane stood next to him. Today, they were a united front, having dropped everything in New York to come down to North Carolina and re-sign the publishing house's most important author. The door opened and Natalie Ratcliff smiled.

"What the *hell* is going on?" Natalie said. "Diane didn't tell me you were coming with her, Kenny."

Kenny Arnett shook Natalie's hand. "Did you think I'd leave this negotiation up to anyone else?"

Natalie shook her head, eyeing Diane through squinted lids before giving her editor a giant hug. "Playing hardball?" she whispered into Diane's ear.

"No," Diane whispered back. "Just bringing the man who signs the checks. And it's going to be a very big one."

"Come on in," Natalie said, releasing her grip.

Kenny and Diane followed Natalie through the sprawling home, decorated to perfection as if Joanna Gaines herself had worked her magic. In the kitchen, a football-field-sized island covered by a slab of treated concrete stood in the middle. Natalie opened a tall wine refrigerator. "I have a Tamber Bey rosé that will be perfect for a hot summer day."

"I hope it's perfect for a celebration, as well," Kenny said.

"You two are really laying it on thick," Natalie said.

"We want you to know how much you mean to us," Diane said.

"Let's sit on the patio."

Natalie placed three wineglasses and the bottle of rosé onto a tray and they all made their way to the back patio, which offered a magnificent view of Lake Norman and the rolling mountain landscape in the distance.

"Wow," Kenny said as soon as he stepped foot outside.

Diane shook her head as she took in the scenery. "Every time I visit you, this view gets more stunning."

"Thank you. We love it, and it never gets old for us, either." Natalie poured the wine. "Don just had some of the trees trimmed back."

"How is Don?" Kenny asked.

Natalie and Don Ratcliff were the definition of a power couple, dominating both the publishing and business worlds. Don was the heir apparent to Ratcliff International Cruise Lines—RICL, pronounced "Rickle" throughout the industry. Most cruise boat enthusiasts had taken a RICL cruise at some point, many were fanatics who cruised with no other company. The Ratcliffs were worth billions. Natalie had married into wealth, and then found her own fortune through publishing novels.

"Good," Natalie said. "He's actually commandeering this house for the Fourth of July weekend and bringing in his top salespeople as a perk or SPIF, or whatever you call it."

"You sound thrilled," Diane said.

"I don't really care. As long as they clean the beer cans off the patio and no one vomits in the fountain. But I have to write, as you know. My deadline is approaching, so I'm heading back to the city, where it will be empty and quiet, to get some work done. That's why I was surprised you made the trip down. I'll be back in Manhattan Friday."

"And miss this view?" Kenny said. "Plus, we didn't want to wait until Friday. We want you to know that you're our biggest priority. You're family to us, Natalie, and we're going to make sure you don't go anywhere."

"Diane gave me my start. Do you really think I'd go anywhere else?"

"We're taking nothing for granted," Kenny said.

"Hemingway is prepared to make an offer for the next five Peg Perugo novels," Diane said. "We've sent a formal offer to your literary agent, but wanted to make sure the offer was in the ballpark of your expectations."

"It exceeds them," Natalie said, nodding her head. "My agent called this morning to discuss the details. I have a meeting planned with her next week."

"If another house comes over the top of us," Kenny said, "we just ask that you give us an opportunity to rework the deal. It obviously has to make sense for Hemingway, but we'll move heaven and earth to keep you."

"I'm really flattered you both made the trip down here," Natalie said. "And I'm more than blown away by the offer and the effort. But I'm going to let you both in on a little secret. I told my agent not to entertain proposals from any other publishers. I'm one hundred percent satisfied at Hemingway, and Diane is a rock star. I'm not going anywhere."

Kenny nodded his head slowly and pouted his bottom lip. "Well, that was easier than I imagined."

"Now that that crap's out of the way," Diane said, "when do I get to see your manuscript?"

Natalie smiled. "When I'm finished with it. I have until October."

"Maybe I should take a peek at the first hundred pages."

"Not a chance," Natalie said. "I'm wrapping up the first draft soon, and then heading to Santorini in September to polish it."

For every novel Natalie Ratcliff had published since *Baggage* took the world by storm, she had gone to Santorini—a quaint and tranquil Greek island where the Ratcliffs owned a hillside villa—to write the final chapters of the story and polish the manuscript before handing it over to Diane.

"It was worth a try," Diane said. "I can't wait to read it. Honestly, Natalie, I'm thrilled that you and Peg Perugo will be with us for many years."

"Me too."

"I also have a favor to ask," Kenny said, as Natalie refilled everyone's wineglass.

"Oh yeah?" Natalie asked.

"I got a call from the LA office. Avery Mason, the host of *American Events*, wants to set up a meeting with you about a story she's working on."

"Avery Mason?" Natalie said with wide eyes. "About what?"

"An old friend and an old case. That's about all I know. Her people reached out to my people, so I don't have the specifics other than the request to talk," Kenny said. "I said I'd ask."

Natalie Ratcliff was not an easy person to reach. Hemingway Publishing was a subsidiary of HAP Media, and strings had been pulled and back channels navigated to make the request. The bid to arrange a meeting with Natalie Ratcliff had finally reached Kenny Arnett.

Natalie nodded. "Sure. Do you have contact information for me?"

"In the car," Kenny said. "I'll give it to you when we leave. In the meantime"—he raised his wineglass—"to five more blockbusters."

Diane raised her glass as well. Natalie smiled and clinked glasses with each of them.

"Did you really think I'd let anyone else publish my books?"

CHAPTER 28

Manhattan, NY
Thursday, July 1, 2021

Ever since leaving Emma's house Avery had been haunted by Victoria Ford's voice. Each night as she settled in her hotel room, Avery considered listening to the answering machine recordings again. So far, she hadn't gotten up the nerve. They were too haunting. A junior high student when the September 11 attacks occurred, Avery knew that each generation dealt with the tragedy in their own way. She had been enrolled in private school in Manhattan, which closed its doors for the week after the attack. When she and her classmates returned, rumors circulated through the hallways about more attacks on the city and that schools would be the next target. Avery still remembered the fear and apprehension she had felt, waiting for an airplane to take down the walls of her school. The morning of 9/11 and her experiences in the days that followed had always been viewed through the prism of a teenager. Until now. She was about to approach the topic, not as a wide-eyed adolescent, but as a journalist. It had her both buzzing with excitement and filled with anxiety.

Listening to Victoria Ford's message to her sister had been personal and emotional, but it hadn't been the first time Avery heard such recordings. Mack Carter had done an *American Events* special for the ten-year anniversary of 9/11. In it, Mack interviewed survivors who had escaped the towers and documented the life and death decisions they made that morning. Many of them, like Victoria, had called home as they tried to navigate their way out of the towers. Avery was about to speak with one of them.

Emma Kind had created a list for Avery of everyone in Victoria's life at the time of her death. It included friends and family, bosses and coworkers, and Roman Manchester—Victoria's defense attorney and the man she had gone to see on the morning of September 11, 2001. Someone who, unlike Victoria, had made it safely out of the crumbling building.

Roman Manchester was seventy-one years old and still a practicing defense attorney today. The list of clients he had represented over the years was long and distinguished, if not infamous. A few notables included his consultation on the O.J. Simpson trial in the nineties, his involvement with John Ramsey, father of JonBenét, and his brief representation of Scott Peterson. Manchester had agreed to meet with Avery when she called, and now she pushed through the entrance of the building in the financial district and rode the elevator to the eleventh floor. She pulled open the glass door on which was stenciled MANCHESTER & PARTNERS, gave her name to the receptionist, and was ushered into the attorney's office.

"Roman Manchester," the man said with a smile as he approached Avery and extended his hand.

"Avery Mason. Thanks for taking the meeting."

"Of course. Have a seat." He pointed to the chair in front of his desk. The attorney took his own seat behind the desk. "No *American Events* cameras?" he asked with a laugh.

In the last twenty-four hours, Avery had watched dozens of videos of Roman Manchester in front of news cameras.

Some were formal news conferences during which the man proudly stood behind a podium and opined about his client's innocence. Others were of Roman Manchester on the courthouse stairs, wheeling boxes of research and courtroom notes behind him, and taking a moment out of his oh-so-busy day to answer reporters' questions about his client. The man, it seemed, never missed an opportunity to be in front of the camera. Avery had watched footage from the nineties, when his hair was black and his face was wrinkle free. She'd also watched footage from his most recent trial earlier this year, when he stood behind the podium with silver hair and droopy jowls. Through the transformation of age, the man's skin carried a perpetual tan and his eyes always looked sharp. The years had mixed gravel into his voice, but it still boomed in the latest video, certain of his client's innocence.

Avery smiled. "No cameras. Just me. I'm trying to get my arms around this story before we start shooting footage. But if the network goes ahead with the special, I'll be back for a formal interview. The cameras will be with me then. If you're willing, of course."

"Absolutely. I'll admit I was intrigued when you called. Victoria Ford was a long time ago, but still so vivid in my memory."

"I'm sure she is, and that's what I was hoping to speak with you about. Victoria's remains were recently identified by the medical examiner's office here in New York, and that started me onto her story. The rest of her history came as a surprise."

"I hadn't heard about the identification until you called. It certainly brought back a flood of emotions."

Avery nodded, and could only imagine what those recollections entailed. Roman Manchester had been in the World Trade Center when the first plane flew into it. He must have terrifying memories of that day.

"Can you tell me about your relationship with Victoria?"

"She initially contacted me to represent her in the Cameron Young murder investigation. We hadn't gotten too far into her defense before she died. I knew the case better than I knew the client."

"Can you tell me about it?"

"I'm seventy-one now, and still active on high-profile cases. Although today I'm extremely selective. Back then I was everywhere and in high demand. Victoria Ford reached out to me in the summer of 2001. I reviewed the case, and as soon as I understood the gravity of the charges against her, I agreed to help. I had back then, and still do today, a personality flaw. The more challenging a case, the more likely I am to take it on."

"And Victoria Ford's case was challenging?"

"Extremely. It became quite a fiasco because of the victim's notoriety. I was working through the details when . . . well, 9/11 happened right in the middle of it all, as you know. But prior to that point, I was collecting my initial documents on the case. Discovery hadn't yet come to me from the district attorney's office, so at the time of 9/11 I was advising Mrs. Ford on her options more than I was preparing an actual defense. It was just too early."

"What was your advice?"

"To find a lot of money so she'd stay out of jail while we prepared a defense. Maggie Greenwald, the district attorney who was running the prosecution, had compiled a substantial case against Victoria and had convened a grand jury to determine if the case had merit. It did. The grand jury was just a formality. I was working with Victoria to figure out if she had the funds to post bail."

"The case was that strong?" Avery asked.

"For that stage in the process, yes. It was strong enough to

secure an indictment and justify formal charges and an arrest. I hadn't gotten into the weeds or rooted through the details to determine if any of the evidence was challengeable. I
only knew what they had, not how they had obtained it or
how credible it was. On the surface, though, it was solid."

"Can you go over some of that information?"

Manchester opened a folder and thumbed through a few
pages before he found what he was looking for.

"The crime scene was the DA's biggest weapon. It contained
Victoria's blood, fingerprints, and urine. DNA analysis confirmed the match and placed her at the scene of the crime. Evidence collected from the Catskills mansion included a home
video of Victoria and the victim, which showed them to be involved intimately. A length of rope recovered from Victoria's
vehicle matched the rope used to hang the victim. All together,
it all made for a very strong initial case.

"Now, I never got into the specifics about how this evidence was recovered, and I never had the chance to scrutinize
the forensic science behind any of it. At the time of September eleventh, I was simply gathering facts about my client
and the case against her. But what I told Victoria at the time
was that the DA's case was substantial, and she should prepare for an arrest. I planned to mount a formidable defense
but knew it would be easier if my client was not in jail while
I did so."

"How much money did she need?"

"All told, she was likely looking at a million dollars initially to post bond and another hundred thousand to pay my
retainer."

Avery took some notes on the pad that rested on her lap.

"Did she have it?"

"The money? She was going to look for it from friends
and family. She didn't have it by herself."

Avery made more notes.

"So the physical evidence, on the surface, was damning. How about circumstantial evidence? What motive did the prosecution offer for why Victoria would have killed her lover?"

"That was strong, as well," Manchester said. "The investigation revealed that Tessa Young was pregnant. *Just* pregnant, about a month or two at the time her husband was killed. Subpoenaed medical records also revealed that a few months earlier Victoria Ford had undergone an abortion."

Avery looked up from her notes. "It was Cameron Young's child?"

"Yes. I spoke with Victoria about it, and she confirmed it."

"So the theory was that she killed Cameron Young because he wouldn't have a child with her, but got his wife pregnant?"

"Partly, yes. Jealousy was a large part of the prosecution's circumstantial case. Cameron Young promised his lover that he'd leave his wife, but never did. And then got his wife pregnant. But there's more to the argument. The subpoenaed medical records also showed that Victoria had experienced a complication during the abortion that left her unable to bear children in the future."

"Christ," Avery said. "That would be a compelling argument to any jury."

"Like I said, the circumstantial evidence was solid."

"The case sounds so overwhelming. Why did you take it on?"

"Like I said, I have an affliction. The more challenging a case, the more tempted I am by it. But there's something else you need to know about the Cameron Young investigation and the district attorney who was behind it."

"Maggie Greenwald?"

"Yes. She was disbarred many years ago."

"Why?"

"Maggie Greenwald had a bloodlust, of sorts, for quickly resolving homicides and adding them as notches on her belt. I'm afraid it's a common syndrome among prosecutors. They're like sharks who can't help themselves after they smell blood in the water. A few years after the Cameron Young case went up in smoke, some folks in her office started complaining that she was cutting corners in order to quickly close cases."

"What sort of corners?"

"Let's just say that Maggie Greenwald was making square evidence fit into round holes. After she left the DA's office and started her campaign for governor, a whistleblower came forward about one particular case and an investigation was launched. It was discovered that she suppressed evidence that might have exonerated the defendant. Nothing happens quickly in the court system, but when new DNA evidence turned up, it proved the defendant was innocent. The conviction was overturned. In the months that followed, two more of her cases were overturned."

"By new DNA evidence?"

"Not new, but suppressed."

"She hid the evidence?"

"Tried to. But the whistleblower knew a lot about Maggie Greenwald's tactics. Rumors were that it was her ADA who came forward, and likely only to save his own ass by promising the truth in exchange for immunity. There's a saying around these parts that if you want all your secrets uncovered, run for public office. Anyway, I thought it was worth mentioning that Maggie Greenwald's career went down the drain. I had heard all these rumors that Maggie cut corners and had a tendency to manipulate evidence. So when you ask why I would take Victoria Ford's case when it looked so unwinnable, it was because Maggie Greenwald was the DA and I couldn't wait to get my hands on the evidence and see it for myself. The case against Victoria Ford was very strong on the surface, but I never got the chance to scrutinize or challenge any of the evidence. Had I, things might have been different."

Avery made notes about Maggie Greenwald, and then paused before she asked her next question. "Can you tell me about the morning of September eleventh? What transpired with Victoria that day? I learned from her sister that Victoria placed a series of phone calls that morning after the North Tower was struck. Can you give me any insight into what happened with you and Victoria that day?"

Manchester nodded. Avery could see his mind spanning the decades, reaching across the years for details he may have tried to forget.

"Victoria arrived that morning at about eight-thirty. I don't have any notes about the meeting for obvious reasons. But I've retold my recollection of events many times over the years for other documentaries that told the story of survivors who made it out of the towers before they collapsed. So I know that I had a meeting with a client that morning at eight-thirty. The client was Victoria Ford. We reviewed the case against her and discussed the implications of the grand jury that was convening that week. We talked about how she might secure the money she was going to need. We'd been talking for about twenty minutes when the first plane hit."

"Where was your office located?"

"On the eightieth floor of the North Tower. Victoria was sitting in front of my desk when an enormous explosion happened. The best way I can describe it is a concussion. The building rocked and thundered. It actually *leaned* to the side and for a moment I thought the tower was going to topple over. Everything broke and shattered. Pictures fell from the walls, items on my desk rattled to the floor, ceiling tiles came down, and the overhead sprinklers turned on. The fluorescent lights went dark and the emergency lighting came on. I remember the sudden darkness outside. It went from a bright sunny morning to midnight. And, of course, the smell. I wasn't able to identify the smell, which was everywhere, and didn't put things together until that night after I had made it safely home. It was then, while I watched and rewatched the footage on the news, that I realized the odor I smelled had been jet fuel."

Avery waited, not wanting to push too hard.

"It's funny how the memories come back to you," Manchester finally continued. "I remember going over to a window and looking out once the dark smoke had dissipated. I remember papers floating through the air like confetti. I remember looking down to the street and seeing the regular crowd of lower Manhattan but noticing something strange. Only later did I figure out what it was. The crowd and the cars and the buses and the taxis, they weren't moving. Everything outside the building had stopped, as if God himself had pointed a remote control at New York City and pressed *pause*. Then I remember seeing this clear sludge slowly running down the window. It looked like gel, thick and soupy. Again, in that moment I had no idea what I was seeing. It was only later that night that I realized it was the jet fuel that was coating the outside of the building."

Avery remained silent. A chill ran through her at the thought of what this man had gone through.

"Anyway," he continued, "after the initial explosion I made sure all my employees and partners were okay, and then we began to evacuate. It was early for us. Some of my partners didn't come in until after nine, so there weren't many of us at the office. We all knew that in case of fire, the elevators were off limits, so we headed to the stairwell and started down."

Avery pinched her eyebrows together. "You started *down*?"

"Yes. Eighty flights of stairs was a daunting task, and we

didn't know which part of the building was on fire, so we prayed we could make it through the floors below us."

"You started down?" Avery asked again, almost to herself this time. "Was Victoria with you?"

Manchester shook his head. "You know, I'm ashamed to admit that I checked on my people—my employees and partners—and we all sort of took a quick head count before we entered the stairwell." He shook his head and momentarily closed his eyes. "I don't remember seeing Victoria Ford after the chaos began. I . . . forgot about her."

There was a sorrow in his voice that was nearly palpable. A survivor's guilt, Avery assumed, that came from cheating death during an event that took so many lives.

"I listened to a recording of an answering machine message Victoria left her sister. In it, she said that she was with a group of people who decided to go *up* the stairwell, not down. Up to the roof where they believed they might be rescued. Do you remember that?"

Manchester nodded his head. "Yes. There were probably a hundred people on my floor and we were all in the hallway and stairwell at the same time. No one person was in charge and things were hectic. There was a lot of confusion and misinformation being shouted, as you might imagine. It's hard for me now, twenty years later, to differentiate what I knew in those moments from what I've learned since. It all sort of mixes together to form its own reality. But for sure, in that moment, none of us knew that a plane had struck the building. We thought it was just some sort of explosion. The idea that a plane had struck the building started being thrown around only after people began calling home. In that chaos, no one knew what to believe or who to listen to as far as a strategy to get out of the building. As soon as the crowd started an orderly descent of the stairs, it was like a vacuum and nearly everyone followed. We made it down twenty flights or so before we ran into congestion. For a long time we barely moved. Just one step every minute or so. Then we heard the second explosion, which I later learned was the second plane hitting the South Tower. When that happened, people started panicking. There was talk about the stairwell being blocked below us, and some people peeled off. Some went back up, some headed to the other set of stairs on the other side of the building."

"What did you do?"

"I stayed put. I didn't stray from that first stairwell. Eventually, the bottleneck ended and we started moving again."

"How long did it take you to get out?"

Manchester shook his head. "I'm not sure. I don't remember looking at my watch that morning, but I'd guess forty minutes to an hour. It was before ten o'clock, I know that. And it's documented that the first plane struck at eight forty-six. When I made it outside, I took in the apocalyptic scene and then started my hike uptown. The subway was not working, so I walked. I'd made it to Washington Square Park when the South Tower came down."

"So after the initial impact, you never saw Victoria Ford again?"

"I saw faces. I had conversations with people but can't remember what was discussed or who they were. After I checked on my coworkers, I hardly remember being with any of them. Victoria could have been one or two heads in front of me but I don't remember. I only remember people shuffling down the stairs."

"When did you find out about Victoria?"

"Not for a while. My law practice was gone—every client, every file, every computer. I don't remember hearing that Victoria Ford had died for weeks. It took that long to salvage the practice, and Victoria was a new client. I hadn't started the process of defending her. She hadn't paid me a retainer. I had more urgent clients to attend to, and court dates to prepare for, once the dust of 9/11 settled. It was some time before I heard that Victoria had died."

Avery nodded. "Well, I don't want to take up too much of your time. Thanks so much for recounting what I'm sure are difficult memories."

"Of course."

"Would you mind if I called you another time, perhaps later this summer, if I get this story off the ground and start formal interviews? By then I will have had the chance to look at all the evidence against Victoria and I would love your opinion on it, and what sort of defense you might have constructed had you been given the opportunity."

"It would be my pleasure."

A few moments later, Avery was outside. She looked in the direction of where the Twin Towers had once stood. She couldn't kick the thought that kept popping into her mind. Roman Manchester and everyone else in his office had gone to the stairwell and started down. Victoria Ford had gone up. Had she simply followed the crowd, would things have been different?

CHAPTER 29

Manhattan, NY
Friday, July 2, 2021

Included in the list of contacts Emma put together was Victoria's best friend, Natalie Ratcliff. Avery hadn't noticed the name until she was back in her hotel room, and had to do a double take. Natalie Ratcliff was one of the best-selling authors in the country. Her books were in every bookstore, pharmacy, and mall kiosk. With over a hundred million copies of her novels sold worldwide, reaching her was not as simple as making a phone call. Avery's research revealed that Natalie Ratcliff's publisher was a subsidiary of HAP Media, so she worked her contacts until a connection was made and a meeting arranged.

Natalie Ratcliff lived in a Manhattan high rise that overlooked Central Park, in the same block of buildings that made up the boisterous penthouses on Billionaire's Row where Avery grew up. Once an emergency room physician working twelve-hour shifts, Natalie Ratcliff was today far removed from her nights in a hospital. She wrote novels now—chicklit mystery that was panned by critics but devoured by her adoring fans. The woman had produced fifteen novels in fifteen years, every one a best seller. Victoria Ford's best friend and college roommate, Natalie Ratcliff was high on the list of folks Avery was interested in talking with.

After her visit to Roman Manchester's office the day before, Avery had stopped at the Strand Bookstore to pick out a couple Natalie Ratcliff novels. She found two shelves of the woman's books and went back to her hotel with a bagful of paperbacks. Despite that she was chasing a story and had plenty of work to do, Avery got sucked into one of Natalie's novels. The protagonist—a portly private eye named Peg Perugo—investigated the shady dealings of a good-looking ER doctor, discovering in the process that good sex trumped Medicare fraud. The story was silly and sophomoric, and kept Avery up until 2:00 a.m. before she forced herself to close the book and get some sleep.

In the morning Avery did some quick Internet snooping and learned that Natalie Ratcliff split her time between New York and North Carolina. She treated herself to a lavish month-long vacation to the Greek isles each year to finish her new book. She was married to an executive at a cruise line, and had three children—two were grown and on their own, one was still in college. She had practiced medicine for eight years before she quit to write novels. She lived on the twenty-second floor of One 57, and her apartment door opened as soon as Avery exited the elevator.

Avery saw the woman laugh and shake her head. "Avery Mason is in my elevator. Is this really happening?"

"I should be asking the same question. *The* Natalie Ratcliff, taking a meeting with me."

"Like I'd ever turn it down," Natalie said. "I'm a huge fan. Please, come in."

The apartment was large, beautiful, professionally decorated, and offered a clear view of Central Park. It was a view

Avery remembered from her childhood. Off the living room was a giant mahogany-studded office outlined by yawning French doors. Avery saw framed covers of Natalie's novels hanging on the walls, and floor-to-ceiling bookshelves lined with her titles. Avery spotted *Baggage*, the slightly trashy and mindless novel that had kept her up most of the night.

"I have to admit," Avery said, "I hadn't read any of your novels when I talked with you, but I picked a few of your books up yesterday and got hopelessly sucked into one of them last night. Couldn't put it down. So you can count me as a new fan."

Natalie put her hand over her heart. "Now, that's about the biggest compliment I've ever received. Avery Mason, a fan of my books. Thank you."

Avery pointed to Natalie's office. "*Baggage*. Honestly, I couldn't stop reading it. Kept me up way too late."

Natalie smiled. "That's one of my favorites. It's my first, so I guess it has to be my favorite since it started everything. Thanks for the compliment. Really, it's a thrill to hear that you're reading one of my books. I'm a huge fan of *yours*, and just love *American Events*. The minivan episode? I thought I'd have a heart attack watching you sink to the bottom of that pool."

"You and me both."

They laughed like old friends.

"Can I get you something to drink?"

"No thank you. I don't want to take too much of your time, I know you're busy. I wanted to talk with you about Victoria Ford. I'm sure it's shocking when the past comes back to us so viscerally."

Natalie nodded and pointed at the dining table. Avery sat down.

"It was quite a shock to hear the news," Natalie said, sitting across from her. "But I was happy for Emma. A little closure will do her good."

"Emma is a rock. I had the pleasure of meeting her the other day. Do you know her well?"

"I've known Emma for years. We still keep in touch. Victoria was such an important part of each of our lives, her absence has sort of been a magnet that draws us together. We see each other once a year to catch up."

"If I'm able to get this project about Victoria up and running, I'll need to interview as many friends and family as I can find. I want to tell Victoria's story—who she was and what she was about—before I get into her death and the events that immediately preceded it. I'm hoping you could fill in some details for me."

"It would be my honor. Victoria was a dear friend."

"Let's start there. How close were you with Victoria?"

"We were best friends."

"Meaning?"

"Meaning if she called and said she was in trouble, I'd show up with body bags and an alibi."

Avery laughed.

"Sorry," Natalie said. "That's the fiction writer coming out in me."

"No, we all need friends like that."

"Victoria and I were close. She was like a sister to me."

"How did you meet? Give me some details."

Natalie nodded, deciding, Avery suspected, where to begin.

"Victoria and I went to college together. She was a finance major, I was a biology major. We were roommates freshman year and just clicked. We stuck together for all four years. After college I went to medical school here in New York. Victoria entered the financial world. We stayed close during all those years, and never really drifted too far apart even as we both became busy with life. I was getting through medical school and residency, and she was starting her career. I got married and had kids. Vic got married and talked about having kids. My husband and I used to see her and Jasper for dinners and that sort of thing. Not as often as we wanted, but that's the way life works."

"Just a curious fan girl question. You went to medical school but now you write books. How did that happen?"

Natalie smiled. "I'm not really sure. I've always loved to read, since I was a young girl. Writing was something I dreamed of doing someday but never figured I'd actually get around to. But finally, I sat down one day and did it. The fact that the first manuscript actually sold is still mesmerizing to me. That I had it in me to write another still shocks me just the same."

"And another and another," Avery said. "You are quite prolific."

"I've had a good run and have been terribly lucky."

"I'm assuming your love of reading and writing also brought you and Victoria together? Emma tells me that she, too, was interested in writing."

"She was. Much more than I ever was, in fact. We both talked about it in school. You know, writing a book someday. Danielle Steel style. But the realities of life got in the way and we both put those dreams on hold as we started our careers."

"And look at you now. A legitimate powerhouse in publishing," Avery said. "Life has a way of coming full circle, doesn't it?"

"I suppose it does."

Avery pulled out a yellow legal pad and scribbled some notes. "Were you in touch with Victoria after Cameron Young's death?"

"Not much. That was obviously a tough time in Victoria's life. I reached out to her, but she didn't return my calls. I knew she was busy mounting a defense and, you know, everything that goes into that."

"Did you speak with her at all about it?"

"Briefly. She had called once to ask if she could borrow money in case she needed it. The cost of her defense was going to be astronomical."

"But that was it? Nothing about the case or . . . her involvement with Cameron Young? Or . . . if any of the accusations against her were true?"

"No. I never asked and she never offered. I had known for some time that her marriage was rocky, and there was a mention about meeting someone else. I never got into the details with her. When the news broke and the media aimed their sights on her, I told her I would always be her friend and that I knew she would never do what she was accused of. I knew it in my heart. I still know it today."

"How about leading up to 9/11? Did you talk with her then?"

Natalie shook her head. "Not for the couple of weeks before. Then, it was a crazy time for me. I was an ER doctor in the city and on 9/11, and for most of that week, it was all hands on deck. It's still just a big blur to me. I didn't find out about Victoria for a couple of days. I was working around the clock and when I finally had a chance to catch my breath, I took inventory of everyone I knew in the city. When I couldn't get in touch with Victoria, I finally reached out to Emma and she told me the news."

"How did you hear about Victoria's remains being identified?"

"In the paper. I called Emma right away, and she filled me in on the details."

Avery checked her notes—a page of scribbled bullet points.

"Would it be too much to ask you to write a chronology of your relationship with Victoria? From meeting in college and beyond?"

"I could do that, sure."

"Great. I'll be in New York for at least another week, but maybe longer depending on what I need. Can I get in touch with you in a few days?"

"Of course. I'll give you my cell. And I'll start working on my history with Victoria right away. It'll be a good exercise for me to remember all the great times we had together."

Avery stood up. "Thanks so much, Natalie. I want to do this correctly. I know there will be some difficult parts to Victoria's story, but I want to show America who this woman was before she was accused of murder. The information you provide will go a long way to making that happen."

They said their good-byes and Avery stepped into the elevator.

"Let me know how you like the rest of *Baggage*," Natalie said before the doors closed.

"I'll be up all night finishing it."

The doors shut and the elevator dropped Avery in the lobby. Her cell phone buzzed as she exited the building. It was Walt Jenkins calling. He wanted to meet tonight for dinner. They agreed on the time and place before Avery dropped her phone into her purse. Her goal was to rip the case against Victoria Ford to shreds. She had the lead detective's ear and the weekend to do it. As she walked through New York City, she realized that she had started so many leads on the Victoria Ford story that she almost forgot the *actual* reason she was back in the city that held so many terrible memories.

It was nice to forget. For just a moment, she was free.

CHAPTER 30

Manhattan, NY
Friday, July 2, 2021

Dinner was at Keens. In traditional Manhattan fashion the city had emptied earlier in the afternoon as residents flocked off the island for the long Fourth of July weekend in the country or at the beach. Consequently, the popular steakhouse was eerily empty when Walt walked in. He spotted Avery at a table tucked into the corner.

"Sorry I'm late," Walt said as he sat down across from her.

"I was just about to call you to ask if I'd mixed up the time," Avery said.

Walt shook his head. "No, my fault. I managed to get my hands on the Cameron Young file and got tied up reading through the case. Lost track of time."

Avery had a glass of white wine in front of her. Walt ordered a rum from the waiter as he scanned the menu.

"Have you eaten here before?" he asked.

"Of course. I might be a SoCal girl today, but I grew up in New York," Avery said.

"Where?" Walt asked, forgetting for a moment that he

was late for dinner because he had lost track of time reading the inch-thick dossier he'd been given on Avery Mason, aka Claire Montgomery. He wondered how she kept her two lives straight—the one she was leading as one of the most popular journalists on television, and her past life as the daughter of the Thief of Manhattan.

"Oh," Avery said. "Uptown. Upper East Side."

She'd been raised in a penthouse on Billionaire's Row, Walt knew. He'd seen the pictures of the building and stock photos of the penthouse that were splashed all over the Internet and linked to Garth Montgomery. He'd also seen the photos of her father being hauled out of the famous building in pajamas and handcuffs. The waiter delivered Walt's rum and asked for their dinner orders, providing an easy segue off the topic of Avery's past. They both ordered steaks—filets, medium, with horseradish crust.

"So, what did you find?" Avery asked. "When you looked back through the Cameron Young file."

"I was able to get the case file and I've spent the last couple of days reviewing it. It's been quite a stroll down memory lane. I have to tell you, as I go back through the case and remember it more clearly, the evidence was overwhelming. Just being straight with you."

"That's all I'm asking for, Walt. I came to New York to learn more about the story of the medical examiner's office discovering the remains of a 9/11 victim at the monumental moment of the twentieth anniversary. But I found something else entirely when I spoke with Victoria Ford's sister. Emma Kind, as we discussed the other night, believes her sister is innocent. But it's more than unconditional love and a sisterly bond that hardens her resolve. Victoria Ford called her sister on the morning of 9/11 and left a series of messages on her answering machine. Emma played them for me. The messages are harrowing, and were placed soon after the first plane struck the North Tower and trapped Victoria inside."

Walt shook his head. "I can only imagine. Each year I relive some part of that day. Everyone does. But to have a loved one so closely tied to the tragedy, and to have a recording from that morning . . ."

"It's more than that, though. On the recording Victoria tells her sister that she's innocent and asks her to find a way to clear her name. Victoria swore that the evidence against her was tainted and couldn't be accurate. She understood she would die that day, and her last words—at least the last ones recorded—were of Victoria Ford begging her sister to make her legacy something other than an accused murderess."

"Her sister has all this on a recording?"

"Yes. Two messages. They're heartbreaking. They're also convincing as hell. So despite the evidence so clearly pointing to Victoria Ford's guilt, she died clinging to her innocence. I at least owe it to Emma to review the case against her sister."

Walt's mind reached back across twenty years to when he was a young, inexperienced detective handpicked to run a high-profile homicide investigation. Things had bothered him back then about that promotion, and he was realizing that they still bothered him today.

"I'm not out to prove Victoria's innocence to the world," Avery said. "This many years later, I'm not sure that would be possible even if it *were* true. I have no plans to paint you or the BCI in a poor light. You conducted your investigation and everything you found pointed to Victoria Ford. Those are the facts. I'm simply asking to review all the evidence and hear about the investigation from start to finish. It will play a crucial role in the exposé I'm planning."

"We can do that," Walt said. "What do you have in mind?"

"My goal is to tell America the story of Victoria Ford. Her life, her flaws, and the tragic day she died along with three thousand other souls. And now, twenty years later, her remains have finally been identified. That she was involved in a sensational murder investigation is simply part of her life's story. That she claimed, until the final moments of her life, to be innocent, is also one of the facts of the case. The recordings are there for everyone to hear, and they form an arc in this story—from the beginning to the very sad and tragic ending—that I want to share with my audience. You and your investigation are part of the story, so even if what you tell me contradicts what Emma Kind believes, I'm okay with that. Yours is a crucial part of the story and I need to hear and understand it all."

"I can see why your show is so popular," Walt said. "You take that approach with all your stories?"

"I do."

"Okay. Let me walk through the case for you, start to finish."

Throughout dinner, Walt covered his role in the Cameron Young investigation—from the moment he stepped foot onto the property of the Catskills mansion, to each bombshell he discovered during his investigation. He discussed the crime scene and finding Cameron Young hanging from the balcony. He covered the blood and urine recovered from the scene, and the fingerprints lifted from the wineglass—all of which matched Victoria Ford. He explained how a thumb drive found in the desk drawer of the office contained a homemade sex video that led him to Victoria Ford. He reviewed the autopsy findings that painted a vivid image of Cameron Young's final moments. He discussed the grand jury that had been convened, the prosecution's argument that Victoria Ford was a jilted lover who'd been coerced into having an abortion that left her unable to bear children, and the imminent indictment that was to come before the morning of September 11 brought a crashing end to the case.

He watched Avery while he spoke, as her fingers jotted notes onto page after page of a yellow legal pad. There was something elegant yet powerful about the way she scrawled her notes, and Walt found himself attracted to her in a way he hadn't allowed himself to be for some time. The situation he found himself in tonight—dining with an intelligent, talented, and attractive woman—made him wonder if he had wasted the last three years on heartache when they might have been better conquered by facing life head-on and allowing the natural progression of time to wash his pain away.

The dinner plates were cleared. They turned down dessert, but each ordered a glass of port as they continued their discussion. Avery paged through her notes and asked follow-up questions until Walt sensed that she was satisfied with the information he had provided.

"I guess that's everything I can think to ask for now," she said. "What are the chances I'd be able to look at the case file myself? Eventually, I'd love to get some of my production team to capture images of the case for *American Events*—photos of interview transcripts, footage from video interviews, images of the crime scene, and even—parts redacted, of course—some footage from the homemade video that helped you break the case."

"I have it all back at my hotel. I'd have to run it past the brass and get them to sign off on anything we share, but I'm sure it could be arranged. Let me make a few calls?"

"I'd appreciate it."

There was a short pause to their conversation, as they both searched for a reason to continue talking now that the purpose of their dinner meeting had ended. They both stared at each other until Avery finally spoke.

"So, Walt, I pride myself on my instincts."

"Uh oh."

Avery smiled. "I'm curious about something you're not telling me."

Walt raised his eyebrows. For a fleeting moment he considered that he'd somehow been blown before he'd done any *ac-*

tual surveillance. That this smart, observant journalist had figured out his and Jim Oliver's and the entire FBI's plan to burrow himself into her life in an attempt to locate her father.

"What am I not telling you?" he asked.

"What really brought you back to New York."

He swirled his port as he mulled the question.

"Come on," Avery said. "You're a good-looking, successful guy who got injured on the job in his forties and then decided to live as a recluse on a tropical island? And suddenly a television journalist calls and you come running back?" She shook her head. "Sorry, I'm not buying it."

"Who said I lived as a recluse?"

"Nice try. And I appreciate the attempt at diversion, but there's got to be more to your story."

Walt lifted his chin and took a sip of port. "Don't let anyone knock your instincts." He stared into the wine before he spoke. He remembered his plan to be as honest as possible. "I was getting bored in Jamaica. I went there to clear my head after I was injured, but I figured out that whatever cobwebs were still present after three years were not likely to be swept away by time. You called and I thought it was a good opportunity to get out of a rut. Plus, I told you. I'm a fan of the show."

He watched her slowly take a sip of port. He got the impression that his answer did not satisfy her.

"You know," she said, "maybe a better question is why you went to Jamaica in the first place."

"You *are* a journalist. Through and through."

"Another dodge. How very *male* of you. I didn't figure you as the typical man, but I've been known to misread people before."

Walt smiled, caught off guard by Avery's sudden probing into his personal life. He understood now, though, that her inquiry came from a natural curiosity and not from any sixth sense she had about his true intentions or the job the FBI had tapped him for. She was simply asking an obvious question. Perhaps he was thrown off because, for the past three years, none of his Jamaican friends—all men—gave a shit about what drove him to their tiny little island. Walt bought their rum and told his stories, and that was good enough for them. He had clearly spent too much time out of the presence of a woman.

"I've got some unfinished business here, and your call made it obvious that now was the time to take care of it."

"Ah," Avery said. "Some sentiment of a human being is in there after all. This unfinished business, anything you want to share with a near-perfect stranger?"

"Maybe," he said. "But a proper drink will be needed to get into the details."

"You need hard alcohol to talk about yourself?"

"No, the alcohol is for you so you don't judge me."

"Is it that bad?"

"I'll let you decide. And it's really not that big of a mystery," he said, standing from the table and pointing to the bar in the other room. "Love or the law. They're man's only two problems in this world."

CHAPTER 31

Manhattan, NY
Friday, July 2, 2021

They moved to the bar. It was nearly empty at 10:00 P.M. on a Friday night and the mass exodus of the July Fourth weekend was on full display. Only one other couple was present at the bar. Dark mahogany lined the walls and ceiling of Keens and cast everything in an auburn shadow. They sat on adjacent stools. Walt ordered a rum, Avery a vodka.

"Since you're part of the law," Avery said, "I'm guessing it's love. Tell me about her."

"It sounds so easy when you put it like that. Simple and direct."

"I blame my bluntness on law school. They teach you to zero in on the topic and push everything else aside."

"You went to law school?" Walt asked, forgetting for a moment that the woman in front of him had a whole other life he was supposed to know nothing about. He sensed a shift in her demeanor as her two worlds overlapped.

Slowly, she nodded. "I did, but the whole attorney thing wasn't for me. I figured that out after school, moved to LA to put my journalism major to use. But those same instincts are part of my job now. When I feel a story, or sense that there is something to be learned, I zero in on it with annoying focus. I apologize if I'm being too direct about this. You don't have to tell me any more if it's private."

"No, I don't mind. It'll probably do me some good to talk about it. That's what a shrink would probably say, anyway."

"I can't analyze, I can only listen."

"Okay. Let's see, the Cliffs Notes version goes something like this: Adultery sank my first marriage. She cheated, not me. We were both young and dumb, and not right for each other, so it was probably best that it blew up so fast. The ending of my second marriage stung a bit more. It fell apart because of children—I wanted them, she didn't. And then, there was Meghan Cobb."

There was a stretch of silence as Walt tried to figure out how to proceed.

"She's the one who sent you to the Caribbean?" Avery asked.

Walt nodded. He took another swallow of rum and allowed the liquor to burn his throat. This last bit of rum pushed him past the tipping point, like it always did, and his mind drifted to the past.

For such life-threatening injuries, Walt's hospital stay lasted only five days. Three had been spent in the ICU after surgery, and the final two in gen pop where he shuffled about with the other post-op patients proving he could walk and talk and pass gas. When the doctors were satisfied, they released him with a long list of restrictions. The discharge had come just in time. His partner's funeral was the following day, and one way or another Walt planned to attend. If he had to pull the IV lines out of his arm and leave against medical advice, he was prepared to do so. But when Walt started to push, no one fought him. He had nearly died in an ambush that claimed his partner. No one was planning to deny him the honor of attending the funeral.

Walt was out of the woods. Dr. Eleanor Marshfield, the sur- geon who had sewn him up, told Walt that the heart was a miraculous organ and as long as he didn't overdo it in the first six months of recovery, he would be fine. The doctor, of course, could speak only to the physical recovery of Walt's heart. She had no idea about the emotional damage he was about to endure.

Jim Oliver drove him home from the hospital.

"Thanks for the lift, Jim."

"You need any help?"

"Nah, I'm good. A little slow but otherwise no worse for the wear."

Walt opened the passenger-side door and slowly climbed out of the car, grunting in the process. After righting himself, he closed the door and leaned down to peer through the open window.

"I'll see you tomorrow?"

"Yeah," Jim said. "You need a ride to the funeral?"

"No, I'm cleared to drive. And, I'm not sure what kind of shape I'm going to be in. I'd prefer to have my own getaway vehicle in case I have to make a stealth exit."

"Understood. It'll be a packed house. All the guys have been asking about you."

Walt forced a smile and slapped the roof of the car a couple of times with strength he didn't have.

"Thanks again, Jim."

The following morning, Walt woke with a foggy brain jum- bled with colliding thoughts and worries. First on his mind was his partner. Walt could not call Jason Snyder a close friend. Other than social work functions a couple of times

each year, and the occasional beer when the timing was right,
Walt had never spent much time with Jason outside work.
Some partners clicked and became thick as thieves. Together
for three years, Walt Jenkins and Jason Snyder had simply
never grown close in that way. All Walt knew about Jason's
personal life was that he was married with no kids, and that
he was close with his father, who had also been an agent back
in the day. A shitty feeling of guilt plagued Walt throughout
the night, causing him to toss and gingerly turn through the
dark hours. By 4:00 a.m. he considered himself a subspecies of
the human race for never showing an interest in his partner's
life. And now that Jason was gone, Walt had the sudden de-
sire to know him better. To be a better friend and a more pro-
tective partner. Walt had always claimed to have Jason's back.
An assertion that was as empty now as it sounded.

He stood in front of the bathroom mirror. The white ban-
dage on his neck denied him the option of a necktie, and the
gauze and tape were positioned too high for the collar of his
shirt to conceal them. He carefully pulled on his suit coat and
examined himself in the mirror. His ashen complexion and
black-rimmed eyes, together with his bandaged neck, made him
look like death warmed over. And though no one would blame
him for that, Walt worried that his presence at the funeral
might take attention away from Jason and his family. He con-
cocted a plan to get in and out as quickly as possible.

He swallowed hard, his Adam's apple rising and falling in
the process and producing a sharp pain in his neck as the
damaged muscles constricted. The bags under his eyes were
evidence of a sleepless night, which was rooted in more than
just survivor's guilt. Something else bothered him. He picked
up his phone and scrolled through the text messages for the
hundredth time. Meghan had not called—no texts and no
voice mails. He had found her mailbox full when he tried to
leave a message during his first coherent day out of the ICU.

All subsequent text messages had gone unanswered. He had heard from both his ex-wives while he was in the hospital, and the irony was not lost on Walt that the two women who hated him most in the world had managed to reach out to check on him, but the one woman who claimed to love him was MIA.

He'd last seen Meghan a week ago, two nights before he was shot. They spent the weekend at a bed and breakfast in upstate New York, and a pang of worry overcame him. He'd justifiably been preoccupied for the last few days by his brush with death, but now he considered that something might have happened to Meghan. He didn't have her parents' phone number, and even if he did, calling would be a bad idea. Walt had never met Meghan's parents. The awkward conversation would likely set off unnecessary alarm. He also scrapped the idea of reaching out to Meghan's sister. It would be a bit dramatic, and even selfish, to worry Meghan's family over a few unreturned phone calls.

As he stood in front of the mirror, he scrolled through his phone and shot her one more text.

"Where are you? A lot's happened since I've seen you. Call me."

He dropped his phone into his coat pocket, looked once more in the mirror but quickly gave up trying to make himself more presentable. He clicked off the lights as he left the bathroom and headed to his partner's funeral.

CHAPTER 32

Manhattan, NY
Friday, July 2, 2021

"You doing okay?" the bartender asked.

Walt looked at his empty glass. "One more?" he asked Avery.

"Sure. I've got to hear the rest of this."

The bartender refilled their glasses. It was now approaching 11:00 p.m. and they were the only ones in the bar.

"You sure?" he asked.

"We're not leaving until I hear it."

Walt took another sip of rum. The alcohol was producing that early effect it always provided when he thought of his partner's funeral—a blunting of the pain that came with the memories. He placed the glass on the coaster in front of him and continued his story.

The parking lot was full, so Walt turned onto the side street that flanked the funeral home. He eased his car to the curb and pulled himself from the driver's seat. It took longer than he wanted to wrestle on his suit coat; his left arm was not yet

*following the commands from his brain, and he was happy to
be without an audience. When he pulled past the funeral
home he had seen a slew of colleagues out front. He didn't
need the razzing he would have taken had they seen him
struggling with his coat. And if his fellow agents had managed to avoid the friendly jeering, the other reaction would
have been worse—pity. This was better, alone on a side street
as he fought with his suit coat. He finally righted himself with
a deep breath that brought a stabbing pain to his chest—a
symptom Dr. Marshfield warned would take weeks of
pulmonary therapy to resolve.*

*Once he had himself settled, he looked at the funeral home
and considered his options. He could walk around to the
front of the building and into the den of his fellow agents,
where he was sure to spend too much time saying hello and
accepting their wishes for a speedy recovery. Or, he could
skate through the side door and sneak into the procession
line, keep his eyes down and avoid anyone he knew until he
reached Jason's family. There, he'd offer his condolences to
Jason's father and tell the man what a stellar partner his
son had been for the last three years. Hug Jason's mother
and introduce himself to Jason's wife, telling them both how
sorry he was for their loss. All the time he'd fight off his survivor's guilt, hope he didn't sweat through his suit coat, and
make a stealth exit before the bandage on his neck grew red
from the seeping wound it covered.*

*The choice was simple. He crossed the street, pulled open
the side door, and entered a quiet hallway. Soft conversations
echoed through the walkway as he slowly made his way
forward. When he reached the end of the dark hallway, he
found himself on the side of the welcoming atrium. The familiar faces of his fellow agents were to his left, surrounding the
front doors. A quick scan into the room to his right revealed
no one he recognized—only Jason's family and a line of
mourners waiting to offer their thoughts before kneeling in*

front of the coffin. Walt slipped through the atrium and into the room. He saw large bouquets of flowers surrounding the casket. The receiving line was against the far wall and he took a spot at the end, slowly shuffling his way to the front of the room. Walt kept his eyes down. His left arm was draped across his chest and supporting his right elbow, his palm over his cheek and mouth. If any of his friends recognized him, no one said a word. He crept along for ten minutes as he slowly edged closer to the casket.

"You made it," came a voice from behind him.

Walt turned to see that Jim Oliver had taken a place in line behind him.

"Yeah," was all Walt said.

"The guys outside said they were waiting to see you."

Walt nodded. "I made a stealth approach through the side door. I don't want to take any of the attention away from Jason's family."

"Understood. But maybe say hi on your way out? It would be good for the crew to see that you're back on your feet."

"Will do, boss."

Together they made their way to the front of the room. Walt swallowed hard as he came closer to the casket, seeing his partner's face in profile. He'd always hated the waxy appearance of dead people in caskets. His childhood, it seemed, was riddled with moments of kneeling in front of sturdy, mahogany caskets that held elderly relatives. He was supposed to say a prayer as he knelt in front of the caskets, his parents had told him, but all Walt had ever been able to do was stare in confusion at the thick makeup smeared across the dead person's face. This childhood quirk had carried into his adult life, and as Walt approached Jason's family he wondered if they were pleased with the way he looked, lying stiff and unmoving in the casket, or if he was as unrecognizable to them as he was to Walt.

"You know Jason's family?" Jim asked.

Walt shook his head. "No," he said just as the couple in front of him finished talking and moved on to the casket.

An older couple were the first family members in the receiving line. Walt reached out his hand and offered his best smile.

"Walt Jenkins."

"Hi, Walt," the man said, taking his hand in a warm embrace. "How did you know Jason?"

Walt swallowed hard, the tape on his neck stretching against the strain. "I was his partner."

"Oh," said the woman. "We're Jason's parents."

"It's nice to meet you," Walt said. "Jason talked about you all the time, sir. About your time in the Bureau. He spoke about both of you. I'm really sorry for your loss."

"Thank you," Jason's father said. "How are you holding up?"

"I'm fine, sir." Walt released the man's hand. "This is Jim Oliver. Jim heads up the field office here in New York."

"Your son was a great agent and a good friend to us all," Jim said.

"Thank you." Jason's father smiled. "Have you met our daughter-in-law?" he asked Walt.

"No, sir," Walt said.

"She had to use the restroom," Jason's mother said. "She'll be right back. I'm sure she'd want to say hi."

Walt smiled and gave a quick nod, beginning a thirty-second span of painful small talk that felt like it lasted an hour. All Walt wanted to do was take a quick knee in front of the casket, pretend to pray, and then get the hell out of there.

"Here she comes," Jason's mother said, pointing over Walt's shoulder.

"Sweetheart," Jason's father said, motioning with his hand. "This is Jason's partner."

Walt turned and felt his knees buckle when he saw Jason's wife.

"*Meghan,*" *Jason's father said. "This is Walt Jenkins.*"

Walt imagined the terrified look on Meghan's face was a mirror image of his own. She stopped a couple of strides away from him, unblinking and unmoving, her mouth agape. It was obvious to everyone—Jason's parents, Jim Oliver, and anyone else within eyeshot of Walt and Meghan—that they knew each other. That they had been sleeping together for the past year and were in love was less obvious, but only slightly.

"*Have you met before?*" *Jason's father asked in a credulous voice.*

"*Uh, no,*" *Walt managed in a strained voice on the brink of cracking. He held up his hand to wave, but it looked more like an act of surrender. "I'm . . ."*

He placed a hand on his bandaged neck and felt the dampness of blood seeping through the gauze.

"*. . . . . very sorry for your loss.*"

It was all he could manage before he turned and walked quickly to the back of the room, through the atrium, and into the dark hallway. He pushed open the door and squinted against the sunlight as he sucked for air. His lungs hurt and his chest heaved. He stumbled to his car and fell behind the steering wheel. Starting the engine, he pulled away even before he had the door closed.

CHAPTER 33

Manhattan, NY
Friday, July 2, 2021

"She was your partner's wife?" Avery asked, leaning close to Walt—a position she found herself in as she hung on every word of his story.

"My *dead* partner's wife, yes," Walt said, taking a needed swallow of rum. "That's why she hadn't returned my calls all week. She was busy dealing with her own tragedy—her husband's death. She had no idea I was Jason's partner or that I was the other agent who'd been shot. We were together for a year and she never told me she was married. She knew I worked in the New York field agency for the Bureau, but she never pressed me for details about my job. I always took it as sort of a separation of church and state. You know, let's not talk about work. Let's just enjoy each other's company. But she didn't want to know anything about my work because she didn't want to know if I knew her husband."

"What happened to you?" Avery asked in a hesitant voice. "What was your injury? It was the same thing that got your partner killed?"

"Jason and I were on a routine surveillance operation. We thought we were just in for another long night of taking photos and gathering intel on a suspected Al Qaeda cell. As we were watching the building across the street, a man in a ski mask approached the front of our van and opened fire. The bullets that found my body somehow managed to avoid all the important plumbing."

"How close did they come?"

"Very. One pierced my heart."

"My God, Walt. And Jason died?"

"He was gone before the ambulance arrived."

"Who was the man? In the ski mask?"

"That's the bitch of the story. He was an asterisk to the whole ordeal. The guy was a strung-out meth addict. We were watching the apartment building of a suspected Al Qaeda sympathizer, tracking his movements to see if we could link him to anyone important. The building across the street was running a meth lab. We had no idea, but the meth-heads caught wind of us and got nervous. So one of them walked outside and started shooting."

Avery's mouth hung open for a moment. "Absolutely nothing to do with the war on terror?"

"Nada."

"Did you talk to her after the funeral? Meghan?"

"Once," Walt said. "To tell her I was going away for a while. The story about the two of us broke soon after the funeral and spread like wildfire through the agency. Everyone assumed I'd been sneaking around behind Jason's back and only when I got to the funeral did I finally crack. And when every one of your colleagues believes that you were knowingly sleeping with your partner's wife, and then that partner is killed in the line of duty . . . Let's just say there was not a lot of sympathy for me."

"Did you try to explain the situation?"

"I never had a chance, and I don't know that anyone would have believed me. I was politely asked to retire. They offered me my full pension and it was a now-or-never proposal. Take my retirement and disappear. The Bureau is extremely sensitive about its reputation. An agent being killed in the line of duty was a big enough scar for them. The scandal of an affair involving the fallen agent's wife and his partner was something they wanted to avoid. They made their wishes very clear to me. I took the money and ran."

"To Jamaica?"

Walt nodded and made it halfway through his drink.

"Whatever happened with Meghan?"

"I ended things."

"Just like that?"

Walt pouted his lower lip and nodded. "Pretty much."

"That sounds vague."

"I see her once a year. I attend an annual survivors meeting here in the city."

"Survivors meeting?"

"It turns out that surviving the night Jason and I were ambushed was a bit of a miracle. Others who have survived similar ordeals and beat similar odds get together each year and celebrate their miracles and the people who saved them. The doctors and nurses and first responders all receive invitations from the survivors. I invite my trauma surgeon each year. If your story deals with others who were not as fortunate, the family members of those who died are also invited. I see Meghan at this meeting once a year, every June."

"And?"

"We hug, say very little, and then I get the hell out of there and find a bar that serves good rum."

"You give her a hug and it's over? You don't talk with her?"

"Small talk, maybe. 'It's good to see you.' 'You look good.' But that's about it. There's nothing else to say."

Avery raised her eyebrows. "There's a shitload to say!"

"It's confusing. I loved her, she betrayed me, and there's no possible way for us to be together. I should just leave it alone, but for some reason I go through this self-sabotage each year and, trust me, I'm no better for it."

"It's because you're looking for a way to forgive her."

Walt blinked as if a piece of debris had flown into his face. "Am I?"

"Of course you are," Avery said with conviction. "You just told me you had unfinished business here in New York. Forgiving her is it."

Having this fact laid so boldly in front of him was shocking, but true. Every time they saw each other Meghan asked what she could do to earn his forgiveness.

"Have you ever told her?" Avery asked.

"Told her what?"

"What it would take to forgive her?"

"No."

"Why not?"

"Because I don't know what that would be."

"I'd figure it out if I were you. Not for her, but for you. It's called closure, and you're in desperate need of it."

Walt took another sip of rum and then raised his glass. "You're more of a shrink than you think."

There was a natural lull to the conversation now that Walt's confession was over.

"Back to what you asked me originally about why I came back to New York. I've been looking for something to get me reengaged and out of my head. Looking into the Cameron Young case has been good for me. It's made me feel like my old self again."

This, along with everything else he had told Avery tonight, was also true.

"Good," Avery said. "And I'm sorry if I was pushy asking about all this."

Walt shrugged his shoulders and pouted his lower lip. "I feel good. It might have been therapeutic to get it off my chest."

"Glad I could help." Avery checked her phone. "It's getting late. Do you think I could take a look at the Cameron Young file tomorrow? See what I could use for my story? The city will be a ghost town this weekend. We could make the most out of it. Go through the case together, start to finish."

Walt nodded. "Yeah. I'll call you tomorrow and we'll figure out a time?"

"That would be great."

Avery stood to leave.

"Sorry to ramble for so long," Walt said.

He felt Avery place her hand on his wrist.

"It's not rambling if you have a captive audience."

He smiled. "Can I make sure you get back to your hotel all right?"

She nodded. "I'd appreciate that. I'm at the Lowell."

They left Keens and walked the quiet streets of Midtown. Ten minutes on Madison Avenue took them to the entrance of Avery's hotel.

"Thanks for walking me back," Avery said.

"Sure thing."

Avery took a step toward him and gave him a peck on the cheek before she embraced him in an unexpected hug. If the pretense of the night had been different, the possibility of being invited up to her room would be on his mind. It *was* on his mind, if he was being honest, but he could not in good conscience sleep with a woman whom he'd met under such nefarious circumstances. Their embrace ended and they stood face to face. There was a moment when it would have been natural to kiss her, but it passed in the blink of an eye.

"I'll call you tomorrow," he said. "And we'll figure out a time to look through the file."

"Yeah," Avery said, nodding her head and taking a step back. "Please do."

He watched her walk through the front door and into the lobby of the Lowell. When the elevator doors opened and she stepped inside, Walt turned and started for his hotel. As he walked the empty streets he realized that for the first time in years, a woman other than Meghan Cobb occupied the folds of his mind.

CHAPTER 34

Manhattan, NY
Friday, July 2, 2021

There was a knock on his hotel room door just before midnight. Sprawled across the bed, Walt used two pillows to prop himself up in a sitting position. A freshly poured glass of rum was on his lap, and ESPN was on the television. He had kicked off his shoes when he arrived back from dinner, and poured himself a nightcap to settle himself after his impromptu confession and the confusing scene that had taken place in front of Avery Mason's hotel thirty minutes earlier.

The knock came again, and his mind spun. He allowed into his thoughts the absurd notion that it was Avery knocking on his door. To check on him, perhaps? He had been a bit rattled after telling her the story about Meghan, one he had shared with no one before. Many knew scattered details about the affair, but no one knew the specifics. Until now. Until he had, for some inexplicable reason, confessed them to a television journalist. The knock came a third time. How had she found him? How did she know where he was staying and what room he was in? And, most urgently, was she here simply to comfort him, or was there another reason for her presence?

Some foreign emotion stirred in his chest as Walt stood from the bed, unsteadily placed his drink on the nightstand, and took a quick look in the mirror. The hazy eyes of a man who'd had too much to drink stared back at him. He ran a hand through his hair, took a deep breath, and walked to the door. When he pulled it open, Jim Oliver stood in the hallway.

"André Schwarzkopf," Oliver said as he walked past Walt and into the hotel room.

Walt leaned his head against the edge of the door and briefly closed his eyes. He wasn't sure what he expected to find on the other side of the door. He wasn't sure he wanted Avery to be there. He wasn't sure what might have transpired between them had he found her standing in the hallway. He felt at once disappointed that she was not there, and foolish for believing she might be. He closed the door.

"Who?"

"The brownstone in Brooklyn," Oliver said. "It belongs to André Schwarzkopf. He flies under the radar but has been known to dabble in procuring false documents. Mostly passports, but also the occasional birth certificate and green card. We had a file on him."

Walt shook his head to clear the cobwebs. He worked hard to change gears. "What's it mean?"

"Garth Montgomery is either trying to get out of the country, or needs to move from wherever he's hiding now—maybe Mexico or South America—to somewhere else. Somewhere new. He needs documents to do it, probably a passport. And his daughter is helping him. How long was she in this guy's house?"

Walt shrugged, thinking back to the morning he followed

Avery to the Park Slope neighborhood. "Maybe twenty minutes."

"Did she have anything when she left?"

"Just her purse, same as when she entered."

Walt walked to the nightstand and picked up his drink. "Put somebody on the guy. Keep tabs on him twenty-four/seven."

Oliver nodded. "Already on it. Tell me about the cemetery."

"The cemetery?"

"Yeah. When you followed her to Green-Wood Cemetery."

"Not much to tell. She took a slow stroll through the grounds. I stayed at a good distance. She approached a grave site, hesitated for several minutes before she actually stood over it. Then she dropped flowers and hurried away. Whose graves were they?"

"Annette and Christopher Montgomery. Her mother and brother."

Walt stared into his rum. "That's sad."

"Her mother died while we were investigating Garth Montgomery. Had a heart attack after he disappeared and all the details about him came out, including his fifteen-year affair with a woman half his age. We thought the death of his wife might cause him to surface, but the son of a bitch stayed in hiding. Can you believe that? Didn't even go to his own wife's funeral. A real son of a bitch, this guy. We've been watching Claire Montgomery for three years now. She visits Green-Wood Cemetery every year."

"Every year?"

"She comes to New York every summer. Usually flies American and stays for a day or two before heading home. The only reason that we've ever been able to come up with for her trips to New York is to visit Green-Wood Cemetery. But this year, she changes things up. She drives instead of using the airlines. And she hasn't used her credit card once since leaving LA. She paid for two weeks at the Lowell using a cashier's check. She's trying not to leave any trails. We're convinced she either sees her father on these trips, or is in contact with him some other way. The trip to André Schwarz-kopf's brownstone is the first piece of concrete evidence we've managed in all the years we've followed her."

"What happened to the brother?"

"Who?"

"Her brother. What happened to him?

"He died in a sailing accident. Claire Montgomery and her brother took out the family yacht, a sailboat that bore her name—the *Claire-Voyance*. A three-million-dollar boat daddy bought for her twenty-first birthday. They ran into bad weather a couple of miles off the coast of New York. The boat sank. She lived, but barely—the Coast Guard pulled her near-drowned and hypothermic body out of the ocean. Her brother died. She visits his grave every year."

"Shit," Walt whispered under his breath, taking a long swallow of rum.

"What's the matter?"

Walt thought back to his confession earlier in the night. His stupid, bumbling, rambling confession, and his explanation of the survivor's guilt that came with making it through the shooting that had taken his partner's life. He spoke as if his situation were unique, as if Avery could never understand the feeling. She surely did.

"Nothing." Walt offered a drunken wave. "Just sounds like a shit situation."

"When are you seeing her again?" Oliver asked.

Walt walked over to the desk in the corner, where papers were strewn across the surface. "Tomorrow. She wants to check out all this Cameron Young stuff to see if any of it can be used on her show."

"Good. Make sure the meeting happens. And if you get a chance to get into her hotel room, take it."

Walt didn't like the implications of what Oliver was suggesting.

"On what pretense would I end up in her hotel room?"

"Come on, Walt. Use those icy blues of yours. We're off the record on this one. Get creative."

Oliver reached into the breast pocket of his sport coat and pulled out a thin, square, metal box, which he placed on the foot of the bed.

"I've got a dozen agents who would kill to be in your current position. But I went all the way to a tiny island in the Caribbean to recruit *you*. You're the only one with the Cameron Young connection, and we need to exploit it."

Oliver checked his watch. "Forty-eight hours. I want another update." He walked across the hotel room and opened the door, then turned before he left. "Good work this week, Walt. This little arrangement is already paying dividends."

The door closed and Walt stood in the quiet of the hotel room. He stared at the small box Jim Oliver had left on the end of the bed. He walked over and picked it up. The brushed metal container was flat and thin. He unclasped the front lock and opened it. Inside were four small, circular devices that looked like silver-oxide batteries. He lifted one out of the seated felt and turned it over to find a 3-M decal covering the pad of tape on the back. Remove this decal, Walt knew, and the tiny listening device could be stuck just about anywhere.

PART IV

Evidence

CHAPTER 35

Catskills, NY
Saturday, July 3, 2021

She steered the Range Rover through the mountain roads as her mind replayed the previous night. Her thoughts continued to return to the moment in front of her hotel when she swore Walt Jenkins was on the verge of kissing her. Avery spent much of the night lying in bed, trying to decide if she had wanted him to kiss her. Of course she did. She was, despite her mind's best attempt to convince herself otherwise, in the midst of a terrible dry spell. Even for her arid standards, eighteen months was something of a record for her. Taking over *American Events* during the last year had left little time for a love life, and she'd gone so long without intimacy that she wondered if perhaps her impression of Walt's intentions was nothing more than seeing an oasis where, really, just more desert sand stood. They had shared an intimate conversation earlier in the night, during which Walt revealed that the love of his life had not only broken his heart, but perhaps his spirit too. Perhaps this innocent confession had given Avery the impression that Walt wanted more from their face-to-face moment in front of her hotel room than reality dictated. Perhaps she had misread the situation entirely.

She pushed Walt Jenkins from her mind when she pulled into the driveway and saw Emma Kind waiting on the front porch, just like the first time they'd met.

"Welcome back," Emma said as Avery climbed from the Rover.

"Good to see you again, Emma."

"Come on in."

Avery walked up the steps and through the front door.

"Can I get you something to drink?"

"No wine today, that's for sure," Avery said.

"Good Lord, no. I'm so embarrassed about that."

"Don't be. I drank as much as you did."

"Still, I'm sorry to have mixed my emotions that day with so much wine. It's never a good idea. But the news about Victoria's remains, and your interest in her story, well . . . the memories just overwhelmed me. The idea that after all these years someone is willing to help me in this quest to prove my sister's innocence, a quest that has felt futile for the last many years, just got to me. And the idea that *Avery Mason* might help shine light on such an injustice . . ."

"I should be the one apologizing," Avery said. "I barged into your life and started asking questions about a very delicate subject. Like you said, mixing wine with emotions is never a good idea."

"Except when it works."

"Except then, yes," Avery said with a chuckle.

"Let's talk out back," Emma said. "Coffee?"

"Sure, thanks. Two creams, two sugars."

It was a beautiful, clear morning in the mountains and the birds were in full chorus as Avery and Emma sat on the patio.

"I'm going to do the best I can on this story about Victoria," Avery said. "If you feel embarrassed about purging your emotions, I feel just as embarrassed about my alcohol-induced confidence that I could prove Victoria's innocence. Now, reality is sinking in. I spoke with Walt Jenkins, the detective who ran the investigation."

"Detective Jenkins. I remember him."

"Yes. He's moved on from the police force and is no longer a detective, but remembers the case well. He's agreed to help me, and has worked his contacts at the New York State Police to gather all the information he can about the case. I'm meeting with him later today to go through it all."

"That sounds promising."

"It will at least provide unfettered access to the details about the investigation. But . . . Walt Jenkins may no longer be a detective, but he still thinks like one. He was steadfast in his opinion that the case against Victoria was strong. According to Jenkins, the circumstantial evidence was powerful. But the hard evidence was overwhelming."

"I'm no detective, Avery. I'm a sixty-year-old retired elementary school teacher who's starting to gray. Many would claim I'm still a grieving sibling whose views are clouded by unconditional love and loyalty. And maybe this many years later I should just move on. But there was something in Victoria's voice when she left those messages on 9/11. A conviction that I'll never be able to get past. So I don't care about the evidence. I don't care how strong a case Detective Jenkins claims he had. Something about the investigation is wrong, and I know Victoria is innocent. I need you to believe that."

"I'm not sure what I believe at the moment. And you don't want me to start a re-investigation of the case believing one thing or another. For me to do my job properly I have to stay neutral and unbiased. I have to collect all the information I can find, analyze it, and then come to my own conclusion. If there is anything that suggests Victoria is innocent, I'll pursue it. I promise. But what I need to do first is learn all I can about your sister, and I need your help on that. I need to figure out who Victoria was so I can form an impression about her and better describe her to my audience. I've already talked with Natalie Ratcliff and she's working on a chronology of her friendship with Victoria, starting with their college days. Together with your testimony, it will go a long way to showing the audience who Victoria was. But I was hoping to dig deeper, even before Victoria's college days. I want to get into her childhood, start from the beginning."

"I'll tell you anything you want to know about our childhoods. And I have boxes and boxes of things in the attic that will help. Victoria's baby albums, school photos, high school yearbooks, her wedding album. Lord, there's so much up there. I packed it all away after she died and haven't looked at any of it for years."

"Would you share those things with me?"

"Of course. It'll take me a little bit to find those boxes. I haven't been up in the attic for some time."

"I'm happy to help."

An hour later, Avery set three old, dusty plastic bins into the cargo area of the Range Rover.

"When are you going to look through the case file?" Emma asked.

"Later today," Avery said. "I've got the entire weekend reserved to review the case and find out as much about the investigation as I can. In my down time, I'll look through all of this and start creating a full history on Victoria."

"Will you keep me posted if you find anything when you review the case?"

"Of course," Avery said as she closed the hatch on the Range Rover. "If I come across anything at all, I'll call you."

"Thank you."

"Have a great Fourth of July, Emma."

A few minutes later, Avery was headed back to the city with a trunk full of bins containing Victoria Ford's childhood and history. Avery had no idea that they would create far more questions than answers.

CHAPTER 36
Manhattan, NY
Saturday, July 3, 2021

After hauling the bins to her hotel room, Avery made a run to Starbucks. She was amazed by the quiet of the city. For a Saturday afternoon, the streets were empty. Traffic lights rotated through their timers, changing from green to yellow to red, sometimes without a single car passing through the intersection. This was, in fact, the first time Avery could remember being in Manhattan around the Fourth of July. Her childhood summers were spent in Sister Bay, Wisconsin. And her adult years had been spent at her family's house in the Hamptons. Staying in the city for the Fourth was something that never occurred to her. It was simply not something people did. Everyone she knew headed to the country or the beach. But now, as she walked the empty streets, she noticed an elegance to the city she had never appreciated before—as if the city were an antique chest that had been stripped of its peeling paint and coarse primer to reveal the true masterpiece underneath.

She relished the feeling that she had the city to herself, tons of work to do, and very little to distract her. At least, she tried to convince herself as much. As she walked the vacant sidewalks, her thoughts drifted back to Walt Jenkins and the foreign sense of excitement she felt about seeing him later today. With so much to do, she couldn't afford these tangential thoughts to distract or confuse her. But the more she analyzed these feelings of excitement, the more Avery realized they were her mind's attempt to shift her focus to something exponentially more thrilling than what waited for her on the other side of the weekend. Her attraction to Walt Jenkins had distracted her, if just momentarily, from the percolating anxiety about heading back to Brooklyn next week to see if Mr. André—she didn't even know his last name—had come through with the falsified passport. If he did, Avery knew the real—and dangerous—work would then begin. As she entered the Starbucks, she realized that even in a near empty city she could find clutter and garbage. She was a Montgomery, after all.

Twenty minutes later she sipped a venti dark roast—two creams, two sugars—while she sat at the small desk in the corner of her hotel room. The dusty bins Emma had pulled from her attic were now empty, the contents spewed across the room covering the bed, coffee table, and floor. Pictures and yearbooks, photo albums and diaries. Avery had spent some time browsing through the pages of Victoria's childhood diary and reading the hopes and dreams of an adolescent girl. The entries were sweet and charming, and covered the crushes Victoria had on grade-school boys, teachers she hated, and her dreams of writing novels when she grew up. Avery felt guilty for reading the private thoughts of a teenaged girl and after a while put the journal aside.

She spent an hour looking through old photos, and imagined her documentary about Victoria Ford including images of these albums and diary—the dreams of a woman who had perished before she had a chance to see them come true.

In one of the boxes Avery found an old USB thumb drive. She plugged it into her laptop and waited for the computer to process the ancient technology. Finally, a file folder appeared on the screen and Avery opened it. There were five files in the folder, all Word documents. She clicked on the first file and a document opened. Avery read the cover page:

Hot Mess
by
Victoria Ford

She cocked her head as she scrolled through the document, realizing that she was looking at one of the manuscripts Victoria had written before her death. The manuscript was four hundred pages long. Avery opened each of the files and found four other manuscripts, all written by Victoria and each about the same length. Scrolling back to the original file, Avery started reading. Two pages into the manuscript, she stopped. There was something familiar about the story. She read another page until it dawned on her. Avery knew the story. She had read it before. Scrolling faster now, her eyes blazed through the prose for another minute until she was sure. Until she came to the main character, introduced at the beginning of the second chapter. A quirky, female private eye who was slightly overweight and unlucky with love. A character named Peg Perugo.

Avery whispered the name aloud. "Peg Perugo. Peg Perugo."

Putting the pages to the side, Avery walked to the closet and took her purse down from where it hung. Inside, she found Natalie Ratcliff's novel that had kept her up late into the night. The book's title—*Baggage*—offered a similar connotation to the title of Victoria Ford's manuscript. *Hot Mess.*

Standing in the entryway of her hotel room, Avery opened the novel and skimmed the pages. The chapters, the paragraphs, the words . . . they were identical to Victoria Ford's manuscript. A manuscript saved on an ancient flash drive and stored in Emma Kind's attic for the past twenty years.

CHAPTER 37

Manhattan, NY
Saturday, July 3, 2021

Her thoughts were disjointed as she walked the lonely streets of Midtown on her way to the Grand Hyatt. Walt Jenkins had called while Avery was racing through the rest of Victoria Ford's manuscripts and finding, astonishingly, that each had been published as a Natalie Ratcliff novel, starring the portly and loveable private eye named Peg Perugo. Avery couldn't quite get her mind around what it all meant, other than that Natalie Ratcliff, in addition to being one of the world's best-selling authors, was also a plagiarizing fraud.

With confusion still clouding her thoughts, she turned on Forty-Second Street and came to the entrance of the Hyatt. She rode the elevator to the twentieth floor and knocked on number 2021. The door opened and Avery quickly forgot about Natalie Ratcliff and Victoria Ford, Peg Perugo and plagiarism. Walt was dressed in jeans and an untucked button-down shirt. Avery noticed a small nick on his freshly shaven right cheek, and for some insane reason had the urge to lick her thumb and press it against his cheek to wipe the mark away. The rational part of her mind intervened with a proverbial slap to the face before she could proceed.

"I think you and I are the only ones left in this city," he said.

Avery pushed the thoughts away and smiled. "It's eerie, isn't it?"

"Very. Come on in."

Avery walked through the doorway and into the one-bedroom suite. "Nice digs."

"I got rid of my apartment a couple of years ago," Walt said, closing the door. "Rent in Jamaica is next to nothing, so I've been sitting on a little nest egg. I didn't know how long I was going to be here, so I splurged. When you and I are done with the Cameron Young case, I think I'm going to stick around and see my parents and brother. It's been a while.

"The case is over on the desk," he said, pointing to the corner where a cardboard box rested on the table by the window. "The hard evidence is still in storage, but this is everything else. The original documents have been digitized, scanned, and transferred to the BCI database. These are copies, but they represent almost all the documents that made up the case against Victoria Ford."

"Almost?" Avery asked as she walked over to the desk and sat down.

"This is everything the Shandaken police had in storage. The Cameron Young investigation was run through their office as a way to keep the peace. The local departments didn't love when the BCI took over a case from them, so as lead detective I allowed the Shandaken chief to be the face of the investigation. I'm still waiting for a call back from the district attorney's office to see if they have any additional documents. Twenty years later, they may be long gone. But trust me"—Walt pointed at the box on the table—"this will keep us busy for a while."

"Can you take me through some of this?"

Walt pulled a chair over and sat next to her. "Sure. We can go start to finish. How much do you know about the murder?"

"Everything you and I discussed last night, plus what Emma Kind told me originally about it. I've also talked with Roman Manchester, the attorney who was set to defend Victoria."

"Sounds like you know a lot then. How much of this stuff do you want to see?"

"Everything."

"Okay," Walt said. "Just a warning. The crime scene photos are disturbing."

Avery nodded. She'd seen many crime scenes in the last few years. "I'm good."

Walt reached into the box and pulled out a folder of photos. Avery imagined her camera guys and production team laying out the contents of this box and taking stills of the documents, highlighting in yellow the areas of transcript interviews and police reports that pertained to the story she wanted to tell. She imagined startling images of crime scene photos flashing onto television screens across America as Victoria Ford's story unfolded.

"Here's the body, the balcony, and the master bedroom of the Youngs' Catskills home," Walt said. "This is what I found when I arrived on the scene."

Avery pulled the photo of Cameron Young hanging from the balcony so that it was in front of her. It was, indeed, disturbing. The lifeless body was suspended in broad daylight as morning fog drifted from the grass beneath him. His head torqued by the rope into a grotesque angle. As she paged through the other photos, they took her from the back lawn of the Catskills mansion, through the house, up the stairs, and into the master bedroom. She saw the rope stretched tight and running taut through the room, from the open balcony doors to the walk-in closet. She paged through the photos until she found the ones taken inside the closet, where the end of the rope was tethered to the leg of a sturdy-looking safe.

"Take me through your findings in the bedroom," she said.

Walt leaned closer, so that he could point at each of the pictures. She noticed the scent of aftershave.

"The rope used to hang Cameron Young was determined to be from an original bundle that was seventy-five feet long when purchased. It had been cut a number of times with a serrated blade." Walt pointed to the photo where an ominous-looking kitchen knife lay on the carpeting next to the safe. A yellow evidence placard stood next to it. "The knife came from a butcher's block in the kitchen and had Victoria Ford's fingerprints on it. Her blood was discovered on the carpet."

Avery felt him lean a bit closer to shuffle through the pictures and find the image of the bloodied carpet next to the safe.

"The blood here was matched to Victoria Ford through DNA. The theory was that in her rush to set up the scene as a suicide, she cut herself while using the knife to sever the rope."

"So this blood," Avery said. "It was the main evidence that put Victoria at the scene?"

"The blood, and urine found in the toilet. Both matched Victoria's DNA."

Avery remembered Victoria Ford's voice from the answering machine recording.

They said they found my blood and urine at the scene. But that can't be true. None of it can be true. Please believe me.

"The knife, as well as a wineglass on the nightstand, held her fingerprints," Walt said, turning his head to look at Avery as they were huddled over the desk. "All of it put her at the scene."

Avery looked back to the photos. "So, at this point in the

crime, when Victoria cuts herself, it was suspected that Cameron Young was already dead?"

"Yes. The theory was that Cameron Young was strangled during some sort of S and M practice. He had whip marks all over his body, so we know whatever was going on that night was quite violent. After he was dead, Victoria Ford attempted to set up the scene to look like a suicide."

"How did you come to that conclusion?"

"The wounds on Cameron Young's neck, according to the medical examiner, suggested that he had been strangled with the length of rope initially. Autopsy findings showed that he had suffered what's called short-drop asphyxiation—congestion in his lungs, petechiae in the eyelids and cheeks, and a host of other findings. We can go over the autopsy results and I can walk you through it. But it was clear that the cause of death was ligature strangulation, possibly the result of erotic asphyxiation. Then, after he was dead, his body was thrown over the balcony. That resulted in what's called long-drop trauma to his neck—deep ligature gouges and a severed spinal cord. But those wounds were determined to have occurred after he was already dead."

Avery ran her hands over the photos to organize her thoughts.

"So Victoria kills Cameron Young because he won't leave his wife."

"And because he got his wife pregnant after he made Victoria have an abortion."

Avery slowly nodded. "And how did you learn about the abortion?"

"We subpoenaed her medical records, and then she admitted during an interview that she had had an abortion."

"And during the abortion there was a complication?"

"Correct," Walt said. "The procedure left her unable to have children in the future."

"And this was the DA's argument for why she killed him?"

"It was."

"Okay," Avery said. "So Victoria kills him. Then she comes up with the idea of making it look like a suicide. She ties a second, longer rope around his neck and runs to the closet to secure the rope to the safe, the heaviest thing in the room."

"Correct."

"As she is rushing to set the stage of suicide and slice the rope so she can tie it to the safe, she cuts herself with the knife."

"Correct."

Avery studied the photo of the bloodied carpeting. "Then she ties the rope and dumps the body over the balcony?"

"Yes, that was the assessment of the crime scene and the prosecution's argument."

"Why did she leave the knife?" Avery asked. "If Victoria was setting things up to look like suicide, why would she leave a knife with her fingerprints next to the safe?"

"She panicked," Walt said with certainty. "Maybe she assumed it would be linked to Cameron. It came from his own kitchen. If we're arguing that she was thinking logically at this point, we'd also ask why she would leave a wineglass with her fingerprints on the nightstand. Or her urine in the toilet. But we never claimed she did any of this perfectly. Quite the contrary. Victoria Ford was very bad at murder. At least, she was at covering it up."

Avery continued to shuffle through the photos. She lifted the image of Cameron Young's bloated body hanging in the backyard.

"Victoria weighed one hundred twenty pounds. The argument was that she dragged a dead man who weighed a hundred pounds *more* than her across the bedroom, lifted him up, and dropped him over a four-foot balcony. Not an easy task."

"But not impossible. Especially for someone supercharged with adrenaline."

Avery watched Walt as he spoke. She thought there was something about his tone, or in his demeanor, that suggested he was less convinced with the case and its conclusions today than perhaps he had been twenty years ago. She doubted that it was her first few questions that caused his skepticism, and Avery wondered if there was something else he knew about the case.

She pointed at the box. "Let's go through the rest of it."

CHAPTER 38

Manhattan, NY
Saturday, July 3, 2021

It was after 9:00 P.M. when they decided to take a break. Avery's eyes were burning and a dull headache had formed at the base of her skull from reading through so many documents, police reports, and interview transcripts. They rode the elevator to the lobby and pushed through the revolving doors into the evening warmth. Neither had eaten lunch so they headed to Public House where they sat at the bar and ordered burgers and beers. Saturday night and the place was empty.

"Have you ever seen the city like this?" Walt asked.

"Never. I've heard stories about how empty it gets over the Fourth. Some of my friends used to love to stick around while everyone else flooded out of the city. When I was a kid I spent my summers in Wisconsin."

"Wisconsin?"

"Yeah. My parents sent me to camp each summer. Eight weeks of sailing camp in northern Wisconsin. So as a kid, I was always gone over the Fourth. When I was older we used to go . . ." Avery caught herself, her two worlds colliding again. "We had a house in the Hamptons. We always spent the Fourth of July there."

"Your parents?"

Avery nodded.

"Do they still have it?" Walt asked. "I mean, if you have access to a house in the Hamptons it begs the question why you're spending the weekend with me."

Avery smiled. "I'm working. But, no, that house is, uh . . . long gone."

Avery didn't mention that the "house" was a ten-thousand-square-foot mansion on the beach, and that it was not "gone" as much as confiscated by the government, like every other piece of property her family had owned. She also skipped the fact that her mother was dead, her father was a crook, and that her time in New York this summer had much greater repercussions than shedding light on Victoria Ford's guilt or innocence. Just life's little details, Avery thought as she sipped her beer. The minor things she kept to herself when meeting new people.

Their burgers arrived. Between bites, Walt asked her, "Spending every summer in Wisconsin . . . was that a drag as a kid?"

"Just the opposite. They were the best times of my life. The sailing school was well known and prestigious. Still is today. At least it is within the small, cultish group of people who want to drill the art of sailing into their children from the time they're old enough to walk. The wait list is years long, literally. Some of my parents' friends jumped onto the list as soon as their kids were born. No kidding. It was the only way to get a spot. That, or your parents had a lot of money and a lot of clout."

"Your parents had that?"

Avery shrugged. "Something like that. But however they

managed to get me there, those summers were special. For me *and* my brother. God, he loved that place."

Memories of Christopher momentarily distracted her. After a stretch of silence, she realized Walt was staring at her, waiting for her to continue.

"It's right on the lake. The camp. Kids from around the country went there to learn to sail. A couple kids from England, too. I used to love their accents. When I was a kid I dreamed of moving to London just so I could talk like them. It was strange, the friends I made. We'd see each other only in the summers and never talk for the rest of the year. But as soon as the school year ended, all I wanted to do was get to Sister Bay. And when my sailing friends and I reunited each summer, it was like we were never apart. Camp kids have that sort of bond."

"You stayed the entire summer?"

"Eight weeks. Every summer."

"What, did you sleep in tents?"

Avery laughed. "You're not a camp kid, are you?"

Walt shook his head. "My summers consisted of baseball in the streets of Queens. Sending me off to camp would have been like a prison sentence."

"Only camp kids understand. No, we did not sleep in tents. We stayed in cabins, complete with bathrooms and even toilets. Yes, Wisconsin has such luxuries as running water and indoor plumbing."

Walt opened his palms. "I'm not ripping on Wisconsin. I just don't know anything about summer camps."

"I'm just giving you a hard time. But the camp really did have these great big, beautiful cabins. A dozen of them—real Northwood Wisconsin log cabins where all the students stayed. Six to a cabin. Some wild things happened in those cabins."

"I can only imagine. Through high school you did this?"

"Through college, too. I went back as an instructor."

"Do you still sail?"

"All the time. I have a small Catalina in LA. I try to get out on the water"—Avery's voice trailed off as her mind flashed back to the crime scene photos—"once a week."

"What's wrong?" Walt asked.

Avery shook her head, put her burger down, and took a sip of beer. She pointed at Walt's glass.

"Finish that up. We need to go back to your hotel. I need to look at the crime scene photos again."

CHAPTER 39

Manhattan, NY
Saturday, July 3, 2021

They hurried back through the empty streets. Avery was silent as she stood next to Walt in the elevator. When he opened the door to his suite, she walked over to the desk and sat down. She pulled the photos in front of her again and paged through them until she found the ones she needed, positioning them side by side on the surface of the desk.

"Look here."

Walt leaned over her shoulder. "What am I looking at?"

"See this knot?" Avery asked, pointing to the knotted rope attached to the leg of the safe. "And these?" She pointed to the knots tied around Cameron Young's wrists.

"Yes. The medical examiner made a note on those. Hold on."

Walt sat down next to her and pulled the autopsy report from the box. He paged through it for a moment.

"Here." Walt placed the report on the desk and pointed at the sentence where Dr. Lockard had made his remarks. "The medical examiner described the knots as *alpine butterfly knots*. He said they were commonly used in mountain climbing."

"He's wrong," Avery said.

"About what?"

"They're not mountain climbing knots, they're sailing knots. I tie them nearly every weekend."

"Sailing knots?"

"Yes. They're bowline knots. I'm sure of it." Avery looked up from the photos and spoke in a singsong voice. "Up through the rabbit hole, round the big tree; down through the rabbit hole and off goes he."

Walt raised his eyebrows.

"It's the jingle used to remember how to tie the knots. I learned it when I was a kid in Sister Bay. Telling you about sailing camp jogged my memory."

"Okay," Walt said, shrugging his shoulders. "So they're sailing knots. What does that tell you?"

"It tells me that whoever tied them had to have used both hands."

"Right. The medical examiner made the same point. The knots could only be tied using both hands, and it was therefore impossible for Cameron Young to have tied his own hands. It's one of the ways we ruled out suicide."

"So, where's the blood?" Avery asked.

"The blood? I showed you." Walt pointed back to the photos. "We found heavy droplets of Victoria Ford's blood in the carpeting next to the safe."

"Yes, I see that. And that's a lot of blood dripped onto the carpeting. But if I have the sequence of events correct—that Victoria cut herself *first*, while she was severing the rope so that she could tie it to the safe in order to drop Cameron Young over the balcony—wouldn't there be evidence of this injury on the rope? If Victoria cut herself to the extent that all this blood dripped onto the carpeting of the closet, where's the rest of the blood in the crime scene?"

Walt cocked his head and leaned back in his chair, Avery could tell, heavy in thought.

"This bowline knot she supposedly tied, for instance," Avery continued. "Just as the medical examiner concluded, she would have had to use both hands to tie it. If one of her hands was bleeding, you'd think the rope would have Victoria's blood smeared all over it. It's a white rope and there's not a drop of blood on it. Or on the safe. And you'd expect somewhere on Cameron Young's body there would also be evidence of this injury Victoria supposedly suffered just before lugging the body to the balcony. No?"

Walt rubbed a palm over his cheek but didn't speak. It was then that Avery knew she had a story she could run with. If a few questions about the crime scene could plant doubt in the mind of the lead detective, it was certainly enough to captivate a television audience of fifteen million. And if a cursory look through the case against Victoria Ford had raised such glaring problems, it was certainly possible that other discrepancies were waiting to be discovered in the Cameron Young file.

Something else occurred to Avery as well. A growing sense of obligation. Victoria Ford's voice echoed in her mind again.

Find a way, Em. Find a way to prove it. Please? Just find a way to prove to the world that I'm not the monster they've painted me to be.

CHAPTER 40

Manhattan, NY
Saturday, July 3, 2021

The online stalking could easily be accomplished on her own laptop, and in her own hotel room—alone and isolated in her own Avery Mason bubble of safety. But tonight she refused to allow rational thought to win out over mirthful. She and Walt felt they had made a small break in the case, and she felt a thrill from working together. She was enjoying his company and knew that working late in his hotel room was a potential conduit to intimacy. When this first occurred to her after they finished reviewing the crime scene photos, Avery's instincts had been to grab her purse and leave, her mind dominated as it were with troubling worries that being intimate with a man would somehow expose her as a fraud. But she decided that her entire existence could not be spent in a perpetual state of flux and fear. At some point she would have to either merge her two lives—the fraudulent with the honest—or decide to leave one of them behind.

This battle was taking place inside her head as she sat next to Walt on the couch while he typed the names into the search engine. They had decided to start with the spouses, and it didn't take long to find Cameron Young's widow and Victoria Ford's widower.

"Jasper Ford is a real estate agent here in New York," Walt said. "That's how they met."

"Who?"

"The Fords and the Youngs. They met when Jasper Ford sold Cameron and Tessa the Catskills home. They became friends after that. Tessa Young mentioned it during one of her interviews."

They stalked Jasper Ford for a while but found nothing interesting. Eventually, they turned their attention to Tessa Young. Cameron Young's widow was a fifty-five-year-old professor of English literature at Columbia. She was remarried and, according to Whitepages.com, lived in a walk-up in Hell's Kitchen. She had a twenty-year-old daughter who was a junior at Boston College.

"Look at this," Walt said. He had Tessa's Facebook page open and was scrolling through her timeline. "Nearly every post from this summer was made on her sailboat. And she belongs to the New York Yacht Club."

Avery leaned over to look at the images.

"That's another part of their history," Walt said. "Tessa and Cameron were avid sailors. They invited Jasper and Victoria out for a sail after they closed on the Catskills mansion. They became friends after that."

"The lady would certainly know how to tie a bowline knot," Avery said. "And if Tessa had found out about the affair . . ."

Walt sat back from his computer and took a deep breath. "Let's not jump to conclusions we can't prove. Other than a flimsy theory on knots, nothing puts Tessa Young at the crime scene."

Avery looked back at the monitor. "Maybe I'll reach out to her."

"And ask about a twenty-year-old homicide you're attempting to tie her to? Really bad idea."

"I'm not tying anyone to anything," Avery said. "But Tessa and Jasper are worth talking to. They're on my list of people to contact."

"Not if you're taking the angle that Tessa Young could be involved with her husband's death. It's a bad idea, Avery."

The way he said her name, staring at her, sent a flutter through her chest.

"Look," he said. "If we really think there's something to any of this, we root out the details and go to the authorities to show them what we have. I still have plenty of contacts. But bowline knots and the absence of blood on the rope are not going to change any minds, especially twenty years later. Getting a case reopened is a monumental task. Before I reach out to any of my old contacts, we're going to need something stronger than a lack of blood on a couple of sailing knots. The fact that Victoria Ford's blood was on the carpeting will trump any lack of blood elsewhere. We need something more."

"Then let's go through the rest of the case," Avery said. "We've made it through, what, half of it? And we've already found some holes."

"*Potential* holes."

"Maybe there are more definitive ones to find."

Walt looked over at the box of files on the desk, paused, and then nodded. "Okay. Let's see what else we can find. Meet again tomorrow evening? Unless you have plans. It's the Fourth of July."

"My only plans are with you." Avery stood. "Thanks for doing this with me. No matter what we find, I appreciate your help."

"I want to make sure we got things right all those years ago. And I need to know if we got them wrong, too."

Walt stood also. They were face to face.

"Say, six o'clock tomorrow?"

Avery nodded. "See you then."

She said the words but didn't move.

"Okay," Walt said, staying as still as her. "See you to-morrow."

His words floated off with little meaning. Then, sud-denly, they moved to each other. The kissing was frantic at first and then slowed to become more passionate. Avery did a quick run-through in her mind. She'd had a single beer at dinner; he'd had two. Neither was drunk, which was both a positive and negative aspect of what was about to happen. She'd never made a habit out of drunken sex, which made accountability the following morning unavoidable. Without drunkenness, there was nothing to blame their behavior on other than mutual attraction and an open willingness to share intimacy. For most, this was a normal result of sex. For Avery Mason, it was a portal that allowed another per-son access to her past.

The worrisome thoughts raced through her mind as she kissed Walt Jenkins. But without too much effort, she forced them away and enjoyed the feel of a man's hands on her hips for the first time in over a year. She pushed him backward as they kissed. They stumbled across the suite, through the bed-room door, and onto the bed. Buttons popped and zippers buzzed.

CHAPTER 41
Manhattan, NY
Sunday, July 4, 2021

On Sunday morning Avery took a long run through Central Park. It was peaceful, quiet, and, unlike any other time she had run these trails, nearly empty. Normally crowded with joggers, bikers, and dog walkers, this morning the park belonged only to the few remaining souls left in the city who were up early on the Fourth of July. Avery nodded at the joggers she passed, sensing an unspoken message in the way they smiled and delivered their good mornings that the once-a-year emptiness and tranquility of the country's most populated city was a secret shared by only a select few, and that Avery was now part of the group.

Thirty minutes earlier she had quietly snuck out of Walt's hotel room while he slept peacefully among the knotted bed sheets. The aftermath of long-awaited sex had filled her with an urge to sweat and run and wring from her body any second thoughts or doubts that would surely surface. For some sophomoric reason Avery had decided on a clean getaway. She had slipped out of bed with catlike poise, and resisted the urge to use the bathroom before leaving for fear that flushing the toilet would wake him. *Why,* she asked herself as she jogged, *is the idea of sharing coffee and breakfast with Walt Jenkins so uncomfortable?* Because those situations always had a way of leading back to her childhood and her upbringing and her parents and her brother, and Avery didn't have it in her this morning to tiptoe through the land mines of her past and figure out what to divulge and what to avoid. She had already managed to share more about herself with Walt than she had with any other man in recent memory, and wasn't sure it was a good idea to offer any more.

In a perfect world—or even just a normal one—Avery would have relished the opportunity to sleep late while lying in bed with a man she found fiercely attractive and more than a little endearing. Walt had shared with her a part of his own past that was riddled with betrayal and secrets. Their histories were so very similar that it would have been a perfect opportunity to share her own scars. If Avery's life bore any semblance of normal, she would have sunk her head deeper into the crook of Walt's shoulder earlier this morning and draped her arm over his chest. Instead, she tiptoed out of his hotel room, and cringed in the hallway when the latch clicked loudly as she tried to silently close the door.

In the end, she stopped the self-analysis and chalked it up to *Avery being Avery.* This was her life and she was stuck with it. Besides, whether she was up for the whole morning-after routine or not was immaterial. This particular morning she had no time. While Walt lay in a postcoital coma the previous night, Avery's mind had drifted back to Victoria Ford. Even during the review of the Cameron Young file and the potential flaws she found, Avery had been unable to stop thinking about Victoria Ford's manuscripts and their connection to Natalie Ratcliff.

She grabbed her phone just after midnight and, on a whim,

sent out a text while Walt softly snored next to her. She hadn't expected a reply so late on a Saturday night—especially on a holiday weekend. But it had taken only a few seconds for Livia Cutty, New York's chief medical examiner and the doctor Avery had met with when she first arrived in New York, to text back. Avery had questions about some of the forensics noted in the Cameron Young case and needed to pick Livia's brain about them. She had other questions, too, about things completely unrelated to the case file she and Walt had paged through, but the forensics would be a good place to start.

She put in three miles, just enough to get a good sweat and burn her lungs, and used the walk back to the Lowell as a cool down. Showered and dressed, Avery grabbed two coffees from Starbucks and hailed a cab for Kips Bay. She saw Livia standing in front of the entrance to the medical examiner's office when the cab pulled to the curb. Avery paid the fare with cash, climbed out of the cab, and handed Livia a coffee.

"Black, two sugars."

"Thanks," Livia said in a questioning tone. "How did you know how I like my coffee?"

"Last time we were together, when you were out in LA, we grabbed coffee with Mack Carter."

"That was two years ago."

"I know. I have a weird thing with coffee."

"Impressive. Thank you."

"Thank *you* for taking time on a Sunday morning, especially over a holiday weekend. And sorry to text you like a lunatic in the middle of the night. I was in a weird place."

"No worries. I was up. I'm on call this weekend, and bored to death. The Fourth is a notoriously slow time at the morgue. No one really dies when the city is so empty, which sounds like a good thing unless your life revolves around people dying. Besides, some of our strangest thoughts and ideas come in the middle of the night. I'm curious to know what's on your mind."

Avery was curious, as well. A revelation *had* come to her, and she needed Dr. Cutty to confirm it.

"Let's head inside," Livia said.

Avery followed Livia through the front entrance of the Office of the Chief Medical Examiner. It was Sunday morning and the building was dark, other than the scattered overhead lights that remained permanently aglow. Livia touched her ID card to the sensor in the lobby to unlock the door. Inside, they rode the elevator to the bottom floor where Livia again scanned her card key to gain access to the long corridor that led to her office. She flicked the wall switch when she walked into the windowless office.

"Have a seat," Livia said. "So what did you find out about Victoria Ford that had you up so late at night?"

Avery sat in one of the chairs in front of the gunmetal desk. She pulled a single page from her purse and handed it to Livia. She had taken it from the Cameron Young file before sneaking out of Walt's room earlier. It was the crime lab's analysis of the DNA found at the crime scene.

"It turns out Victoria Ford was involved in a high-profile murder investigation in the months before she died. My story about her has taken an unexpected turn from her remains being identified to the details about the homicide investigation. I need some help with some specifics about it."

"The woman identified was a suspect in a murder?" Livia said.

"She was. And I've managed to hook up with . . ." Avery stopped herself and shook her head. ". . . To get in touch with the detective who ran the investigation. We've been reviewing the evidence and I'm having trouble with the blood that was found at the crime scene."

"What sort of trouble?"

"Well, I'm stuck on it. I'm working hard to figure out if there's another explanation of the crime scene. If there's any chance things happened differently than how the prosecution presented them. My biggest issue is that droplets of blood recovered from the scene were matched to Victoria Ford through DNA analysis. I need to know how accurate the science is that made that match."

"Very," Livia said. "A specific DNA sequence is sequestered from the blood and then, in a normal investigation, matched against DNA samples taken from the suspect—usually through an oral swab. If the DNA profiles match, it's as accurate as it gets. Statistically, the science is just about one hundred percent."

Avery slowly nodded her head as she considered Livia's words. The fact was that the blood at the crime scene belonged to Victoria. This would be the biggest problem with the theory that someone else had killed Cameron Young, and she could see no way around it.

"The science likely came out at trial," Livia said. "DNA evidence and the science behind it are challenged when it's done badly or if there is even a chance that it's less accurate than normal. If the blood had been contaminated, for instance. Or, if it was not preserved correctly. Was any of the DNA evidence challenged at trial?"

"That's just it," Avery said. "The case never *went* to trial."

"Why not?"

"Because the chaos of September eleventh marked the unofficial end of the case."

"So the investigation was closed?"

"Not formally. It just sort of went away because after 9/11 the main suspect was dead and the case was not pursued. America started chasing terrorists."

Avery's mind returned again to the previous day when she skimmed through Victoria's lost manuscripts. Finally, she looked at Livia.

"The other thing I texted you about," Avery said. "Were you able to find anything out about it?"

"Yes," Livia said. "I called Arthur Trudeau earlier this morning and he told me where to look. It's in the bone-processing lab. Grab your coffee."

Avery followed Livia through the dark hallways until they came to the lab. Livia swiped her card key and the red light on the lock turned green as she opened the door. She flicked on the lights and headed toward a bank of computers lining the far wall. The monitors were dark until Livia sat down at one of the stations and jiggled the mouse. The computer screen woke and brightened with the OCME logo. She logged in and clicked through the screens.

"The identification of Victoria Ford was made on May eighth. It'll take me a second to get back there."

Avery stood next to Livia as she scrolled through the screens.

"Okay," Livia said. "Here we go."

Avery bent over Livia's shoulder and scanned the screen.

"It looks like the specimen was collected from North Tower debris on September twenty-second of 2001."

"Does it tell you more about the original specimen?" Avery asked.

"I'm looking. Let's see . . ."

A few more screens clicked past and then some more scrolling.

"Yes. Here are the original notes on the specimen. Small fragment measuring just three quarters of an inch long and badly charred at the time of recovery."

"That's tiny," Avery said.

"From what I know about the recovery efforts, this was not uncommon. Many tiny fragments of charred bone were recovered. It's really a miracle that from this minute fragment, DNA could be extracted." Livia went back to the report. "It goes on a bit about the damage to the exterior of the specimen—pathology jargon. And then, let's see." Livia pointed to the screen. "The forensic dentists identified the specimen as a central incisor or canine."

"Meaning what?" Avery asked.

"It was a tooth."

"A tooth? From the rubble of the Twin Towers, a tooth was recovered?"

"Yes. We have over five hundred individual teeth here at the crime lab waiting to be identified. Some were recovered as part of a jaw and skull, but many more were single teeth."

"How could a single tooth be salvaged from the rubble of a hundred-story building?"

"Not in the way you're imagining. The recovery efforts in the early days and weeks after 9/11 *did* take place like you're thinking—OCME employees literally walked through Ground Zero and collected bodies and body parts from the rubble. That's true. And it was grisly work, from what I've been told. Many of those victims were identified quickly. But most of the remains the office still has stored today that are waiting to be identified are small bone fragments, and yes, many individual teeth. These small specimens were not recovered *at* Ground Zero, but instead through a sifting program that started a year after the towers fell. When construction and excavating machines cleared the debris from Ground Zero, it was loaded into trucks and transferred to a landfill in Staten Island. All the 9/11 debris was placed to the side in its own section of the landfill. That debris went through various stages of sifting. Think of it as panning for gold. From the rocks and rubble and construction debris, tiny artifacts were teased out. That's how so many personal items like wedding rings, jewelry, wallets, and driver's licenses have been recovered. It's also how small bone fragments and teeth have been found."

"That's amazing," Avery said.

Her mind was racing. Her ludicrous theory, as it echoed in her head, was sounding more plausible. Reading Victoria Ford's manuscripts had sent her thoughts tumbling down a dark rabbit hole toward a wild theory. Until this moment, she believed the idea was fueled by an offshoot of her imagination that constantly searched for the sensationalism her *American Events* stories needed. But the fact that the specimen used to identify Victoria Ford was a tooth not only made her theory realistic, but *possible*.

"Has Dr. Trudeau been able to locate any other remains that matched Victoria Ford?"

"No," Livia said. "The tooth was the only match to date. But the hope is that the new DNA technology will be able to get through the remaining unidentified bone fragments in the next few months. If more of Victoria Ford was recovered in the ruins of the Twin Towers, we'll know soon enough."

Avery suspected that, if her wild theory were correct, none of the other specimens salvaged from the Twin Towers would belong to Victoria Ford.

CHAPTER 42

Manhattan, NY
Sunday, July 4, 2021

He checked his watch and then glanced at his phone on the passenger's seat. He resisted the urge to text Avery. He'd woken this morning to find her already gone, vanished without a trace other than her scent on the pillow next to him. No note. No voice mail. No text. On a different morning or with a different woman, this would have confused or embarrassed him. Perhaps some of that still existed now, but he and Avery had plans to rip through the rest of the Cameron Young file later in the day, so Walt chalked up the disappearing act to Avery chasing down leads sniffed out during their initial review of the case. He was doing the same.

His and Avery's dive into the Cameron Young investigation had him curious, if not worried. Specifically because he knew the box of files sitting in his hotel room did not tell the full story. As soon as Walt woke, he called Jim Oliver and requested some federal bureaucratic pressure be applied to the US Attorney's Office in the Southern District of New York, who had up to this point refused to return Walt's calls. Walt found himself in a unique position of power. Jim Oliver needed Walt's skills in the delicate matter of locating Garth Montgomery, and now Walt needed Oliver's influence to find whatever additional information was out there on the Cameron Young case. Walt's curiosity had nothing to do with the investigation into Garth Montgomery, but he convinced Oliver that it was imperative to locate any lost evidence pertaining to the twenty-year-old case. Walt knew the US Attorney's Office possessed what he needed.

Calls were made, pressure was placed, and over a holiday weekend the right people were pulled from vacation to get it done. Walt had his answer, and locating the missing files was easier than he imagined. Originally confiscated from Maggie Greenwald's office—the DA who was set to prosecute the case—during the investigation into her misconduct, the US Attorney's Office had eventually shipped the evidence back to the BCI headquarters for storage.

As Walt pulled into the empty parking lot at just past 11:00 a.m. on Sunday morning, a wave of nostalgia came over him. He hadn't called the Bureau of Criminal Investigation his employer for twenty years. But he'd cut his teeth here, and the place held good memories. He relished them until he saw the lone car parked in front of the building. He knew it belonged to his old boss. Scott Sherwood was on his shit list.

Walt pulled into a parking spot and turned off the engine. He saw Sherwood standing in front of the BCI building, whose glass facade reflected his image back at Walt as if he were watching himself on a theater screen. He had now seen Scott Sherwood exactly twice in the last fifteen years. Today, and three weeks earlier when Sherwood crashed the survivors meeting at the Ascent Lounge with the sole purpose of figuring out where Walt was spending his time. The "accidental" meeting had given Jim Oliver just enough information to track Walt down in Jamaica and start him on his current course. He no more wanted to talk with Scott Sherwood this morning than he wanted a hemorrhoid removed.

"Walt Jenkins," Scott said with a huge smile as Walt climbed from his car. "Twice in one year. Go figure."

"Fuck off, Scott," Walt said, closing the door and walking up to his old boss. Illogical reasoning allowed Walt to be less angry with Jim Oliver for planting Sherwood at the survivors meeting than he was with Sherwood for going along with it. Perhaps it was because, as a former surveillance agent, Walt appreciated Oliver's cleverness in finding him. The truth was more likely that Walt was frustrated with himself for having taken the bait.

"What's gotten into you?" Sherwood asked.

"I'm not in the mood, Scott. I know our little *run-in* the other day was bullshit. You were a plant. Do you think I'm too stupid to figure it out?"

"Jesus Christ, settle down. The FBI came knocking on my door. They literally knocked on the front door of my house. Was I supposed to turn them away? Sorry, pal, I don't carry that kind of clout. Jim Oliver said he needed to figure out where you were holed up. Said it was important. I didn't know it was going to put you in a bind."

"It hasn't," Walt said in a dismissive tone. "I just don't like being played. Do you have what I need?"

"Yeah," Scott said. "I found it about an hour ago. Hidden way in the back of the evidence room. What's so important about it?"

"It's just an old case, Scott. I was asked to look into it; that's all I can tell you."

"Does it have to do with the Maggie Greenwald scandal?"

"I'm about to find out. Where is it?"

Scott pointed over his shoulder. "Inside. A single box. Looks pretty innocuous."

Scott Sherwood unlocked the door to the BCI headquarters and held it open for Walt to enter.

"Does this mean the invitation to visit you in Jamaica is rescinded?"

"It means it never existed, Scott."

Two hours later, Walt was sitting in his suite at the Hyatt with a second evidence box resting on the table in front of him. He paged through it for fifteen minutes, reading carefully until he found what he needed. Until he found what he hoped wasn't there.

He picked up his phone. Avery hadn't attempted to reach out to him. He typed a short text and sent it off to her.

Found something new in the Cameron Young file. Need to talk asap.

CHAPTER 43

Manhattan, NY
Sunday, July 4, 2021

Avery's laptop sat open on the desk in the corner of her hotel room. The face of *American Events* executive producer and Avery's best friend, Christine Swanson, was on the screen linked through an online meeting app.

"What's going on?" Christine asked.

"You're going to think I'm crazy, but you're the only one I can share this with."

Avery watched Christine on the monitor as she analyzed Avery's hotel room. After her meeting with Livia Cutty, Avery had found a copy shop where she had each of Victoria Ford's manuscripts printed. Now, organized stacks of computer paper occupied the king-sized bed. On top of each stack rested a single paperback book.

"I told you about Victoria Ford's sister, Emma."

"Right," Christine said. "She had the recording of Victoria from the morning of 9/11. I can't wait to get my hands on it. We could do a lot of great stuff with it."

Throughout her time in New York, Avery had kept Christine up to date on her discoveries regarding Victoria Ford and Cameron Young. *Great stuff* meant Christine and her team would produce the hell out of the recordings, making them both chilling and suspenseful. Avery imagined a short clip of Victoria Ford's voice playing just before a commercial break, anchoring fifteen million viewers to their televisions in stunned silence.

"I know you'll make it amazing," Avery said. "But in addition to the recordings, Emma Kind also shared all this with me. Well, accidentally shared it." She motioned to the stacks of paper.

"What is all that?" Christine asked, leaning toward the computer camera so her face filled the entire screen.

"Victoria Ford's manuscripts."

"Meaning *books*?"

"Yes. Victoria was a writer."

"My notes say she was a financial planner."

"Financial planning was her day job. Emma told me Victoria always wanted to write books. It had been her passion since she was a young girl, and was probably what drew her to Cameron Young. But Victoria never found any success. She wrote all these manuscripts but never landed a publisher. I found them on an old flash drive in one of the dusty bins Emma gave me of Victoria's yearbooks and memorabilia. I printed them out earlier today. To the best of my knowledge these manuscripts have sat untouched and unread on that flash drive in Emma Kind's attic for the past two decades."

Christine nodded on the screen. "Okay? How is this related to the Cameron Young case?"

"I'm not sure yet. But here, look at this." Avery picked up one of the paper stacks.

"This is Victoria Ford's first manuscript. The Word document indicates it was written in 1997. Working title is *Hot Mess*. Now look at this," Avery said, placing the manuscript pages back onto the bed and picking up Natalie Ratcliff's paperback novel. "This is a novel published by Hemingway Publishing in 2005 by an author named Natalie Ratcliff."

"*Baggage!*" Christine said. "Peg Perugo. I love those books."

"So you're a fan. Then you're going to love this next part. *Baggage* was published in 2005—the first in the Peg Perugo series, which, as you know, is amazingly successful. One of the most successful series in commercial fiction."

Christine raised her eyebrows as she waited for Avery to continue.

"*Hot Mess. Baggage.* Similar titles, right?" Avery asked. "Similar meanings, anyway."

"Sure."

"So here's the catch. Besides a change in title, the two stories are identical."

There was silence as Christine stared from the computer screen.

"What do you mean *identical*?" she finally asked.

"I mean Victoria Ford's manuscript became the first book Natalie Ratcliff published in the Peg Perugo series."

Christine shook her head. "One hundred percent not following you."

"Natalie Ratcliff was Victoria Ford's best friend. They roomed together in college and stayed close after they graduated. Natalie went to medical school and practiced emergency medicine for eight years. Victoria entered the financial world and started her own career. The whole time, Victoria was writing books hoping someday to publish one of them."

"Yeah, still not following you."

"Victoria died in 2001. For the next four years, Natalie Ratcliff practiced emergency medicine until her first book was published. It took the world by storm and she retired from medicine. That was in 2005. She's written fifteen novels in fifteen years. But here's the problem," Avery said, walking over to the bed where Victoria's other manuscripts were stacked in neat batches, each with a Natalie Ratcliff paperback on top.

"Every one of these piles represents one of Victoria's manuscripts—manuscripts that have sat untouched in Emma Kind's attic for the past twenty years. Each one also happens to be published as a Natalie Ratcliff book."

Christine squinted her eyes. "So you're suggesting that Natalie Ratcliff got a hold of Victoria Ford's manuscripts and plagiarized them, word for word, after Victoria died?"

"No, I don't think so. Emma said Victoria was extremely protective of her work and didn't let anyone read her manuscripts. Emma has never read any of them. Not even Jasper Ford, Victoria's husband, was allowed to see them. Victoria was too insecure to let anyone read them."

"Then how did her work end up in the pages of Natalie Ratcliff's novels?"

"That's where you're going to think I've gone mad."

"Too late," Christine said. "Just spit it out at this point."

"I've spent the weekend reviewing the case against Victoria Ford. It was flawed, no doubt. And I think I can poke some serious holes in it that will intrigue the *American Events* audience. I have more research to do on that front, and plan to go through the rest of the case later today. But despite whatever holes I'm able to find, at the time of the original investigation the hard evidence against Victoria was solid. DNA evidence put her at the scene. The media had all but convicted Victoria in the court of public opinion. There was no doubt that she would be indicted and arrested, and that a trial would follow. One that, based on the evidence Victoria knew about at the time, would have likely ended in her conviction."

"Okay," Christine said. "Again, what do these manuscripts have to do with it?"

"Victoria was in a dire situation. She knew the evidence pointed to her. And she knew, on the morning of September 11 when she met with her attorney, that it was only a matter of time before she was arrested. She knew that she would likely be convicted. According to my interview with Victoria's attorney, he laid out the grim prognosis for her that morning. Then, in the middle of Victoria's meeting with her attorney, the first plane struck the North Tower . . ."

Avery walked over to the desk where her laptop stood. She sat down in the chair and looked at Christine. "And with that plane, an opportunity presented itself."

"An opportunity to do what?" Christine asked.

"To disappear."

CHAPTER 44

Manhattan, NY
Sunday, July 4, 2021

Avery spoke the words with confidence. She knew Christine wouldn't believe that someone would fake their own death and disappear. But Avery had personal experience with someone disappearing to avoid indictment and prison, and she knew it was possible. Desperate people are capable of anything, and often find ways to convince the people who love them most to help.

"Disappear, meaning?" Christine asked.

"Meaning Victoria used 9/11 to solve all her problems."

"You're saying what, exactly, Ave?"

"What if Victoria Ford didn't die that morning?"

"I'm sorry, Avery. I love you and we've been on some wild rides together, but this one might be too crazy for me to jump aboard."

"Just hear me out. She was sitting in Roman Manchester's office when the plane hit the tower. I know this from interviewing Manchester, who, along with twelve of his employees and two of his partners, made it safely out of the North

Tower. *He* lived to tell his harrowing story of escaping the towers. Is it too far-fetched to believe the woman sitting across from him that morning also survived?"

Avery saw the first glimmer of conviction in Christine's eyes, before she shook her head.

"But the medical examiner's office identified Victoria's remains. That's what sent you to New York in the first place."

"They identified a bone fragment that belonged to Victoria, yes. But I spoke with Livia Cutty this morning and we took a closer look into the discovery. The specimen used to make the identification was a tooth."

"A tooth?"

"Apparently the medical examiner's office recovered thousands of bone fragments from the ruins of the towers, hundreds of which were teeth."

"How is that even possible, Ave?"

"By filtering through the debris. Over the years, several sifting projects have been completed. The goal of these operations is to tediously sort through the rubble cleared from Ground Zero in order to find artifacts. Each time a sifting program is completed, more items are discovered. Wallets, driver's licenses, wedding rings, jewelry, bone fragments, and . . ."

"Teeth."

"Hundreds of them."

"Good Lord."

"Livia Cutty tells me that most of these small bone fragments and teeth are still waiting to be matched to victims. So, if Victoria Ford was identified from a single tooth found in the rubble of the Twin Towers, and no other specimens have been matched to her . . . What if Victoria Ford was injured during the chaos of 9/11, as in, she lost a tooth, but still managed to escape the towers?"

When Christine failed to respond, Avery continued.

"Thousands died when the towers collapsed. But thousands more made it safely out of the buildings. What if Victoria was one of them?"

"How? The hospitals were flooded that day. She never sought medical attention?"

"Maybe she didn't need it," Avery said. "And if it were something as minor as a few broken or lost teeth, maybe her friend—who was an emergency medicine physician—helped her."

"Natalie Ratcliff."

"Exactly," Avery said, standing up and walking over to the bed where Victoria's manuscripts rested. "And in a crazy way—yes, a bat-shit-crazy, Avery-Mason-presents way—I think Victoria's manuscripts prove it."

Christine shook her head. "I'll say one thing. Your flare for the sensational is unparalleled. Make the connection for me."

"Before I interviewed Natalie Ratcliff, I bought a couple of her books so I could skim through them. One of them, *Baggage*, hooked me and I read the whole thing. When I met with Emma Kind a second time, she pulled a bunch of old boxes out of her attic. They were filled with things from Victoria's childhood, and I planned to sort through the boxes to see if any of those things were useful for the documentary. To see if any of those items would help me paint a fuller picture of Victoria Ford. In one of the boxes, I found the flash drive that contained Victoria's manuscripts. As soon as I started reading the first one, I noticed the similarities to Natalie Ratcliff's first novel. I went back to the bookstore and purchased Natalie's entire backlist and started skimming them."

Avery pointed to the bed where a Natalie Ratcliff novel rested on top of each of Victoria Ford's manuscripts.

"According to Emma, Victoria wrote five manuscripts. Each of those manuscripts ended up becoming a Natalie Ratcliff novel. Not just a similar storyline, but a verbatim text. It was in Victoria Ford's lost manuscripts that Peg Perugo was born."

"Couldn't the explanation be that Victoria shared her manuscripts with Natalie Ratcliff at some point before her death? Maybe to get a friend's feedback? Then, after her friend died, Ratcliff took the manuscripts as her own? And, out of all this"—Christine pointed at the bed—"the only crime committed was plagiarism?"

"Except that Emma Kind swears Victoria didn't share her manuscripts with anyone. Like I said, not even her husband."

"Okay," Christine said. "You've hooked me. Let's take Victoria Ford's sister at her word. No one ever saw Victoria's manuscripts. That explains the first five Ratcliff books, which represent the five manuscripts Victoria wrote before 9/11. Where did the next ten Ratcliff books come from?"

Avery took a deep breath. "What if Victoria survived the morning of 9/11? She made it out of the North Tower just like thousands of others. She was injured in the process and sought the help of her best friend, who was a physician. Then, as the enormity of events materialized that morning, a thought came to her. What if, in addition to watching one of the most infamous events in American history unfold, Victoria Ford was also watching the opportunity to make her impossible situation go away? She'd already made the calls to Emma. The recordings were proof that she was in the North Tower. Then she asked Natalie, not just for help with whatever injuries she sustained, but to help her disappear. Wherever Victoria is today, she's still writing manuscripts and sharing them with Natalie Ratcliff."

"Wow," Christine said. "That's definitely Avery Mason-esque. But . . . I mean, it's been twenty years. How has an ER doctor and her best friend, a financial adviser, managed to keep this quiet for so long? And how did they pull it off in the first place? Where would Victoria Ford be hiding for twenty years?"

"I haven't figured that out yet, but that's where I need your help." Avery smiled at Christine. "You didn't have plans for the Fourth of July, did you?"

"I work for Avery Mason and *American Events*," Christine said. "My personal life always comes last."

"I can't tell if you're saying that proudly or with a chip on your shoulder."

"Little bit of both. Tell me what you need. I'll do my best."

CHAPTER 45

Manhattan, NY
Sunday, July 4, 2021

Walt was perspiring and the flow of blood through his throbbing carotid was audible inside his head as he walked through the front entrance of the Lowell Hotel on Sunday evening. He carried with him the cardboard box Scott Sherwood had fished from the cobwebbed corners of the BCI evidence room. The front desk clerk smiled as Walt checked in. The woman called up to Avery's room to let her know she had a guest. The clerk nodded her go-ahead, and Walt headed toward the elevator. He stopped at a dispenser to gulp down a glass of iced lemon water, noticing his hand's tremor as he lifted the glass to his mouth. He was either out of practice as a surveillance agent for the FBI, or he knew somewhere inside that what he was about to do was wrong.

In the elevator he pressed the button for the eighth floor. The silver doors closed and reflected his image back at him. He noticed his forehead was covered with beads of sweat and felt his shirt stick to his back. Just prior to the doors opening, he wiped his forehead with his sleeve. He exited the elevator and walked down the hallway, stopping at room number 821. As he knocked, he remembered the question he had posed to Jim Oliver on Friday night. *On what pretense would I end up in her hotel room?*

And now, here he was, the day after they'd slept together, standing outside her room with ill intentions of recording her private conversations. He wiped his forehead one more time, patted the breast pocket of his button-down to feel the small, flat, brushed metal box Jim Oliver had left for him. The door opened and Walt lowered his hand from his pocket.

"Hey," Avery said.

Walt swallowed hard. "Hey."

An ear-piercing concussion of silence followed their high-school-type greeting.

"I, uh, missed you this morning," Walt finally said. "Sorry if I was comatose."

"No," Avery said, shaking her head. "I snuck out."

"Oh. Okay."

"I needed a jog."

"Yeah. Makes sense. I'm just glad, you know . . . everything's okay."

Avery closed her eyes momentarily. "I had an immature moment of panic. I should've told you I was leaving. Look, Walt, if you haven't already guessed, I'm not the greatest at this. And I'm mortified to admit that it's been . . . quite a while since I've been in this sort of situation."

"I'm not sure that's something to be mortified about. And the same is true for me. I've been hiding in Jamaica for three years. Plus, I'm twice divorced, so I'm no better at this than you are."

Avery moved her hands back and forth between them. "Then can we agree that this greeting has been awkward enough? Let's just get back to normal?"

"Done." Walt held up the box. "We've got a lot to cover."

"Good. Come on in."

Walt followed Avery into the room. It consisted of a king-sized bed and, on the far end near the windows, a coffee table in front of a small sofa, as well as a desk and chair.

"Ignore the mess," Avery said, motioning to the bed, where stacks of papers stood in distinct piles on top of the comforter.

"What's all this?"

"Research."

"Looks like you've been busy."

"You too," Avery said as she sat on the sofa. "What did you find?"

Walt sat next to her and placed the box on the coffee table.

"It's a long story. But I made some calls and managed to track down some more files on the Cameron Young case."

"In addition to what we went through last night?"

"Yeah. This was stuff only the DA had. I want to show you something."

Walt reached into the box and riffled through the folders until he found the one he wanted. He placed it on the table and opened it. Inside were photos of Victoria Ford from her initial interview with detectives. Walt fingered through them so they spread across the table.

Avery leaned closer to the photos. "What am I looking at?"

"These are photos of Victoria Ford during our first formal interview with her. They were taken two days after Cameron Young was killed when we brought her into BCI headquarters to question her."

"Intake photos?"

"Yes."

Intake photos were counted as evidence and taken of potential suspects in the early hours and days of an investigation. They were meant to document the presence of wounds, cuts, or bruises a person of interest may have had on their body that would suggest they had been in a recent struggle or altercation. The photos on the table showed Victoria in her bra and underwear. The first showed her standing with arms bent at ninety degrees, as if surrendering at gunpoint. Another captured her in a wide stance, feet shoulder length apart, and her arms straight out to the sides, crucifix style. Other photos were close-ups of her shoulders and neck. The photo Walt pointed to was of Victoria's hands, posed with her fingers spread apart.

"I don't see anything," Avery said.

"Exactly. Your argument last night about the lack of blood on the rope got me thinking. How could Victoria have cut herself badly enough to drip so much blood on the carpeting, but leave no trace of blood on the rope?"

Avery slowly moved her gaze back to the photos of Victoria's hands. "She didn't cut herself."

"It doesn't look like it, and you're looking at the proof. These photos were taken two days after the murder. There's no way a wound would heal that quickly."

"So where did the blood come from?"

"It's a very good question," Walt said. "One that I don't have the answer to."

CHAPTER 46

Manhattan, NY
Sunday, July 4, 2021

Avery continued to look through the pictures. "Where did these photos come from? Why weren't they in the original file?"

"That's the other thing I wanted to talk to you about. Something's been bothering me ever since I dove back into the Cameron Young case and stirred up the memories of that investigation."

"What is it?" Avery said.

"When I was tapped to investigate this homicide, I was young. I wasn't dumb, but I was inexperienced in running a homicide investigation. I was well trained and had been part of other homicides for the BCI, but never as the lead detective. The Cameron Young investigation was my first solo case. And, even looking back now, I don't think I would change much. My job was to present the evidence I found to the district attorney's office. I didn't offer opinions or speculation. I just followed the evidence and then turned it over. I was good at procedure. Find the evidence, log the evidence;

get the warrants, apply the warrants. I did everything by the book.

"What I was bad at were the politics involved in our criminal justice system. The DA was a woman named Maggie Greenwald. She had a reputation as a fierce prosecutor who was on the rise. She was aggressive, demanding, and had political aspirations far beyond the district attorney's office. Rumors had her pegged for the next attorney general or governor. But to get that kind of shot, and gather the support needed to forge a serious run, she needed to make headlines as the DA. Headlines come from quickly resolving cases. And if a high-profile case comes your way, even better. Maggie Greenwald was all over the Cameron Young case from the very beginning and wanted things done quickly. She chose me to run the investigation. I was handpicked and quite proud of it. And I took the responsibility seriously."

"Roman Manchester, Victoria Ford's attorney, told me that Maggie Greenwald had a knack for . . . how did he put it? Fitting square evidence into round holes."

"I didn't know that about her at the time she tapped me to run the Cameron Young investigation. I found that out only after I left the BCI to join the Bureau. She got herself into a little trouble."

"She was disbarred for suppressing evidence, so it was more than a little trouble."

Walt nodded. "One of her biggest convictions got overturned when new DNA evidence was found. The defendant had served years in prison. And it wasn't just *new* evidence that surfaced. It was evidence that had been there from the beginning. Greenwald suppressed it. The only reason the truth came out was because her ADA grew a conscience and blew the whistle on her."

"She withheld evidence?"

"Yes."

"How could she live with herself knowing that she put an innocent man in prison?"

"Prosecutors, some of them, believe the deck is and always has been stacked against them. They see guilty defendants getting off on technicalities. They see rock-solid cases go the other way because of reasonable doubt, despite how *unreasonable* it sounds to them. So, some of them try to even the playing field."

"By lying? Or hiding evidence?"

"Sometimes. And Maggie Greenwald was determined to make a name for herself. Since the whistleblower came forward, some of her biggest cases have been overturned after evidence was found that had been suppressed. The US Attorney's Office from the Southern District of New York got involved and began a formal investigation. They subpoenaed all her cases and all her records. They found four other cases where she tried to make evidence disappear, or where she withheld evidence during discovery. It was enough to get her disbarred and end her career, legal and political. The Innocence Project and other wrongful conviction advocacy groups have taken up all of her convictions and are taking a hard look at them."

"Victoria Ford wasn't one of them?"

"No," Walt said. "First, Victoria was never formally convicted, so there's nothing to overturn. And second, sadly, without a conviction no one really cares about it."

"I care."

"I know you do."

"And Emma Kind cares."

"I know that, too. And she's lucky to have you digging through the case. I just wanted to give you the full picture as to why the files I showed you yesterday didn't tell the whole story. This box"—Walt pointed at the table—"had been in the DA's possession until the US Attorney's Office subpoenaed all of Greenwald's files. They took a hard look at each of them, but passed on digging into the case against Victoria Ford. The Southern District of New York shipped this box back to the BCI, where it has sat for years. And now, as I root back through the details, I can't help thinking that for such a high-profile homicide, I was tapped early on to run the investigation. Maggie Greenwald requested me. At the time, I was honored. I thought I'd made such an impression that she picked me for my talent. But a little time and perspective tells me that maybe she picked me because I was young and green, and because she could manipulate me in ways another, more experienced detective would not have allowed."

"You didn't do anything wrong, Walt. You followed the evidence, and no one can fault you for that. You didn't plant evidence. And you certainly didn't suppress it. The crime scene you found led to Victoria Ford. Not by hunch, not by speculation, but by forensically backed evidence. You didn't make any mistakes. You didn't manipulate the evidence."

"No. But I'm wondering if *I* was manipulated. This case went up in smoke after 9/11, and when the dust settled, everyone had moved on. Soon after, I was recruited into the FBI and I never really put much thought into it after that. But now, twenty years later, with the things you and I have uncovered, I'm starting to wonder if a dead woman was branded a killer when, in fact, she was innocent."

The narrative that twenty years earlier an aggressive district attorney had focused on the wrong woman in the death of Cameron Young was starting to play out in Avery's mind. She had no way to prove who *had* killed Cameron Young, only that there was a very realistic possibility it was not Victoria Ford. Avery knew her viewing audience would salivate over every detail. And things were about to get even juicier.

Walt gathered the files and the photos and returned them to the box.

"There's one more thing I came across in this box of lost evidence," Walt said, holding up a plastic evidence bag. It held a thumb drive.

"What is it?"

"The sex video of Cameron Young and Victoria Ford."

CHAPTER 47

Manhattan, NY
Sunday, July 4, 2021

"It's been twenty years," Walt said, holding up the evidence bag. "But I still remember it vividly."

"I've got to see it," Avery said.

"You sure?"

"I'm sure. I need to see if any of it can be aired in prime time."

"From what I remember, you'll need to blur most of it out."

"I've got a really good technical crew and an even better producer."

"Grab your laptop."

Avery retrieved her laptop from the desk where she had positioned it earlier in the day for her meeting with Christine. She rested it on the coffee table in front of where they both sat on the sofa. Walt placed the drive into the port and clicked open the file. The video started.

"Oh, God," Avery said as Cameron Young's naked backside materialized on the screen.

"I told you you'd have to blur most of it out."

Avery continued to watch until Victoria Ford appeared on the screen. Avery pinched her eyebrows together when she saw the dominatrix outfit, complete with a dangerous-looking spiked necklace and wristbands. Victoria's naked breasts poked through the holes of the leather suit she wore.

"How many times have you seen this?"

"Just once," Walt said. "And only part of it. Once we identified Victoria Ford, I left to interview her."

Avery sat in stunned silence as she watched Victoria Ford pace back and forth next to her vulnerable prey. Avery had trouble reconciling the woman Emma Kind had described, and the one whom Avery had heard on the answering machine recordings, with the woman she saw in the video. Her breath caught when she saw Victoria bring up the tasseled object in her right hand.

"What is that?"

"I believe it's called a flogger whip," Walt said. "That whip, or a similar one, is what caused the violent welt marks on Cameron Young's body that were noted in the autopsy. Should I turn it off?"

"No. So this is how you figured out they were having an affair?"

Walt nodded. "Yes. From the paraphernalia found at the crime scene we knew Cameron Young was at least having a single night of dangerous sex. His wife claimed during my initial questioning of her that she and Cameron had never participated in any type of S and M sex. Discovering the video allowed us to zero in on Victoria Ford as his lover."

Avery cocked her head to the side as she watched the screen and voyeuristically spied on Victoria and her lover. "Where did this video take place?"

"In Cameron Young's writing studio."

"Why is it so off-centered?"

On the monitor, the action took place in the far right-hand

side of the shot, as if the camera were pointed slightly in the wrong direction.

"I don't know," Walt said. "Maybe they didn't have good producers like you. It's a homemade sex tape, not a cinematic production."

On the screen, Victoria Ford slapped the whip against her lover's back and shoulders. To Avery, it looked more playful than violent. She watched Victoria move down Cameron's body and tap him again with the whip, this time on the buttocks and upper thighs. Then, she stopped.

"Wait a second," Avery said. "Rewind it."

Walt looked at the screen. "The video?"

"Yeah. Rewind it a bit."

Walt ran his finger over the mouse pad and clicked the reverse arrow until the movie ran backward for a few seconds.

"There," Avery said.

She watched the screen as Victoria brought the tasseled whip down across Cameron Young's backside. About to strike again, Victoria instead stopped and walked forward where she bent down to place her ear by his mouth.

"Play that part again and turn the volume up," Avery said.

Walt rewound again and increased the volume. This time, when Victoria brought the whip down, the muffled voice of Cameron Young could be heard. The word he spoke was difficult to make out, but as soon as he uttered it Victoria lowered the whip and bent down to speak to him.

"What did he say?" Avery asked.

Walt shook his head. "I couldn't make it out."

He reversed the video again and they both leaned forward to listen more carefully. The whistle of the whip preceded a stinging *thwack*. Then Cameron Young spoke the single word.

Cinnamon.

"Cinnamon?" Walt said. "Did he say *cinnamon*?"

"He did," Avery said.

"What the hell does that mean?"

Avery looked over at Walt. "It's their safe word."

Walt raised his eyebrows.

"Couples who partake in BDSM sex create a safe word—a random word they utter whenever things are getting too rough or dangerous. As soon as the word is spoken, the game is over."

On the monitor, Victoria Ford crouched down next to Cameron Young, dropped the whip on the floor, and unbuckled the restraints that held his wrists to the bottom of the boarding horse. A moment earlier, she was delivering what Avery interpreted as playful punishment. But one slash of the whip had gone too far and they quickly ended things. Now she was rubbing his back.

Are you okay?

Victoria's voice came through loudly from the speakers. Too loudly, as Walt had maxed out the volume a moment earlier trying to capture Cameron Young's muffled voice. He quickly turned the volume down. On the screen, Cameron Young climbed off the apparatus and he and Victoria walked off screen. A door could be heard opening, likely the bathroom. The video played on in silence.

"He got spooked," Avery said. "It looked pretty innocent until that last strike with the whip. It went a little too far."

Walt sat back on the couch, rubbing a hand over his chin. Finally, he looked at Avery. "So their role-playing had limits."

"It appears that way. Which doesn't jive with the crime scene and the violent whip marks noted on Cameron Young's body."

Avery and Walt continued to stare at the monitor. The spanking horse sat in the otherwise empty shot of the studio. Victoria and Cameron had disappeared a few seconds earlier.

"Why didn't they stop the video when they were done?" Avery asked.

"What do you mean?"

"They were supposedly creating a sex tape to watch back later for their own kicks. But when things went too far and the fun ended, why didn't one of them stop the camera?"

The screen suddenly went black. Avery noticed the confused look on Walt's face as he leaned over and tapped the mouse pad to rewind the video to the spot where Victoria and Cameron walked off screen. He pointed to the timer on the bottom of the screen and then fast-forwarded the video until just before the screen went blank.

"Sixty seconds," he said. "Exactly sixty seconds."

"What's that mean?" Avery asked.

"Motion activated cameras are triggered when the sensor detects movement. They continue recording as long as motion is detected. When the movement stops triggering the sensor, the camera shuts off after sixty seconds."

Avery looked over at him, and then it hit her. "That's why the shot was off centered. They didn't know they were being recorded."

CHAPTER 48

Manhattan, NY
Sunday, July 4, 2021

They both needed a break after watching the video of Victoria Ford and Cameron Young. Avery stepped into the bathroom to freshen up after Walt suggested they find a proper bar that served proper drinks. It wasn't the video that had him thirsting for alcohol, but the conclusions they had made during the viewing. Watching the video today, far removed from his role as lead detective on the case, and without the enormous pressures he felt at the time to find answers, it was easy to see that the video had been recorded in secret. It was easy to see that neither Victoria nor Cameron knew they were being recorded.

Walt lifted the plastic evidence bag that had contained the thumb drive and read the writing scrawled across it, indicating the date and time the evidence had been logged. The label on the bag also included the location where the thumb drive had been found—in the desk drawer of Tessa Young's office at the Catskills mansion. Why, Walt wondered, would Cameron Young make a sex video of himself and his mistress and then keep it in his wife's desk drawer?

Combined with the other problems he and Avery had un-covered about the case, the revelations they made about the video were enough to make him believe he'd gotten his first homicide investigation terribly wrong. Was it worse that the accused was dead rather than in prison? If convicted and in-carcerated, at the very least there was hope that some sliver of justice could still be served by bringing the new evidence forward and attempting to overturn the conviction. In this case, though, there was no way to provide Victoria Ford with justice. Posthumous exonerations were as valuable as a win-ning lottery ticket one day past its expiration date.

Walt pulled the thumb drive out of the computer and dropped it back into the evidence bag. Then he suddenly re-alized that with Avery in the bathroom, two hours after he'd arrived at the Lowell, he was alone in her hotel room. He still sat on the small sofa with Avery's laptop open on the coffee table in front of him. He looked around the room. He exam-ined the bed where the stacks of Avery's research rested in separate piles. He noticed a paperback novel on the top of each pile of paper. On the desk near the window was another heap of papers. Next to the laptop on the coffee table were pages containing the details of the Victoria Ford identifica-tion.

Walt reached for his breast pocket. This time he did not just feel for the small, thin box that was there, he removed it and held it in his hand. His heart rate picked up. Simply holding the listening devices caused a visceral reaction in-side him. The past three years of his life had been tormented by deceit. By the ravages of loving a woman who had kept secrets from him and betrayed him in a way that was nearly unforgiveable. As he stared at the listening devices, he won-dered if he were any better than Meghan Cobb. His gaze roamed the room, moving from the nightstand that held the telephone and alarm clock, to the closed bathroom door, and back to the coffee table in front of him. As the analytical part of his mind calculated the most strategic places to secure the listening devices—one under the lip of the nightstand, one under the coffee table, and one in the bathroom in case Avery used her cell phone there—some other part of his mind screamed for him not to do it.

Walt took a deep breath, rubbed the back of his neck, and set the metallic box on the edge of the coffee table. He was lost in conflicted thought when he noticed the postcard among Avery's research. It looked to have been ripped to shreds and then painstakingly taped back together. The pieces mostly fit, at least to return continuity to the postcard, but the edges were poorly opposed and uneven. He lifted it off the table and inspected it. A short message was written on the back of the card:

To the one-and-only Claire-Voyant,
Just hanging out and watching the Events of America.
Could use some company.

On the bottom of the card Walt saw three numbers scrawled innocuously. Almost as if they were an afterthought:

777

Walt flipped the card back over to inspect the front. Pieced together and taped over was a picture of a wooded cabin set among trees whose leaves had been turned ginger by autumn. The handle of the bathroom door clicked. The noise startled him and the postcard slipped from his grip and fell to the floor. Its momentum took it under the couch. Before he had a chance to retrieve it, Avery appeared in the vestibule outside the bathroom.

"You ready?" she asked.

Walt stood quickly. "Yeah."

His heart pounded and the perspiration returned to his forehead. As he walked across the hotel room and toward the door, he passed Avery and headed out into the hallway. She closed the door behind them and checked that it was locked.

"You want to head back to the Rum House?" she asked.

Walt nodded. "Sure. Sounds good."

They stepped into the elevator and Avery pressed the button for the lobby. As the doors closed, Walt again saw his reflection in the clear metal. It was then that he realized he'd left the thin metal box, and the listening devices it held, on the edge of the coffee table.

CHAPTER 49

Manhattan, NY
Sunday, July 4, 2021

A two-man band—pianist and violinist—played in the corner of the bar. After they ordered drinks Avery headed over to put in a request. Walt sat alone at the bar sipping a Worthy Park single estate reserve and contemplating the predicament he'd found himself in. It felt like weeks, not days, since he'd sat in this tavern and met Avery Mason for the first time. Back then he was anxious to get back in the saddle of an operation, get his mind off the wallowing thoughts of Meghan Cobb's betrayal, and work his way out of the funk of self-pity and anger he was in. When he sat in this bar on Tuesday night, Walt was excited to have been tapped by the Bureau to play such an important role in a case that had stumped them. That Jim Oliver had gone to such lengths to find and recruit him had given Walt a sense of purpose. A sense of being needed. It was a feeling that had been absent from the past three years of his life. Now, he couldn't help but make the comparison to when he was a twenty-eight-year-old kid tapped to run a high-profile homicide investigation. The thought crossed his mind that he was being manipulated today in much the same way he had been twenty years earlier. He'd fallen for the romanticism of it all—a delicate case, a top target, and the glory that would come from a successful operation. That he'd have to put his ethics aside and quell any moral objections that arose was simply part of the job, Jim Oliver had convinced him. And now Walt had gone and made a goddamn mess of things. He was sleeping with the woman who was under his surveillance. Worse than that, he was feeling something for her.

The crushing burden of guilt had sat heavy on his shoulders on the walk over from Avery's hotel. Walt worked hard to convince himself that he had not slept with Avery out of any hell-bent effort to obtain information from her. It was spontaneous and unplanned. It had happened in the heat of the moment. *But that was then and this is now,* he thought. The way the rest of tonight had to play out put him in knots. He'd left the listening devices on the coffee table in her hotel room, and had no choice but to return there to retrieve them. Once there, the inevitable would likely follow. It would be then that Walt Jenkins, in his own mind, would have crossed the line.

On top of his guilt was a combination of curiosity and confusion about how his relationship with Avery could end in anything other than disaster. He was on an operation sprung by the Federal Bureau of Investigation and choreographed to intentionally set his life on a collision course with Avery Mason, aka Claire Montgomery, the express purpose of which was to deceive her into believing he was interested in her story about Victoria Ford. All the while, his true goal would be to burrow his way far enough into her personal life so that he might find a scrap of evidence that would shed light on the whereabouts of her father. The entire scenario begged the question of whether Walt was any better than Meghan Cobb.

"Now there's a man lost in his thoughts."

Avery's voice snapped him back from his trance.

Walt smiled at her. "Just zoning out."

Avery opened her eyes excitedly and placed a finger to her ear as the two-man band began to play "The Weight," by The Band.

"I just requested this."

"Great song," Walt said, turning to look over his shoulder at the musicians. "I've never heard it played with a violin. Sounds good."

Avery took the stool next to him. "What were you thinking about?"

A loaded question, Walt thought. He spun his glass a few more times before answering.

"The strange road of life," he finally said. "I was thinking about how we each came to this place in our lives. Sitting with each other here in this empty city."

Avery took a sip of vodka. "*Strange* is one word for that road. Really . . . *screwed up* would be a better descriptor, though."

"Your road is that bad?"

"Not bad, just complicated," Avery said. "I was supposed to be a lawyer for my father's firm. Being on television was never part of my five-year plan."

"Really? How did the *American Events* thing happen?"

"By accident."

Walt noticed her pause, as if she were about to say something before thinking better of it. He felt a sudden urge to tell Avery everything he knew about her, everything he had learned from the dossier Jim Oliver had delivered to him. He wanted to tell her that he knew all about the Montgomery family. That he knew her mother and brother were dead, and that her father had disappeared while under federal indictment. That he knew everything about her past, and that she didn't need to go through the painful process of sharing it with him or figuring out what not to tell him. That he wasn't the person she believed him to be, but something worse. Before any of his thoughts formed to words, Avery spoke again.

"Your story about Meghan the other night got me thinking that you and I have a lot in common."

"How so?"

"We both ran away. You just did a better job of hiding than I did."

Walt said nothing, just waited for her to continue.

"You've been in New York for what? A week now? Have you called her? Does Meghan know you're in town?"

This conversation had taken a sudden turn Walt hadn't expected.

He shook his head. "No."

"Why not?"

"I'm not ready to call her."

"What are you running from?"

"What are *you* running from?" Being pressed on his relationship with Meghan had brought an edge to his voice. He was about to apologize when Avery spoke.

"Ever heard of Garth Montgomery?"

Walt had never been a strong poker player, and bluffing was not his forte. He was sure the shocked look on his face when Avery mentioned her father's name had not gone unnoticed. Still, he did his best to recover.

"The Thief of Manhattan?"

"Shit," she said with a laugh. "I forgot about that nickname. But, yeah, that's him."

"What about him?"

"He's my father."

Walt blinked a few times but couldn't think of a reasonable question to ask.

"Claire Montgomery is my actual name. Claire *Avery* Montgomery. When I moved to LA to write for the *Times*, I used *Avery Mason* in my byline. It stuck."

Walt shook his head. "Start from the beginning."

"After my father was arrested and indicted, I had to get out of New York. On top of stealing billions of dollars from innocent people, my father also had a second life with another woman. I don't know what I hate him more for. To think the man who used to call me *The Claire-Voyant One*— the nickname he gave me for my supposed ability to see through his bullshit—had a secret life away from his wife and kids was a betrayal worse than anything he could have stolen."

Walt's mind flashed to the shredded postcard patched together with Scotch tape he had found in Avery's room. The message on it had been addressed to *the one-and-only Claire-Voyant.*

"I knew my law degree was worthless. No reputable firm was going to hire Garth Montgomery's daughter. So I fell back on my journalism degree. I moved to California and took a job at the *LA Times.* I broke a big case about a missing kid in Florida, and it got a lot of attention. I was invited to appear on *American Events* to tell the story. Mack Carter and I hit it off. Soon, I was guest hosting once a week covering other missing persons stories and the like."

"As Avery Mason."

She nodded. "I found my niche with a strange combination of morbidly fascinating cases and the inspirational."

"Like the lady who crashed into the lake and managed to save her four kids."

Avery smiled. "You really are a fan of the show."

Walt nodded. He waited for her to continue.

"Last summer, Mack Carter died while on assignment and HAP News tapped me to take over. I agreed because there was no way I could turn the opportunity down. It's been a year now, and there have been lots of stories about my success after taking over for one of America's most beloved newsmagazine hosts. I found myself in this sort of whirlpool

I couldn't get out of. No one's made the connection to my father yet. But sooner or later, someone will."

Avery lifted her vodka.

"So that's what I'm running from."

"No one knows about your father?" Walt asked.

"People know. I spent twenty-nine years as Claire Montgomery, creating a life and laying down roots. I'm still very much *Claire Montgomery*. I've heard from plenty of friends and former classmates who watch the show. The network sends my checks to *Claire Montgomery*. It's a common enough name that no one important has made the connection yet. But it'll happen. At some point, it'll happen. The only reason it hasn't yet is because my popularity is too new and came too quickly. If you add up all the people who know me as Garth Montgomery's daughter you might come to, what, a couple hundred? A thousand? Do we each *personally* know a thousand people? The *American Events* audience who knows me as Avery Mason is fifteen-million strong."

"So what happens when it comes out?"

"I don't know. Maybe nothing. Maybe I lose it all. I just finished my first full season as host of *AE*. There hasn't been a lot of time for my past to come out. But the reality is that I can't hide nearly thirty years of life."

"Why would you? You don't need to hide anything. So you have a shitty father—join the crowd."

Avery laughed. "Mine's shittier than most. And infamous."

"So what? None of it was your fault. None of his sins are a reflection on you. You're an investigative journalist who has a wildly popular show. Why are you hiding anything?"

"I didn't plan to hide anything. Not really. This whole thing happened so fast that I haven't had time to right the ship."

"So get out in front of it. That's how these things are handled and put quickly to rest. That this part of your past exists is not the problem. Hiding it is."

"I plan to. Get out in front of it. But . . ."

Walt waited. "But what?"

He saw Avery hesitate, and sensed she was choosing her words carefully.

"But what?" he asked again.

"But I have a few things to take care of first."

CHAPTER 50

Manhattan, NY
Sunday, July 4, 2021

It was 9:30 P.M. when they left the Rum House. Their next destination was not discussed, but they headed back toward the Lowell. As they walked, they heard a pop behind them, turned, and saw the cascading streaks of an arching firework far off in the distance. The fireworks display was staged near the Brooklyn Bridge and set off from barges on the East River. A pinwheel rocketed into the sky and expanded into a burst of brightness. The subtle boom came a second later, delayed by having to travel halfway up the island of Manhattan to reach them. They stood quietly and watched for a minute. Walt felt Avery take his hand and intertwine her fingers with his. After a few minutes they turned and headed to Avery's hotel.

When they reached the front entrance, Avery tugged and he followed her inside. The elevator deposited them on the eighth floor. Walt felt his shirt begin to stick to his back again, and preemptively blotted his forehead with the back of his hand. He followed Avery down the hallway and stood behind her as she unlocked the door. Following her through the entryway, he spotted the thin metal box on the edge of the coffee table. To him, it was as obvious as if another person were standing in the room waiting for them.

"Make yourself comfortable," Avery said. "I'll be right out."

As soon as the bathroom door closed Walt exhaled, allowing his shoulders to relax and his chin to drop to his chest. He hurried over and grabbed the box. If he planned to plant the bugs, now would be the time to do it. It took him only a fraction of a second to decide against it. He would not allow Avery's private conversations to be recorded. Jim Oliver could go to hell. He dropped the box into his pocket just as Avery walked from the bathroom.

He checked his watch. "You know what? I think I'm going to get going."

Avery walked over to him and put her hands on his chest. She kissed his lips, and all the guilt and apprehension Walt had felt earlier in the night evaporated. He pulled her close so their hips touched, then he lifted her off her feet and carried her a few paces until they fell onto the bed. The pages of Victoria Ford's manuscripts flew like confetti into the air. Neither noticed.

CHAPTER 51

Manhattan, NY
Monday, July 5, 2021

They jogged the trails through Central Park on Monday morning. When they had woken thirty minutes earlier, the awkwardness from the previous morning was gone. Avery had felt no need to sneak out. Instead, she had leaned over his sleeping body and whispered in his ear.

"I need a run."

Walt slivered an eye open. "Is that your way of making me leave?"

"No, I just don't want you to think I snuck out again. Want to come with?"

"I'll have to grab shorts and shoes from my hotel."

"Central Park. Meet you at Columbus Circle in twenty minutes."

As they jogged now Avery could see that the paths were more congested than they had been over the weekend. Tuesday would mark the return to normal, and before long the city would be as crowded as always. A tinge of melancholy soured her stomach. The past weekend had felt like some sort of oasis that belonged to just her and Walt—it had started with dinner at Keens and was, sadly, ending this morning. In addition to reviewing the Cameron Young case, they had shared painful secrets about their pasts. Aside from Connie Clarkson, Walt was the first person Avery had discussed her father with. He hadn't seemed stunned or scared or appalled or any of the other reactions Avery imagined people having when they found out who her father was. The truth, Avery finally understood, was that Walt's reaction was *normal.* Her father's crimes were not a reflection of who she was.

They ended their run at 9:00 a.m. and each headed back to their hotel to shower and change. Avery arrived at the restaurant first and was seated at a table for two on the outdoor patio. She sipped coffee and scrolled through her phone. Christine Swanson had gotten back to her on the research Avery had asked her to do on Natalie Ratcliff. Christine believed in only two modes of communication—text messages or face-to-face meetings. And so, when Avery checked her phone she found it filled with foot-long texts from Christine containing links to articles and stories about Natalie Ratcliff, her husband, and his wealthy family, along with Christine's own commentary. As Avery scrolled, she learned that Natalie Ratcliff wrote books for the pure joy of storytelling, not due to any fiduciary obligation to support her family. Her in-laws more than had life's finances covered. The Ratcliffs owned and operated the second largest cruise line conglomerate in the United States, the fourth largest in the world. But unlike the other behemoths in the industry, Ratcliff International Cruise Lines was privately owned with no outside money.

Avery scrolled through the texts and found a link to *Forbes* magazine's 2019 list of wealthiest Americans. The Ratcliff clan held several spots. Natalie Ratcliff's husband,

Don, was worth $1.4 billion and the posh apartment at One 57 suddenly made more sense to Avery. Natalie's father-in-law, and the longtime CEO of Ratcliff Enterprises, held a healthy $3.5 billion net worth. Avery looked up from her phone, took a sip of coffee, and contemplated her far-fetched idea about Natalie Ratcliff and her friend, Victoria Ford. As she mulled the possibilities and worked to connect the dots, she spotted Walt walking along the sidewalk toward the entrance of the restaurant. Out of his running shorts and sweaty shirt, he wore khakis and a dressed-up T-shirt. He had the build of a man who kept himself in shape, and she noticed again how attractive he was. Not for the first time this weekend, Avery wondered what the hell she was doing.

"I'm sorry?" the waitress asked.

Avery, suddenly aware that she had spoken her thoughts aloud, cleared her throat. "Oh, nothing. Sorry. Actually"— Avery turned over the coffee mug opposite her—"my . . . breakfast mate just arrived."

Breakfast mate?

The waitress smiled and poured from a carafe of coffee she carried. Avery emptied two cream containers into Walt's coffee and stirred as her mind continued to run. She had come to New York to procure a falsified passport from the man she had been put in touch with named André. The only person— she was told—who could be trusted for such a task. André didn't have the greatest bedside manner, Avery had been warned, but she should trust him explicitly, and listen to anything he had to tell her. She had come to New York under the ruse of chasing the story of Victoria Ford. Both projects were now in full swing and would command much of her concentration. And yet here she was, starting a relationship with a man who lived in Jamaica and who came back to New York once a year to exorcise the demons that still haunted him from a previous relationship. If there was ever a playbook for failure, Avery was following it. Still, she couldn't stop images from the previous night from flashing in her mind. She quickly shook the memories away as she watched Walt walk onto the outdoor patio. He smiled when he spotted her.

As he sat down across from her, Avery removed the spoon from his coffee mug. "Two creams, no sugar," she said.

Walt's face carried a curious look. "Good guess. But what if I took my coffee black?"

"You don't."

Walt looked at her with a creased forehead.

"It's a weird thing with me. I pay attention to other people's coffee habits. I saw two empty creams on the coffee bar in your hotel room on Saturday. Sugars were untouched."

Walt slowly nodded. "Very creepy, but I sort of like it."

The waitress came and they ordered breakfast.

"Streets are getting full," Walt said, looking at the people who walked past the outdoor café, and the traffic in the street.

"I know. It's sort of sad. The city sort of felt like it belonged to just the two of us for the last couple of days. Now everyone's coming back to intrude."

"We accomplished a lot. And now that our weekend *is* over, we need to figure out where we go from here. This is your project, Avery. I just agreed to provide access to the case files. But we've poked some serious holes in the investigation, and now I feel an obligation to do more. I want to reach out to some people and discuss what we've found. I'm not sure where that might lead, but the Cameron Young case is technically still open. A district attorney or a congressman or a senator somewhere might care enough to put some resources into it. I can work my contacts and see if anyone is willing to listen."

"That would be great. I appreciate anything you can do. And Emma Kind will be thrilled. But despite everything we've uncovered this weekend, I can't get past the fact that Victoria's blood was found at the scene. No matter how many holes we poke in the investigation, or how many other potential suspects we come up with, her blood is a hard obstacle to overcome. Whether we try to get the case reopened, or if I just cover it on *American Events*, the blood is an issue.

"I spoke with Livia Cutty yesterday morning to ask about the science behind DNA evidence. She said that if the blood at the crime scene matched the DNA sample taken from Victoria's mouth swab, it's her blood. One hundred percent, or very close to it. So we might be able to prove that Victoria didn't cut herself with the knife, but that doesn't disprove that the blood at the scene belonged to her."

"You know," Walt said, "I was suspicious this weekend, but I'm convinced this morning. There's something we're missing, and I think I know someone who might be able to help us find it."

"Who?"

"Uh, let's call him an old friend. I tracked him down and he's agreed to meet me. I'm heading there after breakfast."

"About the blood?"

"And a couple other things. Let's chase our leads for a couple of days and touch base later in the week? See what we each come up with?"

"Perfect," Avery said. She needed a little time and space over the next couple of days. In addition to her suspicions about Victoria Ford and what she had just read about Natalie Ratcliff's family, she needed to head back to Brooklyn to see if André had come through on the passport.

After breakfast, she allowed Walt to walk her back to her hotel. Although she couldn't identify what it was, something felt different. Maybe it was the slowly filling sidewalks and the sense that the mass of people coming back to the city were stealing the tranquility she had found over the last couple of days. Or maybe it was the uncertainty about how she and Walt would continue after they finished working together.

Whatever it was, she felt uneasy after she kissed Walt good-bye and walked into the Lowell. She stepped into the elevator and pressed the button for the eighth floor. As she waited for the doors to close, Avery saw Walt on the sidewalk outside. He lifted a hand and waved to her just as the elevator doors came together and reflected her image back at her. An eerie feeling rippled from the pit of her stomach, strange and foreign. She tried to chalk it up to the reality that their weekend was over. An hour later, though, she still couldn't suppress the feeling that something was wrong.

CHAPTER 52

Manhattan, NY
Monday, July 5, 2021

Walt drove through the Queens-Midtown Tunnel and across the East River. Forest Hills was a small community in Queens where he had tracked down the man he was looking for. Walt was not only surprised that Dr. Jarrod Lockard—the pathologist who performed the autopsy on Cameron Young—remembered him, but that the doctor was eager to meet. Twenty years before, Jarrod Lockard was known as the Wizard for his ability to take apart a corpse and magically find the clues it left behind. Walt imagined the doctor now, two decades later, as a stooped-over elderly man who lived alone, never able to marry because so many of his days had been spent so close to death that meaningful connections to the living were impossible. The pit of Walt's gut buzzed with nervous butterflies at the prospect of seeing the Wizard after so many years, but he could think of no one else who could better answer the question he had formed while reviewing the lost Cameron Young files.

He drove along Austin Street and through the center of

town, passing Tudor-styled buildings that lined the quaint shopping area. He turned down a quiet side street and found Dr. Lockard's home—a two-story, half-timbered structure that looked well maintained. He parked in the driveway and walked to the front door, where he rang the bell and wiped his sweaty palms on the sides of his khakis. When the door opened, Walt felt like he was in a time machine. Jarrod Lockard had not changed from Walt's memory of him. The man still sported a head of wild white hair that looked impossible to tame even for the most experienced hairdresser. If this feature embarrassed the doctor, it didn't show. Somewhere in his seventies now, the man's face carried the same cavernous folds that curved like parentheses around his lips and accentuated jowls that drooped like melted frosting.

"Dr. Lockard. Walt Jenkins."

Dr. Lockard's lips twisted subtly, the closest he ever came to smiling. Walt remembered how none of the detectives at the BCI had ever been able to read Jarrod Lockard's mood. His facial expression never veered far from stoic and carried a perpetual look of attending his mother's funeral.

"Detective. It's been a while."

Dr. Lockard offered his hand. Walt took it nervously, remembering that shaking hands with Jarrod Lockard was like squeezing a wet sponge.

"Twenty years," Walt said.

"They look to have treated you well."

"You too." Walt released his grip. "You honestly look the exact same."

"So when we worked together two decades ago, I looked like a seventy-year-old man?"

"No," Walt said, coughing and choking on an errant bolus of saliva. "I meant . . . you look . . ."

Dr. Lockard stared at him without speaking.

"Good. That's all," Walt said, looking for a way out of the awkward reunion. "You look good."

"Was there something on your mind, Detective?"

"Yes. An old case we worked on together."

The doctor nodded. "Come in."

Walt followed him into the house.

"Have a seat," Dr. Lockard said when they entered the kitchen.

The house felt quiet and empty and eerie.

"Can I get you something to drink? I've got coffee still warm."

"That would be perfect," Walt said.

Jarrod Lockard poured two cups of coffee and sat with Walt at the kitchen island.

"What is it that you need my help with?"

Walt took a sip of coffee and felt Dr. Lockard's stare on him. He tried hard to control the irrational nervousness that came from sitting in the man's kitchen.

"Do you remember the Cameron Young case?"

Dr. Lockard shrugged. "Cameron Young. My favorite dead author. I remember some of it. But that was a long time ago, and I've been retired for a decade now. I have trouble remembering where I left my slippers."

About to refresh the doctor's memory, Walt startled when a black Burmese cat hopped onto the kitchen island, appearing suddenly as if it had been conjured from thin air. It slunk along the far edge of the counter, its back arched and its tail straight up like a snake about to strike. Jade-green eyes glowed from the depths of the cat's jet-black face, with vertical slits for pupils staring at Walt as if he was trespassing.

"Walt," Dr. Lockard said, reaching for the cat. "Where are your manners?"

Walt looked, slack jawed, from the cat to Dr. Lockard. "You have a cat named *Walt*?"

Dr. Lockard ran his hand over the cat's back as it purred softly. "Purely coincidence, Detective. I've never married, so in lieu of companionship I have a house full of cats. There are only so many names."

Walt shifted his gaze around the kitchen, imagining other feline eyes staring at him from the shadows.

Dr. Lockard looked blankly at Walt as he continued to pet the cat. The edges of his lips eventually curled again into the subtlest of smiles. "I'm fucking with you, Detective."

Walt stayed still for a moment, confused. "Your cat's not named after me?"

"No. This is Mortimer. He's the only cat in the house and I can't stand the goddamn thing." Dr. Lockard lifted the cat off his lap and dropped it onto the ground where it hissed before scurrying off. "My wife and I are watching it for our daughter, who's away for the Fourth of July holiday. But she's picking the furry thing up this morning. Any minute, in fact. So stop sitting there like a prom queen who shit her dress, and spit out what it is you need, Detective, before my grandchildren swarm this house. Because I won't be able to talk about dead authors from twenty years ago after they arrive."

Walt finally smiled.

"I'm not as scary as you think, Detective. But my wife hates when I talk about old cases, so let's get this show on the road."

"Got it," Walt said, reaching into the breast pocket of his sport coat and pulling out a piece of paper.

"I'm reviewing the Cameron Young case."

"Why?"

"It's a long story. *American Events*, the television show, is planning to produce a documentary about the case. I'm consulting on the project and came across something I need your opinion on." Walt laid the piece of paper on the counter and pointed at it. "I found this forensics report . . . well, not hidden, exactly, but not made available at the time of the investigation."

The doctor squinted his eyes as he looked at Walt. "Who was the prosecutor?"

"Maggie Greenwald."

"Oh, say no more. Square Peg Maggie. She had a knack for making evidence disappear."

"Unfortunately. And this case, because of the unusual circumstances, was not one that came under the scrutiny of the Southern District during their investigation of Maggie Greenwald. But I managed to get my hands on it and I can't figure out a few things I came across."

Dr. Lockard pulled the page close to him and lifted his chin to see through his bifocals.

"Victoria Ford's urine and blood were discovered at the crime scene. The urine was found in the unflushed toilet; the blood was on the carpeting. DNA analysis confirmed that both the urine and the blood belonged to her. But the forensic report has me confused."

"How so?" Dr. Lockard asked.

"The report shows that the urine contained a high level of ammonia, and that the blood had a series of chemicals in it."

"Chemicals?"

Dr. Lockard began to read the report.

"Yeah," Walt said. "Listed in trace amounts in the blood were styrene, chloroform, glyphosate, and triclosan. What are they, and are they usually found in blood samples?"

Dr. Lockard shook his head as he continued to read. "No. Those things are not naturally found in blood."

"How about the ammonia in the urine? Is that normal?"

"No."

"So where did it come from? And what are the chemicals in the blood?"

Dr. Lockard ran his tongue over the corners of his lips. The Wizard, Walt thought, had been conjured.

Dr. Lockard blinked a few times. "The ammonia is easy. Urea breaks down into ammonia after twenty-four hours. So the urine collected from the toilet was more than twenty-four hours old."

Walt considered the timeline. Cameron Young's body was in the early stages of rigor mortis, and had been hanging for much less than twenty-four hours.

"What about the chemicals in the blood?" Walt asked.

"Let's see. Styrene is a chemical used to make rubber and plastic products. Chloroform is a solvent and general anesthetic. Glyphosate is, I believe, a pesticide. And triclosan is an antibacterial and antifungal agent."

"If the blood at the crime scene belonged to Victoria Ford," Walt said, "and we can forensically prove it did, why would she have all those chemicals in her system?"

"She didn't," Dr. Lockard said.

He stood up and walked to the kitchen nook to grab his laptop. He returned to the island, opened the computer, and began tapping on the keyboard. Walt looked at the monitor just as Dr. Lockard finished typing into the search engine. Walt saw the query:

Chemicals found in tampons

Dr. Lockard nodded, pointing at the monitor. "The styrene came from the plastic applicator of a tampon. The chloroform is an anesthetic because, you know, women push babies out of their bodies but corporations don't believe they're tough enough to handle a tampon. Glyphosate is a pesticide used in cotton crops that, sadly, finds its way into cotton tampons. And finally, the triclosan is used as a preservative to prevent contamination."

Walt hesitated as he, too, stared at the monitor, trying to make sense of it.

Dr. Lockard turned from the screen and looked at Walt. "If I were involved with this case, more than simply performing the postmortem exam on the victim, the chemicals found in the crime scene blood, as well as the ammonia in the urine, would raise some serious red flags."

"Red flags for what?"

"That the urine was badly preserved before being placed in the toilet, and that the blood had been harvested from a tampon and planted at the scene."

CHAPTER 53

Manhattan, NY
Monday, July 5, 2021

It was approaching 6:00 P.M. when Avery rode the elevator up to Natalie Ratcliff's apartment and was again met by the author when the doors opened.

"Avery, good to see you again."

"Hi," Avery said. "I didn't think you'd finish so fast."

"I've been done for a day or two. Come on inside."

Avery followed Natalie into the apartment. She had called Natalie after breakfast to ask if she had finished writing the chronology of her relationship with Victoria Ford.

"I wasn't even sure you'd be in town. The city was eerily empty this past weekend," Avery said.

"I know. I actually came back to the city from our Lake Norman house for that exact reason. I'm behind on a deadline and there are too many distractions there. The empty city was a godsend. It kept me focused on my manuscript all weekend because there was nothing else going on."

"I hope my request didn't put you more behind."

"Not at all. I enjoyed putting it together. It was like taking a stroll down memory lane recounting my friendship with Victoria."

Natalie walked through the French doors of her office. Avery again saw Natalie's books arranged on the built-in shelves. Natalie came back out of the office and handed Avery a folder.

"That's a point-by-point overview of my relationship with Victoria, ever since we first met as college freshmen. I hope it answers all your questions and provides some insight into who she was and what a dear friend she always was to me."

Avery took the folder and opened it. Inside were several typed pages.

"Thank you for doing this. It will certainly go a long way to showing my audience who Victoria was. Together with everything Emma has provided, I should be able to paint a complete picture of her. In the fall, are you willing to give a full interview? My team would be with me then and we'd be recording and producing it for *American Events*."

Natalie nodded. "For sure."

"Excellent. I don't want to take too much of your time," Avery said. "So thank you again."

"Of course."

As they walked toward the door, Avery spoke. "I read that when you get to the end of each manuscript, you head to Greece for a month to finish it up."

This bit of information had been provided by Christine in one of her many text messages. The sudden change in subject matter appeared to catch Natalie off guard, which was Avery's point.

Natalie slowly nodded. "That's been my routine for many years, yes."

"How close are you now?"

"To what?"

"To finishing your latest manuscript?"

Natalie smiled and released what Avery interpreted to be a nervous laugh. "Not close enough."

"But you'll be going soon? To Greece?"

"I hope to, yes."

"To Santorini, actually," Avery said in a casual way meant to let Natalie know Avery had been doing some digging. Actually, it was Christine who'd done the digging.

"You have a villa on the small island of Santorini, don't you?"

Natalie gave another nervous laugh. "I try not to talk too much about my private life, or about where I own homes. Some of my readers are . . . let's just say they're very interested in the specifics of my life and I try to stay as private as possible."

Avery nodded. "Understood. I have viewers that are the same way. I'd never release any of that information about your home in Santorini. I was just curious for my own reasons, about whether you'll be visiting there soon."

Natalie smiled. "Yes. I'll be going to Santorini to put the finishing touches on my latest manuscript."

"Why Santorini?"

Avery saw that Natalie became even more uncomfortable now.

"I mean, I'm sure it's beautiful. But so are Napa Valley and Lake Tahoe and a thousand other places. You know, to get away and write a book. Didn't Stephen King finish *The Shining* at a hotel in Colorado?"

"I'm not sure where Stephen King does his writing."

"I'm just wondering what's so special about Santorini? It sounds so far away and so remote."

Natalie shrugged. "It's just where I've always gone. I wish there were a better story behind it."

"Maybe your muse is there?" Avery asked in an offhanded way. She looked back down to the folder and the history Natalie had created about her relationship with Victoria. Eventually, Avery looked up and made eye contact with Natalie.

"Did you know that the medical examiner identified Victoria from a single tooth?"

Avery watched the shock register on Natalie's face.

"Can you believe that?"

There was no answer.

"From the rubble of the Twin Towers, a single tooth was recovered. I didn't believe such a thing could be possible at first, until the methodology was explained to me."

Avery paused a moment but held Natalie's gaze without blinking.

"Nothing else, though. No other specimens were discovered that belonged to Victoria. No other bone fragments. No portions of her jaw. Just that one tooth."

Avery smiled and looked back down at the folder.

"Anyway, I just found it interesting." She held up the notes. "Thanks for the history. I'll let you get back to your writing. Good luck finishing your manuscript."

"Thank you," Natalie said, her voice shaky and hesitant.

"Emma gave me some boxes that contained a bunch of Victoria's old keepsakes. I found a flash drive that had all of her manuscripts on it. Lost manuscripts stored in an attic for two decades."

Natalie cocked her head to the side and feigned a smile. "Is that right?"

"Emma told me that Victoria didn't share her manuscripts with anyone. Not Emma. Not even Jasper. No one, in fact, has ever read them before. So I was a little hesitant to read them myself. It felt like I was intruding on her privacy."

"Did you?"

"Did I what?"

"Read any of her manuscripts?"

"Oh, all of them. They're really good."

Avery turned and opened the door.

"They remind me a lot of your writing."

Avery waited for a reply. When none came, she walked out into the hallway and headed for the elevator.

CHAPTER 54

Manhattan, NY
Tuesday, July 6, 2021

It was just past 8:00 A.M. on Tuesday morning when Avery took the elevator to the lobby, cut across the marble floor, and pushed through the front door. The valet had her Range Rover parked out front with the engine running. Avery climbed in and pulled away. The streets were crowded. Taxis beeped, cyclists darted through traffic as they transported their packages, and a steady stream of pedestrians filled the sidewalks. The long weekend was over and the city had taken back its role as the financial capital of the world. The relaxed and welcoming looks Avery had received on her run through Central Park Sunday morning were replaced by stoic expressions of those on the way to work.

The sun was low and bright when she made it to the George Washington Bridge, and it filled her rearview mirror until she made it into New Jersey and headed north on Palisades Interstate Parkway. Smooth reggae drifted from the car's speakers and was Avery's attempt to calm her nerves. On her mind was the postcard she had ripped to shreds months earlier before painstakingly taping it back together. She had somehow managed to misplace it since she arrived in New York, and she took the card's absence as an omen that what she was planning was about to go wrong.

She had told everyone—her agent, her friends at HAP News, Christine Swanson, Walt Jenkins, and even Livia Cutty—that she had come all the way across the country to chase the story of Victoria Ford. But this morning's drive was the real reason. In addition to her rendezvous planned for tomorrow with the German man named André, whom she had paid thousands of dollars to create a false passport, this morning's trip to the mountains was the reason Avery had come so far. It was the reason she had driven her Range Rover rather that purchased an airline ticket. It was why she had paid in cash for everything she had done on this trip, avoiding her credit card at all costs. She was nearly certain about what she would find, but needed confirmation before she proceeded.

The trip to Lake Placid took over four hours. Avery remembered the tortuous journeys from her childhood. It seemed like days, not hours, to get from the city to the mountains. But she also remembered the joy of finally arriving at her aunt's cabin. The lineage of the property's owners had been immaterial when she was a kid visiting the cabin for the last weekend of summer, just before school was to resume—an annual excursion the Montgomery family took each year to celebrate Avery's and Christopher's safe return home from sailing camp. It was their salute to the end of summer. Back then, Avery was more interested in swimming in the lake and swinging on the long rope attached to the branch of a sycamore tree that hung over the water. A thousand times over, that knotted rope had sent Avery and her brother off the edge of a rock and out into the lake, where they'd release their grip and splash into the water. Time at Ma Bell's cabin came only once a summer but represented significant real estate in Avery's memories because of the glorious time she and Christopher shared there with their cousins.

The cabin was not a Montgomery property. Had it been, it would be three times as large and perched on a lake ten times the size. The latest (and most expensive) trends in architecture would have replaced the cabin's rustic quaintness. A fleet of powerboats and jet skis would have lined the shoreline. Everything would have been ornate and overdone. It also would have been repossessed by the Unites States government, like every other property Garth Montgomery had owned. But Ma Bell's cabin was none of those things. It was simple and charming and far removed from anything Avery's family owned. It was an oasis from the glitz and wealth that followed the Montgomerys everywhere they went. The cabin held for Avery the same appeal as Connie Clarkson's sailing camp. Avery had never been happier than when she was tucked away for summer nights in cabin number 12 in Sister Bay, Wisconsin. She found the same joy each year when she visited Ma Bell's cabin in Lake Placid.

As a child, Avery never knew how she was *actually* related to Ma Bell. The road to get there was too complicated for Avery and her brother to ever explore. Ma Bell was the second cousin of Avery's uncle, and just far enough removed from the Montgomery bloodline to stay off the feds' radar. There was no direct link to the Montgomery family, and as soon as the postcard had arrived Avery knew where her father had been hiding. The three sevens written at the bottom of the postcard represented the cabin's address:

777 Stonybrook Circle, Lake Placid, New York

Welcome to The Sevens, Ma Bell used to say when they arrived each August. How long her father had been there, and in what kind of shape he was in, Avery had no idea. She only knew that she came this far for a reason, and she wasn't going to allow anything to derail her plans. Not her doubts, not her fear, and certainly not her goddamn conscience.

The mountain roads were as serpentine as she remembered when Avery meandered through the final leg of the journey. She slowed when she made the last turn. The road in front of her, which at its conclusion led to the cabin's driveway, was speckled with the morning sun and shadowed by the foliage of the forest around her. She drove to the end of the street and stopped. In front of her was the quaint, A-frame cabin sided with cedar and perched at the precipice of a hill that dropped off to the lake behind it. The driveway was unpaved, and the gravel was packed down in two ruts with a shallow mound of rocks between them. She saw a car parked at the end of the drive. She didn't recognize it. The mailbox, however, held the numbers of the cabin's address. When she came here as a child the three sevens were bright red and vibrant. Today they were ruddy and weatherworn.

There was motion inside the house. A figure passed in front of the window and appeared to pause for a moment. Avery noticed the curtains flutter and she imagined him peering carefully around the window's edge at the fire-red Range Rover stopped in the middle of the street. She almost pulled into the driveway. She almost parked behind the car and climbed the front steps to knock on the door. Almost. Instead, she turned right and pulled away. Speaking directly with her father had never been part of the plan. It couldn't be. But she had to come. She had to see the cabin again. She had to make sure. Confirmation was most definitely part of her plan. The rest, Avery could only hope, would work. She pulled a U-turn in the cul-de-sac and started her drive back to the city.

* * *

Walt Jenkins drove his unmarked government SUV, the keys to which Jim Oliver had handed him on his first night back in New York. He nearly pulled down Stonybrook Circle after he had seen Avery's red Range Rover make the turn. Instincts, however, told him not to. It was a good thing. After he spotted her vehicle stopped in the middle of the road in front of a gravel drive, she had turned around and come back his way. The winding, empty mountain roads did not make the best environment to tail someone.

He watched her turn and head back toward the city. Walt was happy to give her a bit of room. He turned onto Stonybrook Circle now and stopped in the same spot Avery's Range Rover had been a moment before. There was only a single, isolated home on this short stretch of road.

He resisted the urge to park on the shoulder and check the place out. That was not his job. He was on a surveillance operation and his goal was to collect information and pass it on to Jim Oliver. He used his cell phone to take a few photos of the A-frame cabin and the wooded area on either side of it. Then he twisted the steering wheel and pulled close to the mailbox, where he snapped a photo of the address. His mind quickly made the connection between the faded sevens on the mailbox and the numbers that were scrawled on the postcard he had seen in Avery's hotel room.

Walt dropped his phone on the passenger's seat, twisted the car around, and accelerated to catch up with Avery.

CHAPTER 55

Manhattan, NY
Wednesday, July 7, 2021

On Wednesday morning, one week since she met André Schwarzkopf, Avery sat on the F train and bounced toward Brooklyn for her second meeting with the mysterious man she had been put in touch with. The same ripple of worry that had originated when she watched Walt outside her hotel on Monday morning was back again now. This was the crux of the plan. Once she had the passport, everything else had a chance of working. Without it, there was no chance at all. She tucked her purse tight to her side as the subway rocked along the tracks. In her purse was the remaining cash for the purchase. She hoped for a quick exchange this time around. She imagined standing on the front stoop of the brownstone and ringing the bell, André opening the door and handing her the passport in exchange for the rest of the payment. Then she would be off and done with the shady business of procuring false documents. Other things would have to go her way for it all to work, but this was the next critical step in the arduous journey she had started long ago.

Despite an array of empty seats on the subway car, a man sat down in the seat next to her, trapping Avery between him and the window. He wore Bose headphones that barely muffled the music that blasted from them. She tucked her purse closer to her side. The man stared straight ahead and ignored her. The train made a stop and the sliding doors opened. A few passengers exited and were replaced by others who boarded. Avery thought for a moment of telling the man that she needed to exit the train, despite her stop in Brooklyn being thirty minutes away. Before she could muster the nerve, the doors closed and the train rocked back into motion. Music continued to blare from the man's headphones. A few minutes later the train slowed for another stop. The man reached into his backpack, which rested on his lap, and pulled out an envelope. He dropped it casually onto Avery's lap, never looking at her.

"Change of plans," the man said, staring straight ahead.

When the train stopped this time, the man stood abruptly. Before she could ask a question, he was up and through the sliding doors as soon as they opened. She watched through the window as the man pulled the backpack over his shoulders, walked through the turnstiles, and jogged up the stairs. Avery waited for the train to start moving before she picked up the envelope. It was not sealed. She slid the index card from within and read it.

> 9/11 memorial. North reflecting pool. Wait for me there.
> —André

Avery looked around the train wondering what was happening. The image of her making a fast exchange with André on the front porch of his brownstone was replaced now with images of her being arrested and placed in the back of a police cruiser, hands cuffed behind her. She looked up at the map to see where she was. The financial district was two stops away. She thought of calling the whole thing off and ending this nonsense. Of exiting the subway on the next stop and hailing a cab back to the Lowell. But that would mean ending the plan before it had a chance to work.

The train slowed and stopped. She stayed seated and watched the faces of the passengers exiting and entering the car. The doors closed and the train took off. Her right foot tapped away to expel her anxiety. When the doors opened at Fulton Street, she was up and out of her seat and hurrying out of the subway. She walked up the steps of the platform. The empty sidewalks she had known over the weekend were, indeed, gone, replaced now by hundreds of commuters and tourists.

She walked west on Fulton for three blocks, looking over her shoulder as she did, until she came to the 9/11 memorial. She passed the white oak trees that populated the memorial grounds. She stopped when she made it to the north reflecting pool, which occupied the footprint where the North Tower once stood. In its place was now a square hole in the ground lined by granite. Water cascaded elegantly down each side of the memorial and Avery took a moment to listen to its soft murmur. It was easy to hear because, despite the size of the crowd around her, everyone was silent. The tourists were overcome by a natural tendency for calm and respect at this sacred place where so many lives were lost.

Avery ran her finger across the names engraved on bronze parapets that rimmed the top of the reflecting pools. She moved along the perimeter, following the list of names. They were not in alphabetical order, she knew, but instead grouped together to represent whom the victims might have been with when they died. It took a few minutes before she found Victoria Ford's name. Avery traced her finger across the engraving and thought of all she had learned about the woman in the last couple of weeks. Lost for a moment in her thoughts, Avery did not notice the man standing next to her until he spoke.

"There's a food truck on Greenwich Street, one block over," the man said. "Order a Ruben with extra slaw, exactly that way."

The man wore sunglasses and a golf shirt tucked into jeans. He looked like any of the hundreds of other tourists taking in the sights.

"What's going on? Where's André?"

"Ruben with extra slaw. Got it?"

Avery nodded and the man was gone before she could speak another word. She wanted to follow after him, chase him down, figure out what was wrong. *Was* something wrong, or was this just how André did business? But instead she stayed where she was and continued to stare down into the reflecting pool. Her gaze moved back to Victoria Ford's name etched in the bronze. She slowly counted to sixty before she moved. Why sixty and not a hundred? Why wait at all and not just run to the food truck? So far out of her element, she had no idea of the answer to any of these questions, only an instinct that told her something was desperately wrong.

After a minute, she casually walked to Greenwich Street and found the food truck. She was fourth in line. The service was painfully slow and with each passing minute she felt her pulse rising. Her forehead and neck became beaded with perspiration. When she made it to the window, a man stood with a pencil at the ready, hovering it over a pad of paper.

"Ruben with extra slaw."

The man in the truck didn't hesitate. He wore a white apron. Reading glasses hung on the end of his nose. "Fries?"

"Uh, no," Avery said.

"Something to drink?"

"Just the sandwich. Ruben with extra slaw." She spoke the words slowly for the man to hear each syllable.

"Ten-fifty," he said, never once peering over his cheaters.

Avery hesitated before she paid the man, moved to the side, and waited for her order. A few minutes later, a plastic bag was dropped onto the shelf outside the second window of the food truck.

"Ruben, extra slaw," a woman yelled.

Avery walked over and retrieved her sandwich. She looked inside, just a quick glance. It was all that was needed. An envelope accompanied her Ruben. It took all her discipline to stop from reaching into the bag to grab it. Instead, she walked another block and sat on a bench before she opened the bag. She pulled out the envelope and opened it. Another index card.

Old St. Pat's Church. Walk. No subway. No cab.
—André

Avery looked up from the note. Her gaze moved around the sidewalk and street. No one, it seemed, was paying her any attention. Despite this observation, she still felt terribly exposed, as if unseen eyes were watching her. With her heart rate spiking and the perspiration rolling down to the small of her back, she stood from the bench and headed east on Fulton Street. When she reached Broadway, she turned left and started the two-mile trek north to Old St. Pat's Cathedral. It took thirty minutes.

The noon mass was comfortably crowded and well in

progress when Avery found a spot in the back pew. She sang with the parishioners. For thirty minutes she sat and stood and sat again, scanning the crowd for André. She stayed seated during communion. After the final blessing was offered, the church slowly emptied. She failed to recognize a suspicious face. If she were being followed, those who were on the prowl were invisible.

She sat in the back pew of the cathedral, the long center aisle to her left. Ten minutes after the service ended, a few patrons still occupied the church. Some knelt in the front pews, deep in prayer. Others walked the center aisle with necks craned heavenward, admiring the ornate cathedral ceiling and the splendid beauty of the church. A few people snapped photos.

Avery spotted him walking up the side aisle. André moved slowly and acted like the other tourists in the church, looking up at the ceiling and around the cavernous interior. He wore jeans and a sport coat. His midsection threatened to pop the single button holding the coat together. His beady eyes darted around behind the tiny wireless glasses, and Avery noticed a large manila envelope in his right hand. He entered the pew from the side aisle and walked the entire length of it until he sat next to her.

"What's going on?" Avery whispered.

"You're being followed."

"What? How do you know this?"

"You're blown in the worst way. Probably our mutual friend, as well, I'm sorry to say." The German-Brooklyn accent made his rapid speech difficult to follow. André placed the manila envelope on the pew between them.

"Everything's inside."

"The passport?"

André nodded and stood to leave.

"Who's following me?"

He pointed to the envelope. "Everything you need to know is there. Good luck."

"I still owe you money," Avery said.

André shook his head. "I owed him a favor. Let him know we're now even. And whatever it is you have planned, I'd do it quickly. I doubt you have much time."

André skirted past her and into the middle aisle. Avery twisted in the pew to watch him exit the church, walk down the steps, and disappear into the crowd. She sat unmoving for another minute until finally she lifted the manila envelope, resisted the urge to look inside, and quickly hurried out of the church.

It was a straight shot up Broadway near Old St. Pat's, then east to the Lowell. Twelve blocks that she power-walked in ten minutes. Through the lobby and into the elevator, all the while she clutched the envelope to her chest. It wasn't until she bolted and chained her hotel room door that she finally opened the manila envelope. Sitting on the edge of her bed, she fumbled with the envelope's button-and-string clasp. When she finally had the flap open, she poured the contents onto the bed. A blue passport tumbled onto the comforter. She examined it—it looked exactly like a US passport—blue exterior with gold embossed letters. She opened the front cover and saw the picture she had given André last week. She read the name aloud.

"Aaron Holland."

It had a delightful ring to it.

As much joy came from seeing the passport, something else sat in the pit of her stomach. She felt no relief having made it this far. She felt terror and dread, and couldn't stop the sensation that the manila envelope held her worst fears.

She dropped the passport back on the bed and looked into the envelope. She caught the reflection of glossy photos and reached in to retrieve them. Several eight-by-ten photos emerged from the envelope. Avery saw that each was a still photo of Walt Jenkins.

CHAPTER 56

Manhattan, NY
Wednesday, July 7, 2021

Avery sat at the small desk in her hotel room. The photos of Walt lay before her, scattered across the surface. Avery had carefully scrutinized each picture. As André indicated, they told Avery everything she needed to know. The first photo was of Walt in jeans, windbreaker, and ball cap. In the background were the headstones of Green-Wood Cemetery. He had followed her the day after their first meeting when she'd gone to visit her mother's grave. A second photo was of Walt crouching next to Christopher's headstone while he held a cell phone to his ear. The next was an image of Walt standing in the shadows between two brownstones in Brooklyn. Finally, there were photos of Walt sitting behind the wheel of his SUV, sunglasses covering his eyes, and Ma Bell's cabin in the background.

He'd followed her to André's brownstone. He'd followed her to the cemetery. He'd followed her out to Lake Placid. Some combination of disbelief, anger, and embarrassment befell her as she paged through the photos. Had she been so naive to believe that the United States government would

stop searching for her father? Had she believed that her amateurish attempts to fly under the radar on this trip to New
York would really deceive the Federal Bureau of Investigation? The feds had tracked her down in LA a couple of years
earlier and asked a slew of questions about her father. She
hadn't lied when she told them that she had no idea where
her father was. At the time, she didn't. Only after the postcard arrived had Avery figured it out.

Bile bubbled up her esophagus and deposited a bitter taste
in the back of her throat at the notion that Walt had slept
with her in order to gain information about her father's
whereabouts. More acid followed when she admitted that
she had allowed herself to feel something for him. Was she
such a poor judge of character to miss all the red flags? Was
she so desperate for companionship that she allowed his
story of betrayal to resonate with her own? Was that part of
Walt's past even true? Couldn't she see how convenient it all
was? That the detective in the Cameron Young case, now a
retired agent of the FBI, was so eager to help when she
called? Had her ego as a respected television journalist
clouded her reason?

"Dammit!" she shouted as she swiped the photos to the
floor.

Just then there was a knock on the door. She looked up
from the desk and froze. After a moment, another knock
came—three hurried taps. Avery quickly gathered the photos
from the floor, noticing that one had slid under the couch.
She stuffed them back into the envelope and then reached beneath the couch to retrieve the last photo. Coincidentally, or
perhaps an omen of the situation she had found herself in,
when she reached under the couch to retrieve the photo, she
also discovered her father's postcard. The photo that had
skidded under the couch was of Walt in his SUV, studying the
cabin when he followed Avery out to Lake Placid.

She pushed away the worry about what it all might

mean—that not only Walt Jenkins, but the United States government, knew everything about what she had painstakingly planned for the last year. Another knock came from the door. She stuffed the photo and the postcard into the manila envelope and dropped it on the desk. She checked her reflection in the mirror, frustrated that her red-rimmed eyes and bloated face revealed her vulnerability and would allow him to see that his actions had hurt her. Avery hated the feeling of weakness, but there was no way to hide it, and she wasn't about to run from this confrontation. In fact, she longed for it. She walked over to the door and ripped it open.

Natalie Ratcliff stood in the hallway.

"Hi," Natalie said. "Is this a bad time?"

Avery blinked a few times. "Uh, no." She shook her head. "I wasn't expecting to see you, that's all."

"Everything okay?"

Avery recognized the concern in Natalie's voice. Where men may retreat in paranoia at the sight of a woman crying, women pounce on the opportunity to help.

"Working out some man-related crap, that's all," Avery said.

"Is there another kind?"

Avery forced a smile.

"Can I come in?" Natalie asked.

Avery nodded and moved to the side. Natalie walked past her.

"How did you know where I was staying?"

"Pulled some strings," Natalie said.

"Meaning?"

"Meaning I needed to talk with you after how you left things the other day. And I didn't want to wait for a call back, so I figured out where you were staying."

"Fair enough." Avery closed the door. "What's on your mind?"

"You can't do what you're about to do."

Avery opened the minifridge and pulled out a bottle of water, took a sip. "What am I about to do?"

Natalie took a deep breath and exhaled it audibly. "You think you know the whole story, but you don't."

"Oh, I'm sure I don't know the half of it. But I'm pretty sure I figured out the most important part. Victoria is not dead, is she?"

There was a stretch of silence that filled the hotel room, interrupted only by the occasional car horn that penetrated up from the street.

"Victoria was in an impossible position. She was no saint, and I'd never argue otherwise. She was having an affair with a married man. But she was looking at going to prison for a crime she didn't commit."

Avery saw Natalie swallow hard, on the verge of crying.

"She didn't kill Cameron Young," Natalie said.

"I know. Or, at least I *think* I know. I took a deep dive into the case and the evidence, and some other things that were not made public about the investigation."

"How?"

"With the detective"—even peripherally saying Walt's name brought her to the edge of tears—"who ran the investigation."

"Can you prove it?" Natalie asked.

"That Victoria is innocent? No. Not this many years later. But I can certainly make a compelling argument that the crime scene was staged to make it look like she did it. And that's all I need to do for my show."

There was a long pause as they stared at each other.

"She did the only thing she could to survive," Natalie said. "She disappeared because there was no other way, not because she was guilty."

"She couldn't have done it alone."

"She didn't. I helped her."

"And Emma?"

Natalie paused before answering. "No. Emma has no idea."

Avery mulled this over and ran through the possibilities.

"Avery, I'm asking you not to do this. There will be very serious and real consequences if you tell people about this."

"It would ruin your writing career, that's for sure. You'd probably go to prison."

"I don't care about my career. It's not mine to care about. It's Victoria's. I'm just a facilitator."

"She writes the manuscripts, doesn't she? Sends them to you and then you publish them under your name and brand."

Natalie nodded. "It's a collaboration, but yes." She took a step closer to Avery. "But it's not a writing career you'd be ruining. It's a life. A *new* life, fought for and scratched for and obtained against all odds."

"She's in Greece, isn't she? You helped her to somehow get to the island of Santorini. Your husband's family owns a villa there. You see her every year to finish the new manuscript."

Avery saw a look of confusion come over Natalie's face as the twenty-year-old secret was laid before her.

"Please don't expose what you know about Victoria. I'm begging you, Avery."

Avery looked over at the desk and the manila envelope that held the photos of Walt Jenkins. She looked back at Natalie Ratcliff.

"Maybe there's a way we can help each other."

"How?"

"Your husband's family owns a cruise line. It's a private company. No outside money. No outside influences. I think that's how you and Victoria pulled it off. Somehow, you used your husband's cruise line to get Victoria out of the country after 9/11. I can't totally figure it out, but I need to know how you did it."

"Why? If not to expose her, why do you need to know the details?"

Avery looked again to the manila envelope on the desk, then back to Natalie Ratcliff.

"Because I, too, need to get someone out of the country."

CHAPTER 57

Lake Placid, NY
Thursday, July 8, 2021

Close scrutiny of the two hikers making their way through the trails of the Adirondack Mountains near Lake Placid would reveal boots that were too new, gear that was too clean, and rucksacks filled with surveillance equipment foreign to even the most ardent bird-watchers. But thankfully the two hikers—a man and a woman—never saw another soul on the trail.

"I think the blister on my foot just popped," he said.

"You're such a man," the woman said.

"It hurts like a son of a bitch."

"Childbirth hurts. Blisters on your toe are an annoyance," she said, hiking up ahead and forcing him to hurry after her.

They trekked three miles from the national park where they had parked their car. It took nearly an hour, mostly because of her partner's low pain tolerance, to make it to the precipice of the hill that offered a bird's-eye view of the valley below. A trail descended into the basin and wrapped around the lake at the bottom. The peaks of the Adirondacks rose before them and marked the northern border of Lake Placid. It would be, on another day, a time to pause and take in the beauty of the outdoors, the majesty of the morning, and the glory of midsummer Lake Placid. But today was not any morning. The two hikers had information to gather and a deadline to keep. The woman started down the trail. A few minutes later her partner limped after her.

When they made it down to the lake, they had a clear view of the homes perched on the foothills in front of them. The female agent slipped her rucksack off her shoulders and unzipped the top. She removed a long-range Nikon camera with a telescopic lens and had the focus adjusted perfectly by the time her partner joined her.

"How are those new boots treating you?" she asked.

"Like my ex-wife."

She raised her right eyebrow and looked at him out of the corner of her eye.

"Nasty and unforgiving," he said.

"Get your gear out and start looking at birds," she said.

The male agent unzipped his own rucksack and pulled out bird-watching binoculars that looked as innocuous as a child's telescope. The female agent stood behind him for cover and pulled out a much more powerful pair of binoculars. She held them to her eyes and focused the lenses on the A-frame cabin across the lake. Perched at the top of a small hill, the high-range binoculars gave her the ability to see into the windows of the cabin from four hundred yards away.

The cabin's nearest neighbor was ten acres to the north. The terrain on this side of the home consisted of a wooden deck and a long row of stairs that ran down to the water. A sycamore stood at the water's edge, where a rope swing hung from a limb and teetered over the surface of the lake. The agent put the binoculars down and picked up the Nikon.

"Clear?" she asked.

Her partner took a moment to confirm that there were no eyes on them.

"Clear," he said.

The female agent began snapping photos of the A-frame cabin, the lake, and the forested area on either side of the structure. The images would be used to organize the tactical raid the feds were planning on the isolated cabin. But they'd need a warrant before they could crash through the front door. To secure one, they would have to confirm that their subject was present inside, and prove to a judge that it was Garth Montgomery.

"Okay," the female agent said, dropping the camera and binoculars back into the rucksack. "Let's see how close we can get."

CHAPTER 58

Manhattan, NY
Thursday, July 8, 2021

Aknotted towel was twisted on the top of her head and held her wet hair. Just out of the shower Thursday morning, Avery stood in front of the bathroom mirror in jeans and a bra, applying makeup while her mind worked to solve her many problems. Since her confrontation with Natalie Ratcliff the day before, the constant weight of worry sat in her stomach like an indigestible knot of fat and gristle that was sure to do serious harm to her insides. She and Natalie had gone over everything carefully, and spent the entire evening planning and discussing the possibilities. But no matter how they arranged things, there was one missing piece to the very complicated puzzle Avery was attempting to assemble. She was stuck until she figured it out, and she had very little time to do it.

She heard a knock on the door, and paused with the mascara brush an inch from her lashes. When a second knock came she screwed the applicator brush back into the container, walked to the door, and placed her eye to the peephole. Walt stood in the hallway and, despite her attire, she didn't hesitate to pull the door open.

"Wow," he said, shaking his head as if he'd just taken a punch to the jaw.

Avery stood with her hands on her hips, her breasts covered only by her bra. She stared unblinking for a moment, then walked back into the bathroom and closed the door behind her. It was a full minute before she heard Walt's voice.

"Hey," he said through the door. "What's going on?"

The last time he was in her hotel room, the bed had been covered with Victoria's manuscripts. This morning, it was covered with the photos of Walt following her. She wanted him to see them. She wanted him to know that she knew.

"Avery," he said again. "She was set up. Someone planted Victoria's blood at the crime scene. And her urine. I have the evidence to prove it. The blood came from a . . . Do you use cotton tampons, by the way? Because if you do, you have to stop right away."

Avery stood on the other side of the door, thoroughly confused. She wanted to answer him. She wanted to ask what it was he had discovered about Victoria, but she stopped herself from speaking. The Victoria Ford story had taken a backseat to her most pressing issue. More than anything, she wanted him to see the photos that were laid out on the bed. Eventually, she heard Walt close the hotel door. She listened to his footsteps as he walked into the room. She imagined him staring at the photos. It was another minute before she heard him back outside the bathroom.

"Hey," he said in a quiet voice. "We need to talk."

She pulled the door open. "No shit."

Avery walked past him. Walt followed but she made sure to stand on the other side of the bed so that the photos of him were between them. She raised a finger but paused before she spoke, gathering her thoughts and words.

"Did you sleep with me to get information about my family?"

"No," Walt said with some force. "I slept with you because—"

She held up an opened palm to stop him from saying more. It worked.

"Was the story about Meghan even true?"

"Every word of it."

"You promise me?"

"On my life."

"Good. Then I need your help."

Walt paused for a moment. "With what?"

Avery swallowed hard. "My father."

PART V

The Long Game

CHAPTER 59

Manhattan, NY
Thursday, July 8, 2021

The FedEx drop box was located on Madison Avenue, between Fifty-Seventh and Fifty-Eighth Streets. The final pickup was at 3:00 p.m. Avery clutched the overnight envelope to her chest as she left the Lowell and headed south. Her gaze swept across the sidewalks and to the other side of the street, trying desperately to notice if anyone was following her or something out of the ordinary that would stop her from dropping the package off. When she came to the drop box an undefined sense of apprehension made her continue on.

She crossed Fifty-Seventh Street and entered the atrium of Trump Tower. She strode through the lobby and rode the escalator to the upper level, keeping an eye on the entrance as she did. People came and went, but none seemed the least bit concerned with Avery. At the top of the escalator, she walked to the edge of the railing and watched the entrance for several minutes. When she was convinced that no one was following her, she stepped onto the descending escalator and rode to the lobby. She walked back outside, turned right, and crossed Fifty-Seventh Street again. This time, when she came to the drop box, she quickly pulled open the slot. Just before dropping the FedEx package into it, she checked the address label one last time.

Connie Clarkson
922 Hwy 42
Sister Bay, Wisconsin
(Cabin #12)

She released her grip and the parcel fell into the darkness. Inside was the passport belonging to Aaron Holland, and detailed instructions to follow.

CHAPTER 60

Manhattan, NY
Friday, July 9, 2021

He made the call late Thursday night. He made it from Avery's hotel room after he and Avery had had a long, hard discussion. It covered not only what had transpired between them over the last week—the real feelings that had developed, and the sorrow Walt felt for the way he had betrayed her—but also what Avery was hoping to accomplish and how it would all work. *If* it would all work.

The plan now hinged on Walt, and how convincing he could be. The person he called sounded surprised to hear from him, and his request to meet for breakfast Friday morning was met with bewilderment.

"I need to see you," was all Walt said.

"Is something wrong?" she asked.

"Yes."

They settled on a breakfast place on the Upper East Side. Walt sat nervously in the booth and stirred two creams into his coffee, closing his eyes for a moment as he remembered Avery's strange talent of noticing his coffee predilections.

There was something reassuring about Avery knowing his tendencies. No woman had held details about him, intimate or otherwise, for years.

He caught sight of her outside, just a blur as she streaked past the window beside him. Through the blinds, he watched her walk along the sidewalk toward the front of the restaurant. He waited for the normal feelings she elicited in him to materialize. Expected them, in fact. But the usual rush of anger did not come. Nor did the bitter sense of resentment emerge. Even the heartache that went hand in hand with seeing her was gone, replaced this morning with a calm contentment. Things, he knew, would be okay.

When she came through the front door, she spotted him. He lifted his hand in an amicable wave and offered a heartfelt smile. He stood when she came to the booth and they embraced in a warm hug.

"I was shocked you called," Meghan Cobb said, her mouth near his ear.

"Sorry to spring this on you without warning," Walt said.

"How long have you been in town?"

"A couple weeks."

He sensed her pain that he had not called her before now. He equally detected her comprehension that something was different about him.

"Why didn't you call me sooner?" Meghan asked, but there was no conviction in her voice. "We could have spent some time together."

Walt shook his head. "This is about something else."

Neither spoke for several seconds.

"What's her name?" Meghan asked.

"Who?"

"This change," she said. "Only a woman could have caused it."

Walt didn't answer.

"I like it. This version of Walt Jenkins. It reminds me of the old you. The man I used to love. It's good, Walt. I'm happy for you." Meghan cleared her throat before she spoke again. "You said something was wrong. What is it?"

"I need your help."

CHAPTER 61

Manhattan, NY
Friday, July 9, 2021

It was Friday evening before she gathered the courage to call him. Her hand shook when she lifted the cell phone and placed it carefully on the coffee table. She hit the speaker button and then tapped the phone number she remembered from childhood. It, too, contained the three sevens from the address, and Avery hadn't known the number still rested in the folds of her mind until she decided that this was the best move she could make. She hoped to God it worked.

She pressed *send* and waited. Four long rings chimed through her hotel room, each one causing her heart to pound harder in her chest. Then, he answered.

"Hello?"

Avery tried to speak, but couldn't. The sound of his voice after so long caused her vocal cords to seize.

"Hello?" he said again.

"Dad? It's me."

Now her father paused. The sound of her own voice surely causing the same reaction for him.

"Claire?"

"Yes, it's me."

"You got the card," he said. "I knew you'd know what to do."

"I have to see you, Dad. I don't have a lot of time."

"I'd love that. Where?"

"I'll come to you. To the Lake Placid cabin. It's safest that way."

"When?"

"Sunday."

"Okay."

Neither spoke for a moment.

"Claire, I wanted to tell you—"

"Not over the phone, Dad. Get off the landline. I'll see you Sunday."

"Okay."

Avery ended the call, her hand shaking now more than it had been a moment earlier.

"Do you think it will work?" she asked.

On the coffee table next to Avery's phone was the thin metal box containing the listening devices Jim Oliver had given to Walt. Moments earlier, Walt had removed one of them, activated it, and placed it next to Avery's phone so the entire conversation could be recorded.

"I'm not sure," Walt said. He was sitting on the couch next to her. "But it's your best shot if you want to keep the feds occupied and focused on the cabin."

Walt lifted the device from the table, stood, and placed it in his pocket.

"Now the hard part starts. Are you sure you're up for it?"

Avery nodded. A few minutes later they hailed a cab outside the Lowell. From the backseat Walt told the driver where they were headed.

"Javits Federal Building. Twenty-Six Federal Plaza."

FBI headquarters.

CHAPTER 62

New Orleans, LA
Sunday, July 11, 2021

When things happened, they happened quickly. Months of limbo had been suddenly replaced with action. Years of planning had been changed at the last minute. He had only a small window to pack his belongings and get moving. It all came down to this moment. There was no time to think it through. No time to plan it out. No time to use logic or critical thinking to make sure things would work. They either would, or they wouldn't. But staying put and hunkering down at the cabin was no longer an option. The feds were on the prowl, and closer than they'd ever been. It was now or never.

Fueled by half a dozen energy drinks, he drove through the night. He wanted to speed and race and put miles behind him, but couldn't risk a ticket. He drove in the middle lane and pegged the cruise control right at the speed limit designated by each state he drove though. It was five in the morning when he finally made it to New Orleans. The timing was good. Had he arrived earlier, he'd have too many hours to burn. Any later, and he'd be cutting it close.

He ditched the car in a Target parking lot about a mile from the terminal. His legs were stiff from the drive, which was nonstop other than bathroom breaks. When he reached the Julia Street Cruise Terminal, he walked over to the railing and looked out at the Gulf of Mexico just as the horizon was starting to burn with dawn. The brightening sky and the orange glow of the ocean filled him with hope that soon he would be free. That maybe, perhaps, this could work.

God, he hoped Claire knew what she was doing.

CHAPTER 63

Manhattan, NY
Sunday, July 11, 2021

The two federal agents pulled to the curb in front of the judge's residence early Sunday morning and climbed from the car. The female agent wore slacks and a blazer, and just like when the two hiked through the mountains of Lake Placid earlier in the week, she was in charge. Her partner, wearing a crisp gray suit, followed her to the front door. He limped slightly from his blisters. Sunday mornings, the agents knew, were a time for coffee and newspapers before the judge headed to church with his family. Their presence would not be well received, but there was simply no more time to wait.

The female agent knocked on the front door and a moment later Judge Marcus Harris opened it. The judge was wearing a T-shirt and work-out shorts. Open-toed slippers covered his feet, and a look of annoyance covered his face.

"Good morning, sir. I'm special agent Mary Sullivan. This is my partner, James Martin."

"Is this really necessary on a Sunday morning?" the judge asked.

"I'm afraid it is, sir."

The Federal Bureau of Investigation had a bead on one of its most wanted white-collar criminals, and years of searching had finally produced his whereabouts. Waiting for Monday morning and office hours and chambers time was not an option.

Judge Harris waved them both through the door. "Come on. Let's see what you have. I'm leaving for church in an hour."

Ten minutes later, the judge's kitchen island was covered with the surveillance photos the agents had taken of the Lake Placid cabin, including a couple of long-range shots through the windows that captured the hazy figure inside. For thirty minutes the agents presented their evidence to the judge, who sipped coffee as he listened. They took him through the operation and brought the judge up to speed on the Bureau's hunt for Garth Montgomery, and how they had, just this week, turned over the most damning evidence yet that convinced them the fugitive was hiding in the cabin featured in the photographs.

"Listen, Agent Sullivan," Judge Harris said, "it's a compelling case, and the Bureau should be applauded for the hard work it's put in on this. But in order for me to sign off on a warrant, I'm going to need more than hazy photos of an unrecognizable figure in that cabin. I'll need proof that it's Garth Montgomery before I permit a SWAT team to crash through the front door."

"We have it, sir," Agent Sullivan said. "These"—she gestured at the photos on the kitchen island—"were just to show you that we've put in the legwork. *This* is our proof."

Agent Sullivan removed her phone.

"Jim Oliver met with Claire Montgomery, Garth Montgomery's daughter, on Friday afternoon. She provided us with proof that her father had attempted to contact her with a postcard that revealed his location. This was confirmed by a phone call she made to her father at the Lake Placid cabin. A call that she recorded herself and then delivered to the Bureau, on her own and without coercion."

Agent Sullivan tapped her phone and Avery's voice was heard.

Hello?
Dad? It's me.
Claire?
Yes, it's me.
You got the card. I knew you'd know what to do.
I have to see you, Dad. I don't have a lot of time.
I'd love that. Where?
I'll come to you. To the Lake Placid cabin. It's safest that way.
When?
Sunday.
Okay.
Claire, I wanted to tell you—
Not over the phone, Dad. Get off the landline. I'll see you Sunday.
Okay.

Agent Sullivan stopped the recording. "We know Garth Montgomery is at that cabin, and we know he's there today. Tomorrow, he might not be."

Judge Harris put his coffee down and flicked his index finger at her.

"Give me the warrant. I'll sign it."

CHAPTER 64

New Orleans, LA
Sunday, July 11, 2021

He sat at an outdoor café and waited. The last two days had been filled with movement—hurrying, packing, and speeding along the dark highways. Now he waited, and it was driving him mad. The copious amounts of caffeine and taurine surging through his veins from the energy drinks were not helping.

A dozen round tables occupied the outdoor courtyard next to the cruise terminal. He wore sunglasses that hid his blood-shot eyes as he scanned the crowd. He had been careful over the years to trust only a select few people, in whose hands he was comfortable placing his life. But that had all changed in the last forty-eight hours. He waited this morning on a stranger—a woman he had never met, but whose presence was vital to the next leg of an impossible journey that began years ago.

He wore casual slacks and a collared button-down under his baby blue sport coat. Deck shoes covered his feet. No socks. He looked the part. The waitress approached and offered to refill his coffee. He accepted, but asked for decaf. He was wired enough. He checked his watch. Boarding would start in ten minutes. He looked around the café as his forehead beaded with perspiration. The chair across from him rattled across the pavement as it was pulled away from the table. A woman sat down casually.

"Meghan?" the man asked.

Meghan Cobb's face stayed expressionless. She nodded.

The man sat back in his chair and dropped his head in relief. "Thank God. I thought we missed each other."

"No, I was just doing what I was told to make sure no one was following me."

"And?"

"How the hell am I supposed to know? I'm a goddamn interior decorator. This whole thing was sprung on me two days ago."

"Okay, I'm sorry," the man said. "I've been here for an hour. I think we're fine." He looked at the dock. "They're starting to board. We better get going."

He dropped cash onto the table to pay his breakfast bill, then they both stood and walked toward the giant cruise ship. Meghan took his hand as they joined the line of passengers waiting to board.

CHAPTER 65

Manhattan, NY
Sunday, July 11, 2021

The cabin, Jim Oliver had learned during his meeting with Claire Montgomery, was owned by Annabelle Gray, a cousin-in-law once removed from Garth Montgomery. The lineage was not difficult to follow once it stared him in the face. Garth Montgomery's brother was married to a woman whose uncle had owned the Lake Placid cabin located at 777 Stonybrook Circle. The uncle died years ago and willed the property to his daughter—Annabelle Gray, the cousin of Garth Montgomery's sister-in-law. The hours-long interview Claire Montgomery had given on Friday night revealed that Annabelle Gray was called "Ma Bell" by the Montgomery children. Her cabin had been an end-of-summer destination for the Montgomery clan.

Confirmation that Garth Montgomery was, indeed, the cabin's current occupant came from the recorded phone conversation Claire had provided to the FBI. It was priceless. If a warrant were going to be granted, the recording—in addition to Claire Montgomery's cooperation—would be what made it happen.

The call came through at 9:00 a.m. Sunday morning.

"Oliver," he said into the phone.

"We got it," Agent Sullivan said.

"No shit?"

"Judge Harris signed it while wearing his pajamas and slippers as he sipped coffee at his kitchen table. We're on our way now."

"How long?"

"Ten minutes."

Jim Oliver had his team on standby. They waited only on the warrant. He placed the call to set them in motion. It would take four hours to get out to the Lake Placid cabin. In the meantime, since Thursday morning, agents had been dispatched to the hiking trails around the cabin. Their job had changed from surveillance to security. Their objective now was to make sure Garth Montgomery did not leave the cabin.

Thirty minutes later, Jim Oliver and his team were en route. A caravan of SUVs tore out of Manhattan and headed to the mountains of Lake Placid. His phone rang again.

"Oliver."

"Sir," the agent said. "We have a visual on the cabin and confirmation of a single occupant inside."

"Hold tight," Oliver said. "We're on the way. No one leaves that cabin, understood?"

"Yes, sir."

CHAPTER 66

New Orleans, LA
Sunday, July 11, 2021

They waited nervously in the line of passengers preparing to board *The Emerald Lady*. He had bent and unbent the top of the boarding pass protruding from his passport so many times that the corner was a withered mess. Meghan reached over and gently pulled his hand away to stop his fidgeting. There were only a few things his level of anxiety could relay: He was nervous about climbing onto a cruise ship for fear of it sinking. Or he was apprehensive about tropical storm Bartholomew, which was swirling in the eastern Caribbean, and which meteorologists were predicting would twist its way into the Gulf of Mexico. It was too early in the season for hurricane concerns, but the storm promised a deluge of rain and rough waters. Either supposition was better than the truth—that he was uneasy because he was fleeing the country under an alias, and if caught was facing years in prison.

He stemmed the fidgeting just in time to come face to face with the pretty, young deckhand dressed in a crisp white uniform that sported gold stripes on the shoulders as if she carried some level of military rank. She smiled warmly at them, expecting the same in return. After all, every passenger she encountered this morning was about to embark on an epic vacation cruising the open waters of the Caribbean and visiting its fabulous islands, which included Grand Cayman, Jamaica, Cozumel, Belize, and Roatán in Central America. What was there not to be happy and excited about? He and Meghan smiled back at her.

"Passport and boarding pass, please," the woman said.

Meghan took the lead, handing over her information. Her papers were real, and there was no worry as she confidently waited while the deckhand scanned the document. The woman smiled a moment later and handed the passport back to Meghan.

"Ms. Cobb, welcome aboard *The Emerald Lady*."

"Thank you," Meghan said.

With a subtle tremor to his grip, the man handed over his documents. If things were going to fall apart, the scanning of his doctored passport would be the start of it. But all that happened after the woman placed the document facedown on the scanning machine was that a pleasant ring sounded and a green light brightened on the podium.

"Mr. Holland, welcome aboard *The Emerald Lady*."

"Thank you," Aaron Holland responded with a barely audible stutter in his throat.

"You're in cabin thirty-three-eighteen. How many bags will each of you be carrying?"

"Just one for each of us," Meghan said.

"Very good," the woman said, looping an *Emerald Lady* tag around the handle of each suitcase.

"You can leave your bags here." She pointed to the growing collection of luggage that was organized off to the side. "It will be delivered to your cabin shortly."

Aaron Holland and Meghan Cobb smiled and deposited their bags with the others.

"Carlos will escort you to your quarters. Enjoy your stay."

"Thank you," Mr. Holland said in a considerably more relaxed tone than just a few minutes earlier.

They followed Carlos to cabin 3318. The first obstacle had been cleared. Many more waited. So far, Claire was batting a thousand.

CHAPTER 67

Lake Placid, NY
Sunday, July 11, 2021

The no-knock warrant authorized federal agents to storm the cabin without warning. The motorcade consisted of two Humvees and three black Suburbans with tinted windows. The caravan looked so out of place in the quiet mountains that even without sirens blaring or lights flashing, other cars pulled to the shoulder to allow them to pass. Eight agents clad in riot gear occupied the Humvees. Ten more agents, including Jim Oliver, rode in the Suburbans and were dressed in SWAT gear with FBI windbreakers over their Kevlar vests. Firearms were strapped under their arms. And each of them, per the terms Claire Montgomery had negotiated that made this raid possible, had been fitted with body cameras and microphones that would capture every move and every word.

The small brigade pulled down the shaded street until the two surveillance officers who had been watching the cabin came into view. They pointed at the canopied drive and the caravan screeched forward. Before the Humvees came to a full stop, the doors opened and agents poured out. They were armed with submachine guns across their chests and Glocks strapped to their sides. They hid beneath Kevlar helmets and shatterproof face shields. The two lead agents hurled themselves up the front steps and used a battering ram to splinter the front door. They slid to the side to allow the stream of heavily clad federal agents to storm the cabin.

CHAPTER 68

New Orleans, LA
Sunday, July 11, 2021

Aaron Holland planned to stay in the room for most of the cruise. It was small and cramped and there wouldn't be much to do besides watch television and worry. He'd much prefer to lounge out by the pool, or maybe grab a drink from the bar. But that would expose him to other passengers, and every venture out of the cabin presented an opportunity for some memorable incident to occur. Whether it be a casual conversation that someone later recalled, or a minor mishap like spilling his drink, there was no way to know what another passenger might remember. The fewer people he saw, the better the chance that Aaron Holland could exist for only a short few days before disappearing from the world.

Of course, without Meghan Cobb, the vanishing of Aaron Holland would be impossible. The staff and crew, as well as the housekeeping team assigned to every cabin onboard the ship, were well trained. If Mr. Holland simply disappeared and his cabin went empty, it would raise red flags. The housekeeping crew would know to follow strict protocols if a cabin went dormant. A vacant room was to be reported. Fear of passengers, especially overserved vacationers, falling overboard was always a concern. There had been enough negative publicity over the years about cruise lines and passengers disappearing for strict, industry-wide procedures to have been put in place to identify such peculiarities.

But Meghan Cobb solved that problem. Her presence would prevent any red flags from rising. She would be visible on every day of the ten-day cruise. That her recluse travel companion rarely left the cabin would go unnoticed. That she would eventually depart the ship without him at the conclusion of the cruise would be immaterial, because by that time she would be listed as a solo passenger. If Claire was able to pull off what she promised, sometime during the cruise's ten days at sea, Mr. Aaron Holland's name would disappear from the formal register of passengers.

CHAPTER 69

Lake Placid, NY
Sunday, July 11, 2021

With their Glock .40-caliber sidearms trained in front of them, the SWAT team cleared each room of the A-frame cabin. Front room, clear. Kitchen, clear. Bedroom, clear. With each empty room, the possibility dawned on Jim Oliver that perhaps, somehow, his intel was bad. Either they had the wrong cabin or his agents had missed their subject escaping the property. On the run for so long, it was not unbelievable that Garth Montgomery would have in place precautions for this exact moment. And as much as Oliver believed he'd run a flawless operation, he knew it was rushed. If more time were available, he'd have put surveillance in place for longer than just three days. He'd have insisted on more definitive confirmation of the subject's presence instead of relying on the half-assed and blurry photos they had managed to obtain through dirty and curtain-clad windows.

All at once Jim Oliver felt his career slipping away. He'd hung everything on his promise of pulling Walt Jenkins out of retirement and delivering Garth Montgomery. The operation had gone better than predicted, and was a greater triumph than what he'd sold to his superiors. Claire Montgomery had, in the end, provided the critical information needed on her father's whereabouts, and was the reason a warrant had been secured so quickly. But now, here he stood in an empty cabin in the mountains—either completely incorrect about what he thought was inside, or just a moment too late. He tried not to allow the other possibility into his thoughts—that he'd been played. He didn't dwell on it, because whichever situation was unfolding, it spelled the end to his career.

"Bathroom!" one of the agents yelled.

Jim Oliver blinked his eyes and came back to the present. He raised his Glock and moved through the front room, past his agents who were poised and ready for action, muzzles pointed at the closed bathroom door. Audible now in the hushed interior of the cabin was the sound of pressurized water whining through the pipes. Jim Oliver took his position outside the bathroom, his back flat against the wall. He nodded and the battering ram agents appeared. In the silence just prior to the sound of splintering wood, a showerhead could be heard spitting water.

CHAPTER 70

New Orleans, LA
Sunday, July 11, 2021

The majesty of one of the world's largest cruise ships was the draw, and the brochures laid out magnificent photos of the spacious deck, massive swimming pool, and grand ballrooms. The tiny living quarters, where passengers slept after a full day out and about, didn't get much attention in the RICL brochure. Cabin 3318 was small and cramped. After an hour of bumping into each other, Meghan Cobb laid down some ground rules. A line of pillows separated the bed into two halves. Their suitcases were stored underneath. He sat in a chair crammed in the corner. Meghan took a spot on her side of the bed.

"Thanks for doing this," he said. "However it is you got roped into it."

"I owed someone a favor," Meghan said.

They ran through the plan and what they hoped to accomplish during the next couple of days.

"So, you're not allowed to leave this cabin?" Meghan asked.

"It would be best for me not to. I'll walk the halls each day when housekeeping comes to clean, but I'll stay out of sight as much as possible. You, on the other hand, should get out and about. Make yourself seen."

Meghan nodded. "I plan to at least get a hell of a tan out of this deal."

"I'll be out of your hair in two days. Then, you'll have the cabin to yourself."

"Do you think this will work?"

"I'm not sure, but I'm trusting the person who set it up."

"Your name's not really Aaron, is it?"

"No."

"What should I call you then?"

There was a short pause before he answered.

"Aaron," he said. "It's probably best for you to just call me Aaron."

CHAPTER 71

Lake Placid, NY
Sunday, July 11, 2021

The bathroom door disintegrated under the weight of the battering ram, and agents poured into the room. Steam wafted from the door frame and fogged their face shields, which they quickly lifted out of the way.

"Federal agents!" they shouted. "Put your hands in the air. Hands in the air!"

Oliver caught glimpses through the bodies and the steam as he stepped into the room. A man stood naked in the shower. He did not put up a fight, or any resistance at all. He simply raised his hands in a frightened and defeated manner. Two agents manhandled the naked figure out of the shower and forced him to the ground, where they cuffed his hands behind his back.

"Clear," another agent yelled before shutting off the shower.

The agents took the man by the elbows and lifted him to his feet. Naked and dripping wet, he looked pathetic. It would have been appropriate, since he put up no resistance, to offer the man a towel to cover himself. But Jim Oliver had no intention of lessening this man's humiliation.

Oliver walked up to the fugitive he had been hunting for years. Even with sopping wet hair clinging to his ears, Oliver recognized the Thief of Manhattan.

"Garth Montgomery," Oliver said, "I want you to know two things. First, you're under arrest. And second, your daughter is the reason we found you."

CHAPTER 72

Montego Bay, Jamaica
Tuesday, July 13, 2021

The Emerald Lady made landfall just after twelve noon on the third day of the cruise. Aaron Holland watched from the balcony of the second deck as hordes of passengers bottlenecked the exits to storm the island's tourist traps, eager to buy cheap jewelry and handbags and knickknacks for their grandchildren. He waited patiently for the crowds to thin, then walked back to Cabin 3318. Meghan Cobb sat on the bed.

"Well," he said, "I guess this is it."

"Will you be okay?"

He shrugged. "I've made it this far. Thanks for everything. I don't know how you got involved in all this, but I couldn't have gotten this far without you."

"What if someone asks about you? The staff or crew?"

"They won't."

"Are you sure?"

"No."

Meghan nodded. There was nothing left to say. "Good luck."

He zipped his suitcase and left the cabin. He walked down the long hallway and entered the elevator that deposited him on the main level. When he made it to the exit, he registered with the cruise ship employee by handing over his passport. It was scanned and logged into the ship's databank—a careful record of every passenger who disembarked from the ship. This ensured that the exact number of passengers made it safely back onboard before *The Emerald Lady* pulled out of port. It was here that another opportunity for failure presented itself. If Claire were not able to pull this off, then a hunt for Aaron Holland would ensue later today. Montego Bay would be put on alert. The Jamaican authorities would be called, and when they failed to locate the missing American, by protocol *The Emerald Lady* would contact the US authorities. A progression through the chain of agencies would follow, starting at the US consulate in the Caribbean and eventually involving the Department of State. The international branch of the FBI would eventually get involved.

Come on, Claire, he thought as he walked down the stairs and stepped onto the dock. *Work your magic.*

Without looking back, he walked along the pier until he stepped foot onto the mainland of Jamaica. He had studied the map and knew the route by heart. Forgoing the taxis and buses, he chose to cover the three miles into town on foot. It was hot and humid and by the time he reached Jimmy Buffet's Margaritaville restaurant he was sweating through his shirt. At the bar, he ordered a Red Stripe and drank greedily.

As was the plan, he blended in with the other tourists. After he cooled down, he paid his bill with cash and headed into the market where he haggled with street vendors for fifteen minutes. When he was sufficiently comfortable, he disengaged from the crowd and crossed the main thoroughfare until he found Hobbs Avenue. He walked for a quarter of a mile, as instructed, with his small suitcase doing its best to keep up behind him. It contained all his possessions in the world. His entire existence reduced to a single suitcase.

As he rounded a bend in the road he saw the neon-green Jeep Wrangler on the shoulder. The vehicle was without a top or doors. A dreadlocked Jamaican man sat behind the wheel. He walked up and waved.

"Yeah, mon. Aaron Holland?"

"Yes, that's me," he said.

"No problem, mon. Come on."

The man gestured for him to get in. The green Wrangler pulled a U-turn and headed off into the heart of Jamaica. *The Emerald Lady* disappeared behind them.

CHAPTER 73

Trelawny, Jamaica
Tuesday, July 13, 2021

In the town of Trelawny, Jamaica, the man drove the Jeep Wrangler across unpaved roads until they came to the edge of an enormous property. From his research, and all the information Claire had provided in the FedEx package that had arrived at cabin 12 in Sister Bay last week, he knew he was looking at the Hampden Estates, one of Jamaica's oldest rum distilleries. He gripped the handle strap as the Wrangler turned onto a dirt road that consisted of two ruts separated by a patch of grass and bounced its way onto the property. The straight trunks of palm trees lined the path and blurred past. They eventually emerged into a clearing where an ivy-covered home stood. The brakes whined as the Jeep stopped in front of the house.

"Yeah, mon. All set."

"This is it?"

"Yeah, mon. Jerome, he will help you from here."

Aaron Holland pulled an envelope of cash from his pocket and handed it to the driver.

"Thank you."

"Yeah, mon. No problem."

As soon as he lifted the suitcase from the back of the Jeep, the vehicle was gone with the rev of its engine and a plume of dust. He walked from the cloud and headed for the house. Before he could knock, the door opened.

"You made it! I am Jerome." The Jamaican accent gave the name a distinguished *Gee-roam* pronunciation. "We can have lunch and then I'll give you a tour. Maybe we will taste some rum before you leave?"

"Maybe," he said, although rum was the furthest thing from his mind. He had a long drive ahead of him through the hills of Jamaica, and only a slight grasp of where he was headed. To make it, he'd need a clear head not fogged by rum. He was, however, starving, so he accepted the generous offer of lunch but declined the numerous offerings of Hampden Estate rum.

An hour later he climbed behind the wheel of a well-used Toyota Land Cruiser and twisted the key in the ignition. After a few seconds of protest, the engine sputtered to life.

Jerome stood with both hands resting on the open passenger's side window.

"Good luck, my friend," Jerome said.

"How do I get the Land Cruiser back to you?"

"No problem, mon. Mr. Walt is a good friend, he will make sure it gets back to me. I will let him know that you have arrived. Feed his dog when you get there. It will save me a trip. The dog's name is Bureau."

Aaron Holland nodded as if any of this made sense to him. He had needed luck to get to this point, and would surely need more in the weeks to come. This first spell, he hoped, would continue long enough to get him through the interior of Jamaica and to the west end of the island, into the parish of Negril and to the house that belonged to a man named

Walt Jenkins. With no cell phone, and the Land Cruiser's gas gauge pegged at just under half a tank, he figured he'd need all the luck he could find. Finally, he put the Toyota into gear and pulled away.

He was pulling away from more than just a rum distillery in Jamaica, and from more than just a stranger who had willingly surrendered his vehicle to him. Christopher Montgomery was pulling away from his old life. From the stress of spending years in hiding. He was pulling away from the role he unknowingly played as a portfolio manager at his father's hedge fund.

But now, perhaps, he could be free of all that. As free as a man on the run could ever be.

PART VI

Repayment

CHAPTER 74

Westmoreland, Jamaica
Thursday, October 21, 2021

The boat's journey had started in Sister Bay, Wisconsin, where it headed north out of Green Bay before wrapping around Washington Island and trekking down the entire length of Lake Michigan. It passed through the locks in Chicago where the boat rose and fell with other vessels and ships. The sails were never raised. Instead, the boat's motor burned through gasoline and oil. It was the fastest way. The purpose of this journey was transport, not adventure.

Once through the Chicago locks, the crew pointed the Moorings 35.2 south and chugged down the Illinois River. From there they connected to the Mississippi and eventually found the Tenn-Tom Waterway, which took them to Mobile, Alabama. During one leg of the voyage, the masts had to come down to clear low-hanging bridges. But finally, after fourteen days of grunt travel, the Beneteau glided into the Gulf of Mexico. From there, it motored to the southern tip of Florida where, finally, the crew set the sails. By then the boat needed to spread its wings. America disappeared behind them. The island of Jamaica did not become visible for three more days.

Walt Jenkins sat for lunch at a local tavern on the southern end of the island. He ate jerk chicken and plantains and washed it down with a Red Stripe while he watched the efficiency of the crane operators and listened to the creaking of the ships. There was only the infrequent tourist in the Jamaican parish of Westmoreland. Far removed from the sandy white beaches and pristine resorts, not much happened in Westmoreland to attract vacationers. The tiny parish was a hub to the commercial industrial workings of the island. After tourism, Jamaica's economy was fueled by the export of bananas. Much of the island's exportation business happened here at the Savanna-la-Mar port, where tankers docked and cranes lifted thousands of crates of fruit onto ships for transport to foreign lands.

On the north side of the port was a small marina where recreational vessels were moored. There were not many. Wealthy tourists chose other, more scenic and practical locations to park their massive sailboats and yachts. Montego Bay and Ocho Rios were among the most popular. There was a sought-after harbor on the north side of Negril that required clout to secure a slip. But here in Westmoreland, the marina was occupied by small motorboats and fishing vessels that had stopped for service. It was, Walt promised, the perfect location for the delivery.

He finished his lunch and nursed a second Red Stripe, the whole time checking his watch and watching the marina. After thirty minutes he saw the sailboat appear out of the west, its sails full and majestic. A sailing novice, to Walt the boat looked far too big for its purpose. He paid his bill and walked out to the dock, watching as the boat drew closer to land. The sails came down and the boat took a more direct approach toward him. He stood at the end of the pier and waved as the crew of four expertly steered the boat into the slip, roping it off and securing it before Walt could think to offer a hand.

He read the name of the boat, stenciled on the stern, and confirmed that this was, indeed, the boat he was waiting on. The crew looked haggard. All four men sported thick beards and shaggy hair that sprouted from beneath their hats. Their skin looked bronzed and windburned.

"Gentlemen," Walt said, "looks like you've had a helluva journey."

The captain of the crew jumped onto the pier, removed his hat and sunglasses, and wiped his hand across his brow to clear the perspiration.

"Let's just say the flight home is going to be a lot easier. You Jenkins?"

"Yes, sir," Walt said, handing over both his American driver's license and his passport.

The captain took the documents and secured them under the clasp of his clipboard. He scribbled information from Walt's ID onto the delivery slip, checked a few boxes, and handed everything back to Walt.

"Signature at the bottom."

Walt signed.

"Let me go over a few things about the boat. Nothing major, but there are a few mechanical issues that will need attending to. Nothing structural. She's a beast, that's for sure."

"Good to hear," Walt said, as if he had any idea about what made a sailboat a beast or a burden.

For twenty minutes he followed the captain around the boat and nodded as the man inspected the sails, the winches, and the topside equipment. Walt followed him into the engine room and pretended to comprehend the things that were mentioned about the fuel pumps, the propellers, and the drive system. There was a glitch in the electronics, Walt was told. He made a show of making a mental note of it.

"We made a list as we traveled," the captain said. "I know I'm cruising through a lot of things, but our flight leaves in three hours."

Walt waved his hand. "As long as you made a list, I can go over everything after I get you guys to the airport."

Two hours later, Walt dropped the four men at the airport in Montego Bay. As soon as they disappeared into the terminal, he shifted the Land Cruiser into drive and headed toward Negril.

CHAPTER 75

Negril, Jamaica
Friday, October 22, 2021

Avery felt the thick humidity of the Caribbean as soon as she stepped onto the tarmac. Her flight was six hours, direct from Los Angeles into Montego Bay. She made it through customs and wheeled her suitcase outside. The airport was busy with tourists waiting in long lines to pour onto buses and vans that would deliver them to the island's beaches, where they would drink rum and try hard to bronze their pale skin.

Avery walked out of the terminal and heard a horn beep twice. She made her way through the crowd and saw Walt standing in the crook of the open driver's side door and waving to her over the roof of the Land Cruiser. It was the same vehicle, Avery knew, that her brother drove three months earlier when he first arrived in Jamaica. Avery hustled over and climbed into the passenger's seat while Walt threw her bag in the trunk.

"How was your flight?" he asked as he pulled out of the terminal.

"Long. How is he?"

"Settled and enjoying island life. I may or may not have turned him on to single batch Jamaican rum."

Avery smiled.

"He's really anxious to see you."

"Did the boat get here?"

"Yesterday, right on schedule. Christopher wanted to inspect it, but I told him we had to wait for you."

"How did it look?"

"The boat? Great, but I don't know anything about boats."

"It's a beautiful boat," Avery said, remembering the day in June when she and Connie Clarkson had taken it for a sail through Green Bay. That morning's sail had been a final inspection during which Avery made sure the vessel could do what it needed to.

"I'll take your word for it," Walt said.

Then, it was quiet for a long time as Walt navigated out of the airport and onto the main highway that would take them to Negril. He finally spoke after thirty minutes.

"I missed you," he said.

Avery looked over at him. "I still think you're an asshole."

"No argument from me on that front. Just know that I'm working really hard on changing that."

A minute of silence passed before Avery spoke.

"I missed you, too."

"I'll take that," Walt said, keeping his eyes on the road. "I'll take that any day of the week."

Walt reached over and took her hand. She didn't resist.

Most of the drive to Negril was on the main road, which was populated with tour buses, vans, and motorcycles that slithered in and out of traffic. The ocean was to Avery's right. The water was crystal clear nearer to shore, offering a glimpse of coral deep beneath its surface. Farther from land the water turned a rich cobalt. Palm trees were everywhere. In the city of Negril they exited the main road and headed toward the interior of the island—away from the tour buses and far from the ocean and beaches. The roads on this leg of the journey were narrow and shaded by heavy foliage. In some spots the road was so slight that Walt had to pull to the side to allow oncoming traffic to pass.

The farther into the rain forest Walt drove, the more excited she became. She didn't speak for the last thirty minutes of the trip. All Avery wanted was to get there and see him.

"Five more minutes," Walt said.

Those minutes felt like hours until Walt finally slowed the car, made a right turn, and pulled up the driveway of a well-kept blue house tucked into a nook of mangroves and palm trees. The closest neighbor was two acres away and very much out of sight. This had been the perfect place for Christopher to stay while Avery finished the last of her plans. Walt had promised that it would be.

"Thank you," she said.

Walt nodded, and then pointed at the house. "Get in there."

Avery opened the door and stepped onto the pebbled driveway. A dog ran down the driveway to greet her. The front door of the house opened and Christopher walked onto the front patio. Avery ran for him.

CHAPTER 76

Negril, Jamaica
Friday, October 29, 2021

Christopher Montgomery was three years older than his little sister. Age, however, provided little leverage and no advantage. Avery was better than him at most things—she had been a better student and was a better sailor. She was more charismatic and outgoing. She could likely, if things ever got out of control between them, overpower him in a wrestling match. But there was one thing Christopher beat her at. Math. He was a savant when it came to numbers. Math and all its derivatives came easily to him. In fact, he had never felt the need to learn the subject. The knowledge was somehow already in his brain. He was born with it. All he had to do was organize the information and apply it to any version of math. In college, he majored in mathematics. After college he earned a master's degree in applied and computational mathematics. If he had had a normal father, perhaps Christopher Montgomery would have become a professor or an actuary for the insurance industry. Instead, he took his mathematical brain to Wall Street and joined Montgomery Investment Services as an analyst.

Christopher applied himself to studying the market and determining the probabilities and statistical analysis of making money by trading stocks and commodities. Surprising to no one, he was very good at it. So good, in fact, that he rose to the top of the food chain at his father's firm and was soon offering his advice not just to his father, but to every partner, about which industries to place the hedge fund's assets into. Christopher became so lost in the statistical analysis of the firm's funds that he couldn't see the forest for the trees. Until one night when he was alone and working late. His mind functioned best when the offices of Montgomery Investment Services were empty. That was when he first began to unravel the fraud that was taking place. It took him weeks of working through the night to dissect the firm's financial misdeeds.

The offices of Montgomery Investment Services occupied the entire fortieth floor of the Prudential building in lower Manhattan, and once Christopher smelled corruption, he didn't care how many chances he took. Late at night, after the cleaning crew was gone, he entered his father's office and searched through his computer. He did the same to each of the partners. What took the feds two years to uncover, Christopher had learned in two weeks. Montgomery Investment Services was dirty as sin, and Christopher's name and brainpower was behind nearly every deal that had been made.

As quickly as he pieced together the fraud, Christopher also figured out that he would be considered as guilty as anyone else at the firm. His digital fingerprints were on nearly every trade. He would be implicated in the Ponzi scheme as much as his father or any of the partners. Implicated, prosecuted, indicted, and imprisoned. And the feds were coming, he knew. An old friend with whom he had studied applied mathematics worked for the IRS and had confirmed Christopher's suspicions. Christopher asked for a favor, and his friend obliged. While Christopher spent two weeks unraveling the financial crimes at Montgomery Investment Services, his friend made a few calls and did some snooping of his own. The friend didn't know much, he told Christopher, but he *had* learned that there was an active investigation going on that involved the FBI's Math Geeks—the nickname used for the forensic accountants who worked for the government. His friend had even managed to get the name of the operation: House of Cards.

There were many choices Christopher Montgomery could have made. He could have gone to the feds and cut a deal. He could provide all the access they needed. He could have been a siphon to it all. He could have confronted his father and demanded that things change, but he knew things were too far gone. He could have attempted to erase his fingerprints from the trades and plead ignorance. But each of those choices had flaws. Attached to all of them was the likelihood that he would go to prison. So, instead, he had told Claire about their father's hedge fund and the fraud and the billions in assets that were nothing but a mirage. He told her how he was neck deep in it all, even though until recently he knew nothing about any of it. Then, he had asked for her help.

There was no perfect way to fake your own death. But he had been adamant that he needed to do it before the feds busted down the doors. Because to fake your death *after* an indictment was too suspicious. To fake your death a year before anyone at Montgomery Investment Services came under federal indictment was possible. If they did it the right way.

Sacrificing her Oyster 625 took some convincing, but after Christopher explained that the boat—and everything else in their lives—had come from dirty money, Claire had agreed. Knowing that the marina had surveillance cameras, he and Claire had climbed aboard the *Claire-Voyance*, prepared the boat for a sail, and pushed off. It was only after they were a mile offshore that Christopher boarded the dingy and made it back to land—a different marina where surveillance was less severe. Then, he had prayed that Claire would survive.

The storm was as brutal as forecasted, and Christopher did his best to keep track of the news as he drove. It was sixteen hours from Manhattan to Sister Bay, Wisconsin, and Christopher stopped only for gas. When he did, he kept his sunglasses on his face and his ball cap pulled low over his eyes. By the time he reached Connie Clarkson's sailing camp it was six in the morning and the sun was rising. When he opened the door to cabin 12 he was met with the smell of fresh brewed coffee and pancakes, and said a silent prayer of thanks that he had Connie in his life. He clicked on the news and ate like a wild animal.

His biggest regret—even greater than asking Claire to sacrifice the Oyster 625, and risk her life for him—was that the money Connie Clarkson had given his father for safekeeping was gone. Like many of his father's victims, Connie Clarkson was blind to the fraud until she learned the cold, hard truth that any money given to Montgomery Investment Services had disappeared like smoke in the wind.

It was noon before Christopher found the story on CNN's Web page. A sailboat had sunk off the coast of Manhattan during a violent storm. One passenger, a woman, had been rescued by the Coast Guard. A search and rescue operation had been launched for a second passenger.

Up to that point, things had worked. He had planned to hide at Connie's for a couple of weeks. He never imagined it would take three years to leave cabin 12 and the sailing camp.

CHAPTER 77

Westmoreland, Jamaica
Friday, October 29, 2021

The port of Savanna-la-Mar was a thirty-minute drive from Negril. Avery sat in the front seat as Walt drove the Land Cruiser toward the ocean. A week earlier Walt had accepted receipt of the sailboat at the small marina there. The slip had been rented for a month, paid in full and in advance. It only took three days to spin through the checklist of repairs the boat needed after making the long journey from Sister Bay. Over the last three days they stocked the vessel with nonperishable food, water, and everything else someone might need to spend weeks on the water.

Christopher's goal was to disappear for a year to make sure no one was looking for him. By then they would be certain that his escape had, indeed, been flawless. The only worry was that their father, facing the rest of his life in jail, might mention to the feds that he believed his son was still alive. Neither Christopher nor Avery believed that their father knew the truth. Still, it was safest for Christopher to take to the sea while their father was prosecuted. There was no telling the extremes he might go to to lessen his sentence. That his own daughter had betrayed him and turned him over to the feds was surely a bitter pill Garth Montgomery would not swallow easily. But it had been part of the long game Avery concocted the moment her father's postcard arrived in the mail. The final details had come together with Walt's help. The best way, Walt had told her, to make sure the eyes of the FBI were off the airports, borders, and ports was to divert the agency's attention. And the apprehension of one of their highest targets was the best way to do it.

In a year, when the coast was clear, the plan was for Christopher to return to Jamaica and start his new life. His job at Hampden Estates distillery would be waiting for him, and there were worse ways to spend time as a free man. Holed up in a cabin in Sister Bay, Wisconsin, working at Connie Clarkson's sailing camp had been a temporary arrangement that had run far past its course of practicality. Here in Jamaica, Christopher Montgomery—aka Aaron Holland—could truly be free.

Avery stared through the windshield as Walt pulled into the marina's parking lot. The masts of other sailboats poked into the sky, but she recognized Christopher's boat immediately. Avery led the way with Walt and Christopher following. She walked down the dock and stopped when she came to the stern of the boat. The name was printed in cursive, and Avery was thrilled with how it turned out. Connie had done a spectacular job.

Claire-Voyance II

She felt Christopher's arm wrap around her shoulder.

"I've told you before, but I just want to make sure you know how grateful I am for everything you've done," he said.

"I know."

"I'll pay you back somehow."

"No you won't."

He smiled. "Probably not."

"But when things calm down, you can show me the Caribbean on this gorgeous boat."

"Deal."

"You think you'll be okay?"

He nodded and continued to stare at the boat. "I'll be fine. Is it hard to get used to a new name?"

"Depends on why you changed it."

"To find freedom."

"Then it's easy. You're Aaron Holland from now on. You live on a sailboat and sail the Caribbean. Every few months you come back to Jamaica to work at a rum distillery. There are worse things than that."

"I'm worried about the money. I don't feel right taking it from you."

"It's already done," Avery said. "Too late to worry now."

Her contract from HAP News had been finalized earlier in the fall. It named Avery as the host of *American Events* for the next five years. Dwight Corey had negotiated tirelessly and Mosley Germaine and David Hillary had signed off on the final details of the contract that would pay Avery $3 million a year for five years. Even at that number, Avery argued that she was undervalued. The show's most recent numbers had proven she was correct. The Victoria Ford special, which spanned three episodes, had brought the second highest ratings in *American Events* history. That Avery's investigative reporting, and the new evidence she unearthed, had spurred the re-opening of the Cameron Young investigation only added notoriety to her already powerful name. Cameron Young was back in the news, and serious questions were being raised about who had killed him. The evidence that had once so clearly pointed at Victoria Ford was now being questioned. The idea that the blood and the urine had so clearly been manipulated and planted came under immense scrutiny. The Innocence Project had even gotten involved, promising to continue the crusade to prove Victoria Ford's innocence.

The *American Events* special had not named names as to who might have planted the evidence, because to do so was a liability the network was not prepared to take. And it had never been Avery's goal to solve the case. She'd made just two promises. The first was to Emma Kind that Avery would do her best to show the world that Victoria was innocent. The second was to Natalie Ratcliff that, in exchange for Natalie's help, Avery would stay silent on the truth about Victoria's disappearance. She had made good on both.

The Victoria Ford special was topped in the ratings only by Avery's exposé on her father, the Thief of Manhattan. The two-part series covered the life of Claire Montgomery, aka Avery Mason, and detailed how Avery had worked with the FBI to track her father down and bring him to justice. During the negotiations on how Avery would deliver her father, she had insisted that the federal agents wear cameras and microphones. The body cam footage from the SWAT team as they crashed through the front door of the isolated, lonely cabin in the mountains of Lake Placid was something not to be missed. And no one did. Twenty-two million viewers tuned in to watch the episode. For Avery, the episode was cathartic on many fronts.

In the end, despite her mild protests, Avery knew the contract from HAP News provided everything she had asked for, and more. Dwight structured the deal to be front-loaded, and it paid Avery a signing bonus of $3 million. She did two things with the bonus. First, she opened an account at Cainvest Bank and Trust on Grand Cayman in the name of Aaron

Holland, with a starting balance of $100,000. It would be enough for Christopher to start his new life. The second thing Avery did was pay for the sailboat. She sent the cashier's check certified, overnight, and knew it would arrive later today.

Avery looked around the marina. "Better get going, big brother."

There were no surveillance cameras here and Avery knew no one in the government was interested in her whereabouts any longer—Walt had made sure of that before allowing her to come to Jamaica. Her fame, however, drew the odd paparazzi, and the last thing Avery needed were photos of her and her dead brother showing up in the tabloids. She wasn't too concerned. This port was off the beaten path and far from the touristy areas of the island. Still, even with no one paying attention to the three Americans standing on the dock, Avery knew if they waited much longer one of them might back out of the plan. They had come too far to get cold feet now.

Christopher nodded. He turned to Walt.

"Thanks for all your help."

"Sure thing," Walt said. "You know where I live if you need anything."

Christopher turned to Avery. She felt him kiss her forehead. He didn't say anything more. There was nothing left to say. Instead, he climbed onto his new vessel. Avery untied the lines as the engine rumbled to life.

"Stay safe," she said.

Ten minutes later, *Claire-Voyance II* was motoring out of the marina. Once it was in the open water, Avery saw the main sail climb the mast and fill with air. The front sail followed and the boat heeled slightly to the left as it took on an eastern tack and headed into the morning sun.

"So," Walt said. "How long are you staying?"

"I'm off for a week."

"Then what?"

"You tell me," Avery said.

Walt took her hand as they walked along the dock. "I was thinking I should start spending some more time in the States."

Avery looked at him with slivered eyes. "I thought you hated New York."

"I do. I was thinking California is more my style."

CHAPTER 78

Sister Bay, WI
Friday, October 29, 2021

The brown UPS truck drove north through the Door County peninsula. The driver's stops included the towns of Fish Creek and Ephraim before heading up to Sister Bay. It was 2:30 p.m. when he turned into the parking lot of Connie Clarkson's sailing camp, grabbed the overnight envelope from the stack next to him, scanned the bar code, and dropped it on the front porch of the main office. He rang the bell and hustled back to his truck. He was pulling away when the front door opened.

Connie looked down to see the UPS envelope on the ground. She picked it up and walked back into the kitchen, where she dropped it on the table. A kettle of water was on the stove and had just started to whistle. She turned the burner off and poured the boiling water into a mug with the strings of two tea bags hanging over the rim. She allowed them to steep for two minutes, then pulled the tea bags from the mugs and dropped them in the garbage. She brought her mug to the kitchen table and sat down. She tore the thread from the top of the UPS envelope. Pushing the edges together, she saw that there was a single piece of paper inside, along with a business-sized white envelope.

She turned the package over and the contents slid onto the table. Lifting the paper, she unfolded it. It held a short, hand-written message:

> *Dear Connie,*
> *You've done more than anyone else would have done.*
> *More than either of us expected. We owe you*
> *everything, and can never repay you. But we can at*
> *least give you what was taken.*
> *Love,*
> *Claire & Christopher*

The boat, Connie assumed, had made it safely to Jamaica. She put the paper down and reached for the envelope. She stuck her finger under the edge and ripped it open. Inside was a cashier's check. After she pulled it from the envelope, she looked long and hard at the number printed on it. She had trouble comprehending that it was real. It was made out for $2 million, the exact amount she had handed over to Garth Montgomery years ago.

CHAPTER 79

Santorini, Greece
Wednesday,
December 15, 2021

For the first time in nearly twenty years Natalie Ratcliff was late delivering a manuscript. Her impeccable track record of punctuality had been broken this time, and for good reason. So much had happened since summer to thwart her creativity and productivity. But now, finally, she was attempting to put the finishing touches on her latest Peg Perugo story. And just in the nick of time. The world was waiting. The book was slated for publication the following spring.

Over the years, Natalie Ratcliff and Victoria Ford had developed a routine. Victoria wrote the first draft of each manuscript and sent it off to Natalie, who reworked the story, picking out the flaws and inconsistencies. This many years later they both knew Peg Perugo equally well. But they each knew her *differently*. The advantage Victoria held from having originally created the affable character more than twenty-five years earlier was matched by Natalie's understanding of how to mold Peg Perugo's character for maximum commercial appeal. Together, they had developed a smooth back and forth that, while never fully escaping disagreement, always avoided argument. Until this year. Until the sixteenth Peg Perugo novel. This time there were deep disparities on how they each thought the plot should be structured. E-mailing their opinions and attempting to work through the problems from thousands of miles away had only added fuel to the fire, so Natalie arranged a trip to Santorini to sort out the details.

Victoria and Natalie sat in the splendid Ratcliff-owned villa on the tiny island of Santorini. They had spent the week reading and rereading the manuscript, tweaking and reworking the story in an attempt to find common ground on which they could both agree. Natalie had fought hard to convince Victoria that they should stick with the formula that had produced fifteen best sellers and had sold a hundred million copies. Victoria, on the other hand, wanted to go in a different direction. A darker, edgier direction that had been absent from all the previous Peg Perugo stories.

Natalie had noticed this change to Victoria's writing since summer. An edge to Victoria's writing that didn't match the voice from the previous decade and a half of work. They wrote hard-boiled mysteries, not dark thrillers. And they had been spectacularly successful at it. Their readers expected a certain genre, and using their beloved protagonist in such a dark way would not be well received. But no matter how many times Natalie pointed this out, Victoria refused to listen. She simply came back with darker ideas still.

Natalie was sitting on the veranda of the villa and reading the latest version of the manuscript Victoria had produced. Victoria walked out and popped the cork to a bottle of Dom Pérignon. The Aegean Sea was in front of them, and the air was chilly. It seemed to Natalie to fill Victoria with vigor. More than that, actually. Natalie sensed defiance in the way

Victoria carried the bottle of champagne and filled their glasses.

"Well?" Victoria asked. "What do you think? Is it our best yet?"

Natalie felt a strange shiver climb up her spine. There was something in the way Victoria asked the question that made Natalie hesitant to voice her true opinion. Still, she tried one last time.

"Vic, this is not what our readers want from us. It's not what they want from Peg Perugo."

Victoria handed Natalie a champagne flute filled to the brim.

"Why do you say that? It's okay if Peg gets an investigation wrong. It will build her character in future books."

"Sure," Natalie said. "It's just that . . . the way it happens. I'm not sure we should go in that direction."

"Of course we should," Victoria retorted. "It's the only way Peg Perugo could be fooled. It goes hand in hand with the title I've come up with."

Victoria reached over and touched her glass to Natalie's.

"Besides, it's too late to change things now. I've already sent the manuscript to New York."

Another chill ran through Natalie's body when Victoria smiled at her. It felt like Victoria was daring her to protest. Something told her not to, so she didn't. Instead, Natalie lifted the champagne and smiled back at her friend.

CHAPTER 80

Santa Monica, CA
Saturday, April 16, 2022

Walt had not made the formal move from Jamaica to California, but it was inevitable. He visited more and more often, to the point that Avery had given him a key to her place. She was getting used to the Friday afternoons that she came home from the studio to find a rental car in the driveway and Walt making dinner in her kitchen, a glass of wine waiting for her. After spending most of his life on the East Coast, Walt pledged never to spend another winter anywhere the temperature dipped below fifty degrees. He rather enjoyed, he told her over the last year, bouncing between the Caribbean and Southern California.

He was staying for a week this visit, and they were taking advantage of rare downtime Avery had before she would be busy recording the last few episodes of her second full season as host of *American Events*. After this weekend, they wouldn't see each other again until Avery headed to Jamaica in July to spend a month during her summer break from *AE*. She hadn't seen Christopher since the previous October and was anxious to hear about his adventures at sea. Walt had provided updates over the months, reporting back to Avery every time Christopher returned to Jamaica to restock supplies. *Claire-Voyance II* was proving to be as formidable a vessel as Avery had predicted, and Christopher was enjoying his new life as Aaron Holland.

Avery and Walt returned home from a late dinner. Walt turned on the Yankees game. They were playing the A's and they had made it home for the ninth inning. Avery poured them each a glass of wine and, while Walt became engrossed in the game, she returned to the book she was reading—the latest Peg Perugo novel, which was proving to be as unputdownable as all the others she had read over the last few months. This one, though, had her on edge in a way the other books in the series hadn't. It was darker than the previous ones, and more intense. She was lost in the pages.

The Yankees game ended. Walt clicked off the television.

"I'm heading to bed," he said.

"I'll be up in a little while," Avery said. "I just have another couple of chapters."

Walt kissed her and disappeared up the stairs. Avery reached for her glass of wine before returning to the pages. As her eyes skimmed through the final chapters, time seemed to stop and the pages flew past with no effort at all. The ending materialized and Avery anticipated the twist as she read. It would be the first time in Peg Perugo's storied career that she got a homicide investigation wrong. It would be the first time the loveable character got duped. The way it happened brought goose bumps to Avery's skin. It was clever and cunning, and the only way for the endearing heroine to be fooled. Not even Peg Perugo would suspect that the killer planted her own blood at the crime scene to lead detectives in the wrong direction.

Avery's mind spun as she read the final page. Finally, she

closed the book and looked up at the blank television where the Yankees game had been playing a few minutes earlier. Then she turned the book over and looked at the cover. The wineglass dropped from her hand and shattered on the floor when she reread the title with a new understanding of what it all meant.

The Perfect Murder
A Peg Perugo novel

EPILOGUE

The Night of Cameron Young's Death
July 14, 2001

Victoria Ford walked back into the bedroom wearing nothing but a silk robe that was unclasped and open in the front, covering her breasts but revealing her cleavage, her smooth midsection, and the fact that she was wearing nothing else. She kept her right hand hidden behind her back. Cameron was lying on the bed with his hands tied to each bedpost. She had made sure to secure the knots tighter than normal.

He was still breathing heavily from what she had done to him. The normal lightheartedness of their role-playing was gone tonight, and Victoria saw the deep purple welts wrapping around his thigh and shoulders as he lay on his back. She had been particularly violent with the whip, but he hadn't protested. She needed his body to look very different from the home video she had secretly taken of both of them. She walked over to the bed and climbed on top of him, straddling his waist. The silk robe slid off her shoulders and crumbled into a pile behind her. She leaned over and put her lips to his ear, whispered in the seductive way she knew would turn him on.

"I want to make sure you know how I feel about you to-night."

As she kissed his ear, she slowly dragged the length of rope she had hidden behind her back along the side of his face and over his head until it was around his neck. She immediately felt his arousal and knew this would be easier than she imagined. She pulled the rope upward and the slipknot tightened down on his skin. His hips rose up into her. Victoria laid the end of the rope on the bed. It curled over the pillows like a serpent's tail. Then she kissed him again, this time on the mouth. It was a deep, forceful kiss—almost violent. She could feel that it sent him into a state of euphoria. Then she kissed his chin and his neck and his throat and his chest. She continued her descent along his sternum and down to his navel, where she paused for a moment to look up at him. He was panting like a dog. Waiting. Wanting. So vulnerable and distracted that he would never have a chance.

She finished her descent and heard him moan. She wanted to bring him to the edge of ecstasy, but no further. Victoria wanted him to die at the same proverbial place where he had killed her—on the cusp of bliss and joy, and completely blindsided. When she felt that he was close to climax, she stopped and quickly jumped off him. Two quick steps put her at the head of the bed, where she grabbed the rope before Cameron's eyes were open. She wrapped the rope in her hands and pulled with all her strength. With his hands bound to the bedposts, Cameron was helpless. It went on for close to a minute before the rope binding his right wrist broke free and he clawed at his throat, trying but failing to loosen the rope that Victoria was strangling him with.

It took another full minute before his body relaxed. Another minute more until she was sure he was dead. When she finally released her grip and looked at Cameron's lifeless body, his face was purple and his lips were black. His penis was engorged but deflated, and fell pathetically across his hip. It was the perfect way for him to die.

Victoria quickly got to work. From her bag she removed the items she needed. Her urine was in a sealed Tupperware container. Her research told her that by now the enzymes would have broken down into ammonia, tipping off investigators that there was no earthly way possible the urine could have come from her body in the last twenty-four hours. It would be the first clue to investigators that the scene had been staged. The tampon was in a plastic ziplock. Ever since the abortion Victoria had bled frequently and heavily. The idea of planting her blood tonight in an effort to lead investigators to Tessa Young had been conjured as the remnants of Victoria's unborn child poured from her body. Tessa carried the child Cameron was meant to give Victoria, and they both should be punished. This blood, Victoria knew, was contaminated with the toxic chemicals found in cotton tampons. It would be another clue to investigators.

The next item she removed was the wineglass that was coated with her lipstick and fingerprints. Victoria had stashed it away over the Fourth of July weekend, at the end of the night after Tessa had placed all their glasses into the dishwasher. The fact that this glass also held Tessa's fingerprints would further lead investigators to her. The culinary knife Victoria had used over the Fourth to chop vegetables also held both hers and Tessa's prints. The last item in the bag was the thumb drive that held the homemade sex tape. Victoria had planned the video carefully to make it look like neither she nor Cameron knew they were being recorded. It turned out even better than she imagined. She planted the thumb drive in the desk drawer of Tessa's office.

By themselves, each item may not be enough. But all together, and added to the bowline knots Victoria had spent hours learning to tie, they would paint a clear picture of a jilted wife attempting to frame her husband's lover for his murder. Victoria was certain of it. She believed she had calculated everything perfectly. But Victoria never planned on a district attorney refusing to follow the evidence, or a sycophant detective refusing to trust his instincts.

When Victoria was finished staging the scene, there was only one thing left to do. She turned her attention to Cameron. Moving his lifeless body was like lifting a heavy garbage bag filled with waste. But she managed, and eventually she hoisted Cameron Young over the balcony and dropped him into the night.

ACKNOWLEDGMENTS

A big *Thank You* to all the folks who helped make this book a reality. Especially to my family, who have for years dealt with the ups and downs of the emotional rollercoaster that is part of the writing process. I couldn't do it without you, and wouldn't really want to.

To Amy and Mary, my First Readers, you were instrumental in making this story what it is.

To my literary agent, Marlene Stringer, for her support and speed-reading skills.

To my editor, John Scognamiglio, for helping me get what's in my head onto the page.

To Mark Desire, the assistant director of forensic biology at the Office of Chief Medical Examiner in New York, for taking my calls and explaining so eloquently what you and your team do to honor the victims of the 9/11 terror attacks. Your efforts are heroic.

And to the readers—as always, I'm grateful that you have plucked my novel out of a sea of entertainment options.

From the #1 internationally bestselling author and master of modern suspense comes a brilliantly twisting and propulsive standalone novel about a woman whose dark past as the lone survivor of her family's slaughter collides with present-day crimes.

Alex Armstrong has changed everything about herself—her name, her appearance, her backstory. She's no longer the terrified teenager a rapt audience saw on television, emerging in handcuffs from the quiet suburban home the night her family was massacred. That girl, Alexandra Quinlan, was accused of the killings, fought to clear her name, and later took the stand during her highly publicized defamation lawsuit that captured the attention of the nation.

It's been ten years since, and Alex hasn't stopped searching for answers about the night her family was killed, even as she continues to hide her real identity from true crime fanatics and grasping reporters still desperate to locate her. As a legal investigator, she works tirelessly to secure justice for others, too. People like Matthew Claymore, who's under suspicion in the disappearance of his girlfriend, a student journalist named Laura McAllister.

Laura was about to break a major story about rape and cover-ups on her college campus. Alex believes Matthew is innocent, and unearths stunning revelations about the university's faculty, fraternity members, and powerful parents willing to do anything to protect their children.

Most shocking of all—as Alex digs into Laura's disappearance, she realizes there are unexpected connections to the murder of her own family. For as different as the crimes may seem, they each hinge on one sinister truth: no one is quite who they seem to be . . .

**Please turn the page for an exciting sneak peek of
Charlie Donlea's
THOSE EMPTY EYES
coming soon wherever print and e-books are sold!**

McIntosh, Virginia
January 15, 2013

Sin has always been a conundrum.

Some believe their sins go unnoticed, and can be committed without consequence. Others repent in the conviction that an omnipotent god sees all discretions and forgives unconditionally. The shooter, dressed in boots and a long, sweeping trench coat, believed something else—that the most egregious sins should always be noticed and never forgiven, and that those who commit them should be punished.

The shooter conquered the stairs silently while the family slept. At the top of the staircase, the figure used the barrel of the shotgun to push open the bedroom door of the master suite. The hinges creaked and disrupted the otherwise silent home. The door came to rest with just enough space to pass through the doorframe. The shooter slipped inside and walked to the foot of the bed. The soft breathing of the woman could be heard between the animalistic snores coming from the man lying next to her. The shooter lifted the rifle and secured it to their shoulder. The right cheek fell into place against the cold metal as the barrel pointed at the snoring man. A finger settled over the trigger, paused momentarily, and then twitched, unleashing a deafening blast. The sleeping man's flesh exploded as buckshot tore into his chest. Disoriented, his wife sat up quickly. In her confusion, she never saw the shooter standing at the foot of the bed or the barrel of the shotgun rotating toward her. A second blast sent the woman's torso ricocheting off the headboard.

Reaching into the pocket of the trench coat, the shooter removed several pages of documents and photos, and then dropped them onto the bed and around the bodies. As the ringing of the gunshots dissipated, floorboards creak outside the bedroom. Quickly, the shooter cracked the barrel of the shotgun open, allowing the spent shells to sail into the air. With hands protected by latex gloves, the shooter retrieved two live shells from the second trench coat pocket, inserted them into the smoking chamber, and snapped the barrel closed before aiming toward the bedroom door. An eternity passed until the hinges whined again and revealed a young boy standing in the doorframe.

Raymond Quinlan was thirteen years old, a troubling age for the shooter—old enough to be a viable witness, but young enough to make the next decision challenging. As Raymond struggle to understand the scene before him, the shooter allowed no time for the boy to orientate himself. The barrel of the shotgun was trained at the boy's chest, and a third deafening blast filled the home.

As the concussion ricocheted off the bedroom walls, melancholy should have settled in but was quickly brushed aside. There would be time for despondence when the mission was over. A job that moments earlier had been finished was now only three-quarters complete. The shooter walked quickly to the hallway. Raymond lay in an expanding pool of blood that seeped across the hardwood. A quick glance back into the bedroom allowed the spent shells to stand out on the ground where they'd landed. But they were not a worry. Nor was the gun itself. In fact, the plan had been to lay the weapon at the foot of the bed when the night was over, but Raymond had spoiled everything. Stepping over his body, the shooter hurried down the hall to the far bedroom. There was another family member in the house that now demanded attention.-

Reaching the end of the hallway, the barrel of the shotgun was again used to push open the bedroom door. This time, however, the door did not budge. It was latched shut. Twisting the handle and finding the door locked, the shooter lifted a knee and aimed a boot heel at the doorknob. The wood splintered but did not give. A second effort burst the door open and sprung the top hinge from the frame so that the door hung crooked from the jam. Entering the room, the shooter saw that the bed was empty but the covers were tussled. Placing a palm to the sheets, the bed was warm from where someone had been sleeping just moments earlier. Turning from the bed, the shooter's attention fell to the closet. The wicker door was closed. Walking over, the shooter used the barrel of the shotgun to tap on the door.

When no answer came, the shooter turned the handle and slowly pushed the door open. The closet, like the bed, was empty. It was then that the cold chill of night drifted across the back of the shooter's calves, below the hem of the trench coat. Across the room, the window curtains twirled as they filled with the night air that passed over the sill. Rushing across the room, the shooter ripped the curtains to the side and pushed the window fully open. The screen lay on the walkway below, broken free from the frame when the final family member escaped through the window.

It was a problem. A serious error created by careless miscalculation, but not the only one the shooter committed that night.

Visit our website at
KensingtonBooks.com
to sign up for our newsletters, read
more from your favorite authors, see
books by series, view reading group
guides, and more!

Become a Part of Our
Between the Chapters Book Club
Community and Join the Conversation